A *Rose* and a *Promise*

Katie Flynn is the pen name of the much-loved writer, Judy Turner, who published over ninety novels in her lifetime. Judy's unique stories were inspired by hearing family recollections of life in Liverpool during the early twentieth century, and her books went on to sell more than eight million copies. Judy passed away in January 2019, aged eighty-two.

The legacy of Katie Flynn lives on through her daughter, Holly Flynn, who continues to write under the Katie Flynn name. Holly worked as an assistant to her mother for many years and together they co-authored a number of Katie Flynn novels.

Holly lives in the north east of Wales with her husband Simon and their two children. When she's not writing she enjoys walking her two lurchers, Sparky and Snoopy, in the surrounding countryside, and cooking forbidden foods such as pies, cakes and puddings! She looks forward to sharing many more Katie Flynn stories, which she and her mother devised together. with readers in the years to cor

Keep up to date with all her la
Katie Flynn Author

Also available by Katie Flynn

The Forget-Me-Not Summer
A Christmas to Remember
Time to Say Goodbye
A Family Christmas
A Summer Promise
When Christmas Bells Ring
An Orphan's Christmas
A Christmas Candle
Christmas at Tuppenny Corner
A Mother's Love
A Christmas Gift
Liverpool Daughter
Under the Mistletoe
Over the Rainbow
White Christmas
The Rose Queen
The Winter Rose

Available by Katie Flynn writing as Judith Saxton

You Are My Sunshine
First Love, Last Love
Someone Special
Still Waters
A Family Affair
Jenny Alone
Chasing Rainbows
All My Fortunes
Sophie
We'll Meet Again
Harbour Hill
The Arcade
The Pride
The Glory
The Splendour
Full Circle

KATIE FLYNN

A Rose and a Promise

PENGUIN BOOKS

PENGUIN BOOKS

UK | USA | Canada | Ireland | Australia
India | New Zealand | South Africa

Penguin Books is part of the Penguin Random House group of companies
whose addresses can be found at global.penguinrandomhouse.com

First published by Century in 2023
Published in Penguin Books 2023
004

Copyright © Katie Flynn, 2023

The moral right of the author has been asserted

Typeset in 11.74/14.9 pt Palatino LT Pro
by Integra Software Services Pvt. Ltd, Pondicherry

Printed and bound in Great Britain by Clays Ltd, Elcograf S.p.A.

The authorised representative in the EEA is Penguin Random House
Ireland,Morrison Chambers, 32 Nassau Street, Dublin D02 YH68

A CIP catalogue record for this book is available from the British Library

ISBN: 978–1–804–94008–2

www.greenpenguin.co.uk

For Sharon Matthews

A Rose and a Promise

Prologue

March 1944

Cadi woke with a start as the air raid siren blasted its mournful wail across the base. Swinging her legs out of bed, she reached for her greatcoat and threw it over her shoulders, then headed for the Anderson shelter.

'They should build decent shelters *before* setting up these new bases,' mumbled Ethel, one of the recent arrivals, as she settled on the bench next to Cadi.

'With the Luftwaffe destroying airfields faster than we can build them, we have to make do with what we've got,' said Cadi. She smiled kindly at the other girl. 'Helping to build new airfields does come with one advantage.'

Ethel eyed her doubtfully. 'Oh?'

'We aren't on any maps, so the Krauts don't know we're here,' said Cadi.

'I hadn't thought of it like that,' replied Ethel, glancing at the wedding ring that adorned Cadi's finger. 'Is your husband in the services?'

'Jez is a mechanic in the RAF, so he has both feet firmly on the ground – something for which I shall be for ever grateful.'

Ethel swallowed hard as a series of sickening thuds sounded in the distance. 'How close are they, do you think?'

Cadi tilted her head to one side as she considered the new girl. 'I take it this is your first posting?'

Ethel nodded nervously. 'First air raid too.' She continued before Cadi had a chance to express her surprise. 'I come from Llangollen, a village not far from—'

'Wrexham!' Cadi beamed, interrupting Ethel mid-sentence.

Astonished that Cadi had heard of Llangollen, Ethel's lips rose into a small smile. 'You know it?'

Cadi nodded fervently. 'I was born in Rhos.'

Delighted to be in the company of someone local to her own area, Ethel's smile widened. 'Talk about a small world.' Her eyes fell to the corporal's stripe that adorned Cadi's arm. 'You've done ever so well for a woman from a small mining village.'

Cadi glanced at the stripe with pride. 'I love my life in the WAAF, although it's a far cry from what I'm used to.' As she spoke, Cadi realised that Ethel was no longer paying attention to the bombs that continued to fall. Not wanting her to turn her attention back to the Luftwaffe, Cadi continued to talk, telling Ethel how she and her best friend Poppy had left Rhos for Liverpool when they were just sixteen.

'We hadn't been in Liverpool for more than a few days when we got attacked by a man called Eric

2

Taylor,' she said. 'He was a real brute – someone who liked his drink.'

The Waaf's eyes rounded. 'What happened?'

Cadi went on to explain how Jez – the man who was now her husband – had come to their rescue. 'He fought Eric off with one punch before escorting us to his friend Maria's pub, where I could clean my bloodied head before catching the train back to Rhos.' Cadi sighed happily. 'Maria was the answer to all our prayers. Not only did she see to my wounds, but she gave Poppy and me jobs at the Greyhound, running the upstairs as a B&B.'

'Every cloud,' said Ethel

'Or fate?' suggested Cadi. 'After all, if we hadn't stayed in Liverpool, we'd never have rescued Eric's daughter Izzy from him.'

Ethel's jaw dropped. 'The man who attacked you?'

Cadi nodded. 'It seemed we weren't the only women Eric had raised a hand to – only in Izzy's case he used his belt, leaving her scarred below her eye.'

Ethel tutted disapprovingly. 'Where is she now?'

'In the WAAF, same as Poppy.' Cadi paused before continuing, 'She's gone from being frightened of her own shadow to giving orders. She's a sergeant.'

Enthralled by Cadi's tale, Ethel shuffled eagerly in her seat. 'Is that why you joined, or were you conscripted?'

Cadi grimaced. 'The Luftwaffe destroyed the Greyhound whilst we were sheltering in the cellar.'

Ethel held a hand to her mouth as her eyes grew ever rounder. 'Was anyone killed?'

Cadi nodded sadly. 'Jez's adoptive grandmother, Carrie.'

Ethel pulled a sympathetic face. 'To lose someone you love is bad enough, but to lose your home and job on top of that?' She shook her head. 'It must've been dreadful.'

'It was,' agreed Cadi, 'but sometimes you just have to pick yourself up and get on with things, and that's why I joined the WAAF.'

Ethel stared at Cadi in awe. 'I think you're marvellous. It's no wonder you made corporal.'

Cadi blushed as a smile tweaked her lips. 'I'm sure most people would've done the same in my position ...' She was interrupted by the siren sounding the all-clear, and got to her feet. 'That was mercifully short.'

Ethel rose from the hard wooden bench. 'Thanks for taking my mind off things. I thought I was going to go to pieces for a minute back there.'

Cadi led the way out of the shelter. 'I think we all feel that way at first, but don't worry, you'll get used to them in time. And keep it in mind that we're not the target.' She flagged down an airman who was jogging past. 'Any news?'

He nodded grimly. 'They've destroyed the runway at RAF Connington.'

Cadi cursed softly beneath her breath. 'Good job our runway's operational; at least they'll have somewhere to use in the meantime.'

Bidding the airman goodnight, she entered the billet ahead of Ethel, taking off her greatcoat and hanging it up before sliding between the sheets. When all the

Waafs were back in their beds, there was a general murmur of goodnights before Cadi pulled the light cord above her bed. As she settled down to sleep, her thoughts turned to her forthcoming trip to Lincoln, where she would meet up with Poppy and Izzy for the first time since her wedding the previous December.

Having always believed that wartime weddings were a bad omen, Cadi had only agreed to marry Jez after talking to Izzy's estranged mother Raquel. They had traced the missing woman just over a year back, and Cadi still found it hard to comprehend everything that had transpired as a result. Not only had it turned out that Izzy's mother was alive and well, but to their horror they learned that she had been pushed into working as a prostitute. The girls had marched into the brothel determined to take Raquel back to Liverpool, but during the altercation that followed Cadi's friend Kitty had thrown the nearest object to hand, which turned out to be an oil lamp. Fortunately everyone got out in the nick of time, and Cadi had believed there was nothing left to discover until Raquel had revealed that not only was she Izzy's mother, but she was Jez's as well. There had been many tears, some of sorrow, some of joy, but for the first time in a long while it looked as though everything had come up trumps.

Chapter One

Seeing the outskirts of the city looming into view, Cadi removed a compact mirror from her handbag and checked her appearance. Her fair curls were still neatly nestled in place, and the merest dab of lipstick was just visible on her lips. Informing the clippie that she wanted the next stop, she placed the mirror back in her handbag and readied herself to get off as the bus drew to a halt.

The mirror had been a wedding present from Jez, who'd had the outer lid inscribed with the date of their wedding. In return Cadi had given him a wallet with a picture of the two of them inside. Jez had treasured it, saying that it was the perfect fit for his breast pocket, and as such would mean he would be keeping her close to his heart. A reminiscent smile crossed her cheeks. Her husband could charm the birds out of the trees, and she loved him for it.

Thanking the clippie, she stepped down on to the pavement. She was very much looking forward to seeing her friends, and with the pub being only a short walk from the bus stop it wasn't long before she ducked through the small doorway of the Horse and Groom.

Casting her eyes around the bar, a broad grin spread across her face as she spied Poppy and ... 'Ronnie!' she cried.

Turning in her seat, Ronnie beamed. 'We thought it would be nice to surprise you.'

'And what a nice surprise it is too,' said Cadi. She walked over to the bar and spoke directly to the landlord. 'Hello, Alfie. The usual for me, please.'

Alfie took the bottle of R. White's lemonade and unscrewed the lid. 'Another fleeting visit, I assume?'

Cadi nodded. 'You know me, here one minute, gone the next.' She turned to face her friends. 'Where's Izzy?'

'Call of nature,' said Poppy, glancing in the direction of the Ladies. 'We've already ordered our meals, but Alfie's waiting for you before serving up.'

Taking the hint, Cadi thanked Alfie for the drink, then ordered a plate of fish and chips before handing him the money and joining her friends at their table. 'It's wonderful to be back in Lincoln.' She turned to Ronnie. 'Are you here for a visit, same as me?'

Ronnie shook her head. 'If you remember, I was supposed to be posted to Waddington not long after we found Raquel, but with one thing and another it got put on the back burner, and I've only just moved.'

'That's the WAAF for you,' said Cadi, 'tell you one thing, then do something else. How long have you been there?'

'I arrived the day before yesterday,' Ronnie told her. 'First person I bumped into was Mike.' She quickly corrected herself. 'I mean Flying Officer Grainger.'

Cadi waved a dismissive hand. 'He's always insisted we call him Mike when off base. He hates formalities.'

'I remember the first time we met him in Innsworth,' Ronnie went on. 'I thought he was a corker then, and I still do. Izzy's a very lucky girl.'

'She certainly is,' agreed Cadi, and grinned at Poppy. 'Remember the first time Izzy met Mike? What a night that was!'

Poppy raised her eyebrows. 'That was when we found out that Eric had been murdered.'

'It was quite an adventure,' Cadi recalled, 'rushing off to Liverpool in the middle of the night.'

Exiting the Ladies, Izzy walked towards them, smiling. 'And finding out that my mam was alive.'

Remembering how painfully thin Izzy had been when they first met her, Cadi welcomed her friend with open arms. 'I swear you look better every time I see you.'

'I feel it too,' Izzy beamed. 'Mam's been in touch; she said to say hello.'

Cadi smiled. 'I love hearing you talk about your mam.'

Izzy sank down on to a chair next to Cadi's. 'And I love talking about her.'

Alfie approached the table and placed Cadi's meal down, along with two plates of sausage and mashed potato and a fourth containing liver and onions.

'Best fish and chips in Lincoln,' said Cadi as she sprinkled salt over the chips. She grimaced at the plate in front of Ronnie. 'Urgh! I don't know how you can eat that stuff.'

Ronnie paused, a forkful of liver before her lips. 'It's good for you,' she said, before popping the fork into her mouth.

'Full of iron,' said Alfie approvingly. 'A plate of that is all you need to give you the energy to keep you goin' whilst you're running round like a headless chicken.'

Cadi pulled a face. 'I'll stick with fish and chips, thanks all the same.'

Chuckling, Alfie left the girls to eat their meals in peace.

'Has anyone heard from Kitty?' asked Cadi, slicing her knife through the gold and crunchy batter.

Ronnie nodded. 'She's still in RAF Little Snoring, although she wishes she was closer to the rest of us.'

'Same here,' Cadi affirmed. 'I'll not deny that I really enjoy setting up the new bases, but there's nowt like having your pals around you to help brighten up your day.'

Poppy smiled before swallowing her mouthful. 'We miss you too! As for Kitty, I can't see that the officers at Little Snoring are going to let one of their best cooks leave in favour of pastures new, nor would I blame them ...' She clapped a hand to her forehead. 'I've got a head like a sieve at times.' She stared at Cadi. 'I forgot to tell you that I saw Marnie the other day.'

'Aled's girlfriend?'

Nodding, Poppy continued, 'I didn't know it was her at first, but after we got chatting she asked where I was from, and when I said Rhos, she asked whether I knew Aled. Of course I said yes, and that's when she asked if I knew about his new posting.'

'Oh?' said Cadi. 'What new posting is this?'

Poppy eyed her in a speculative manner. 'RAF Finningley.'

'The same base as Jez.'

'Indeed. I know you said they were on friendly terms now, but I'm not sure how Jez will welcome the news.'

Cadi shrugged. 'Only one way to find out; I'll call him when I get back to my base later this evening.'

'I can't see him objecting,' said Ronnie, 'not after everything they've been through.'

'Neither can I,' said Cadi, 'but I don't want Jez thinking I'm holding anything back from him, not after the last time.'

'That bloomin' Daphne's got a lot to answer for,' said Izzy bitterly. She began counting Daphne's misdemeanours off on the tips of her fingers. 'First she fixes Aled's pilot's exam papers, then she sends Jez a rotten letter full of hogwash ...'

Cadi interrupted her friend mid-flow. 'I agree Daphne shouldn't have fiddled with Aled's papers, but she only did it to stop him gaining his wings.'

'Not because she was in love with him, though,' interjected Izzy. 'She did it because she wanted a farmer for a husband, and Aled fitted the bill.'

'Granted,' Cadi conceded, 'but the letter wasn't entirely hogwash. I did give Aled a peck on the cheek, as well as agreeing to let him show me around Lincoln ...'

'So? That's still no excuse for her to behave the way she did,' said Poppy.

'Maybe not, but I shouldn't have let her get under my skin, because that's what gave her the ammunition to tell Jez that I was chasing Aled in the first place.'

Ronnie frowned. 'Why are you defending her?'

'I'm not!' insisted Cadi. 'But I do believe that she thoroughly regretted fixing his papers, and had I not deliberately set out to rile her, she might never have sent that letter to Jez.'

'And what about when she met Jez on the docks?' Poppy went on doggedly. 'Telling him how you and

Aled had been whispering in corners and keeping secrets behind his back?'

Cadi shrugged. 'We had.'

'Because he was going to Africa, and you didn't want him to worry needlessly,' Izzy put in, her tone rising with exasperation. 'You were doing the right thing by Aled *and* Jez!'

'I know, but if I'd've said something sooner …'

'Could've, should've, would've,' said Poppy simply. 'Nobody knows what effect it would've had on Jez if you *had* said something sooner, so lay blame at blame's door. Daphne caused all this.'

Izzy nodded wisely. 'And let's not forget that her meddling put Aled in the worst position of all; rear gunner on a Lancaster Avro.' She paused before adding, 'Plus had it not been for Daphne, Aled and Jez would never have been in that dreadful car crash.'

'And if Jez hadn't acted as quickly as he did, things could've turned out very differently,' said Poppy.

Cadi nodded slowly, deep in thought. 'I suppose there's always been a small part of me that felt sorry for Daphne, even though I know she brought everything on herself.'

'You've got a big heart, as well as a forgiving nature,' said Ronnie, before hesitating as a sudden thought entered her mind. 'Hang on a mo – isn't Daphne on the same base as Jez? If she is, I think someone should warn Aled.'

Cadi shook her head fervently. 'She was, but she put in for an immediate transfer after accosting Jez down the docks.'

Poppy spoke through pursed lips. 'Not surprising. She was probably worried that Jez might get his own back by telling everyone what she'd done.'

11

'People in glass houses, and all that,' Cadi agreed.

Poppy continued, still annoyed at the thought of Daphne's behaviour. 'What sort of person lights the flame then scarpers before the fireworks?' she snapped, before answering her own question. 'A coward, that's who.'

'I still think Aled was a fool for letting sleeping dogs lie,' said Izzy. 'I'd have shouted it from the rooftops if it were me.'

'I think he was just glad to get shot of her,' said Cadi simply, 'and what's more, I don't blame him. If I never see that woman again, it'll be a day too soon.'

Izzy pulled a face. 'If she's any sense, she'll have asked to remuster from the WAAF to one of the other services.'

'They say you reap what you sow,' concluded Ronnie, 'and boy oh boy did she ever plant some seeds!'

As soon as Cadi returned to her base, she headed straight for the NAAFI to telephone Jez.

Lifting the receiver, she waited patiently for the operator to put her through to RAF Finningley. Hearing Jez's voice come down the line, a smile flashed on her lips.

'Mrs Thomas! To what do I owe the pleasure?'

Cadi giggled. 'I don't think I'll ever tire of hearing you call me that.'

Jez grinned. 'I think it rolls off the tongue nicely. How did your lunch go with the girls?'

'Lovely. Ronnie's finally moved to Waddington, so she joined us, which was a nice surprise.'

'I'm glad she's moved further inland. Those coastal bases don't half take a battering.'

'The bullseye of Jerry's target, that's what Ronnie used to call them,' said Cadi. She paused briefly. 'Talking about people getting new postings, have you heard about Aled?'

'No ...?'

Cadi went on to recount how Poppy had bumped into Marnie, and the subsequent conversation.

'I knew we had a new bombing crew coming in, but I didn't think much of it, save to say I hoped they'd have better luck than the last lot.'

Cadi nodded silently. The RAF were forever replacing aircraft as well as the crew who hadn't made it back to Blighty. 'That's why I've always been grateful that you have both feet firmly on the ground,' she said, 'and why I wanted you to know about Aled, not because I thought there'd be a problem ...'

Jez intervened. 'I know, queen, and I appreciate you keeping me in the loop, but there really isn't any need, not after everything Aled and I have been through.'

'That's a thought. You'll be able to show your pals the man whose life you saved.'

Jez laughed. 'Blow my own trumpet, you mean?'

'I don't see why not. You should be proud of what you did. I know *I'm* proud of you.'

'I pulled an unconscious man from a car that was about to burst into flames,' said Jez. 'If I'd left him to perish what would that have made me?'

Cadi tutted. 'I know what you're saying, but not everyone would've rushed to his rescue. Some people would've put their own safety first.'

Jez felt his chest begin to swell with pride, but he was far too modest to allow Cadi to continue. 'I wonder how he is?' he mused. 'I've not seen him since the crash, and I know he took a fair old crack to the head.'

'He was lucky to get away with a few scrapes and bruises – you both were – and you heard what his father said: Aled was soon up and at 'em, which was why he couldn't make our wedding.'

'Doesn't say much; you know what these fellers are like. Take that Douglas Bader chap: lost both his legs, and yet he still gives the Luftwaffe a run for their money!' He hesitated as a thought entered his mind. 'Here, I wonder if I'll be working on Aled's plane? I worked on the one it's replacing.'

Cadi grimaced. 'Do you know what happened to that one – the plane, I mean?'

'Gunned down over the Channel,' said Jez briefly.

The operator cut across their conversation, letting them know that their three minutes was up. Aware that she could see fit to end their call at any moment, Jez went on hastily. 'I'm due some leave next month. If I let you know when, maybe we could spend a bit of time together?'

'I'll see what I can arrange—' were the only words Cadi managed to get out before hearing the click as the operator terminated the call.

'Honestly! You could've waited,' huffed Cadi, but it was no use; she was talking to empty air.

Tutting at the unfairness of it, Cadi headed for the house she was sharing with five other Waafs. She had only been sent to help get the base up and running, and she supposed it wouldn't be more than a couple of weeks before she would be moving on to yet another satellite station, not that that bothered her. She thoroughly enjoyed the challenge of starting from scratch. It meant she was always meeting new people, and seeing the bases go from derelict pieces of land to working airfields gave her a sense of achievement.

She entered the house and checked the kitchen to see who was about, but it seemed the girls were either out or in their rooms. Taking the kettle, she filled it with water before putting it on the range. She had stayed in many places over the past year, some of which had been rat-infested and derelict, the worst one being served by a well which instead of a pump had a bucket on a length of rope. She had thought fishing newts out of the bucket was bad enough until she came across an unfortunate rat, and now she pulled a face as she re-called watching the bucket plummet back into the well, rat and all. But, just as she had with the others, she had soon got things shipshape, arranging for a proper water supply as well as freeing the site of vermin. By the time she left, the airfield was one of the best she'd ever organised.

Now, as she waited for the kettle to boil, she gazed out over the open fields. The view reminded her of Rhos, with its rolling countryside, and meadows bursting with wild flowers, but here she wasn't having to share a bedroom with her three older brothers. Cadi had no idea how her mother managed to keep every-thing clean with four miners living in a two up, two down.

She glanced around the quaint kitchen with its beamed ceiling and thick walls. She had never envis-aged herself wanting to move back to the country, but she quite fancied the idea of herself and Jez in a house much like this one, with her making the Sunday roast whilst Jez read his paper in one of the chairs that flanked the fireplace.

Seeing wisps of steam rising from the kettle's spout, she took a tea towel and poured the hot water into the pot. Absentmindedly scooping the tea leaves in, she stirred the contents and left them to brew.

Cadi was a great believer in fate, and so far every cloud had had a silver lining. Maybe Aled was being sent to Finningley for a purpose which hadn't presented itself to her yet, but if past events were anything to go by, she was sure it wouldn't be long before the reason behind his posting was revealed.

It was over a year since Aled had last been home, and with his new posting being even further away than the previous one, he was currently sitting beside the fire in the kitchen of his parents' farmhouse.

'It's a shame Marnie couldn't join you,' remarked Aled's mother, Gwen, looking up from her knitting. 'Such a nice girl, and she's a real help around the house.'

Aled stretched his legs out. 'She's not long been posted herself, so she can't take any more leave just yet.'

John Davies looked at his son over the top of his newspaper. 'Am I right in thinking that Fiskerton's not too far away from Finningley?'

'You are indeed.'

Gwen moved her hands to release more yarn from the ball of wool. 'That's nice. You'll get to see a lot more of each other now that you're being posted nearby.'

'Have you given any more thought to your plans for when all this is over?' John asked, before glancing down at his newspaper again.

'What is there to think about? I certainly don't want to stay on in the RAF as tail-end Charlie.'

The news that his son planned to return home was music to John's ears. 'It'll be good to have you back.'

Arching a single eyebrow, Gwen continued to knit whilst eyeing her son over her needles. 'And are we to take it that you'll be returning with Marnie as your wife?'

Leaning forward in his seat, Aled used the poker to stir the coals in the fire. 'I shan't be asking Marnie to marry me until all this is over.' He held up a hand to quell his mother's objections. 'We won't be living here in sin, if that's what worries you.'

'Then what?' asked Gwen testily. 'A long-distance relationship? How's that going to work when you're busy on the farm?'

Aled leaned back in his seat. 'As soon as peace is declared, I shall ask her to marry me, and not a moment before.'

His mother gave a snort of contempt. 'I hope you're not holding out in the hope that Cadi will leave Jez? Because—'

Aled tutted irritably. 'What sort of fool do you take me for? That ship has long sailed, and I'm pleased for Cadi. If you must know, I'm waiting until the war is over because there are too many young widows ...' He didn't get a chance to finish his sentence. Hurriedly placing her knitting needles down, Gwen left the room before her son could see her tears.

Aled had half risen out of his seat when his father waved him back down. 'You wait here. I'll see to her.'

Gwen was standing at the foot of the staircase, drying her eyes. 'I can't help it, John,' she murmured through trembling lips. 'The thought of our boy …'

John put his arms round his wife. 'I know, cariad.'

Aled arrived in the hallway. 'I'm sorry if I upset you. I'm just trying to do the right thing by Marnie.'

Gwen left her husband's arms for Aled's. 'I know you are, cariad. I shouldn't have poked my nose in.'

Aled winked at his mother. 'Isn't that a woman's job?'

Laughing raucously, John clapped a hand on his son's shoulder. 'You've hit the nail on the head there, son.'

With the atmosphere lightened, Gwen smiled. 'I'll have you know I don't gossip, but I do take an interest, and the good news here is that our son will be returning home, and in time he will marry Marnie, and they will continue running the farm, just as we have.'

'Aren't we jumping the gun rather?' said Aled. 'After all, we don't know for certain that she'll say yes.'

Gwen gave him a playful pat on the chest. 'As if she'd say no to you.'

Aled roared with laughter. 'You're biased!'

Gwen shook her head. 'I saw how she looked at you when you brought her back home the Christmas before last, and she was smitten.'

John pushed his hands into his pockets as he rocked on his heels. 'I'm just glad to hear you're coming home.'

'Wild horses couldn't keep me away,' replied Aled, and he meant every word. Having completed countless operations, he knew that he and the crew of the *Ulysses* had had more than their fair share of luck. He would just have to hope that it would hold out until the end of the war.

Cadi waved goodbye to her housemates as she set off on the long trip to Northumberland. The officer in charge of her next posting had assured Cadi that she would only be there for a couple of weeks, but Cadi knew from past experiences that the WAAF could turn weeks into months at the drop of a hat. The station she was bound for had been used as a dummy airfield, but the powers that be wanted to turn it into a training base, and they needed someone like Cadi to make sure that everything ran smoothly. She glanced at the brand new sergeant's stripes that now graced her arm. She had only ever hoped to reach the rank of corporal, so to be promoted to sergeant was a real feather in her cap. Up until now, she'd told no one of her promotion, wanting Jez to be the first to hear the news. As her route would take her in the direction of Finningley, she had informed him that she would be popping in on her way past, but she had mentioned nothing about her stripes. She smiled. Northumberland was a world away from Lincoln, but if it meant she got to see her husband en route, then it would be worth the journey.

With Cadi due to arrive within the next couple of hours, Jez had swapped shifts with one of his friends. It would be the first time he had seen his wife since their wedding, and he intended to make the most of every minute.

19

'Blimey, will you look at the smile on your face!' remarked Craig, one of Jez's fellow engineers. 'Doesn't take a genius to work out who you're seeing today.'

Jez held his hands up. 'What can I say, apart from guilty as charged.'

Craig chuckled softly. 'Married bliss, eh? You can tell the two of you are newly-weds.'

Jez winked at his fellow airman. 'You're nowt but an old cynic. I love my Cadi more and more with each day that passes.'

Craig, who was considerably older than Jez, laughed. 'That's cos you ain't been married long enough.' He pointed to the ring on his wedding finger. 'You'll change your tune after you've had ten years of earache.'

Jez wagged a reproving finger. 'Don't give me that. We all know you dote on your Maisie.'

'Only because she'd swing for me if I didn't.' Craig tapped the side of his nose. 'Do you want to know the secret to a good marriage?'

Jez stretched his legs out in front of him. 'Enlighten me.'

'Two words,' said Craig, holding up two fingers. 'Yes dear.' He grinned. 'If you can remember them two words, you'll not go far wrong.'

Jez laughed. 'So the secret to a long marriage is to agree with whatever your wife says?'

Craig gave him the thumbs up before adding, 'Take it from one who's had years of practice. And besides, just because you say yes it doesn't mean that you agree with her, but it will make for a peaceful life.'

'Cadi's not like that,' said Jez loyally. 'In fact, we never really argue.'

Craig coughed on a chuckle. 'Never really argue? I seem to remember you havin' a right old barney over that bird.'

Jez rolled his eyes. 'I take it you're referring to Daphne, but that was different.'

'Still an argument though,' said Craig evenly, adding, 'and a humdinger it was too, as I recall.'

'But only because of that interfering ...' Jez bit back the words without finishing his sentence. 'Now I come to think of it, we've only ever argued over summat that woman said or did.'

'Nasty piece of work by all accounts,' Craig agreed. 'At least she had the decency to skedaddle before you come back here. I take it she's well and truly out of the picture?'

'Long gone,' said Jez.

Craig clapped a hand on his shoulder. 'Good riddance to bad rubbish. And when it comes to Cadi, I'm only teasin'. I may've only met her a couple of times, but she seems like a grand lass to me.'

'She certainly is,' said Jez, before adding, 'She'd have to be, to put up with all the nonsense Daphne threw our way.'

'A woman that stands by her man is like a gift from God,' said Craig. 'I might make light of my Maisie, but I know she'll always stand by me.'

'Cadi's the same,' said Jez. 'I just wish I'd learned that sooner, as it would've saved a lot of heartache.'

Craig popped a peppermint into his mouth before proffering the bag to Jez. 'Marriage isn't a bed of roses; you have to work at it, and that doesn't stop just because you get older.'

'That's what my nan used to say,' said Jez, 'but I honestly think Cadi and I have seen the back of our troubles.'

Craig pushed the small bag of sweets back into his pocket. 'I must admit, I certainly think you've had your fair share!'

Cadi cursed beneath her breath. Road closures were the bane of her existence. Not only did she have to plot an alternative route, but a blocked road could add hours on to a journey. Getting out of her car, she walked over to the fallen tree to see if there was any possibility of getting past, but with the main bulk of the trunk lying across the road she realised she would have to look for another way.

Climbing back into the car, she opened the map and began tracing her finger along the different options. Concluding that there were only two, she chose the shorter one, turned the car round, and headed back on to the main road. Keeping her eyes peeled for the new turning, she slowed down as it came into view, and pulled a disgruntled face as she reached it. *Hardly a road*, Cadi thought to herself. *I've seen bigger tracks.* She glanced in the rear-view mirror. If she were to take the longer route, she reckoned she could be looking at adding another hour on to her journey, but if she did turn here she might discover the road to be unfit for anything other than a horse and cart. Torn between the two decisions, Cadi decided to do something she hadn't done in years.

'Eeny meeny miny moe...'

Finishing the rhyme, she smiled at the track ahead of her. After all, what was life without a bit of adventure?

Whether the new route was any quicker than the original one Cadi couldn't say, but it was a lot more windy than it had appeared on the map, and some of the blind bends were slowing her progress considerably. As for the state of the car, she dreaded to think what it looked like on the outside, but since she'd had to use the wipers to clear thick mud from the windscreen she could only imagine that it must be caked in all manner of detritus. Seeing a fork in the road ahead of her, she pulled into the car park of a pub so that she might take another look at the map. Locating the pub on the road she was currently on, she confirmed that she should turn left at the fork, then folded the map and put it back into the glove compartment. Glancing in the rear-view mirror, she began to reverse, and felt the car hit something.

Yanking the handbrake up, she got out quickly and ran round to the back of the car, but to her surprise there was no evidence of an accident. She was dumbfounded for a moment, but then her heart fell as she saw a large drop of blood on the ground not too far away. Feeling sick to her stomach, she spotted another drop a little further off. Whatever she had hit, it appeared to be heading in the direction of the pub. Fearing that she might have injured a child, Cadi followed the trail of blood to the door at the back of the pub, and it was here that she saw a beautiful Irish setter with a glossy red coat. Bending down, she looked into the animal's soulful eyes, and the tip of its tail wagged a timid greeting. Reaching out, she gently stroked the dog's head to let it know that she meant it no harm.

'You poor thing, I'm so sorry,' she said softly. Looking to see where the blood was coming from, she saw that it was oozing from a gash on the dog's hind leg. Standing up, she knocked firmly on the back door of the pub. 'Hello? Is there anyone home?' She waited for a reply, but with none coming she tried turning the handle. It was no use – the door was locked. She decided to try the front, but when she began to walk that way she heard a noise behind her. Turning, she saw that the dog had got up to follow her. 'Stay here whilst I go for help.' Cadi instructed, but the dog took no notice, and limped after her as she hurried round to the front door. She tried the handle, but it seemed that the pub was closed. Tutting beneath her breath, she knocked loudly to see if she could gain anyone's attention, but there was no response. Frustrated, she peered through the square pane of glass in the middle of the door, and her heart skipped a beat. There was someone home, but he was sprawled on the floor, and it looked to Cadi very much as if he'd collapsed. Banging her fist against the glass, she did her best to rouse the recumbent figure, but he was dead to the world. Not wanting to waste another second, she picked up a rock and hurled it through the small pane, then grabbed another stone and knocked out the remaining fragments of glass so that she could fit her hand through. Turning the knob of the Yale lock, she pushed the door open and ran over to the man she had seen. When she knelt down she could see that he was in his late sixties, and he was still conscious, but only just. His face was beaded with sweat, and seeing the way he was clutching his chest Cadi felt certain that he must be having a heart attack.

She smoothed his matted hair back, speaking in what she hoped were reassuring tones. 'I'm going to ring for an ambulance. Is the phone behind the bar?'

The man managed a small nod before closing his eyes.

Cadi ran round to the far end of the bar and located the phone. She dialled 999 and was thankful to hear the operator's voice after the first ring. She explained the situation, and was assured that help would be on its way very shortly. Relieved, she replaced the receiver and fetched the man a glass of water, which she held to his lips.

'Try not to worry,' she said soothingly as the man managed a few small sips, 'the ambulance is on its way.' She looked at the dog, which was wagging its tail fervently as it settled next to him. 'Is this your dog?'

The man gave a small nod. 'Annie.'

Cadi smiled. 'Because of the red hair?'

His lips tried to twitch into a smile. ''S right.'

Holding the man's hand in hers, Cadi admired the dog. 'She's a beauty.'

The man looked earnestly into Cadi's eyes, and spoke clearly for the first time. 'Look after her for me.'

Cadi's eyes rounded. 'I'm sorry, but I can't,' she said, before adding, 'Besides, you'll be able to look after her—' She broke off as he clutched his hand to his left breast, his face contorted with pain, and to spare him any more stress or anxiety Cadi made a promise she knew she couldn't keep. 'I'll look after her, I swear it.'

She felt his fingers go limp in hers. Panic rising in her chest, she repeatedly tapped the back of his hand, begging, 'Please wake up, the ambulance will be here any minute now,' and fighting back tears as she prayed for the ambulance to arrive. Annie shuffled towards her owner and licked the side of his face, as if she too were encouraging him to stay with them.

Hearing the crunch of stones as a vehicle pulled into the car park, Cadi called out to the ambulance crew to let them know where she was, and when they entered the building she felt an enormous sense of relief sweep over her. Swiftly getting to her feet so that they might see to the man, she told them how she had found him.

Nodding her understanding, one of the ARPs spoke to her patient as they transferred him on to a stretcher. 'Phil? It's Gail. We're goin' to take you to hospital.' She glanced up at Cadi. 'He's lucky you came along when you did. How on earth did you know what had happened?'

Cadi grimaced. 'I didn't. I was on my way to RAF Finningley when I accidentally hit Annie.'

The ambulance driver tutted irritably. 'I always said that dog would be the death of him.'

Cadi wrinkled her brow. 'It's not Annie's fault, surely?'

Gail indicated the lead which had fallen out of Phil's hand. 'Annie's frightened of her own shadow. I'd wager Phil was in the process of putting her lead on when summat spooked her, and she hared off before he had a chance to secure it.'

Cadi pulled a doubtful face. 'But she was outside, and the door was locked …?'

Gail counted to three before she and the driver lifted the stretcher. Walking out of the pub, she spoke to Cadi over her shoulder. 'It probably swung shut behind her. That's the trouble with Yale locks.'

Cadi followed them out to what she had assumed was an ambulance, but was in fact a hearse. 'Isn't that a bit inappropriate?'

The driver shrugged. 'Beggars can't be choosers, and as you know ...'

Cadi nodded, finishing his sentence for him. 'There's a war on.' She looked at Annie, who was sitting beside the hearse, whining. Breathing a resigned sigh, she opened the back door of her own car. 'Come on, Annie, you'd better come with me.' She had half expected the dog to ignore her, but to her surprise she happily leapt on to the seat.

With their patient secure in the back of the hearse, the driver turned to Cadi. 'Where will you take her?'

'RAF Finningley for now. I'm hoping someone there will look after her until Phil gets better.'

Wishing her luck, he took his place behind the wheel, and pulled out of the car park.

Cadi started the engine of her car before getting in behind the steering wheel. Annie promptly jumped from the back to the front, and began licking the side of her face. Laughing softly, Cadi gently pushed her away. 'I said I liked a bit of adventure, and boy did I ever find one! C'mon, Annie, let's get you to Finningley.'

Cadi turned in to the parking area reserved for visitors and pulled an exhausted face as she opened the car door, but her expression lightened when she saw Jez hurrying towards her. 'Sorry I'm late, but I've had rather an eventful journey.'

Jez appeared intrigued. 'Sounds interesting.' He held out his hand to help her from the car, and noticed the extra stripe on her arm. 'Why didn't you tell me you'd made sergeant?' he cried.

With all that had gone on, Cadi had completely forgotten her husband was yet to learn of her promotion. 'I wanted it to be a surprise.'

'So why do you look so glum?' Then his eyes fell on Annie, and with a broad grin etching his cheeks he jerked his head towards the dog. 'You didn't tell me you had company.'

Cadi rolled her eyes. 'She's the reason why I'm late.' Explaining the circumstances in which she'd acquired Annie, she finished, 'I completely forgot she'd be needing her lead. I don't suppose you've got anything we could use? Only apparently she's easily spooked and we can't have her running around the base like a headless chicken.'

Jez scratched the top of his head. 'I can easily come up with something, even if it's just a belt ...' He hesitated. 'The pub you found her at, was it the Bull and Heifer by any chance?'

Cadi nodded. 'I take it you know it?'

'I certainly do; it's our local watering hole.' He turned his attention to Annie, who was wagging her tail at him from the front passenger seat. 'Poor old Phil, he'll be lost without her.' He turned on his heel. 'Wait here, and I'll see what I can fashion into a lead.'

Whilst he was gone, Cadi stroked Annie's silky head, and took a quick peek at her leg. She was thankful to see that it was no longer bleeding, but it would still need a good clean. Jez was hurrying back with the cord of his dressing gown, and Cadi watched as he fashioned a loop and placed it over the top of Annie's head. 'C'mon, old girl, let's see if we can't get you some food and water.' As he spoke, his gaze fell to the gash on the dog's leg. 'And we'll take a look at that wound of yours whilst we're about it.'

'It's stopped bleeding, so I'm rather hoping she won't need stitches,' said Cadi as they led the setter round to the back of the cookhouse.

Jez took Cadi's hand in his. 'She can walk, so at least nothing's broken.' He knocked a brief tattoo on the cookhouse door, and within moments one of the cooks appeared in the doorway, her welcoming smile fading as she noticed Annie's leg.

'Oh, you poor thing,' she cried. 'What have you done to yourself?'

'Beryl, this is Cadi,' Jez said quickly. 'She can tell you what happened.'

Her cheeks turning crimson, Cadi relayed the incident to Beryl, who smiled sympathetically. 'If it's any consolation, I very much doubt you caused that wound. It probably happened when she legged it out of the pub.'

'But I hit her,' said Cadi, a puzzled frown crossing her brow, 'I know I did.'

'I'm not doubting that,' said Beryl, 'but I should imagine you can't have been going very fast, or she'd not be here to tell the tale.'

Cadi nodded slowly. 'I was reversing, so no, I wasn't going fast at all.'

Jez agreed with Beryl. 'She probably saw you sitting in the car, so came to say hello,' he conceded. 'Wrong place, wrong time, and it's pure bad luck that you hit her.'

'Or fate,' suggested Cadi. 'Because if I hadn't Phil would still be on the floor of the pub.'

Beryl nodded approvingly. 'There you are, all's well that ends well. As for Annie, I'm afraid we probably all saw this day coming; she's notorious for runnin' amok. She's a lovely dog, but she needs a lot more exercise than Phil can give her, which is why she takes herself off for a good run whenever she can.' She indicated the dried blood on Annie's leg with a chubby finger. 'I'll get some salt water for that cut, and a few scraps for her to eat.'

Thanking Beryl for her help, Jez stroked Annie's ears as he spoke to Cadi. 'So, what do you plan on doin' with her?'

Cadi shot him a pleading glance. 'I was rather hoping RAF Finningley might like to have her, at least until Phil's out of hospital.'

Jez looked startled. 'Crikey Cadi, this is an airfield, not a kennel. Where do you propose she sleep?'

Cadi sighed miserably. 'I don't know, but I promised Phil I'd look after her because I thought he was going to die in my arms, and now I'm going to have to keep that promise.'

Beryl emerged with some food for Annie and a bowl of salt water. Taking a cloth, she instructed Jez to hold the dog still while she cleaned the wound.

As Jez comforted Annie he nodded a greeting to Craig, who had come over to see what was going on. 'Hello, Cadi.' He grimaced as he saw Beryl gently cleaning the dried blood from Annie's leg. 'Dear oh dear, what's happened to you?'

Not wishing to go through the details again, Cadi looked to Jez, who explained how the accident had occurred. 'We're just discussing what to do with her,' he finished.

Craig pushed his hands into his pockets. 'I don't think Cadi's suggestion's so outlandish. I've seen other bases with dogs, and I don't see why she couldn't stay here until Phil gets better.'

Cadi heaved a sigh of relief. 'Do you really think they'd agree?'

'If it were any other dog than Annie, I'd not be so sure, but she's ever so popular with them that frequent the Bull and Heifer,' said Craig, adding, 'which is ninety per cent of the folk on base.'

Squatting, Jez placed his arm around Annie's shoulders as he hand-fed her some of the scraps which Beryl had rustled up. Hungry from her ordeal, Annie began to wolf the food down, whilst Beryl finished cleaning the wound. Cadi waited for her opinion with nervous anticipation. 'How is it?'

Beryl smiled up at her. 'Not bad at all. I honestly don't think you caused this – it's barely the size of a sixpence, if that.'

Craig muttered a mild expletive before hissing, 'Heads-up, looks like we've been spotted. Best hope this 'un knows our Annie.'

Concern etched on her face, Cadi turned, only to find herself standing face to face with the corporal who'd trained her in RAF Innsworth. 'Corp...' she hesitated as her eyes fell on the extra stripe adorning the Waaf's arm. 'Pardon me; *Sergeant* Moses!'

The woman smiled at Cadi. 'It appears I'm not the only one who's made sergeant. Well done, Sergeant Williams!'

Jez coughed, and with a smile Cadi corrected the other woman. 'It's Thomas now. I got married' – she turned to Jez – 'and this is my husband, Airman Jeremy Thomas.'

Sergeant Moses exchanged greetings with Jez before she turned her attention to Annie. 'And who does this magnificent beast belong to?'

Cadi swallowed. 'Good question.' She explained the situation for what seemed like the umpteenth time, and Sergeant Moses nodded as she listened. 'So you see,' finished Cadi, 'I was rather hoping that you would have her here at Finningley, if only until the landlord recovers.'

The sergeant leaned down to stroke Annie behind her ears. Seeing the anxious quartet of faces looking hopefully at her, a slow smile crossed her cheeks. 'I know Officer Bailey's one for dogs, *and* he frequents the Bull and Heifer so he'll know Annie.' 'I can't see him turning her away. Leave it with me; I'll see what I can do.'

Jez tousled Annie's ears. 'I promise I'll take full responsibility; you won't even know she's here.'

Sergeant Moses held her hands up in a cautionary manner. 'I can only try.'

Jez and Cadi thanked her, and as she walked away Jez turned to Cadi. 'How do you two know each other?'

'She was the first corporal I ever had,' Cadi explained. 'She was the one who recommended me for promotion to NCO, as well.'

'Fingers crossed she can persuade Officer Bailey to let Annie stay,' said Beryl.

Cadi stroked Annie's smooth fur. 'I feel so guilty, but I can't take her to Northumberland—' She broke off as Sergeant Moses approached with a tall man in officer's uniform.

To Cadi's relief, the newcomer wasted no time before fussing Annie. When he had finished, he looked at the sea of expectant faces. 'Which one of you said they'd take care of her?' He smiled as Jez, Craig and Beryl shot their hands into the air.

Jez stepped forward. 'My wife brought her here, so I think it's only right that I should take the bulk of the responsibility.'

The officer cocked an eyebrow. 'You do understand that you'll be held accountable for anything she does?'

Jez nodded curtly. 'I'm an engineer, so I can make her a kennel, and I'll give her plenty of exercise, so she won't feel the need to go wandering.'

The officer smoothed the tips of his moustache between his forefinger and thumb. 'She can stay, but only on a trial basis,' he concluded. 'You've got a month to prove she won't make a nuisance of herself.'

Jez beamed. 'Thank you, sir. I won't let you down.'

The officer gave Annie a final pat goodbye before heading back to the officers' mess.

Sergeant Moses waited until he was out of earshot before speaking. 'As soon as he heard it was Annie, he couldn't wait to come over and see her. I'm not so sure he'd have been the same if it had been a different dog.'

'Thank you so much,' said Cadi. 'I was dreading her being turned away, because I don't know what I'd have done with her.'

Sergeant Moses smiled. 'My pleasure. Besides, it'll be nice to have a dog around. She can be our camp mascot.' Glancing at the watch on her wrist, she quickly excused herself. 'It was good to see you again, Sergeant Thomas; safe travels.'

As the sergeant walked away, Annie found herself engulfed by a mass of hands, all congratulating her on her new home.

Cadi glanced at her wristwatch. 'Damn! I'm sorry, Jez, but I'd best be making tracks.'

Jez held the makeshift lead out to Craig. 'Would you mind looking after Annie whilst I say goodbye to Cadi?'

Craig took the lead without hesitation. 'Not at all.' He turned to Cadi. 'Make sure you take care on those roads.'

Cadi smiled. 'I will, and I promise not to hit any more dogs!'

Cadi and Jez walked the short distance back to her car, where Cadi retrieved the crank handle from under her seat. 'What a palaver,' she said, as she pushed it into the slot. 'Trust me to choose the wrong road.'

Jez was shaking his head. 'If you'd gone the other way, it could've been hours before someone came across Phil, and who knows whether he'd still have been alive.'

Cadi spun the handle round until the car roared into life. 'Do you realise that our lives have been full of grey clouds with silver linings?'

'It certainly seems that way,' admitted Jez, as he slipped his arms around his wife's waist. 'Take good care of yourself, Mrs Thomas. You're a precious commodity.' He kissed her softly before drawing back. 'I'll let you know how Annie is when you call to tell me you've arrived safely.'

She glanced back at Craig, who was only just visible within the group of people that had gathered to fuss Annie. 'Annie's going to be just fine.'

Jez followed his wife's gaze. 'She wins the heart of all those who meet her, same as the woman who rescued her.' His eyes twinkled as he gazed down at her. 'When's your next bit of leave?'

'I'm due four days on the twenty-eighth,' said Cadi promptly.

He pulled out a pencil along with a piece of scrap paper from his pocket and jotted the date down. 'On the assumption that I can get the same dates, where would you like to go?'

'How about the Belmont? I've not been back to Liverpool in ages,' she suggested.

'The Belmont it is.' Jez took his wife in his arms and kissed her tenderly.

As their lips parted, Cadi rested her forehead against his chest. 'I can't wait.'

He tightened his arms around her. 'Ditto.' He kissed her again, softly at first, but with growing passion until Cadi reluctantly broke free from their embrace.

'I'd best get a move on. It's going to be dark by the time I reach my destination, and I hate driving in the dark.'

'Of course.' Jez kissed her on the forehead then pushed his hands into his pockets whilst Cadi got into the car. 'Make sure you telephone as soon as you arrive.'

Winding the window down, she nodded. 'I always do.'

'I love you, Mrs Thomas.'

Cadi called out 'I love you too' before driving away. She hated saying goodbye to her husband, and she was finding it harder each time she had to do so.

After what seemed like an eternity behind the wheel, Cadi finally arrived at RAF Boulmer. Having checked in at the hut which was serving as the office, she trooped over to the billet earmarked for Waafs, hoping that it would be clean if nothing else. She was relieved to find that whilst it was basic, there were no signs of rat droppings, or large spiderwebs. Being the first to arrive, she had her pick of the beds, all of which looked pretty rickety. She selected the one closest to the door, and pushed it gently with her fingers to make sure it didn't fall apart at the slightest touch. Satisfied that it was sturdy enough, she placed her kitbag down on the lumpy mattress, and withdrew her vanity mirror from the recesses of the bag to check her appearance before heading back out to the hut which the men were using as the NAAFI, the cookhouse, and everything in between. After duly locating the phone, she rang RAF Finningley.

She smiled as she heard Jez's cheery voice come down the line. 'Hello, queen. How was your journey?'

Cadi hid a yawn behind her hand. 'Tiring, but I'm here now.' She glanced around her. 'Not that there's much here. How's Annie?'

'Getting spoiled rotten,' Jez laughed. 'I don't think we've encountered anyone yet who doesn't already know her.'

Cadi gave a relieved sigh. 'Well, that's one weight off my mind.'

Jez continued, 'I've taken her for a long walk in the woods. I even tried her off the lead, and she was brilliant, apart from when she heard a loud bang.'

Cadi's face dropped. 'What happened?'

'One of the cars backfired,' Jez explained. 'She was fine, but it took me a while to coax her out of her kennel.'

Cadi's brow rose. 'Kennel?'

'I wasn't short of volunteers, so it didn't take us long to build her one.'

Cadi felt her shoulders relax. They really were a good bunch at Finningley. Her thoughts turned to Annie's previous owner. 'Has anyone heard how Phil's doing?'

'From what I gather he's still on dodgy ground,' said Jez, 'but if you hadn't come along when you did, the staff at the hospital reckon it would've been curtains. So you really did save his life.'

'Not me, Annie,' said Cadi sincerely. She heard a soft whining coming down the line. 'Have you got her with you?'

'She's right beside me; I was about to take her out again when you rang.'

'It's a good job they allowed her to stay. She'd not be safe here in Boulmer.'

A look of concern crossed Jez's face. He hated the thought of his wife staying in some of the rotten places the RAF saw fit to send her to. 'Is it that bad?'

'There's nothing here, so I really can't see this being only a two-week job,' said Cadi truthfully.

Jez tutted beneath his breath. 'They shouldn't rely on you so much. When are the other Waafs arriving?'

'It's supposed to be tomorrow, but you know what it's like.'

'I certainly do. Just you make sure you tell them that you're not a one-woman band, otherwise they'll leave you to do all the work on your own, and that's not fair, luv.'

'I will, not that I expect them to listen. I don't suppose you've had a chance to ask about getting the same leave as me?' she asked hopefully.

She could tell from the sound of his voice that he'd been successful. 'I've managed to book the same time as you, and what's more I can take Annie with me, because I've already squared it with Maria and Bill.'

'But what about the train?' said Cadi cautiously. 'I very much doubt she's been on one before, and they can be quite loud, especially when they blow the whistle.'

'She'll be fine,' said Jez confidently.

Cadi wasn't so certain, but she would just have to hope that he was right. 'You sound pretty confident.'

'She's a grand dog,' said Jez. 'I have to admit, I've taken a real shine to her. I always wanted a dog growing up, but Nan worried that she would be the one taking care of it, so the answer was always no.'

'Well, you've got one now, and what a corker she is too.' Cadi stifled another yawn with the back of her hand, and Jez, hearing it, brought the conversation to an end.

'You sound absolutely whacked, so I shall say good-night and leave you to get some rest.'

Cadi smiled sleepily. 'Ta-ra, Jez. I love you.'

'Not as much as I love you. Goodnight, sweetheart.'

Cadi replaced the receiver, then headed off to find something to eat. She might be tired, but she hadn't had anything since breakfast, and she'd need at least a snack before she could sleep.

Seeing the guard on duty at the gate, she walked over to him. 'What does one do for food around here?'

The guard stood to attention. 'There's a makeshift pantry in the hut, ma'am. We're a bit short on supplies until tomorrow, but we've got bread, butter, corned beef and cheese, as well as milk.'

Thanking him for his help, she soon found the pantry he had spoken of. She made herself a corned beef and tomato sandwich and ate it hungrily. It had been one heck of a day, but at least it had ended well.

Chapter Two

Through his earpiece, Aled heard the pilot announce that they were getting ready to land at RAF Finningley. He knew from the whole Daphne business that Jez, too, had served at Finningley, though whether he was still here was another matter. Glancing at the airfield below, he saw several Waafs making their way across the runway. Was one of them Daphne? He fervently hoped not, because whilst he might've been prepared to leave things lie, it didn't mean to say that he'd forgiven her.

As the plane touched down, Aled turned his thoughts to what he would say to his ex, should he bump into her. *I'll be polite*, Aled told himself, as the pilot taxied the plane down the runway, *but I'll make sure she knows that our relationship will be purely professional*. When the plane came to a standstill, he took his belongings and followed the rest of the crew off the plane to greet the officer who had come to meet them. Aled listened with half an ear as they walked, keeping a keen eye out for Jez, but the airfield was a hive of activity, and with everyone wearing the same uniform it was like trying to spot a needle in a haystack.

Officer Bailey showed them to their hut before leaving them to settle. The crew from the *Ulysses* trooped into their new accommodation, where selecting their beds and putting their belongings away took no more than a few minutes.

Aled stretched audibly. 'I'm off for summat to eat. Do any of you fellers want to join me?'

The skipper picked up his cigarette case and placed it in his pocket. 'Seeing as it's pretty much the law to check out the food at each new base, how could we say no?'

Once they were outside, they took a few minutes to get a sense of their whereabouts before heading off towards the NAAFI. Chatting to the *Ulysses*' mid-gunner, Tom, Aled hadn't been paying too much attention to those around him until he heard someone call out his name. Turning to see who had hailed him, his face split into a large grin when he saw Jez waving to get his attention.

Aled turned back to face the rest of the crew, who'd stopped to wait. 'I'll catch you up in a bit,' he said, and peeling away from the group he made his way over to Jez. 'Long time no see.'

Jez put the wrench he'd been using back into the box. 'Cadi told me you were coming.'

Aled looked at him in surprise. 'She did? How on earth did she know?'

'Marnie's at RAF Fiskerton, with Poppy.'

Aled pushed his hands into his pockets. 'I see! Talk about a small world.'

Jez chuckled softly. 'You know what the services are like: you can't sneeze without everyone knowing about it.' He hesitated. 'We missed you at the wedding; it's a shame you couldn't make it. Your dad explained you were busy on operations.'

Aled rubbed the back of his neck with the palm of his hand. 'Life seems to be one big op at the moment.' He glanced down as a soft wet nose pushed itself into the palm of his hand. 'Hello! Where did you come from?'

Annie wagged her tail, and Jez patted her rump absentmindedly whilst explaining the circumstances behind her unexpected arrival.

'Good job Cadi pulled over when she did,' Aled commented. As he'd been listening he'd been keeping an eye out for Daphne, something which hadn't gone unnoticed by Jez.

'Are you expecting someone?'

Aled pulled a grimace. 'I hope not. Is Daphne still at Finningley?'

'Long gone, mate. I haven't got a clue where she went, and nor do I want to know.' He jerked his head to where *Ulysses* was parked up. 'Is this a permanent move?'

Aled smiled. 'As permanent as it gets with the RAF.' He watched as the rest of his crew disappeared into the NAAFI. 'Do you fancy catching up properly over a pint? Only I'd like to grab a bite to eat before reporting to the office.'

Jez picked the wrench up from the box. 'Sounds good to me. Just let me know where and when.'

Aled gave him the thumbs up and said 'Will do' before striding away to join the rest of his crew.

As he entered the NAAFI, he scanned the tables to see where the others were sitting. Seeing Tom waving to gain his attention, Aled acknowledged him with a raised hand before selecting a plate of stew with mashed potato. Taking his food over to his pals, he sat down in the chair which Tom had drawn up for him.

'Who was that?' Tom asked inquisitively.

'Cadi's husband, Jez,' said Aled, before taking a large forkful of mashed potato and stew.

'The famous Cadi,' said Tom. 'It's been a long time since I heard her name being mentioned.'

'I've not seen or heard from her in ages,' agreed Aled, 'but I guess that's life. People move on.'

'Granted,' conceded Tom, 'but I always thought the two of you would end up together, no matter how unlikely it seemed.'

Aled pulled a face. 'I'd have agreed with you in the early days, but Cadi made it perfectly clear that Jez was the man for her, ergo I gave up on that dream a long time ago. Marnie's the one for me now.'

Tom gave him a sidelong glance. 'And are you happy with her?'

Aled contemplated this as he finished the mouthful of stew he'd just taken. 'Cadi's a real corker, but so is Marnie.'

Tom mopped the last of his gravy up with a slice of bread and butter. Aled had thought about his answer before replying, and Tom knew for certain that if he'd asked the same question about Cadi, way back when, Aled wouldn't have hesitated. 'But that's not what I asked you.'

A smile twitched the corner of Aled's mouth. Tom knew him inside out, but that could be said for any member of the crew. Placing your life in the hands of your fellows made for a close-knit group of men.

'I'm happy, and if it makes you feel any better, I plan to ask Marnie to be my wife as soon as peace is declared.'

Tom nodded approvingly. 'Good. I'm glad to see you've moved on, because there was a time when I didn't think that was going to be possible.'

Aled shrugged. 'I'll always love Cadi, but it's Marnie I'm in love with.' Considering the conversation to be at an end, he continued to eat his meal in thoughtful silence. In the past, he'd have agreed with Tom, because even Daphne hadn't taken his mind off the woman he regarded as his true love. But, as he'd known many moons ago, if you truly love someone you set them free. And since Cadi had wanted to be with Jez, that's exactly what Aled had done.

Cadi thanked the Waaf who handed her the receiver. 'Hello?'

'Hello, Cadi. It's me, Poppy.' Her friend's tone was dull and lifeless, a far cry from the happy-go-lucky girl Cadi had grown up with.

Cadi frowned. 'Is everything all right? You sound as though you're a bit down in the dumps.'

'I suppose I'm getting a bit fed up with the same old thing. Nothing exciting ever happens here. But that's enough of that,' said Poppy, her tone brightening. 'How's Annie getting on?'

Cadi grinned. None of the girls had met Annie, but they were all eager to do so. 'From what Jez has told me, she's fine. The camp sweetheart, by all accounts.'

'I wish we had a dog at Fiskerton, if only to take our mind off the bloomin' war.' Poppy paused. 'How are you getting on at Boulmer?'

'It's coming along at one heck of a pace, mainly because the girls they've sent over are experienced Waafs, which makes my job a lot easier.'

Poppy brightened. 'So you could be back in Lincoln soon?'

'Not until April, I'm afraid.'

'April!' cried Poppy. 'That's not two weeks!'

'I knew it wouldn't be two weeks as soon as I arrived, probably before, if I'm honest with myself,' admitted Cadi. 'The WAAF are always expecting us to perform miracles, so I'm used to taking their timescales with a pinch of salt. Having said that, I should be all right to take my leave in Liverpool on the twenty-eighth.'

Poppy pouted. 'I wish I was going to Liverpool.'

'It's not like you to sound so glum. Are you sure nothing's happened?'

Poppy heaved a sigh. 'I think the tediousness of war has set in. We had such an exciting time when we were looking for Raquel, and then there was your wedding, of course, but now that's all behind us it seems like we've nothing left to look forward to.'

Hating to think of her best friend being miserable, Cadi spoke without hesitation. 'Why don't you join us in Liverpool?'

'And play gooseberry?' Poppy laughed ruefully. 'No thanks.'

'Bring Geoffrey. In fact, I don't we see why we can't make this into a reunion. If Izzy could bring Mike ...'

A suddenly eager-sounding Poppy cut Cadi short. 'I know they're both due some leave, as are Raquel, Ronnie and Kitty,' she chattered excitedly. 'Oh, Cadi, it would be marvellous if everyone could make it. Life's always good when we're all together.'

'Then that's what we shall do,' said Cadi. 'I'll give Jez a quick call to let him know what's going on; could you sound out the others?'

Poppy breathed a happy sigh. 'Of course. It would be my pleasure. Thanks for this, Cadi; I could really do with a break. I'm fed up of people saying that the end's in sight, because it gets my hopes up, and then nothing happens.'

'I think there's definitely light at the end of the tunnel,' said Cadi, 'but I'd say we've still a long way to go.'

'Which is why I'm hoping this reunion will be the tonic I need to pep me up,' said Poppy. 'A break in the clouds as it were.'

'We all need some of that,' said Cadi. 'Let me know how you get on with the others, won't you?'

Poppy agreed, and Cadi terminated the call before asking the operator to put her through to RAF Finningley. 'Jez?'

'Cadi!'

Cadi grimaced. 'I've a confession to make. I've been on the blower to Poppy ...' She went on to explain how Poppy had been down in the doldrums. 'As soon as she heard I was going to Liverpool, she said she wished she could come too ...'

Jez interrupted her with a soft chuckle. 'Let me guess: Poppy's joining us?'

'Sorry, sweetheart. I know I should've asked you first.'

He laughed. 'Don't be daft. Our Poppy's always welcome, and the same goes for the rest of them.'

Cadi drew in a guilty breath. 'I'm glad you said that, because Poppy's inviting everyone: your mam, Ronnie, Kitty, the whole shebang. We thought we could turn it into a reunion.'

She could hear the grin in his voice as he said, 'We really are one big happy family, and I wouldn't have it any other way. As far as I'm concerned, the more the merrier.' He paused briefly as a thought entered his mind. 'Have you checked with Maria? Only she might be fully booked.'

Cadi was confident. 'Maria's always said she'll keep a couple of rooms spare in case we want to go back—'

He interrupted without apology. 'I don't want to bunk down with Mike and Geoffrey. I'd rather it was just the two of us.'

Cadi felt herself blushing. She had completely forgotten that she and Jez would be sharing the same bed. 'Ah! Good point. I'll telephone Maria, make sure she can hold back enough rooms.'

'Tell her I'll pay for ours too, seeing as we'll be using up one of the guest rooms—'

The operator cut across, letting them know their time was up.

'Will do. Ta-ra, Jez. I love you.'

She heard Jez replying that he loved her too, before clicking down his receiver. Cadi asked the operator to put her through to the Belmont, promising her fervently that there was no one waiting to use the telephone.

'Maria? It's me, Cadi.'

'Hello, Cadi love. How's tricks?'

'Good, thanks. How's everything at the Belmont?'

'Not too bad. Mustn't grumble,' said Maria.

'I'm phoning to ask you a favour ...' Cadi quickly went on to recap the phone calls between herself, Poppy and Jez. 'So you see, if everyone can make it, you're going to have a houseful. I hope that's all right?'

It sounded as though Maria was beaming. 'Just the way I like it, and as for Jez paying for your room, he can forget it. I'm not having family pay to stop over.'

'This is a bit different, though,' said Cadi reasonably, 'because we'll be taking up a paying guest's room.'

But Maria was adamant. 'I'll be grateful to have my family around me. There's not many that can say that nowadays, and I'll not be accepting payment from any of you.'

Whilst none of them were strictly family, Cadi knew that Maria and Bill still counted them as such, and so she thanked Maria for her generous hospitality and hung up the receiver. As she walked across the base she turned her thoughts to the twenty-eighth. Poppy was correct: it was occasions like these that kept them all going, and Cadi couldn't wait to be reunited with those she held dear.

Jez had been whistling the theme tune to *Jitterbugs* when the air raid siren split the air. Dropping his tools, he called Annie to follow him and started to run to the nearest shelter. His heart pounding in his chest he was about to dive into the entrance when he realised that Annie was no longer behind him, but heading for the safety of her kennel. Cursing beneath his breath, he veered away from the shelter, his feet pounding against the concrete as he chased after her. He knew that if Annie made it to her haven he didn't stand a cat in hell's chance of winkling her out, not with a dogfight now raging in the skies above them.

She had almost made it inside when Aled appeared out of nowhere. Grabbing her by the collar, he gathered the dog in his arms just as Jez skidded to a halt beside them. Seeing one of the Messerschmitts beginning to turn, the pair flung themselves against the side of one of the buildings while Aled adjusted his hold to stop Annie from struggling free.

'Let's get out of here before he comes back for round two,' yelled Jez. Aled stuck his thumb up in response, and they fled towards the shelter with Annie clasped tightly in Aled's arms. Jez grimaced as he heard the Messerschmitt behind them open fire, and they dived through the doorway just in time, tumbling across the floor as the bullets ripped and zinged into the sandbags. Both men lay panting, and Annie, who was whimpering with fear, tucked herself beneath the bench that skirted the walls of the shelter.

When he had regained his breath, Jez helped Aled to his feet, and the two men sank down on to the bench above Annie. Lowering his voice so that the others couldn't hear, Jez spoke quietly. 'Thanks for that, mate.'

'Don't worry about it, but you really should keep her on a leash; at least that way you wouldn't have to go chasing after her.'

'I've tried, but she clearly doesn't like being tied up, because she's chewed straight through them all,' said Jez, glumly.

Aled kept his voice lowered. 'Well, you're goin' to have to do summat, because if the wrong person gets wind of today's performance, they'll make you get rid of her.'

Jez shot Aled a sidelong glance. 'You won't say anything, will you?'

'No, but I'd wager I wasn't the only one who saw her.' He tutted irritably. 'You knew she was a flight risk when you got her. It's a miracle she hasn't done this before.' Seeing the guilty look that crossed Jez's face, he spoke slowly. 'Jez?'

'Not during an air raid,' mumbled Jez, 'but she's legged it a few times over cars backfiring and stuff like that.'

Aled rolled his eyes. 'You must've realised summat like this was bound to happen?'

Jez nodded miserably. 'But air attacks are few and far between – thank God – so I thought ...'

'Only you didn't, did you?' said Aled, as kindly as he could manage. 'Because if you had, you'd have done summat about it by now – both for her safety and for yours.'

Jez cursed himself inwardly. He knew he'd been lackadaisical regarding Annie's being tethered, but he'd been hoping that she'd calm down over time. He turned to Aled. 'I'll make her a proper leash, one she can't chew through. I know she won't like it, but it's better than the alternative.'

Aled clapped his hand on Jez's shoulder. 'Good man. You know it makes sense. I'd hate to think what could've happened had she made it to her kennel.' His eyes turned to the roof of the shelter. 'Can you hear anything?'

Jez shook his head. 'Nothing. I reckon our boys have sent them packing.'

The men continued to ponder the dilemma as they waited for the all-clear. 'What you need is a chain – nothing too heavy, but summat she can't chew through,' Aled said slowly.

'I'll go into town,' said Jez, 'see what I can find—'

The all-clear sounded, cutting Jez short. He took Annie by her collar, and as they left the shelter Aled caught his eye. He was glancing meaningfully in the direction of Annie's kennel, which now lay in shreds.

Thanking his lucky stars that Aled had got to her before she'd made it to her kennel, Jez grimaced. 'Bang goes that theory. There's no way she can stay in there.' He looked around. 'I need summat to use for now, because I've got to get back to work.'

Aled held up a finger before disappearing towards the ablutions, calling out 'Wait there' to Jez over his shoulder.

Wondering what the other man was up to, Jez broke into a smile when Aled returned a few moments later brandishing the chain from one of the cisterns. He grinned back at Jez. 'What can I say? It came off in my hand.'

Chuckling, Jez fixed the end of the chain to Annie's collar. 'Thanks, mate. I owe you one – more than one, in fact.'

Aled ruffled Annie's ears. 'Call it payback for the time you pulled me out of the car.'

Jez thanked Aled again before returning to his work, with Annie trotting at his heels.

Aled strode off, trying not to think of what could have happened had he not got to Annie in time. He knew that Jez was soft-hearted when it came to his four-legged friend, but if he wasn't diligent his beloved hound might end up being the Luftwaffe's next victim.

It was the twenty-eighth of March and Cadi was on the train with Poppy, Geoffrey, Kitty, Ronnie, Izzy and Mike.

Glancing across the overcrowded carriage to Izzy, who was sitting on Mike's lap, Cadi reflected on how far her friend had come since running away from her father all those years ago.

Having entered the WAAF a skinny wretch, Izzy had filled out beautifully, and the scar that ran below her left eye – courtesy of her father – was barely visible. In fact, the more time went on, the fainter it got. Having a brute like Eric for a father, Izzy had understandably sworn off men, until Flying Officer Mike Grainger walked into her life. Cadi felt a small smile twitch the corner of her lips as she recalled the day her friends met for the first time.

Cadi and Poppy had been waiting for Izzy in the Horse and Groom when Mike had turned up unexpectedly. They had been chatting about Cadi's recent promotion to corporal when Izzy arrived. The attraction between the two had been immediate and obvious, and it wasn't long before they were seeing each other romantically.

She turned her attention to Geoffrey and Poppy. Poor old Poppy had been another of Eric's victims, and she too had been reluctant to put her trust in the opposite sex, but after joining the WAAF her confidence had grown, and romance had blossomed when she met Geoffrey on the train to Liverpool. The gentle giant was a perfect beau for Poppy, and Cadi knew her friend felt safe with Geoffrey by her side.

Her gaze then fell on Ronnie, who had drawn a line under wartime romance after meeting too many war widows. Cadi would have argued that life was for the living had it not been for her own feelings about wartime weddings.

Lastly, she looked to Kitty. Kitty had been desperate for a boyfriend, and had often whined that she thought she'd never have one, until she found love in the form of one of her co-workers in the canteen of the officers' mess. Cadi fell deep in thought as she tried to recall Kitty's boyfriend's name. Daniel, Derek ... *Dave*. That was it. Kitty hadn't been courting him for long, but she was already smitten; having said that, Poppy had pointed out that Kitty would be enamoured with Frankenstein if he asked her for a date.

Mike's voice cut across her thoughts. 'Penny for them?'

Cadi smiled. 'I was reflecting on how much our lives have changed since the war broke out.'

'Mostly thanks to you,' said Izzy. Seeing her friend about to protest, she continued, striking her reasons off on her fingers as she did so: 'It was you and Poppy who helped me to escape my father, but it was just you who found my mam, and you who introduced me to Mike.'

'And if you hadn't persuaded me to go to Liverpool I'd still be in Rhos,' said Poppy, 'because I'd never have had the guts to go on my own.'

Cadi felt her cheeks grow warm. 'Maybe I'm the taper that lights the fire, but I couldn't have done any of those things without the rest of you.'

'Maybe not,' conceded Izzy, 'but you never gave up, even when I walked away.'

Cadi laughed. 'My dad always used to say that I was like a dog with a bone when I got an idea into my head.'

'You're a doer,' said Poppy; 'always have been, always will be.'

'And thank goodness you are,' said Izzy, 'cos I'd never have found my mam otherwise.'

Cadi leaned back in her seat. 'Talking of your mam, do you know what time she's getting to the Belmont?'

'She should be there already, considering she's based in Burtonwood.'

'Jez reckons she's sounding more American than British nowadays, what with all the Yanks stationed there,' said Cadi.

Izzy glanced down at the nylons which graced her legs. 'Mam got me these from one of the fellers, so you won't find me complaining. She got me some chocolate too.' She fished in the recesses of her handbag before pulling out a large Hershey bar. 'Would anyone like a piece?'

Everyone wanted a share except Kitty, who was resolute that she was watching her figure. 'I'm not like the rest of you. I only have to see a piece of chocolate and I instantly begin to pile on the pounds,' she pouted. 'It's not fair.'

Cadi rolled her eyes. 'You're not overweight, and I don't know why you think you are.'

'It's because I'm short,' moaned Kitty. 'I don't need as much food as everyone else, but at the same time I don't like to waste the portions they dish out.' She paused thoughtfully before adding, 'It's not so bad when Dave's with me, because he has my leftovers, but left to my own devices ...' she blew her cheeks out, making her face look round.

Izzy wagged a reproving finger. 'It's what's on the inside that counts.'

'You need a decent worm to hook a fish,' retorted Kitty promptly, causing the others to laugh. 'Well, you do!' she said indignantly. 'Dad always said you needed the right bait for the right fish.'

Ronnie smiled. 'Only you've already hooked your fish, so why do you think you need to keep dieting?'

'Cos I want to keep him,' said Kitty stoically, 'and there's loads of thinner, more attractive Waafs out there.'

Ronnie shook her head chidingly. 'And did Dave ask you out because you were a blonde bombshell with a tiny waist?'

'Well no, but ...'

'But me no buts!' said Ronnie, adding, 'Dave's with you because he likes *you*, so let's hear no more of this dieting nonsense.'

Kitty looked hopefully at Izzy, who chuckled softly as she retrieved the chocolate bar from her handbag.

She broke a piece off and handed it to Kitty. 'Men like women with meat on their bones,' she said. 'Take it from one who knows.'

Kitty savoured the chocolate as it began to melt on her tongue. 'I forgot you used to be a Skinny Minnie.'

'I wouldn't want to be with a man who was only with me for the way I looked, because looks don't last for ever,' Cadi put in. 'Has Dave ever mentioned your weight?'

'Only to say that I'm fine the way I am.' She shrugged. 'It's me that has a problem with the way I look, not him.'

'Then you need to stop being so hard on yourself, because you're a lovely girl with a wonderful personality, and when all's said and done, that's the only thing that matters,' said Ronnie. She paused before continuing. 'Take the Finnegan brothers, for example; they're both handsome, and immaculately turned out, but would you want one of them as your boyfriend?'

Kitty stared at her, aghast at this reminder of the pimps from whom they had rescued Izzy's mother. 'No, I jolly well wouldn't.'

'There you are then,' finished Ronnie simply. 'Looks aren't everything.'

Cadi glanced out of the window as the train began to slow. 'Are we in Leeds, do you think?'

Mike peered through the window to the platform they were approaching. 'I'd say so.' He counted the previous stops off on his fingers. 'In fact, I'd put money on it.'

Kitty emitted a small squeal of excitement, as she spotted Jez and Annie on the platform. Cadi was waving frantically in order to gain his attention, and both girls beamed as Jez waved back.

With the train being standing room only, it took a while for the departing passengers to leave before the next set could get on. Breathless with anticipation, Cadi gave a small whoop of joy as Jez and Annie eventually entered the carriage, where Annie found herself engulfed by a sea of hands all eager to welcome her on board. With everyone fussing over the setter, Cadi and Jez enjoyed a quiet kiss hello. Leaning back from their embrace, Jez smiled round at his friends. 'I wish I had a welcome like that wherever I went.'

'Ah, but you're not adorable like Annie,' chuckled Poppy.

Settling into Cadi's vacated seat, Jez motioned for her to sit on his lap. 'Cadi thinks I'm adorable.'

Cadi laughed as she settled herself. 'I certainly do, but I think Annie's got the edge, especially when it comes to those big brown puppy-dog eyes.'

Hearing Cadi mention her name, Annie snuffled her way over for a fuss.

'Will you look at that!' Cadi exclaimed. 'I think she remembers me.'

'She's a very intelligent dog,' said Jez, his voice tinged with pride.

'What about Phil? Is he any better?'

'He telephoned me at the base to say that he was feeling better, but wouldn't be returning to the pub,' said Jez. 'He also said that he'd be grateful if I could keep Annie on a permanent basis because he's not fit enough to look after her himself. Phil's not daft: he

57

knows that things could've been a lot worse had you not turned up when you did, which is probably why he asked me to thank you for everything you did for him and Annie.'

A guilty look crossed Cadi's face. 'Does he know I reversed into her? Only I didn't tell him on the day, to save him from further worry.'

Jez smiled kindly. 'He does, but he agrees that Annie probably got hurt running off the way she did. Besides which, if you hadn't hit her, he'd as likely as not be pushing up daisies by now.'

Cadi ran her fingers along Annie's lead. 'Is this new? It's very snazzy.'

Jez chuckled softly. 'It's miles better than the one Aled got for her.'

Cadi arched an eyebrow. 'Aled got her a lead?'

Jez explained Annie's ability to chew through every lead she had, and the consequences. When the girls heard about Aled's temporary solution to the problem they fell into fits of laughter, but after she had calmed down Cadi tutted beneath her breath. 'Honestly, Jez, you're lucky Aled came along when he did.'

'I know. That's why I got her this.' Jez ran his finger across the links of her new lead. 'You should've seen her kennel – or rather, what was left of it.'

'I wonder how many lives dogs have?' commented Poppy's boyfriend, Geoffrey. 'If it's the same as cats then Annie's used up two of her nine already.'

Cadi fingered the stainless steel chain with its leather strap. 'I'm glad you got her this, I wouldn't fancy walking her around Sefton Park on the end of a loo chain.'

Jez grinned. 'I got her an identity tag too.' He swivelled Annie's collar round so that they could see the shiny disc. 'It's got her name on one side and the telephone number of the base on the other – just in case.'

Poppy stroked Annie's ears. 'She's so lovely. I'm going to get a dog when all this is over.'

As the train crossed the open landscape, Cadi turned to Jez as the others fell into their own conversations about the joys of owning puppies.

'Didn't anyone notice that Annie was wearing a toilet chain?'

'Of course they did, but this is Annie we're talking about, so they all turned a blind eye. Besides, it wasn't long before we put it back.'

She rested her head against his shoulder. 'Do you see Aled much?'

'Nigh on every day,' said Jez, 'because I'm part of the team who service the *Ulysses*.'

Cadi grimaced. 'It can't be easy for you, knowing what happened to its predecessor.'

'It's all part and parcel of being in the RAF – Aled knows the score, same as the rest of us.'

She slid her hand into Jez's. 'At least you've got both feet safely on the ground. And as long as you keep Annie firmly leashed, there's not much to stop you getting through this blessed war.'

It was much later the same day when they finally arrived at the Belmont. Maria and Bill welcomed their guests with open arms, and Annie proved to be the star of the evening with the pub customers.

'She's such a sweetheart,' Maria cooed as she fed Annie a few scraps. 'If they ever change their minds at Finningley, she's more than welcome here.'

Raquel – who'd arrived well before the others – pushed her arm through Jez's. 'I reckon she's good enough to win at Crufts.'

Jez slid his hand over Annie's smooth head. 'She'd win best in show, I'd lay money on it.'

Watching Annie in a thoughtful manner, Cadi pursed her lips to one side. 'Where's she going to sleep?'

'Bagsie she sleeps in the girls' room!' cried Poppy, before anyone else had a chance. 'Please, Maria? I swear we won't let her on the beds.'

Maria laughed. 'I think she'll have to, as I can't leave her down here unattended, so as long as it's all right with Jez …?'

Jez placed his arms around Cadi's waist. 'Fine by me, because I don't intend sharing my bed with anyone other than my beautiful wife.'

Poppy clapped her hands together excitedly. 'Now that we've got that settled, can I take her for a walk?'

Jez looked doubtfully from Annie to Poppy. 'She can be quite strong, especially if summat scares her …'

Geoffrey placed his arm around Poppy's shoulders. 'Don't worry, I'll make sure nowt happens to either of them.'

Instructing Annie to 'be a good girl', Jez handed the lead to Poppy who was grinning like the cat that got the cream as she attached it to Annie's collar.

Maria jerked her head in the direction of the stairs. 'If everyone would like to follow me, I'll show you your rooms so that you can get yourselves settled in.'

They followed Maria up the stairs, and she showed the girls to the room which used to be Poppy and Cadi's before taking Mike to the room that he would be sharing with Geoffrey. Leaving everyone to put their belongings away, she led Cadi and Jez to the back of the building.

Beaming proudly, she stopped outside the last door. 'I've put you in the honeymoon suite.'

Jez looked surprised. 'Honeymoon suite?'

'It was your wedding that gave me the idea,' said Maria, her voice full of enthusiasm. 'When we got back to the Belmont the regulars were eager to hear how things went, and it was as I was telling everyone how fabulous the wedding breakfast was that it suddenly dawned on me that we could do the exact same thing here, especially with us being so close to the register office in Brougham Terrace. Anyway, Bill got his paintbrushes out, and …' she waved her arm in a sweeping motion as she opened the door to the honeymoon suite, 'ta-dah!'

'A four-poster bed,' breathed Cadi. 'Oh Maria, it's beautiful.'

Maria smiled proudly. 'I'm glad you like it – believe it or not, Bill made it.'

'Like it? I love it!'

Jez blew a low whistle as he took in the beautifully decorated room. 'Bill's got a real talent when it comes to carpentry.' He turned to Maria. 'It's very good of you, Maria, but are you sure it's all right for us to take your best room?'

'It's our pleasure.' Turning to leave, she called out to them over her shoulder, 'Supper will be ready in half an hour.'

'Sounds perfect,' said Jez, closing the door behind her.

Cadi sank on to the bed. 'I feel like a princess.'

Jez took her hand in his as he sat down beside her. 'When we get a home of our own, I shall make us our very own four-poster bed.'

'A home of our own,' Cadi cooed. 'It makes us sound so grown up, but I don't feel it, do you?'

Jez laughed. 'According to Maria, men never grow up.'

Remembering her father and brothers, Cadi smiled. 'I think she might have a point.'

Holding her hand up, he kissed the back of her knuckles. 'You always worried that you'd end up like your mam if you got married. How do you feel about it now?'

'Silly,' admitted Cadi, 'because I'm not living in a poky terraced house with a gaggle of kiddies. I'm the same as I always was, only with a husband.'

'Do you think marriage changed your mam?'

Cadi shrugged. 'I always assumed that Mam had left behind an exciting life in Liverpool in order to marry my dad. Now that I'm older, I realise that Mam left Liverpool because it wasn't for her. Just because you're born in the city doesn't mean to say that city life's for you. And on the contrary, I was born in a little village, but I didn't want to be a villager.'

'Different strokes for different folks,' said Jez. 'And as I've not kicked the bucket, I'm guessing you've also scrapped your view of war weddings being a bad omen?'

'Please don't tempt fate,' said Cadi quietly. 'It still worries me – it's silly, I know, but I can't help the way I feel.'

Jez chucked her under the chin before kissing her softly. 'Well stop your worrying, because I'm not going anywhere.'

They were two days into their four-day break, and Maria and Bill had closed the pub so that they could spend the day together as one big family.

With everyone having different ideas as to where they should go, Kitty had put her thoughts to the group.

'I know the Greyhound's not there any more, but I've heard so much about it that I think it would be nice to see where it used to be?'

Cadi nodded slowly. 'It was a huge part of our lives, and I must admit, I'd quite like to see what it looks like now.'

Maria threaded her arm through the crook of Bill's elbow. 'Then that's where we shall go.'

They had been walking for quite some time, buried in mutual conversations about life and war in general, when Raquel stopped dead in her tracks.

Izzy put her hand on her mother's forearm. 'Mam?'

Raquel was staring glassy-eyed at a street which ran off to one side. She put her hand on top of her daughter's. 'I've not been round these parts since Eric threw me out.'

Jez placed his arm around his mother's shoulders. 'Do you want to turn back?'

Raquel shook her head. 'It's about time I faced up to my past.' Gazing at the house she had once called home, she voiced her thoughts. 'When I married your father, I was the happiest woman in Liverpool.'

Izzy was staring aghast at her mother. 'Why? Surely you must've realised what he was like?'

Raquel shot her daughter a wry glance. 'Do you think I'd have married him if I knew the truth? Of course not. When we were courting, your father was the perfect gent. Only after he put a ring on my finger did he show his true colours.' She glanced down to where her wedding band used to be. 'Things went downhill from that moment on.'

Jez eyed her inquisitively. 'What difference did your wedding ring make?'

'When Eric's parents abandoned him as a baby, he was taken first to the orphanage, then to the workhouse. When he broke free of the workhouse, he vowed that if he ever got married he would see to it that his children lived in a grand house with fine pieces of furniture, and his family would want for nothing. He had a good paying job when we first married, but he was accused of skimming money, and got fired as a result. The only work open to him was down the docks, and as you know, a docker's pay doesn't go far, so we had to move into a small house with barely any furniture. He spiralled into debt, and that's when he became bad-tempered and violent. I told him I was happy the way we were, but he was convinced that I would leave him, just as his parents had done.'

Jez gave a low whistle. 'I guess that kind of explains why he went for your friend Colin – he must have thought him a threat, a man with his own business.'

'Do you suppose that's why he didn't put me in the orphanage?' said Izzy thoughtfully. 'He was always saying he should have, and I often wondered why he didn't.'

'He probably couldn't bring himself to hand you over, knowing what it was like himself. He didn't go into too much detail, but I know he had scars from where the governor caned him.'

Izzy stared at her mother in disbelief. 'So why on earth did he do the same to me?'

'Because he didn't know any different,' said Raquel. 'To Eric, that's how you discipline a child.'

Izzy blew her cheeks out. 'I wish I'd known all this when I lived at home. It wouldn't have changed anything, but at least I'd have understood why he was the way he was.' She glanced up at the underside of Mike's chin. 'Not that I'd dream of treating my own children that way.'

'And that's the difference between you and him,' said Mike. 'He might have had a reason, but it was no excuse.'

Cadi slid her arm through Raquel's. 'Out of curiosity, what made you go to Portsmouth? Surely you could've gone just about anywhere?'

Raquel gave a short, joyless laugh. 'It was the destination of the first train leaving Lime Street Station.'

Cadi gaped at her. 'And that's the only reason?'

Raquel nodded. 'Once I'd made my mind up, I didn't want to hang about. Something I bitterly regret, because had I been better prepared, with a bit of money behind me, I wouldn't have ended up in such dire straits.'

'As it was, you jumped out of the frying pan and into the fire,' said Kitty.

'Hindsight's a wonderful thing,' agreed Raquel.

'Talking of hindsight, I wonder what's happened to the Finnegans?' Poppy mused.

Raquel smiled happily. 'They've not set foot in Portsmouth since Dolly threatened to spill the beans.'

Geoffrey, who had been quiet until now, spoke up. 'Spill what beans?'

Also feeling confused, Mike added, 'And who's Dolly when she's at home?'

Poppy brought him up to speed. 'Dolly used to work for the Finnegans, the same as Raquel, but when everything went up in smoke Dolly stayed in Portsmouth so that she could help the rest of the girls to get proper jobs and accommodation.

'And the chief of police was one of Dolly's clients,' said Raquel.

Mike shook his head. 'No wonder he didn't want people finding out. What a world we live in, eh?'

'But if the Finnegans aren't in Portsmouth, where are they?' asked Kitty. She was looking around her as though expecting to see them walk round the corner at any minute.

'I don't care as long as it's a long way from us,' said Cadi.

Raquel straightened her back. 'Let's leave this place behind us and get to the Greyhound. It's time for me to move on, in more ways than one.'

The small group sauntered off in the direction of the old pub, all thoughts turning to what they expected to see when they arrived. But when they rounded the corner to Burlington Street, Cadi stared in dismay at the rubble that was once their beloved pub. 'Why haven't they rebuilt it?'

Bill nudged a brick with the toe of his boot. 'It's not worth them starting until the war's over. No sense in building them up for Jerry to knock 'em down again. All you can do is make it safe.'

Cadi peered at something which glinted in the sunlight. Bending down, she fished the object from between some pieces of mortar. Holding it up for closer examination, tears pricked her eyes. 'I don't believe it. It's the key to the pub.' She held the key, which was slightly bent, out to Maria. 'You should have this.'

Maria closed Cadi's fingers over the key. 'You take it. The Belmont's my home now.'

Cadi looked at Jez, who was staring solemnly at the pile of rubble. 'How about a trip to the park?'

There was a general murmur of agreement, and as they headed to the park Cadi hung back with Jez. She pushed her hand into his. 'Your nan would've been ever so pleased to know we'd got married.'

A faint smile crossed his lips as he turned his head to look back at the spot where his grandmother had met her maker. 'I wish she could've been at the wedding. She loved a good knees-up.'

'She'd have had a whale of a time,' said Cadi, 'and probably drunk most of the guests under the table.'

A laugh escaped Jez's lips. 'She certainly knew how to have a good time.'

'The life and soul,' agreed Cadi. Slipping the key into her pocket, she gave his hand a cajoling jiggle. 'C'mon, let's go show the rest of them how to skim stones.'

'Considering Nan never had any children of her own, she made a brilliant grandmother,' remarked Jez, as they followed after the others. 'I reckon you're going to make a great mum.'

Cadi's brow shot towards her hairline. 'Where did that come from?'

He shrugged. 'We're bound to have them one day.'

'That's as maybe, but I really think we should wait until the war ends before we start planning a family, don't you?'

'I do, but I'm hopeful that the war will end sooner rather than later. Besides, it doesn't hurt to think about it.'

Cadi relented slightly. 'I suppose not,' she said, 'but you do know that I'd still want to open a tea room, whether we have children or not.'

'Of course! I think that's a splendid idea, and when we do have children, they can be part of the business.' He placed his hands in the air as though indicating a banner. 'Thomas's Tea Rooms.'

'A family business?'

He smiled. 'We could even have our own pub. I know you used to be against the idea, but that was before we got married. Now we're official, we could run it together – just like Maria and Bill.'

Cadi imagined them living somewhere like the Belmont. It might be a grand pub, but it was too close to the city for her liking. 'If I were to run a pub, I'd rather it was on the outskirts of the city.'

'A country pub?' mused Jez.

She nodded. 'The Greyhound will always hold my heart, but it got bombed because of its location. I know we won't have to fear that kind of thing once peace is declared, but I've stayed in a wide variety of places since joining the WAAF, and I reckon something like the Bull and Heifer would be ideal if it were closer to Liverpool.' She tucked her arm into the crook of Jez's elbow. 'It would be a wonderful place to bring up a family.'

Jez chuckled softly. 'Sounds like you've got it all worked out.'

'A boy and a girl,' said Cadi promptly. 'One of each.'

'I'm not sure it works that way,' said Jez, 'but I don't mind trying until we get it right.'

She slapped his bicep in a playful manner. 'Cheeky!'

'Can't blame a feller for wanting to give his wife her heart's desire,' said Jez, 'and if you want to keep going until we have one of each, then I'm prepared to give it my all until we do.'

She shook a chiding finger. 'Hold your horses. The war's not over yet.'

But Jez wasn't giving up. 'So, what about names – for our children, I mean? Have you thought of any?'

'Carrie Anne, if it's a girl ...'

Jez smiled. 'Carrie after my nan, I assume, but Anne?'

'After my grandmother,' said Cadi.

He nodded. 'And for a boy?'

'Oscar Dewi,' said Carrie promptly.

His smile broadened. 'Oscar because it's my middle name, as well as being Carrie's husband's – God rest his soul – and Dewi after your dad, because it'd be a cold day in hell before we named him Eric?'

She laughed. 'Precisely!'

Once in the park they walked round to the lake, where they found the others gathering stones.

'I ain't done this since I were a young lad,' said Bill as he bent to pick up a particularly flat one.

Jez weighed his stones in his hand. 'How about a competition to see who can skim their stone the farthest?'

Izzy stood up. 'I think that's a fabulous idea.'

They spent the remainder of the morning skimming stones across the surface of the lake, with Cadi being crowned the overall winner. As lunchtime approached, they bought fish and chips which they ate down by the floating road, and after that they headed back to the Belmont where they got themselves ready for an evening's dancing in the Grafton.

As Jez led Cadi on to the dance floor, he reminded her of the time they had shared their first kiss.

'You made me the happiest man alive,' confessed Jez. 'I felt as though I could've won the war single-handed that night.'

She laughed as she gazed up into the deep brown eyes shining down at her. 'Was I worth the wait?'

'A million times over,' said Jez. 'They say that all good things come to those who wait, which is why I'm happy to hang on until the war is over before we have children. We're going to make brilliant parents, Cadi, I just know it. And we'll have no shortage of babysitters, with our extended family.'

Cadi imagined herself, Jez, their two children and Annie living in a pub with a thatched roof and beamed ceilings, only a bus ride away from the city. Sighing happily, she closed her eyes as Jez guided her with ease around the floor. She had married the man of her dreams, and they had the most wonderful future planned. Life couldn't be any more perfect!

Chapter Three

The short break had come to an end and they were currently waiting for their train to arrive at Central Station.

'Four days isn't long enough,' said Maria as she rested her cheek against Bill's shoulder.

'It's better than nothing,' said Bill, 'and no doubt we'll be seeing them all again soon.'

'Just you try keepin' us away,' said Jez. 'It's the only time I actually get to be with my wife.'

'I can't wait to see the end of the war and all its madness,' said Cadi. 'We'll be together all the time then.'

Jez winked at her. 'Maybe even have us a little company.'

'Grandbabies,' cooed Maria. 'How wonderful would that be?'

Poppy caught Cadi's eye. 'I'd rather enjoy being "Auntie Poppy".'

Cadi wagged a reproving finger. 'Sorry to disappoint, but you won't be hearing the pitter-patter of tiny feet for a long time yet.'

'Unless Annie has a litter of puppies,' suggested Jez.

Poppy's eyes rounded, as did the rest of the girls'.

'What a wonderful idea. We could have one each,' said Ronnie excitedly.

Jez had voiced his thoughts without thinking, so was quick to put them straight before they got too excited. 'Sorry, but I think RAF Finningley would draw the line at puppies. Besides, we've only got Annie, and it takes two to tango.'

Cadi stroked Annie's silky head. 'Who'd have thought my little detour could prove to be so popular?'

Standing behind his wife, Bill placed his arms around Maria's shoulders. 'Just you make sure you keep her on a tight leash. I don't want to be hearing any more tales of how you nearly lost your life saving Annie.'

Jez pulled a guilty grimace. 'Don't worry. I won't be making the same mistake twice.'

'I'm glad to hear it,' said Maria testily. 'Annie's a beautiful dog, but not worth risking your life over.'

Hearing the train whistle as it approached the platform, Jez gripped Annie's leash as she tried to dart off. Squatting on his haunches, he smoothed the setter's fur down. 'Steady, old girl, it's only our ride home.'

'Heart of a lion, that one,' chortled Bill. 'It's a good job you're not using her as a guard dog.'

As the train drew to a halt, Maria and Bill found themselves surrounded by their extended family, all of whom wanted to bid them goodbye. Maria dabbed at her eyes with a tissue, whilst Bill gathered everyone for a group photograph. Instructing them to say 'cheese', he took a couple of snaps and gave a satisfied nod. 'I'll send each of you a copy.'

As the others were boarding the train, Jez hurried to Bill, his hand held out for the camera. 'May I?' he asked. Bill lifted the strap over his head and handed it to him, and Jez stepped back a few paces whilst Bill placed his arm around Maria. The two of them smiled for the camera and Jez took the picture, then wound the film on before taking another. The guard called, 'All aboard who's going aboard,' and Jez hurriedly passed the camera back to Bill before taking Maria's hands and holding them tightly.

'Ta-ra, Maria, and thanks for everything. I know I speak for everyone when I say that we've had a wonderful time, and can't wait to come back so that we can do it all over again.'

Maria's lip wobbled. 'Take care of yourself, luv.'

Bill kissed the top of his wife's head as he took her in a comforting embrace: 'C'mon, luv, it's not like you're never goin' to see him again.' He winked at Jez. 'She's never been one for goodbyes. I'll send everyone a copy of the photo.'

Jez touched his temple with two fingers, giving a mock salute. 'Please do. I'd also like a copy of the photos I took of you and Maria, if that's all right?'

'Course it is. Now get you gone before the train leaves without you.'

Giving Maria a final hug, Jez quickly kissed her on the cheek before hurrying over to the train, boarding just as the guard came along to shut the door. Signalling to the driver with his flag, the guard blew his whistle, and the train began to slowly pull away.

Walking arm in arm, Maria and Bill followed the train along the platform until it was out of sight.

Turning to her husband, Maria fought to keep her bottom lip from trembling.

'Every time we say goodbye, I worry that our luck's going to run out. I know we lost Carrie, but she's the only one. I don't know anyone else who's only lost one of their family *and* friends. It's as if we're continually dodging a bullet.'

Bill tutted irritably, not least because he was worried that his wife might be right. 'Stop being so pessimistic.'

'I don't mean to be,' mumbled Maria, 'but neither do I want to be lulled into a false sense of security.'

He thought for a minute, then smiled. 'I know what you need.'

'Oh aye, and what's that then?' asked Maria dubiously.

'A night out on the tiles with yours truly.'

A wry smile forming on her lips, she arched an eyebrow. 'Two nights out in less than a week? Are you sure your hip can take it?'

'Never you mind my hip,' chuckled Bill. 'And we're hardly likely to be doing the conga on our own, now are we?'

'I s'pose not, but we can't keep closing the pub when we want to let our hair down,' Maria pointed out reasonably.

'No, but that Edie Wainwright from down the market's after an evening job, and this would suit her down to the ground. She's local, so she's already familiar with most of our customers, and she needs the extra cash.'

'It would be useful to have an extra pair of hands behind the bar,' Maria mused.

'*And* she's too old for conscription,' added Bill, 'so you needn't fear that she's going to get whisked away to do war work.'

Maria looped her arm through Bill's. 'Do you really think she'll be interested?'

Bill tapped the side of his nose. 'Her husband was in the other night, hinting that you looked as though you needed some help, and his Edie was looking for a job. I never said owt, cos the kids were here, but maybe now?'

Maria nodded. 'I'll put it to him when he comes in tonight.' She squeezed his arm in hers. 'It'll be the first date we've had since before the war.'

'Give her a week to learn the ropes, and if all's good,' Bill paused whilst he contemplated his proposal, 'I'll take you down the Rialto, followed by a chip supper.'

Maria beamed. 'A proper night out, just like the good old days.'

As Raquel got down from the train she was closely followed by Jez, Cadi and Izzy, all of whom had come to give her a proper goodbye, whilst the others looked after Annie.

'Why don't you ask to be transferred?' suggested Cadi. 'It would be marvellous if you could come Lincoln way; we'd all be close together then.'

Raquel held up her hands. 'I've asked, but they say they want me where I am for the time being, though should summat come up I'll be the first to know. But seeing as one of the girls has been wanting to move for over a year, I shan't be holding my breath.'

Fearing the train might start off without them, they each hugged Raquel, with Jez being the last. 'I'll give you a bell as soon as I'm back. Take care of yourself, Mam.'

Releasing her son from a tight embrace, she slid her hands down his arms and gazed lovingly at him. 'You too.' She saw Cadi standing in the carriage doorway in order to prevent the guard from closing it, and gave him a final kiss. 'Goodbye, luv.'

With everyone back in the carriage, Cadi slipped her hand into Jez's as she settled herself on to his lap. 'It's your turn next.'

He nodded woefully. 'True. But we've still got a way to go yet.'

She screwed her lips to one side. 'I don't know when I'll see you again, what with me gallivanting up and down the country.'

Jez shrugged. 'There's not a lot you can do about that, though.'

'Unless I asked to be based somewhere permanently.'

He turned his shoulders so that he could look her in the eye. 'But that would mean giving up your current role.'

She gave a wistful sigh. 'I know, but if it means we get to see more of each other, that's what I shall have to do.'

He eyed her doubtfully. 'I'm not sure that's a good idea, queen.' Seeing the surprised look on her face, he continued hastily, 'I'd love to have you close by, of course I would, but I don't think you'd be happy doing the same thing day in day out.'

'I'd still get to travel,' said Cadi reasonably, 'but I'd be based somewhere – hopefully close to you and the girls – and that could make all the difference.'

'Are you sure it would be enough?' asked Jez, his voice laced with uncertainty. 'You've always wanted to be your own boss, and you get to be that in your current role.'

Cadi nodded confidently. 'Independence and freedom can make for a very lonely life, and I don't want to be on my own when I've a husband stationed near Lincoln.'

'I still worry you'd get bored.'

She entwined her fingers in his. 'I suppose I'm saying I want to settle down.'

A smile slowly traced its way up his cheeks. 'Are you telling me that my little suffragette wants to lay down her placard?'

She nibbled the inside of her bottom lip. 'Is that so bad?'

'Not at all,' said Jez, 'but do you really think they'll listen?'

She crossed her fingers. 'I can but try.'

Jez rubbed his thumb over the top of hers. 'This is such a big change of heart; are you sure you'd be doing the right thing?'

She cupped his chin in the palm of her hand. 'Positive.'

She knew what Jez was getting at, and could even understand his reservations, but all the chat about children, homes and businesses had given Cadi the urge to nest, just like her mother.

Paddy Finnegan scooped the water up in his hands and threw it over his face. Glancing in the mirror above the sink, he watched as the water ran down over his cheekbones, then took a towel and rubbed his face dry before throwing the towel over his shoulder and walking out of the ablutions. Striding the short distance to the Nissen hut, he flung the door open in a heavy-handed manner.

'Oi! You'll have it off its bloody hinges if you keep doing that,' warned one of the men, whose bed was furthest away from Paddy's.

'And what if I do?' growled Paddy. 'You goin' to stop me, are ya?'

The man shook his head. 'Why're you always picking a fight, Paddy?'

'Because it's not my bloody war,' spat Paddy. 'I shouldn't even be here.'

Having had a gutful of Paddy's constant bellyaching, one of the younger men spoke up. 'So you keep sayin', yet you're still here. Why don't you do us all a favour and sod off back to the Emerald Isle where you belong?'

The speaker sprang to his feet as Paddy rounded on him. Suddenly realising that he was confronting the station's boxing champ, Paddy backed down, mumbling, 'I've never run away from a fight in my life.'

The young man didn't bother responding. It was pointless arguing with someone who held their cards so close to their chest.

The man who had first spoken to Paddy gathered his wash kit. 'I don't know what your problem is, but you'd best get it sorted before it comes back to haunt you.'

Paddy shot him a withering glance. 'I don't have to explain myself to the likes of you – or anyone else,' he snarled.

Turning his back to the others, he put his wash kit away before gathering his tobacco tin and heading outside for a smoke. Since he had joined up the other men in his hut had done their best to befriend him, but Paddy was positive they'd soon change their minds if they knew what he'd previously done for a living. So he had purposely distanced himself from them, because the very idea of them looking down their noses at him would enrage him, considering that a lot of them probably frequented brothels themselves, if the clientele of Hillcrest House was anything to go by.

He turned his mind back to the night of the fire. Finding himself confronted by an angry mob of Waafs, he had been on the verge of giving them what for when one of the women – a short, dumpy Scouser – had thrown an oil lamp at him, causing the whole place to go up in smoke. After a brief attempt to douse the flames, Paddy had rushed to the safe, and together with his brother Micky had emptied the contents into two suitcases. The fire would bring unwanted attention from those not on the payroll and they would be left having to do some very awkward explaining. So the pair had fled the building, hurrying to one of the seedier B&Bs down by the docks, where they found themselves a room to hole up in until the coast was clear.

As soon as they had entered the room, Paddy had thrown his suitcase on to the bed, clutched Micky by the throat and pinned him against the wall.

'This is all your fault,' he had roared, 'lyin' on the floor like a bleedin' coward. Yer useless.'

Micky had grabbed hold of Paddy's hands in an attempt to push him off, but his brother was by far the stronger of the two. Struggling to breathe, Micky spoke in a strangled voice. ''S not my fault,' he croaked, and realising that he might accidentally kill his brother Paddy quickly cast him to the floor.

'Oh aye? Then whose fault is it?'

'You kept provokin' them,' said Micky. Massaging the life back into his throat, he continued, 'You should've let them walk. None of this would've happened but for your stupid pride.'

'Stupid pride?' bellowed Paddy. 'If we ain't got a reputation, then we ain't got nothin'.' He pointed a trembling finger towards the docks outside the window. 'If word gets out that we've gone soft, folk'll walk all over us.'

Micky got to his feet. 'Why? Because we let two women leave when we was outnumbered?'

Paddy was clenching and unclenching his fists. 'If we'd have just let them go we'd have been kissing the whole operation goodbye.'

Micky tutted beneath his breath. 'We don't know for certain they'll say owt to anyone.'

Paddy's jaw clenched. 'And you think folk would be prepared to take that risk?' He shook his head. 'They'd have dropped us like hot cakes, for fear of what that Dolly and Raquel *might* say. Running a

81

brothel is one thing, but money-launderin' and smugglin' is a different ball game altogether. Like they said, we might own the police, but we don't own the local rags, and if they'd have got their hands on summat like this we'd have lost all credibility.'

Micky rolled his eyes in a sarcastic fashion as he placed a cigarette between his lips. 'Like we haven't now?'

Paddy punched his brother, knocking the cigarette clean out of his mouth. 'Because of *you*. A blind man could've seen what that cow was goin' to do, but not you, oh no, you just stood there and let her knee you in the knackers.'

Rubbing his mouth from the punch his brother landed him, Micky picked the cigarette up off the floor. 'If you're so bloody clever, why didn't you stop her?'

Paddy threw his hands up in exasperation. 'Because I was blocking the door to stop them from leaving. Not only that, but I shouldn't have to protect you from some stupid tart!'

Micky straightened the cigarette, and placed it between his lips. 'I had Raquel. All you had to do was turf them out, but you couldn't even do that.'

Paddy launched himself across the room and the pair fell to the floor with Micky yelling out for Paddy to leave him be.

Taking Micky's head between his hands Paddy stared into his brother's eyes, spittle gathering in the corners of his lips. He held on to his temper, but only just. 'How could I do that when you was on the floor, whimpering like some snivelling coward?' He thrust Micky's head out of his hands then spat in his face.

82

'I'm ashamed to call you my brother.' Getting to his feet, he wiped his mouth with the sleeve of his jacket as he walked over to one of the suitcases and opened it up. Taking a wad of money and a tin of cigarettes, he headed for the door.

Micky picked himself up off the floor. 'Where are you goin'?'

Paddy answered without turning. 'To see if I can salvage summat from the carnage you've caused.' He formed his fist into a ball. 'If I stay here any longer, I swear I'll swing for you.'

Stepping out into the frosty air, Paddy turned his collar up against the wind and headed into the dark. Taking a pre-rolled cigarette from the tin, he stopped briefly to light it. If he had any hope of getting himself and Micky back on track, he would have to go and see the man who held the most authority. He rolled his eyes. He was also the man who stood to lose the most should word get out.

Taking a long drag on his cigarette, he continued to walk, and soon arrived outside the smart entrance with its black and white tiled porch and pillared doorway. He knocked a brief tattoo against the door before slinking back into the shadows to wait for someone to answer.

He hadn't been there long before the door opened and a maid stood peering into the darkness. 'Hello?'

Paddy came out from behind the shelter of a bush. Briefly touching the brim of his fedora between finger and thumb, he asked if he might speak to the master of the house.

The maid cast him a disapproving glance as her eyes travelled from his shoes to the crown of his hat. Lifting her chin, she spoke haughtily. 'And who should I say is enquiring?'

When Paddy smiled, the moonlight glinted off his gold incisor. 'Tell him I've come with news of Hillcrest House. He'll know who I am.'

Taking care to close the door firmly behind her, the maid disappeared, but it was only a few moments before a rotund, blustery man with a walrus moustache took her place in the doorway. Hastening down the steps, he pulled Paddy away from the house and made sure he was out of earshot before speaking in hissed tones. 'What the bloody hell are you doing here?'

Paddy wrenched his arm firmly, but politely, from the man's grasp and briefly summarised the situation. 'We've had a fire.'

'I don't give a rat's behind what's happened, you should know better than to come here,' spat the old man irritably.

'Do you think I'd be here if I weren't desperate?' snarled Paddy. 'Hillcrest House is nowt but ashes ...' He went on to explain exactly what had happened, although he was careful to leave his and Micky's incompetent attempts to stop the girls out of the conversation.

The old man stared at him, his face turning puce as the gravity of his situation sank in. Lifting his fat forefinger so that it was millimetres away from Paddy's nose, he spoke in a shaking voice as he tried to keep himself from being overheard. 'Do you mean to tell me that there's two tarts with an axe to grind running free round my city?'

Paddy's jaw flinched. 'I could hardly stop them, not when the bleedin' house was on fire.'

The older man gripped Paddy's elbow. 'They know who I am,' he said harshly. 'How long do you think I'll remain in power once they'd had their tuppence worth?' He pointed to the house behind him. 'I'll lose my house, my wife, *and* my place in the cabinet.'

Paddy swallowed. He'd known it wouldn't be easy. 'I'll find them, make sure they keep their mouths shut.'

The ends of the man's walrus moustache trembled as his anger rose. 'How the hell are you going to do that when you couldn't stop them leaving in the first place?' he spluttered, adding, 'Hell's teeth, you don't even know where they are!'

Paddy rubbed the back of his neck with his hand. 'Raquel's daughter's a Scouser. They were sayin' summat about puttin' Raquel and Dolly up with a friend of theirs. As none of them are from around these parts, I assume they were talking about somewhere in Liverpool.'

The old man nodded quickly. 'Further away from here the better.' He scowled at Paddy. 'Stay out of the way until the dust settles, and we'll go from there,' he snapped, and returned to the house without so much as a backward glance. He loathed the Irish brothers, but he needed them in order to keep his dealings afloat. If the girls really had left the area, then he saw no reason why they couldn't continue as before.

Paddy returned to the B&B to find his brother missing, along with both suitcases. Leaving the room in a blind rage, he headed for the train station, hoping to catch Micky before he absconded with their life savings. He ran up and down the empty platforms, but there was no sign of him. When a guard ventured over to see who was running around, Paddy grabbed him by the elbow. 'When did the last train leave, and did you see a feller carrying two suitcases get on board?'

The guard attempted to snatch his arm back, but there was a look of murderous intent in Paddy's eyes. 'L-lots of people got on,' he stammered, 'and most of them had suitcases.'

'You'd remember him,' snarled Paddy. 'Did anyone try and get on without paying?'

The man nodded nervously as he remembered the encounter with the Irishman who had tried to board the train without buying a ticket first. He'd confronted him, assuming that the man had made a genuine mistake, but it had been clear from the look on his face that he had never intended to pay. It was only when the guard threatened to call the police that the Irishman swore loudly and purchased a ticket. As an image of the man, trying to take some money from one of his suitcases whilst hiding the contents from prying eyes, entered the guard's mind, he told Paddy all he knew.

'Where was the train headed?' snarled Paddy.

The guard swallowed. 'Birmingham.'

Cursing out loud, Paddy released his grip on the frightened man. He hadn't a cat in hell's chance of heading his brother off, but at least he knew the destination.

As he headed back to the B&B he chastised himself for being stupid enough to leave Micky with all the money, especially after having threatened his life. His brother was the sort of man who acted on impulse, and

Paddy should've realised that his harsh words might have caused Micky to run.

The morning after the fire Paddy had gone to take a look at Hillcrest before returning to the house he had visited the previous evening. When he arrived, he saw a police car pulling away from the kerb. Wondering why the police had been visiting the house, he looked up to see the man with the walrus moustache staring out of a first-floor window after the car. As his gaze fell, his eyes settled on Paddy, and he gestured furiously for him to get out of sight before dropping the curtain.

Paddy stepped behind the hedge and waited for the man, who appeared within moments. Pushing Paddy further behind the hedge, he spoke through gritted teeth. 'I thought you said Raquel and Dolly had left the city?'

'Why? What's happened?'

'That bloody Dolly sang like a sodding canary. Told them all about you and your brother, and the kind of business that went on at Hillcrest House.'

Paddy's face paled. 'They've got no proof ...'

The other man cut across him. 'No? That's not what Dolly reckons. In fact she's got a flamin' list! Birthmarks, tattoos, freckles, even circumcisions ...' He shot Paddy a withering look. 'Dolly knows marks on my body that even my *wife* doesn't know about. What's more, she's written everything down and handed it to a friend for safeguarding, so that if anything happens to her the information can be made public.' With his face turning beetroot, his cheeks wobbled as he tried to contain his temper. 'She's also threatened to hang the bloody lot of us if you and your brother don't leave Portsmouth.' Seeing the fire that flashed in Paddy's eyes, the man continued, 'No one's goin' to miss you or your brother should you disappear one day, so don't even think about trying to blackmail or threaten me. You and Micky are to be out of the city by sundown; any later than that, and I'll arrange for your removal. There's bigger fish out there than you, Paddy Finnegan. I know a lot of people in very low places who won't need much persuading once they know the pecking order's changed.'

Paddy stared at him open-mouthed. 'You can't! You're ...'

The man came so close, Paddy could see the thread-like veins on the bridge of his nose. 'You'd be amazed what I can do. You know for yourself that you only got away with running a brothel – as well as your other "business" – because I saw to it.' His eyes darted wildly in their sockets. 'Don't test me, Finnegan.'

Paddy was desperate to retaliate, to put the old fool in his place, but it was pointless. Pushing his hands into his pockets, his fingers curled around the crisp notes he had taken out of the suitcase the night before. It wasn't much, but it was better than nothing. With no belongings to speak of, other than the clothes he stood up in, he headed straight for the train station. His only hope now was to hunt his brother down in Birmingham, and at least recover some of the money before Micky blew the lot.

Arriving at his destination, it soon became clear that Micky had made quite the impression in Birmingham, but for all the wrong reasons.

'I remember him,' said Paddy's informant sullenly. 'He was acting as if he had money to burn, and he was carrying two suitcases rumoured to be stuffed with cash.' He gave Paddy a disapproving look. 'Folk round these parts don't take too kindly to foreigners actin' as though they think they're cock of the walk, when the rest of us are strugglin' to put food on the table.'

Paddy raised an eyebrow. 'Cock of the walk?'

'Aye. He were living out of a hotel room, and from what I heard, he was holding nightly poker sessions. They reckon the drink was flowing, and there were girls aplenty – if you know what I mean.'

Paddy rolled his eyes. He knew exactly what the man meant. 'So where is he now?'

'If he took the advice given him, he's lost himself in the services; if not, he's at the bottom of the cut.' Seeing the blank look on Paddy's face, he elaborated. 'The canal.'

Paddy's face darkened. He might want to kill his brother, but he didn't like the idea of him being threatened by complete strangers. He grabbed the man by his collar. 'You'd better tell me everything you know, or *you'll* be at the bottom of the cut.'

The man's eyes bulged as he gasped for breath. Paddy relaxed his grip and allowed him to talk.

'Don't shoot the messenger, mister. I wasn't involved in none of this – poker's too rich for my blood. I only know what I was told.'

'Which was?'

'He was cheating, and they reckon he'd been doing so for some time. From what I heard they took everything he had, and he only escaped a bullet because the coppers raided the room they were holding the games in.'

'Are you sure he wasn't arrested?'

'Definitely not. The coppers ain't stupid. Once they realised who was in the room, they made sure they had a chance to escape before trying to arrest anyone.' The man narrowed his eyes. 'I don't know who you are, mister, but I can guarantee there's worse than you in Birmingham, and this is their stomping ground, not yours.'

Paddy rolled his eyes. 'I'm not trying to tread on anyone's toes, I'm trying to find out what happened to my brother.'

'Like I said, he was given a friendly word of advice to join up.' He shrugged. 'It's easy to hide in the services, especially from men like that, cos there's no way they're going to sign on the dotted line.'

Paddy released his informant and headed off to have a think. If the man was right, and Paddy very much suspected he was, Micky was in the forces, which meant Paddy would never find him.

Whilst he considered what to do about his brother, Paddy turned his hand to petty theft, but that came to an abrupt halt when he was discovered sliding backwards out of a window. As it turned out, he was stealing on a patch run by a gang of thugs, quite possibly the ones who'd threatened his brother, and they soon let him know that his presence wasn't welcome. He was left not only beaten and bruised, but with a warning to never return or face the consequences.

With his options running out, Paddy turned his thoughts back to Micky. In Paddy's opinion there was no way Micky would've stayed in the services, and neither would he have returned to Ireland, because even he must know he'd be dead as soon as his foot touched Irish soil.

He wreaks havoc everywhere he goes, Paddy told himself. *It was his fault we had to leave Ireland in the first place.* He remembered the day his brother had decided they should join the IRA. Paddy had been against it from the start, but Micky was convinced that the brothers could profit from the organisation by double-dealing in firearms.

Paddy had warned his brother that he was playing with fire, but Micky had remained determined. So Paddy had kept a close eye on things, and when he got wind that some members of the IRA were indeed looking for Micky he had made sure that he and his brother were out of the country before they could be found. Once they were safely across the water, he telephoned one of his associates to see if he had any news, and that was when he'd been told that the IRA had found out about Micky's shenanigans and as a result was wanted by one of the most powerful organisations known to Ireland.

He frowned. Was it possible that his brother had really believed he could make a bargain with the IRA? A vision of Micky pleading for his life in return for handing over their loot entered his mind. It would be typical of him to assume he could buy his way out of trouble, but Paddy knew full well that the IRA would take the money with one hand and shoot Micky dead with the other.

Paddy himself certainly wouldn't be going back to Ireland, or to Portsmouth, and seeing as he'd outstayed his welcome in Birmingham he could only see one choice left to him. The services were taking men on in their droves. It wasn't what he wanted, but beggars couldn't be choosers, so he had joined the RAF and done his training in the MT.

The pay was pitiful and the work dire. Paddy had been about to jump ship when a new opportunity presented itself in the form of a spiv who had approached him whilst he was repairing a puncture at the side of the road. Being in the RAF meant Paddy had access to things that civilians couldn't get hold of. Not only that, but it was easy for him to transport items up and down the country without fear of being stopped. It hadn't been the best earner, but it certainly beat the wages of an airman in the RAF. Paddy's intentions were to continue on his current path until he found his brother. Despite their differences, they worked better as a team than on their own, and with Paddy's new connections he felt sure they could start again.

April 1944

Cadi was on the move once more, only this time she was heading to RAF Chivenor in Devon; not to start another airbase, but to transport an officer to an unknown destination.

She loved Devon itself, but she wasn't so keen on the narrow, windy roads which added copious amounts of time to the journey – especially if tractors or livestock were involved. As she passed by the Stag's Head inn, with its thatched roof and deep-set windows, Cadi turned her mind back to the conversation she had had with Jez on the train ride back to Lincoln. Jez might have thought her decision to be sudden, but in truth she'd been thinking about settling somewhere closer to Lincoln ever since they married. She was officially based at RAF Coningsby, and thought it would be ideal if she could remain there without the constant travelling, but she doubted the RAF would see things her way. Kitty had once remarked that the RAF were forever trying to place a square peg into a round hole. Cadi had thought her friend's comment to be ludicrous, but she soon learned that Kitty had the RAF down pat.

Turning on to a main road, she saw the main gate to the base looming ahead of her. She pulled up in front of it and flashed her ID at the guard, who waved her through, indicating a parking space opposite the place where she would be signing in.

Cadi parked and drew her small compact mirror out of her handbag to check her reflection. Smoothing an errant strand of hair beneath her cap, she popped the mirror back into her handbag and made her way over to the office. Inside, she smiled at the young Waaf who sat behind one of the desks. 'Sergeant Thomas. I'm here to transport one of your officers.'

The Waaf looked down at a sheaf of papers in front of her. Thumbing through the top few pages, she traced a pencil down the list of names, then nodded. 'I'll inform Officer Harris of your arrival.' She glanced at the clock on the wall behind her before adding, 'He's been in a meeting. If you'd like to wait here, I'll get one of the girls to nip over to see if he's ready.'

Cadi gave her a brief smile. 'Thank you. I'll just nip to the ablutions whilst I'm waiting.' As she left the office she heard the Waaf instructing the woman beside her to run and tell Officer Harris his ride had arrived.

Cadi soon located the ablutions, and had just exited the cubicle when she bumped into the one woman she had hoped she would never see again: Daphne. For a moment, the two women stared at each other in stunned silence. Daphne was the first to move. Snorting her contempt, she swept past Cadi, and Cadi, flabbergasted that Daphne had the audacity to act as though she were the one in the right, was determined not to let her walk away before she'd had a chance to voice her thoughts.

'How dare you look at me as though I were the dirt beneath your shoe,' she snapped. 'Especially after what you did to Aled.'

Daphne folded her arms across her chest as she turned to face her. 'I *knew* it was you and your little pals who blabbed.'

Cadi stared at her, aghast. 'Don't bring Kitty into this. She didn't know Aled from Adam. If you're going to lay blame, then you should point the finger at me.'

'Kitty might not have known him, but Poppy did.' Her eyes narrowed. 'Why didn't she tell him that I very much regretted my actions? I only told them in the first place because I was trying to stop them from making the same mistake.' She pouted petulantly. 'I should've kept my nose out, and let them learn the hard way – just as I did.'

Cadi gaped at her in disbelief. 'Kitty and Poppy would never have *dreamed* of doing what you did.'

Daphne took a step forward. 'How do you know? I bet you'd have jumped at the chance to stop Jez from going if an opportunity arose. It's all well and good to look down your nose at me, but I reckon you'd have done exactly the same thing.'

'I'm nothing like you,' said Cadi. 'I'd never have meddled in Jez's affairs to suit my own needs. And that's the difference. Aled was desperate to be a pilot, and he would've made it too, but for your interference.'

'I wanted to keep him safe,' said Daphne, 'which according to you is the crime of the century.'

'Only you didn't, did you?' snapped Cadi. 'You put him in the worst possible danger.'

'It's obvious I didn't mean to,' said Daphne loftily. 'It's as though you're hanging me for having a heart.'

'You may have convinced yourself that you were doing the right thing as far as Aled goes,' said Cadi, 'but you were being malicious and spiteful when you went running to Jez.'

'I was being truthful,' said Daphne evenly. 'I didn't tell that man a single lie. Much the same as you when you went to see Aled – apart from the fact that you didn't bother to tell him how much I regretted my decision.'

'That's where you're wrong. Poppy told me how much you regretted what you'd done, as did Kitty, and I told Aled, because he had a right to know,' said Cadi. 'But he reckoned you weren't a couple when he took his exams, and you'd only done it in the hope that he'd help you run your parents' farm when the war was over.'

Daphne blinked. She hadn't realised Aled had been so open with Cadi. What's more, he'd more or less hit the nail on the head. Daphne had only interfered because she wanted a farmer for a husband, and it was only later that she fell in love with him. Her silence was speaking volumes.

'He was right, wasn't he?' said Cadi.

'I'm not about to start discussing the ins and outs of our relationship with the likes of you,' said Daphne primly, 'especially as we're no longer together, although I dare say you were privy to that information before I was.'

'Can you blame him?' said Cadi. 'He'd be forever watching his back.'

Daphne looked down to a thin circle of silver which adorned her wedding finger. 'With hindsight you did me a favour.'

Cadi followed the other woman's gaze. 'You're married?' she breathed, hardly able to believe her eyes.

'Engaged,' said Daphne. 'To a wonderful man who didn't hesitate to ask me to be his wife.' She gave a haughty sniff. 'It was love at first sight.'

'Bully for you.'

'We'd only known each other for a few weeks,' Daphne admitted, 'but when you meet the right one, you just know ...' She glanced at the ring on Cadi's finger before adding, spitefully, 'I wonder why it took you and Jez so long to tie the knot?'

'Because only fools rush in,' said Cadi levelly.

'I don't see the point in hanging back when you know you've found *the one*,' retorted Daphne. She pushed the door to an empty cubicle and disappeared inside, making it clear that as far as she was concerned the conversation was at an end.

Turning to the sink, Cadi soaped her hands as she ran them under the tap. She knew it was none of her business, but she couldn't help wondering which poor sap had captured Daphne's heart. As she shook the water from her fingers she glanced at the door to Daphne's cubicle before stepping outside.

Hearing the outside door close, Daphne checked to make sure that Cadi had really gone before stepping out from her cubicle. Talking to her had brought back some pretty nasty memories which Daphne would have preferred to remain buried. After her failed romance with Aled, she had vowed never to date again, but that had all changed when she met her fiancé for the first time. Being new to the RAF he had been seeking directions to the camp cinema when he approached her. As Daphne was going there herself, she had offered to lead the way, and it seemed only natural that they should sit together. They had watched *A Day at the Races*, during which he had told her that he was a country boy at heart who'd always dreamed of running his own farm. Daphne had told him about her father's farm and the two had chatted merrily for hours. From that day on they spent all their free time together, and when he proposed a few weeks later Daphne found herself saying yes without giving it a moment's thought. It was a fresh start with no secrets, and as far as Daphne was concerned her break-up with Aled had been for the best, even though it hadn't seemed like it at the time. She had put her past behind her, and if she never saw Cadi again it would be a day too soon.

Having returned to the office only to be told that Officer Harris would be some time yet, Cadi now sat in the NAAFI, eating a cheese and pickle sandwich. She supposed it was highly likely that she would have bumped into Daphne sooner or later, what with her constant moves around the country, but she only wished it had been from afar.

The audacity of the woman, she thought as she ate the last of her sandwich. *Everything is always someone else's fault as far as she's concerned. I can't imagine who her fiancé is, but I hope he's got a strong backbone, because Daphne will walk all over him if not.*

She drained the dregs of her tea just as the Waaf from the office approached to tell her that Officer Harris was ready to leave.

Glad to be quitting the NAAFI in case Daphne turned up, Cadi went to meet the officer, who was waiting by her car. Having greeted him she took the crank handle from under the driver's seat and pushed it into the slot. 'May I ask where we're headed?'

'RAF Ilfracombe,' he replied.

Cadi stared at him. 'But that's barely twenty minutes from here.'

He slid into the back seat of the car. 'So you know the way then.'

Cadi cranked the car into life with more force than usual. She had just driven the best part of six hours to ferry an officer twenty minutes up the road. Surely someone at Chivenor could've taken him? She tutted beneath her breath. Daphne was a driver; why hadn't they sent her? Wordlessly, she took her place behind the wheel and waited for the guard to open the gate before setting off. The lane was narrow, and she had only driven a short way when she was forced to stop for a lorry that was coming towards them. She reversed the car to the nearest passing place, and waited for the lorry to pass. The driver raised his hand in thanks, and when Cadi looked up to acknowledge him her heart skipped a beat. She might have been mistaken, but she was almost positive that she'd just seen Micky Finnegan. She stared after the lorry in her rear-view mirror. Surely she must be mistaken? What would Micky be doing driving a military lorry?

She started as the officer tapped his cane on the back of her seat. 'What's the hold-up?'

Cadi apologised as she slipped the car into gear and pulled out on to the road. 'Sorry, sir. I thought I recognised the driver of the lorry.'

'O'Connell?'

Cadi glanced at him in the rear-view mirror. 'Is that his name?'

The officer laughed. 'I should bally well know, considering the number of times I've had to reprimand him.'

Cadi breathed a sigh of relief. 'In that case it's not the same person.'

He shrugged. 'Everyone looks the same in uniform.'

Only I've never seen Micky in uniform, thought Cadi, before scolding herself inwardly. There was no way the RAF would allow a man like Micky to join their ranks, and nor would he want to. Men like him preferred to make their money by foul means not fair.

You're tired after the long journey here, Cadi told herself; *you've already been on the road for the best part of three days. What you need is a good night's kip.*

Delighted to receive a phone call from his wife, Jez picked up the receiver.

'Hello, Mrs Thomas, and what can I do for you?'

Cadi smiled. 'We've been married for over four months. When are you going to stop calling me Mrs Thomas?'

'Never!' cried Jez, before adding, 'I still have to pinch myself, cos it took me long enough to get you down the aisle.'

'Certainly longer than Daphne – she's only known her fiancé for a few weeks.'

Jez interrupted without apology. 'Do you mean Daphne as in Aled and Daphne?'

'I do indeed,' confirmed Cadi. 'I bumped into her earlier today. You should've seen the look she gave me! Like I was summat nasty that she'd stepped in. There was no way I was going to allow her to look at me like that without giving her a piece of my mind.'

'No more than she deserves,' said Jez.

'I know. Yet she tried to make out we were the villains and she was the injured party. When that didn't wash, she tried to claim that it was all for the best because she'd found the man of her dreams.'

'He must need his bloody head examining,' said Jez stoutly.

'With them only being together a few weeks before he popped the question, they obviously don't know each other very well.'

Jez gave a dark chuckle. 'Boy is he in for a nasty surprise!'

'Talking of nasty surprises, you'll never believe who I thought I saw earlier today.'

'Who?'

'Micky Finnegan.'

Just hearing the other man's name caused Jez to splutter. 'Where? When?'

'As I said, I *thought* I saw him, but it turns out I was mistaken – thank goodness.'

Jez was immediately on his guard. 'How can you be sure?'

'The officer said his name was O'Connell.'

'You thought he was in the *RAF*?' asked Jez incredulously. 'Even I could've told you you'd got that wrong, and I wouldn't need to see him in order to come to that conclusion, either.'

'You're right, and with hindsight of course I know it can't have been him, but just for a few seconds I was almost positive.'

'Well for God's sake don't tell me mam,' said Jez, 'she'd have kittens if she thought Micky might turn up on her doorstep. Could you imagine what it would be like for her if the girls on her base knew what she used to do for a living?'

Cadi's eyelids fluttered at the very thought. 'My lips are sealed.' Wishing that she'd never brought the matter up, she turned the conversation back to Daphne. 'Are you going to mention Daphne's new love interest to Aled?'

'Yes. He was quite concerned that she might still be in Finningley when he first arrived, so I'm certain he'd want to know that she no longer has him in her sights.'

101

The operator cut across them in the usual manner.

'Time to go,' said Jez. 'Love you with all my heart.'

'Love you too, cariad.'

Hearing the click as the operator terminated the call, Cadi replaced the receiver and made her way out of the NAAFI. She turned her mind to the following day, when she would be taking Officer Harris back to Chivenor. She knew she was being silly, but there was a niggling doubt in the back of her mind that she'd truly seen Micky, and she wouldn't be satisfied that she had made a mistake until she saw this O'Connell up close for herself. Only how would she go about arranging that?

Mulling the thought over, she made her way to the billet where she would be staying overnight. Cadi had deemed it ridiculous that she had been called from afar only to drive an officer twenty minutes up the road, but if this O'Connell proved to be Micky, then maybe fate had played a hand in the appointment? And if that were the case, then who could say the same thing wouldn't happen again when she took Harris back?

The thought of a man like Micky in the RAF made her skin crawl. A hunter amongst his prey; what would his effect be on the unsuspecting Waafs? Surely even Micky wouldn't try to prostitute servicewomen, but she feared he would find some way of profiting from their misery. Her mind instantly turned to Raquel, and what Micky would do if he were to come across her … she shook her head. It didn't bear thinking about. He would make Raquel's new life a complete misery by blackmailing her into buying his silence, and he'd be able to command whatever price he wanted.

She cursed herself inwardly for giving the matter so much thought. It didn't make sense that someone like Micky would join the RAF, and even if he had, he'd not last more than five minutes. Micky didn't take orders, he gave them. A picture of the man driving the lorry formed in her mind and she felt her stomach jolt unpleasantly. Sometimes common sense didn't come into it. Cadi knew in her bones that she'd seen Micky, and only speaking to this O'Connell would convince her that she was wrong.

A frown appeared on the brow of Daphne's fiancé as he placed his arm around her shoulders.

'Bad day?'

She nodded. 'I bumped into someone I hoped I'd never see again.'

'Anyone I know?' he asked curiously.

She shook her head. 'She was only here on a flying visit – thank God.'

'Yet she still found time to upset you?' he noted, before adding sarcastically, 'That was nice of her.'

'Typical of Cadi, mind you,' mumbled Daphne. 'She's always making trouble, raking over the past, and bringing up matters that had been dead and buried until she showed her face.'

He eyed her curiously. 'Sounds ominous – anything I should know?'

'Not really,' said Daphne hurriedly. Having snared the man of her dreams she had no intention of frightening him off. 'More like Chinese whispers.'

'You get plenty of them in the RAF.'

Eager to put the matter to rest before he could ask any more questions, she brought the conversation to a quick conclusion. 'We got everything off our chests, and I rather think I came out on top, because you should've seen her face when I said I was engaged.'

He kissed the top of her head. 'You told her about me?'

'Not everything,' admitted Daphne, 'but when she spied my ring I couldn't resist telling her that I was going to marry a wonderful man.'

He huffed on his fingernails before pretending to polish them on the lapel of his jacket. 'A prince amongst men.'

She slid her arm around his waist. 'You are to me.'

He gave a lopsided smile. 'Maybe so, but I bet there's a few out there who'd disagree with you.'

'They're just jealous,' said Daphne confidently.

'You said she was only around for a short while; what was she doing here?'

'Dunno, but I did see her getting into a car with Harris.'

'Officer Harris?'

She nodded. 'I don't know where they were going, and I don't care either as long as it's far away from here.'

He stopped outside the door to the cinema. 'How can you be sure she's not coming back?'

Daphne froze. 'I'm sure she would've said if she were being posted here, don't you think?'

'Not if she thought it were obvious. How did you leave the conversation?'

104

Daphne rolled her eyes. 'I walked off before she had a chance to say anything else.' Daphne had cut Cadi off purposely, but with hindsight had that been a wise move? If she'd seen the conversation to its end, Cadi might've said what she was doing there. The thought of being on the same base as the wretched woman, who would undoubtedly tell everyone what she had done, had Daphne on the brink of tears. 'You don't really think she's been posted here, do you?'

He shrugged. 'No idea. I suppose her friends would know. Could you ask one of them, maybe get the heads-up?'

Daphne laughed scornfully. 'I wouldn't ask them if you paid me.'

His eyes widened. 'Just what went on between you and these women?'

She pouted defiantly. 'They're nothing but a bunch of interfering busybodies.'

That sounded typical of most women as far as he was concerned. 'I take it you knew each other before the war?'

'Not at all. I met them by accident, when I went to RAF Little Snoring.'

'Little Snoring?'

Daphne continued absently. 'That's when my troubles started. If it hadn't been for that Poppy and her pal Kitty ...' She tutted beneath her breath. 'Cadi might *say* Kitty had nothin' to do with it, but as far as I'm concerned her pals are as thick as thieves, and I wouldn't trust any of them as far as I could throw them.'

'Who's Kitty?'

'She's a short, fat, dumpy Scouser with frizzy hair who likes to tattle-tale on innocent people, and I wish I'd never gone to her stupid station.'

He pointed to the screen as the silvery light began to flicker across it. 'Looks like the film's about to start.' He pulled her close. 'Don't worry about this Cadi or her pals. If they start giving you gyp, come and tell me, and I'll soon put an end to their shenanigans.'

Daphne settled her cheek against his shoulder. It felt wonderful to have a man on her side; not like Aled, who would have taken anyone's word over hers. As far as Daphne was concerned, Kieran was heaven-sent.

Jez knocked a brief tattoo on the door to Aled's hut before entering.

Aled pushed the letter he had been writing to Marnie to one side and looked expectantly at Jez. 'To what do I owe the honour?'

'Fancy goin' for a swift one?'

Aled slapped both his thighs before standing up. 'You must've read my mind. Where to?'

'The Bull and Heifer?'

Aled slid his wallet into his trouser pocket. 'Lead on Macduff.' Stepping outside, he wasn't altogether surprised to see Annie tied up. He gave her a friendly pat. 'Is she our plus one?'

Jez laughed. 'Everybody loves a redhead – or they do this one, at any rate.'

Aled took his place behind the wheel of the car, and waited until Jez had settled Annie in the footwell of the passenger's side before setting off. Very soon, the setter had climbed on to Jez's knee so that she might put her head through the open window. Smiling, Aled shot Jez a chiding glance. 'You let that mutt get away with murder.'

Jez cocked a superior eyebrow. 'You'll not be calling her a mutt when she wins best in show at Crufts.'

'She's a beauty, but she'd not hold a candle to my collies in the brains department,' said Aled. They both glanced at Annie, who was still staring happily out of the window.

Jez smiled. 'She might not be the sharpest knife in the drawer – or certainly not compared to a collie – but she's loyal to her core.'

Aled ruffled Annie's head. 'She certainly makes for a good companion. Which is more than can be said for some of the females I've had in my life recently.'

Jez looked shrewdly at Aled. 'If you're referring to Daphne, then I don't think her fiancé would agree with you.'

Aled stared at Jez open-mouthed. 'Her *what*?'

Jez gave an alarmed cry as Aled's lack of attention caused the car to drift on to the opposite side of the road. 'Her fiancé!'

Hastily veering back on to his own side of the road, Aled stared doggedly ahead. 'I take it you've seen her – she's not back at Finningley, is she?'

Jez shook his head. 'Not me; Cadi.' He went on to relay his wife's telephone conversation from the previous evening.

'Well, I'll be blowed,' said Aled faintly.

'I must admit, I was a tad surprised myself,' said Jez, 'but not half as much as Cadi.'

Aled turned into the car park of the pub and drew to a halt. 'I just hope she's learned her lesson.'

Jez alighted from the car, closely followed by Annie. 'She told Cadi that they'd only been together for a matter of weeks before he proposed.'

Aled held the door of the pub ajar for Jez, and they ordered two pints of Burtons, which they took to one of the tables. 'I hope he knows his way around a farmyard, because if he doesn't he'll have to learn quickly, and life on a farm is very different from that in the services. Which is another reason why I'm hanging fire with Marnie.'

Jez frowned. 'How d'you mean?'

'Marnie's in love with the man in air force blue who flies off into the sunset; she's never met the man who spends his day in tatty overalls, up to his knees in pig manure.'

Jez laughed at the two images in his mind. 'Quite a difference, I'll grant you, and not just for Marnie, but for you too. Are you sure you've thought this through properly? About going home, I mean.'

'I've promised my parents that I'll return when the war's over, and I intend to abide by that promise, but it will be with a heavy heart.' He paused whilst he took a sip of his drink. 'What about you? Are you still planning to be a mechanic?'

'Cadi's decided she'd like to run a pub.' Jez glanced around the interior of the establishment they were in. 'A bit like this one, but on the outskirts of Liverpool.'

'You do surprise me. I'd have thought Cadi would want to be in the heart of the city.'

Jez shrugged. 'She doesn't want to bring kids up in the city centre – too busy. She'd prefer to be on the outskirts, so that they'd get the best of both worlds, and the pub would provide a living for us both, of course.' He arched his shoulders as a shiver ran down his spine.

'What's up? Someone walk over your grave?'

'I hope not! It makes you think, though. Here we are talking about our futures, yet we don't even know if we're going to make it to the finishing line.'

Aled looked out of the window as a plane roared past. 'Course we will – we've made it this far, haven't we?'

Remembering that Aled was in a far more dangerous position than himself, Jez nodded fervently, holding up his glass. 'To making it to the finishing line.'

Aled clinked his glass against Jez's. 'Hear, hear.'

Chapter Four

Cadi bade goodbye to Officer Harris, then headed for the cookhouse. On every base the kitchen was the bed of all gossip, and one of the cooks was bound to know if it was Micky that she'd seen.

When she reached the front of the queue she ordered the cottage pie, and while the cook was ladling it on to a plate she asked, 'I wonder if you could help me? As I was driving out of here yesterday, I could have sworn I saw a man who looked very much like someone I've seen before, who goes by the name of Micky Finnegan. Have you heard of him?'

The cook pulled a face as she mulled this over, before nudging one of her workmates. 'I haven't; have you heard of a Micky Finnegan, Tessa?'

Tessa pulled a face, whilst shaking her head. 'Unless he's new?'

'I suppose he could be,' mused Cadi, before quickly dismissing the idea. 'I was driving Officer Harris at the time, and he seemed to know him, but he said he was called O'Connell.'

A knowing smile crossed the cook's face. 'We all know Kieran O'Connell – I shouldn't imagine you could get him mixed up with anyone else.'

'Sounds intriguing,' said Cadi.

The cook shot Cadi a meaningful glance. 'He's a bit of a hit with the ladies – if you know what I mean.'

Tessa began plating pie and mash for the next person in line. 'Not so popular with the fellers, though.'

The cook tutted beneath her breath. 'They're only jealous, cos our Kieran's got the gift of the gab when it comes to the ladies.'

'More likely cos he's a sulky git what's never done a day's work since joinin' up,' said the man who had ordered the pie and mash.

The cook handed Cadi her plate, whilst glancing in the direction of the man who was walking away with his pie and mash. 'See what I mean? Jealous.'

The man overheard the cook's words and turned on the spot. 'Jealous my eye! Stuff started to go missin' as soon as he arrived, and we never had that problem before.' He walked away stiffly, shaking his head.

'Whatever the weather, he's not the same feller,' said Cadi, adding in the privacy of her own mind *and a good job too* as she walked away. Settling down to eat her lunch, she relaxed in the knowledge that wherever the Finnegans were, it wasn't in the RAF.

'Friday means fish and chips,' said Daphne, as she and Kieran moved up the queue for their lunch.

'Best day of the week,' said Kieran. He winked at the cook who was doling the food on to their plates. 'Made even better when Irene's in charge of portion control.'

Irene rolled her eyes. 'A silver-tongued devil, that's what you are Kieran O'Connell.'

Tessa watched Irene shovel more chips on to one of the plates. 'We were only talking about you the other day.'

He shot them a glance full of Irish charm. 'Should I be blushing?'

'Some woman was in here asking after you – or rather someone she'd mistaken you for.'

He pulled a mischievous face. 'Two men as handsome as me? Surely not!'

The cook put the fish on to the plates, handing Kieran the one with the larger portion of chips. 'She seemed pretty convinced, despite Harris telling her she'd got it wrong.'

He clicked his fingers. 'She must've been looking for Prince Charming; it's an easy mistake to make.'

The cook laughed raucously. 'Close, but not quite.' She fell silent for a moment or two whilst she tried to recall the name. 'From what I remember she was after a man by the name of Micky ...' Her voice trailed off as she saw a look of utter shock cross Kieran's features. She shot him an enquiring glance. 'Do you know him?'

Kieran laughed sarcastically. 'Does an Irishman know a man by the name of Micky?'

Thinking that she must have misread his expression, she shrugged it off. 'I suppose it is a fairly common name.'

'Did she not give you a surname?'

'Fagan,' said Tessa promptly, 'because I remember thinking of Oliver Twist.'

The cook shook her head. 'Not Fagin. Finnegan, that was it.'

112

Daphne narrowed her eyes. 'This woman, was she blonde with a slight Scouse accent by any chance?'

'She was indeed a blonde, and I suppose she did have a bit of an accent, yes.'

Daphne folded her arms across her chest. 'Did she mention me?'

Tessa shook her head. 'Just this Micky Fagan, or Finnegan, or whatever.'

'Did she say what she was doing here?'

The cook nodded as she doled chips on to another plate. 'She'd taken Harris somewhere the day before.'

Daphne was about to turn away with her tray when another thought sprang to mind. 'Was she a sergeant?'

'You know her, then?' said the cook, as she held the plate towards the next person in the queue.

'Yes, I flamin' well do,' snapped Daphne, 'and she's nowt but a troublemaker.' She turned to Kieran. 'I bet you anything you like it's that Cadi, the one I told you about.'

Kieran followed Daphne over to a table. 'Why on earth would she be asking after this Micky feller?'

'She must've seen us together, so did some digging to find out who you were – she didn't know your name so she made one up, knowing that the cook would set her straight!' She paused momentarily before adding, 'What's the matter with that woman? Why can't she leave me alone?'

Kieran placed his tray down as Daphne continued wittering about Cadi. Could it be possible that one of the women who'd turned up at Hillcrest was this Cadi? He'd like to think not, but what were the chances of two blonde Waafs, both with slight Scouse accents, knowing him by name as *well* as knowing Daphne.

He pushed his peas around the plate. 'What's your beef with this Cadi?'

'She's always wanted what I've had,' said Daphne irritably. 'First Aled, now you.'

'Well, she can't have me.'

'That's what I thought about Aled,' said Daphne sullenly. 'Didn't stop her from trying though.'

'So that's the reason why the two of you fell out,' said Kieran. 'Because of this Aled?'

Daphne nodded. 'She'll never admit it, but she wanted him for herself despite the fact she already had a feller of her own.'

'Is Aled a Scouser?' He pushed the prongs of his fork into some of the peas. If Aled had a strong Scouse accent, the same as the lad who'd come to take Raquel, then he'd know for certain who the blonde Waaf was.

'No. He's from a little village called Rhos, somewhere in North Wales.'

Kieran breathed a sigh of relief. It couldn't be the same woman, although there was a niggling doubt in the back of his mind. 'If Cadi got Aled, why would she be after me?'

'That's the stupid part,' said Daphne. 'She married someone else – now *he's* a Scouser.'

Kieran felt his stomach drop into his boots. It *had* to be the same one. 'Do you think she'll come back?'

'I flamin' well hope not,' snorted Daphne, 'but if she does I shall tell her to keep her nose out of my business for the last time.' She was momentarily silent, before mumbling, 'I'm sure this could count as harassment.'

Kieran sliced a piece off the end of his fish. The Finnegans were talented at easily identifying women who were down on their luck, and as soon as he'd laid eyes on Daphne he'd realised that she fell into this category. He had taken her to the cinema, where they had chatted at length about the many acres her father farmed. Kieran knew little about farming, save to say that farmers had to be considerably wealthy to own their own land. He quite fancied the idea of being a landowner himself, and if this Daphne woman was stupid enough to fall for his charms, he would marry the land from under her. A devilish smile formed on his face as he imagined himself as the lord of the manor.

Daphne cut across his thoughts. 'What are you grinning about?'

He placed his hand over hers. 'Just thinking how wonderful our life is going to be once we're married.'

Daphne beamed. 'It truly is, and I just know you're going to make the perfect farmer.'

'You've said that you're an only child. Does that mean it'll be your father that teaches me to farm?' He hesitated. 'Only I've got no experience and I wouldn't like to make a pig's ear of things. I should imagine that the farm with all its stock is worth a bob or two?'

'Golly yes, but not to worry: Dad'll teach you everything from ploughing the land to balancing the books.'

Kieran nodded slowly, deep in thought. Up until now, he had thought his marrying Daphne a done deal, but if this Cadi continued to stick her oar in she could very well scupper his plans before he had a chance to get his feet under the table. He needed to come up with an idea of how to ensure her silence, but how could he do that when he didn't know where she was based? He thought for a moment. Hadn't Daphne said that all her troubles had begun in RAF Little Snoring with a woman called Kitty? His face clouded as Daphne's description of a rotund Scouser with curly hair came back to him. The woman sounded identical to the one who'd set fire to the brothel. A wicked smile tweaked his lips. He might not know where Cadi was, but he could certainly pay Kitty a visit.

Once again, Daphne interrupted his thinking. 'We keep talking about getting married, but what's holding us back? It seems silly to wait when we've no idea what tomorrow might bring.'

'I'm not the sort of feller who weds without asking a father's permission,' lied Kieran. 'We can set a date once I've spoken to your father in person.'

Daphne smiled, but said nothing. As far as her father was concerned, the potato famine of 1849 told you all you needed to know about Irish farmers. It was utter nonsense, of course, but he was a proud Englishman who'd worked hard to turn the farm into a reasonably profitable business, and she was pretty sure it would be a cold day in hell before he let some Irishman come along and run it into the ground. He'd have accepted a fellow farmer like Aled in a heartbeat, but Kieran? Her best bet was to marry Kieran, *then* introduce him to her father when it would be too late.

Kieran, on the other hand, wanted to hold back until he'd seen the extent of her father's farm. He had no intention of marrying a woman he couldn't stand in order to gain a quarter of an acre.

May 1944

When Cadi arrived in Lincoln, she could hardly contain her excitement as she caught sight of Jez watching out for her from the platform. Gathering her belongings, she rushed to the carriage door and jumped down on to the platform. Jez was hurrying in her direction, and as they came together he took her up in his arms and they sank into a deep kiss, forgetting the world around them.

As their lips parted, Jez was the first to speak. 'God, it's good to see you!'

Still holding him close, so that there wasn't a sliver of light between them, Cadi sank her head against his chest, murmuring softly, 'I wish I never had to leave, and we could stay like this for ever.'

Jez bent his neck so that he could kiss the top of her head. 'You say that now, but you'll be sick at the sight of me after we've been living together for a few years.'

She nuzzled her cheek against him. 'I'll never get sick of seeing you.'

'What? Even after you've found my underwear on the floor for the millionth time?'

Cadi giggled. Jez always knew how to cheer her up. Leaning back from their embrace, she glanced around her. 'Where's Annie? I thought the two of you were joined at the hip.'

'Still at Finningley. I wanted it to be just the two of us.'

Cadi looked surprised. She had thought Annie far too precious to Jez to be left behind. 'Who did you leave her with?'

117

'Aled's the only person I trust with Annie,' said Jez. 'When we're on different shifts, one of us will look after her whilst the other's working. It means that she's rarely on her own, and she gets plenty of exercise.'

Cadi smiled. 'It's nice to know that you don't have to worry about her.'

They had been walking out of the station as they talked. Approaching the line of cabs, Jez motioned to the drivers, who were standing around smoking and chatting. The driver of the car at the front hastily stubbed his cigarette out with the toe of his boot, and strode towards them. 'Where to, guv'nor?' he enquired as he opened the back door of the cab.

'The Adam and Eve,' Jez replied, following Cadi on to the back seat as the driver took his place behind the wheel. He turned to Cadi and took her hand. 'I know we could've walked, but I think we deserve a treat. We've been married for nigh on five months and we still haven't had a honeymoon – in fact this is the first break we've had on our own since I don't know when.'

Cadi smiled as Jez's fingers curled around hers. 'I rather like being the one who's being chauffeured round for a change,' she said. 'It makes me feel special.'

Jez twinkled at her. 'You are special.'

The Adam and Eve was only a short distance from the train station and it wasn't long before the driver had pulled up outside the inn. Thanking the man, Cadi stepped down on to the pavement whilst Jez paid the fare and collected their bags.

Inside the tavern, Jez informed the young girl who came to greet them that he had made a reservation under the name of Thomas. Taking a key from a board behind the bar, she showed them to their room, informing them that breakfast would be served between seven and nine. She waited until Jez had approved the room before heading back down the stairs, while Cadi went to admire the view of Lincoln Cathedral, just visible from their window. Gazing at the Pottergate arch, she addressed Jez over her shoulder. 'What do you want to do first?'

The image of his wife's trim figure silhouetted against the sunlight which was pouring through the glass was too much for Jez. Dropping their bags to the floor, he wasted no time in scooping Cadi into his arms. His lips meeting hers, he carried her over to the bed.

Melting under the warmth of his kisses as they descended her neckline, her heart began to race as she surrendered herself to his caress.

With dusk descending, Kieran flashed his pass at the airman guarding the gate to RAF Little Snoring, and handed him the clipboard beside him. The airman scanned the list before handing it back to Kieran with a nod. 'Park up on the right, and someone will be with you shortly.'

Kieran did as he had been instructed before descending from the cab of his lorry. Effortlessly rolling a cigarette between his fingers, he glanced around to see if he could spot Kitty anywhere; the last thing he wanted was for her to spy him before he'd had a chance to speak his piece. Leaning against the truck, he lit the cigarette before waving the match out and throwing it to the ground.

He hadn't been there long when an airman approached with an expectant look on his face. 'You the feller with the supplies?'

Kieran nodded. 'Where do you want them?'

The man pointed to another airman who was waiting outside a hut further along. 'See the chap over there?'

Kieran nodded.

'He'll see you right.'

Taking a couple more pulls of his cigarette, Kieran nipped the end between his fingers and placed the remainder behind his ear. He drove the lorry to where the airman was waiting, and it wasn't long before they had unloaded the contents. Kieran fastened the tailgate as the airman bade him a safe journey back.

'I was hoping to see a friend of mine before I left,' Kieran told him. 'Her name's Kitty; do you know her?'

The man pointed towards one of the buildings. 'She works as a cook in the officers' mess, although I'm not sure whether she's on shift or not.'

Kieran thanked him, and jogged over to the rear of the hut. He ran his tongue over his bottom lip. If his plan went well, then all to the good, but if Kitty screamed blue murder he'd have to hightail it out of there before anyone could stop him. Taking a deep breath, he knocked a brief tattoo on the kitchen door.

A large woman with floury hands opened the door with one hand whilst using the other to pull the blackout curtain across behind her. 'Yes?'

Confident that she wouldn't be able to see his face clearly, he smiled. 'Can I have a quick word with Kitty, please? I promise I won't keep her long.'

The cook tutted irritably before yelling for Kitty to come and see to her visitor. As she closed the door behind her, Kieran could hear her telling Kitty that she was to hurry up.

Kieran stepped back into the shadows whilst he waited.

Kitty opened the door and quickly stepped out. Peering into the darkness, she tutted under her breath. 'Don't mess about, Dave—' She gave a small squeal as she felt a hand cover her mouth. Still believing it to be her boyfriend playing a prank, Kitty tried to break free, but it soon became evident that this was no prank when the unknown assailant viciously dug his fingers into her cheeks whilst twisting her arm up her back.

'One word from you and I'll snap your bleedin' neck,' hissed Kieran. He dragged her to the side of the hut where they would be completely hidden from passers-by and placed his lips next to her ear. 'Tell Cadi to keep her nose out of my business or I'll tell everyone what Raquel used to do for a living.'

Kitty's blood ran cold as realisation dawned. The man threatening to snap her neck had to be one of the Finnegans. Clueless as to what had gone on with Cadi, all Kitty could do was nod her head, as the tears trickled down her cheeks.

Pushing her roughly away, Kieran still kept a hold of her wrist, preventing her from running back to the safety of the kitchen. He wagged a warning finger under her nose. 'And don't even think about reportin' me, cos if you do, I'll return the favour.'

Kitty glared at him, angered by his empty threat. 'By reportin' me? Go ahead. I've not done anything wrong.'

Kieran tutted irritably. 'Do you not remember settin' fire to my house?' He narrowed his eyes. 'That's the favour I was referrin' to.'

Kitty swallowed. 'I – I didn't mean to.'

He pulled a face. 'Too little, too late; or as some might say, an eye for an eye.'

Shoving her roughly away, he swaggered back to his lorry, leaving Kitty to dry her tears on the backs of her hands. She knew if she went back in now it would be obvious that she had been crying and people would want to know why, so she quickly headed to the ablutions where she could wash her face and gather her thoughts.

Standing over the nearest sink, she began throwing cold water on to her face. The Finnegans weren't the sort to make idle threats, but what had Cadi done to infuriate them so, and how had they found out where Kitty was based? She would have to speak to Cadi and find out exactly what was going on.

She frowned at her reflection in the mirror above the sink. Why on earth hadn't Cadi warned her that the Finnegans were back and that one of them at least was serving in the RAF? It wasn't like her friend to be complacent, yet surely she must have realised the danger they posed? Kitty knew that she would get in trouble for using the phone when she was meant to be on duty, but she had to try to speak to Cadi.

Hurrying over to the NAAFI, she telephoned RAF Coningsby to find out where her friend was currently based, and was disappointed to find that Cadi had gone on a forty-eight. Thanking the Waaf for her help, she asked for a message to be passed on, and for Cadi to telephone her as soon as she returned.

It was the first morning of their weekend away, and Cadi and Jez were just finishing their breakfast.

'Not as good as the one Maria serves in the Belmont, but not far off,' remarked Jez, as he mopped the last piece of toast around his plate.

'When we have a pub of our own, we shall have toast racks and butter dishes,' said Cadi, 'and I shall curl the butter with one of those fancy spoons.'

Jez drained the tea from his cup before speaking. 'You've obviously been giving this some thought.'

'From the napkins to the bedsheets,' said Cadi. 'And I want the pub to have a thatched roof and hanging baskets above the door come summertime.'

He rubbed his chin. 'You've just described the Coach and Horses back in Rhos.'

'Only our pub will be somewhere like Formby,' said Cadi, 'close to the city *and* the sea.'

Jez's brow shot towards his hairline. 'I didn't know you did the pools.'

Cadi shot him a wry smile. 'So maybe I'm reaching for the stars when we can only afford to bathe in their light, but it's lovely to dream, don't you think?'

'I do indeed,' he agreed. 'There's nowt wrong with aiming high, and who knows? We might fall lucky.'

Cadi crossed her fingers. 'Here's hoping.'

'As good a method as any,' chuckled Jez. Standing up, he held his hand out to her. 'Where would you like to go today?'

Cadi slipped her fingers through his, allowing him to pull her to her feet. 'How about the cathedral?'

He nodded approvingly. 'Good choice.'

As they made their way out of the pub, they began to climb the steep hill across the road from the tavern.

'That was certainly a good way of working off our brekker,' said Jez, as they completed the ascent.

Cadi turned to him as they entered the cathedral. 'I wish we'd married sooner; it feels as if we wasted so much time.'

'Being married any earlier wouldn't have made an ounce of difference to the amount of time we spent together,' said Jez reasonably.

'No, but I let my fears and superstitions get the better of me, and I shouldn't have. All that worrying over what might happen stopped me from following my heart.'

He kissed the back of her hand. 'You can't live your life with regrets. We're together now and that's all that matters.'

Cadi tucked her arm into the crook of his elbow as they continued to walk through the church. 'It's so peaceful in here – it takes you away from the madness of war.'

He squeezed her arm in his. 'I reckon we're nearing the finishing line; I can feel it in my bones.'

She whipped round to look him square in the eye. 'Have you heard summat?'

He tapped the side of his nose. 'No one's prepared to say too much, but the general feeling amongst the pilots has lifted, so I'm guessing they know summat we don't.'

'Has Aled said anything?'

'No, but I've noticed a difference in their attitudes when they're going off on operations: they seem more confident somehow. I guess they must see more than we do because they cross over into Europe.'

Cadi felt her heartbeat quicken in her chest; the very thought that the war might soon be coming to an end was music to her ears. 'I hope you're right.' She hesitated as a thought entered her mind. 'What do you suppose your mam will do when the war's over?'

'Last time we spoke, she said she'd go back to work for Maria.'

Cadi mulled this over. 'When you stop to think about it, there's going to be a lot of people looking for employment when peace is declared.' She nodded thoughtfully as she continued, 'A lot of women will find themselves back where they started when the men return to their jobs. No work, no money, no independence. All that freedom whisked away in the blink of an eye.'

'That's a bit of an exaggeration,' said Jez. 'The Chinese laundries will still be employing women.'

Cadi shook her head. 'Women's work, Jez; thankless tasks that hold no prospects.' She turned to face him. 'I'm a sergeant in the WAAF, but if I were to go back to Rhos I'd be on the line with all the others.'

'But you won't be going back to Rhos,' Jez pointed out.

'No, but others will, because they won't have a choice – either that, or they'll be returning as war brides, and a lot of them will be living with men they barely know. We were lucky because we got to know each other before the war. I know that I'm a different person in the WAAF from who I am on civvy street.'

Jez was about to disagree when he remembered what Aled had said about Marnie being in love with a hero who flew off into the sunset. He said as much to Cadi.

'There you are: case in point, and I'm afraid Aled could well be right. Farming isn't a glamorous lifestyle – far from it.' She smiled as she remembered the day Aled had driven past her in a dirty great tractor, accidentally covering her in a substance she'd rather forget. 'I'm pretty sure that's why Aled wanted to join the RAF in the first place.'

'So the end of the war is going to bring troubles in itself,' said Jez; 'something I'd not thought about until now.' He placed his arm around her shoulders. 'Thank goodness we've got each other.'

Saying goodbye to Jez was always hard, but today's parting had been made a little easier when he presented her with a surprise gift.

Taking the jewellery box, she peered at the exquisite locket inside before opening the tiny clasp and gasping at the photograph of herself and Jez on their wedding day. 'Oh, Jez, it's beautiful, but what's the occasion?'

He shrugged. 'Does there need to be one?'

Placing the chain around her neck, she turned so that Jez could fasten the clasp. With the locket in place, she continued to admire it before tucking it out of sight. 'I didn't realise we were doing presents, or I'd have got you something,' she said.

'It's my job to shower you with gifts,' said Jez, 'not the other way round.'

'I love it,' Cadi cooed, 'and I shall treasure it always.'

Seeing the train approach, he pulled her close. 'I believe this one's yours.'

Cadi wrapped her arms around his waist. 'Why is it they're always late setting out, but they're bang on time when it comes to going back?'

Cupping her face in his hands, he kissed her with such love that Cadi felt as though the world around her had come to a stop. So lost was she in the kiss that it seemed as if no time had passed when the guard called for the last of the passengers to board.

Breaking away from their embrace, Cadi looked ruefully along the platform, which had almost emptied since the train's arrival. She turned back to say goodbye, but the words caught in her throat.

Jez picked up her kitbag and walked her over to the train. 'Chin up, queen. It's not as though it's for ever.'

'I know, but ...'

She stopped short as the guard bellowed for everyone to board the train. Giving Jez the briefest of kisses, she whispered, 'I love you, Jeremy Thomas.'

It was dark by the time Cadi arrived back in Coningsby. She flashed her pass to the airman on the gate and headed for her billet. Stifling a yawn, she stopped as a Waaf trotted over with paper in hand.

'The caller said it was urgent,' said the Waaf, before ripping off a salute and walking away.

Hoping that it wasn't bad news, Cadi read the note asking her to telephone Kitty as a matter of urgency. She turned on the spot and headed for the NAAFI, where she kept her fingers tightly crossed as she called Little Snoring.

'Kitty! I just got your note after a weekend away. Is everything all right?'

Kitty got straight to the point. 'I don't know what you've done to annoy the Finnegans, Cadi, but they're out for blood.'

Cadi stood in stunned silence before finding her tongue. 'I haven't done anything to them, I haven't even seen—' She stopped short as the image of Micky behind the steering wheel of a lorry came to the forefront of her mind.

'Cadi?'

Licking her lips, Cadi swallowed. 'I thought I'd seen Micky a while back, but when I asked around, everyone said I was mistaken, and that the feller I'd seen was called Kieran O'Connell.'

'The feller I saw definitely wasn't Kieran O'Connell, whoever he might be. He told me that you were to stop asking questions, or he'd let everyone know what Raquel used to do for a living. He also said that if I reported him he'd – he'd ...' She faltered, unable to repeat his threat.

'He'd what?' cried Cadi.

'He'd return the favour. He was talking about my accidentally setting fire to Hillcrest.'

Cadi gasped out loud. 'Bloody hell!'

Her mind raced whilst Kitty continued to talk. 'You must've said or done summat, Cadi.'

'I swear to you, all I've done is ask if anyone knew of a Micky Finnegan, and that's it.'

'Well, he's really worried that you're goin' to keep askin', otherwise he wouldn't have come and threatened me.' Kitty hesitated. 'Which brings me to another point …'

Cadi voiced the question before Kitty had a chance. 'How did he know where to find you?'

'Not just me. He must have guessed that Raquel's in the WAAF, and if he knows about her, then he'll know where to find Ronnie, Poppy and Izzy.'

Cadi clapped a hand to her forehead. 'I wish I'd kept my big mouth shut.'

'Hardly your fault,' said Kitty. 'You were only asking what any of us would've asked had we thought we'd seen him. Question is: do we tell Raquel?'

Cadi heaved a miserable sigh. 'I told Jez that I thought I'd seen Micky, and he said not to mention it to his mam because she'd go spare. I'd rather talk to Jez first, see what he thinks, then go from there.'

'As you can imagine, I've given the matter a lot of thought, and I reckon Micky would walk the other way if he saw her,' said Kitty helpfully. 'He's as much to lose from this as she has, if not more. As far as I'm aware being a you-know-what isn't grounds for dismissal, but lying about your identity? That's bound to raise a few eyebrows.'

'Which is why he's bandying threats around,' agreed Cadi. She hesitated. 'Did he mention his brother?'

'No, probably because you'd only been asking about him and not Paddy.'

But Cadi didn't think this to be the case at all. 'When they came outside to threaten you and Ronnie, they did it together, which suggests to me that one never goes far without the other. Yet he only wants me to stop asking questions about him?' She shook her head. 'Summat's gone on there, summat we don't know about. Whatever it is has got Micky running scared.'

Kitty's lips parted. 'So there's more to this than meets the eye?'

'A lot more,' said Cadi.

'It certainly would explain why he went off the deep end,' said Kitty. 'So what now?'

'I'm going to telephone Jez and tell him everything. It's too late to call him now, so I'll do it first thing in the morning. I'm so sorry Micky decided to pick on you.'

'Don't worry about it. I'm sorry you had to come home to this news, and so late at night too.'

'I'd rather know no matter what time of day or night, so I'm glad you told me. I'll telephone you when I get to my new base tomorrow.'

'Right you are. Goodnight, Cadi.'

Bidding Kitty goodnight, Cadi replaced the handset and headed for the ablutions, where she had the briefest of washes before continuing to her billet and getting ready for bed. As she stripped, she tried to shake the image of Micky – or should they be calling him Kieran? – out of her mind. The cook and her assistant had seemed to think highly of him, but the feller in the queue behind her hadn't reckoned much to him at all. Snuggling between the sheets, she pulled the blanket over her. How she wished that Jez was cuddling her to sleep, as he had done the previous night. As her eyelids began to droop, she wondered what he would say when she told him Kitty's news. When she fell to sleep, it was only to dream of Micky standing in front of a burning hut, a wicked grin on his face.

The following morning Cadi was up betimes, hoping to catch Jez before he started his shift. As she waited patiently for him to come to the phone, she was still trying to imagine how he was going to react when his voice came down the line.

'Can't keep away, eh?' he chuckled.

Cadi sighed heavily. 'I'm afraid I've got some bad news.'

He stopped laughing in an instant. 'What's happened?'

Cadi caught him up on everything Kitty had told her, finishing with, 'So it *was* Micky I saw.'

Deep in contemplation, Jez was silent for a moment or so. 'What the hell is he doing in the RAF?'

'I don't know, and what's more, I don't think we should ask,' said Cadi. 'But I do think we should tell your mam, and the others.'

Jez heaved a reluctant sigh. 'Forewarned is forearmed. Mam's going to be devastated when she hears.' He hesitated. 'How the hell did he know where to find Kitty?'

'Not the foggiest,' admitted Cadi. An image of herself arguing with Daphne entered her mind. 'Oh God.'

'What?'

'Daphne knows where Kitty is, because that's how we got to find out about Aled. It must've been her that told him.'

131

Jez was aghast. 'Why on earth would she do that? I know she hates us, but surely she'd not tell him?'

'More to the point, *why* would she tell him?' mused Cadi. She tapped her forefinger against her chin as she tried to come up with a plausible explanation. 'The only people I spoke to about Micky were Officer Harris – and I can't see him gossiping – and the two cooks. I never mentioned him to Daphne, because I'd not seen him by that stage.'

'Then the answer's simple: it must've been one of the cooks who gave Micky the heads-up.'

'Then where does Daphne come into it?'

'Search me.'

'So where do we go from here?'

'First things first, tell me mam.' He paused. 'I hate to ask, but is there any chance you could tell her? Only you've spoken to Kitty, and you were the one who saw Micky, so …'

Cadi was already nodding. 'Leave it with me, although I won't be able to contact her until I get to my new base. I'm running late as it is.'

'Where are you off to, or don't you know?'

'Hopefully not miles away,' said Cadi, 'but they don't tell me until I'm ready to leave.'

'Well, take care, and let me know what happens after you speak to Mam.'

'Will do. Ta-ra, Jez.'

'Ta-ra, queen.'

Heading out of the NAAFI, Cadi ducked into the office to get her orders.

The Waaf looked down at the paper in her hands. 'You're off to RAF Fiskerton.'

Cadi stared at the woman, a wide smile splitting her cheeks. 'How long for?'

The Waaf glanced at Cadi's instructions again before handing them over. 'Looks like you're going to be there for the foreseeable, which is why they want you to catch a train, rather than drive.' Seeing Cadi's smile widen even further, she added, 'I take it you're happy with their decision?'

'I am indeed,' said Cadi. Grinning like the cat that got the cream, she pocketed the paperwork and headed out of the office. After hearing the worst news possible, it was a refreshing relief to have some good tidings. She had asked to be posted to Lincoln as soon as she came back from Liverpool, but not for one moment had she thought they'd grant her request. The whole business with Micky would be much more easily sorted out with her friends beside her, and her husband just over an hour away.

Poppy drummed her fingers against the steering wheel as she waited for the train carrying their new sergeant to arrive. Hearing the squeal of brakes as the approaching train entered the station, she checked her reflection in the rear-view mirror. The last thing she wanted was some stuffy officer giving her a dressing down for having a crooked tie.

Turning her attention back to the train, she scanned the passengers who were descending on to the platform, until her attention was caught by a familiar figure. Leaning across the passenger seat for a better look, she gave a whoop of joy before jumping out of the driver's door and racing round to greet her friend with a hug.

'Why didn't you tell me you were coming to Fiskerton?' she cried.

'I thought it might be a nice surprise. Well, that and the fact I couldn't wait to get here,' said Cadi.

Poppy beamed at her friend as they got into the car. 'I can't wait to see the look on Izzy's face. Will you be with us for long?'

Cadi sighed happily. 'The foreseeable, and I'm hoping that means until the end of the war.'

Poppy's smile broadened as she pulled away from the kerb. 'This is going to be just like the good old days. What did Jez say? I bet he was disappointed that you weren't going to Finningley.'

Cadi told Poppy of her earlier phone call to Jez, and the conversation surrounding Micky. 'So I shall tell Jez of my new posting *after* I've spoken to Raquel.'

Poppy nodded slowly. 'Jez telephoned Izzy a few minutes before I came to pick you up. She wanted to talk to me as soon as she hung up, but I had to leave in order to meet your train, so I said I'd see her in the NAAFI just as soon as I got back.'

'Poor Izzy,' said Cadi. 'It seems to be one thing after another for her and Raquel.'

'I must admit, I thought we'd seen the last of the Finnegans. Why on earth have they joined the RAF? I'd have thought that would be the last place they'd want to be.'

'Me too, but as far as we know it's only Micky who's signed up.'

Poppy gave a disbelieving snort of reproval. 'I doubt it. Those brothers are joined at the hip. It took two of them to come and have a word with Ronnie and Kitty when they were standing outside Hillcrest House – the cowards.'

'That's what I said to Jez, yet Micky was definitely on his own when I saw him, *and* when he went to visit Kitty,' said Cadi. 'Not only that, but Kitty said that when he threatened her he didn't mention Paddy.'

They showed their passes to the airman on the gate duty, and he waved them through. Poppy waited outside while Cadi reported to the office. When she reappeared, she took her kitbag from the car and turned to Poppy. 'Let's go and find Izzy. I won't bother putting my things away until I've spoken to her and Raquel.'

They entered the NAAFI to find Izzy sitting at the far end, gazing mournfully into a cup of tea. Hearing the girls approach, she lifted her head, and her face brightened when she saw Cadi.

'Cadi! Jez never said—'

'He doesn't know,' Cadi interjected. 'I'll phone him after we've sorted out this business with Micky Finnegan.'

Izzy's face fell. 'I felt sick to my stomach when he told me what Micky had done. I don't suppose you've anything to add?'

Cadi shook her head. 'I'm afraid not. We're clueless as to how he comes to be in the RAF. I can only assume that something must've gone horribly wrong after the night of the fire.'

'I'm amazed he didn't have a go at Kitty over setting the place alight,' said Izzy, 'especially as it seems to have led to his signing up.'

Cadi mulled this over. 'You've got a point. You'd think he'd be spitting feathers over that fire, yet all he said was he'd return the favour if Kitty reported him.'

'Sounds like he has bigger fish to fry,' said Izzy darkly.

Poppy nodded. 'Doesn't it just.'

'There's no point in us trying to work out what's going on. If anyone knows, it'll be Raquel,' said Cadi. She placed her kitbag on one of the empty chairs. 'No time like the present. I shall be back shortly.'

She headed for the telephone and asked the operator to put her through to Raquel's base. It was a minute or two before her mother-in-law could come to the telephone, and Cadi wondered how she would take the news. She wouldn't be pleased, that was for certain, but other than that ...? Her thoughts were interrupted as Raquel's voice came down the line.

'Hello?'

'Raquel? It's me, Cadi.'

'Hello, Cadi love. How are you?'

'I'm very well, thank you,' said Cadi, quickly adding, 'and I don't want you to panic, but I'm afraid I've got some bad news ...'

When Cadi had finished relaying her tale, she waited for Raquel's response.

'If one of those two has joined up the other one has as well,' she said at last, 'so they must've been posted to different parts of the country.' She hesitated. 'Either that, or they've had the mother of all fall-outs.'

'But why join up in the first place?' queried Cadi.

136

'They must have been desperate for money,' Raquel told her. 'They'd not have done it otherwise, and of course the services could prove highly profitable for the wrong sort of people.'

'I don't understand.'

'Black market,' said Raquel simply. 'The services can get hold of most things, and if I know those two they'll be pilfering stock and selling it on the side.'

Cadi stood rooted to the spot. 'One of the fellers in the lunch queue said summat about things going missing after Micky arrived.'

'There you go.'

'But why is he telling everyone he's called Kieran O'Connell?'

'I can tell you that. It's because Micky Finnegan wasn't the name on his papers.'

'Sorry, you've lost me.'

'Dolly started working for the Finnegans when they first came to Portsmouth. She said when they first arrived she often heard Micky calling Paddy "Seamus", and she was curious as to why, so she went rooting and found their passports. The one with Micky's photograph was for Kieran O'Connell, and the other for Seamus O'Connell.'

Cadi nodded slowly. 'So Kieran O'Connell is Micky's real name?'

'It is indeed. They must have changed their names as soon as they got to England. Not sure why, but there again we are talking about the Finnegans, so there's probably a list of reasons as long as your arm.'

A slight frown furrowed Cadi's brow. 'Only why isn't Kieran using his new alias?'

'I don't know, but I'd put money on it that he's trying to hide from people who knew him in Portsmouth – or even from Paddy.'

Cadi blew her cheeks out. 'He must've done summat really bad to Paddy if that's the case.'

'I don't know why they left Ireland, but I always got the impression that it was summat to do with Micky. He's a real snake in the grass; far worse than his brother. If I had to guess, I'd say that Micky has double-crossed Paddy somehow. Perhaps grassed him up and done a runner before Paddy can find him.'

'So you think he's hiding from Paddy in the RAF?'

'That's only a guess, because of course Paddy knows both names, but it's the only explanation I can think of for hiding from people looking for Micky Finnegan, because his identity is watertight,' said Raquel. 'You could say that you know him as Micky Finnegan until you're blue in the face, but Kieran O'Connell's passport is kosher, and if they wanted to dig further they'd find that his date and place of birth all check out. Quite frankly, you'd be the one with egg on your face, not him. So he's nothing to fear from the authorities.'

'Then why is he so scared? Because he must be, to threaten Kitty the way he did.'

Raquel gave a fleeting, mirthless laugh. 'Do you really think that Micky – or rather Kieran – will have been honest with his comrades about what he did prior to joining up? Not a chance! He'll have told them a pack of lies, and not just them, but the women around him. If I know Kieran, he'll have his feet under the table somewhere and he won't want his belle finding out the truth.'

'You can't really believe he wants to settle down?' Cadi asked incredulously.

'If he finds himself a rich woman – and we both know there're plenty of women from wealthy backgrounds in the WAAF – he'll marry his way into her money.'

'I don't think a woman like that would go for a man like him,' said Cadi, but Raquel thought differently.

'We know Kieran for the man he truly is, but to someone who doesn't know him he's a charming Irishman with roguish good looks. I should imagine that's like nectar to many women in the upper classes.'

Cadi spoke slowly, deep in thought. 'So why fear what I have to say?'

'Do you know anyone on his base?'

Cadi shook her head. 'Only Daphne. Why?'

'He's obviously worried that she might take your word over his.'

Cadi tutted beneath her breath. 'She wouldn't believe me if I told her the world was round.'

'But he doesn't know that,' said Raquel reasonably, 'and he'll be worried that you might scupper his plans to wed himself rich. Believe me, once he's got a ring on some unfortunate woman's finger, he won't give two hoots what you say or do because it'll be too late.'

Cadi grimaced. 'I couldn't imagine anything worse than marrying a Finnegan.'

'Me neither, and once he's got his feet under the table the true Kieran will come out, and that poor woman will be in for the biggest shock of her life. The kindest thing you can do is tell this Daphne what he's really like and ask her to pass the word on. Whether she believes you or not is another matter, but at least you'll have tried.'

Cadi looked uncertain. 'But what about you? If Kieran finds out I've been speaking to Daphne, he'll tell everyone about Hillcrest.'

Raquel laughed. 'Have you not listened to a word I've said? Kieran doesn't want anyone digging into his past, so he'll keep his mouth shut.'

'But he won't have anything to lose once the cat's out of the bag,' Cadi reminded her.

'He'll call you a liar, deny it to the hilt, and bring it down to your word against his, because to do anything to the contrary would be admitting his guilt,' said Raquel.

The operator cut across the women, letting them know their time was up.

'Please, just one more minute,' begged Cadi. 'There's no one wanting to use the telephone this end.'

'Nor here,' confirmed Raquel.

The operator grudgingly gave them one more minute, but insisted that would be the limit.

'What about Kitty? Do you think he'll take it out on her?'

'Not a chance,' said Raquel, 'because Kitty won't have anything to lose by reporting him. Kieran thought he could scare Kitty into silence, but it didn't work, so he'll steer well clear for fear of what else she might do. His plan has well and truly backfired.'

Cadi smiled. 'It certainly has, and I can't wait to scupper his next plans.'

'Do let me know what happens,' said Raquel, adding, 'and make sure you're not alone should you decide to confront him.'

'Will do.'

'Ta-ra, Cadi. Take care.'

'You too.'

Hearing the click, Cadi replaced the receiver and headed over to the girls, who were awaiting her return with anticipation.

'You've been gone ages!' cried Izzy.

'Sorry, but as you can imagine, we had quite a lot to discuss.'

Poppy was on the edge of her seat. 'What did Raquel say?'

Cadi ran through the entirety of the phone call, finishing with, 'I promised I'd let her know the outcome.'

'She's got Kieran bang to rights,' beamed Poppy. 'I hope you give him both barrels, Cadi, because he deserves it.'

'First things first: I'll tell Kitty that she has nothing to worry about, and should Kieran come near her she's to scream blue murder and tell all.'

'And after that?'

'I'm not going to confront Kieran, because it'll be his word against mine, and forewarned is forearmed. I need to speak to Daphne.' She raised a hand as Poppy started to object. 'I know she's not my biggest fan, but she'll know I've got nothing to gain by grassing him up, and I'm hoping she'll tell his belle.'

'He'll just move on to another woman,' insisted Izzy.

'Not once word gets out,' said Cadi, 'and you know what the WAAF's like for gossip. Kieran's goose will be well and truly cooked!'

It was the following day and Cadi was delivering a parcel to RAF Lindholme, via Finningley which happened to be en route. Having telephoned ahead to make sure that Jez knew of her intended visit, she now flashed her ID at the guard and he waved her through.

Jez, who had been waiting for her to arrive, ran over with Annie to greet her as she exited her vehicle. Taking his wife in his arms, he gave her a welcoming kiss.

'I hope you keep getting jobs like this 'un,' he said. 'We'll get to see a lot more of each other if you do.'

'Being a sergeant means I can earmark runs like this for myself,' said Cadi. Reaching down, she gave Annie a welcoming ear rub.

Jez nodded approvingly. 'Does that mean you'd be able to call by on your way home? Only I thought it would be nice if I could take you out to lunch.'

Cadi threaded her arms around his waist. 'How could I refuse such a tempting offer!'

Jez beamed. 'If you give me a call before you set off, I'll come down to meet you at the gate.'

Cadi gave him a brief peck on the lips. 'Will do.' Getting back into her car she wound the window down. 'TTFN!'

Leaning in through the open window, Jez kissed her goodbye before standing back. 'Ta-ra, queen. See you soon.'

Waving goodbye, Cadi pulled on to the main road. With Lindholme only being a short drive away from Finningley, she arrived at her destination only ten minutes later. Taking the package into the office, she was delighted to learn that she wasn't required to wait for a response, and was heading to the NAAFI to telephone Jez when the wail of the air raid siren split the air.

Holding her cap to her head, she rushed over to the safety of the nearest bunker. Diving through the door, she held her breath as she listened keenly, and to her relief she heard no sound of thrumming engines, or gunfire. If they were lucky, it was another false alarm.

After they had been in the bunker for a good twenty minutes, Cadi turned to the Waaf next to her. 'I wish they'd give us a clue as to what's going on. I'd have thought they'd have let us out by now.'

The Waaf nodded. 'It's a pain in the proverbial, but better to be safe than sorry. Are you in a rush to be off?'

Cadi grinned. 'My husband's taking me out to lunch. He's based at RAF Finningley, and I'm to ring him before I set off.'

'I see!' The woman pulled a face. 'I can't imagine they'll keep us here much longer.'

'I hope not, because I hate being in shelters,' Cadi confessed. 'It reminds me of the time we got bombed in the B&B where I used to work. Worst day of my life.'

The Waaf made a clicking noise with her tongue. 'I can see how that could make you claustrophobic.'

The two women continued to chat about their lives, and after a further twenty minutes the all-clear sounded. As they emerged, Cadi waylaid a man who was jogging past them. 'What was all that about?'

'False alarm, or at least that's what it looks like,' said the airman.

Cadi furrowed her brow. It seemed a long time to keep them underground if it was a false alarm. She cast an eye to the sky above her. If someone hadn't made a mistake, it meant the Luftwaffe could still be in the area and she could be driving across open country with a Messerschmitt haunting the skies.

'Are they sure?'

He shrugged. 'We've not heard owt to the contrary.'

Thanking him for the information, Cadi hurried over to her car, where she started the engine before settling into the driver's seat. She was about to drive out of the gate when she heard someone yelling at her to wait, and realised she had forgotten to ring Jez. She put the car into neutral and opened the door to get out, smiling as the woman she had been talking to in the shelter came pelting towards her. 'I know. I forgot—'

The woman cut her off. 'It was RAF Finningley.'

Cadi nodded, but the woman shook her head. 'They were the ones the Luftwaffe were attacking.'

Chapter Five

It seemed to Aled as though the world and his wife had been outside when the air raid sounded. The Messerschmitt had been on them before they had a chance to take action, and with the main targets being the runway and the fighter planes all hell broke loose as pilots scrambled to get their kites off the ground before the Messerschmitts could destroy either.

Those who had a job to do ran to their posts, but others, such as the bomber pilots and the mechanics, ran for shelter. Every fibre in Aled's being wanted to run to the *Ulysses*, but a heavy bomber was no match for an agile fighter plane.

Ducking into the safety of the bunker, he was quick to cast an eye round for Jez and Annie, until he remembered that Jez had been meeting Cadi. He glanced at the watch on his wrist, and felt his stomach lurch unpleasantly. He was certain Jez had said he was expecting Cadi around eleven thirty, and it was only ten to twelve. What if she was running late? What if she was just arriving? An image of Cadi exiting her car as the Luftwaffe descended entered his mind. He turned to the woman beside him.

'Did you see Jez or Annie?'

The woman shook her head. 'I know they weren't on the runway, because he'd gone to meet his wife by the gate, but that was ages ago.'

'Didn't he come back?'

'Not that I know of, but he certainly wasn't at his post when the air raid sounded.'

Removing his cap, Aled ran his fingers through his hair. His eyes kept darting towards the exit as he struggled to stop himself from running outside.

It seemed like an eternity before the all-clear finally sounded, but as soon as it did, Aled had only one thing on his mind: to find Jez and make sure Cadi had been nowhere near the station at the time of the attack.

As he emerged from the bunker, he saw a fire engine hosing a burning plane, while off to one side a human chain was extinguishing the flames engulfing one of the huts.

Seeing a Waaf hobbling towards him with blood gushing out of her leg, Aled ran over and caught her just as she fell into his arms. He carried her to the hospital, keeping a keen eye out for Cadi as he went.

Jez had been walking Annie at the far end of the base when the air raid siren sounded. Being a fair way from the nearest shelter he was praying for it to be another false alarm, but his hopes were shattered when he heard the Messerschmitt dive towards the airfield.

Running hell for leather towards the shelter, Jez praised Annie for being a good girl as she kept pace with him. The Messerschmitt was coming in for another attack, so he veered off towards the bushes and flung himself to the ground, clutching Annie close to him as he prayed that the Messerschmitt wouldn't waste its bullets on a lone airman. Feeling a sharp sensation of heat streak up the left-hand side of his body, he threw his hands over his head, drawing Annie's leash taut. He heard the plane pass above him and tried to stand, but it was no use. Blood was flowing freely from his wounds. He let go of Annie's leash and shouted at her to go, but she stood frozen to the spot. The Messerschmitt was turning to come back for another round, and by sheer strength of will Jez dragged himself into the bushes, despite the excruciating pain searing through his body. Instead of running for safety, Annie followed him into the undergrowth, trembling with fear, and shuffled up next to him, the tip of her tail wagging ever so slightly.

Reaching out, he smoothed her ears as she barked at the planes. As she nestled closer he placed his arm around her neck. 'Not to worry,' he soothed, 'they'll soon be gone.' He smiled weakly as she licked the side of his face. 'Cadi'll come and nurse us better,' he told her, 'and I'll tell her what a good, brave girl you've been.' Looking out from under the branches of the bush, Jez frowned as his vision began to blur. And then darkness enveloped him.

As soon as Cadi heard that RAF Finningley had been the station under attack, she dropped back into her seat and her foot hit the accelerator. Barely stopping for the guard to lift the gate, she pushed her way up through the gears, but the car still wasn't going fast enough. Jez could be anywhere on base, but with him being an engineer it was more than likely he'd be near the runway, which is exactly where the Luftwaffe would aim to strike. She just had to hope that they'd had plenty of warning.

As she raced towards the base, she saw a bloom of black smoke on the horizon, and her heart sank. The Waaf had been correct. An image of Aled clambering into his plane entered her mind. How could she have forgotten that he was also in danger? Willing the car to go faster, she practically pushed the accelerator through the floor.

Seeing the gate to the base come into view she flashed her ID at the guard before pulling to one side. She got out of the car and glanced wildly around her before rushing off, only to be brought up short by the guard, who had caught hold of her by the arm.

'Sorry, ma'am, but you can't go runnin' off without stating your business.'

'My husband's Jeremy Thomas,' said Cadi, yanking her arm free from his grip. She stared at him incredulously. 'You saw the pair of us together no more than an hour or so ago.'

The guard took her to one side as another car pulled up outside the gate. 'You know I have to ask. If you wait here, I'll deal with this...' But he was talking to thin air. Cadi had seized the distraction to flee.

Protocol be damned, she thought as she belted towards the runway. Skidding to a halt, she caught the attention of a Waaf who was hurrying in the opposite direction.

'I'm looking for Jeremy Thomas. Have you seen him?'

The Waaf shook her head. 'Sorry.'

'How about Aled Davies?'

The Waaf pulled a downward smile. 'Sorry, but no.'

As the Waaf continued on her way, Cadi turned her attention to Annie's kennel. If Annie was there, it was a good indication that Jez was safe. Her heart plunged as her eyes fell on Annie's chain lying loose on the ground. Turning full circle, she desperately scanned the area for a sign of Jez, Annie or Aled. Frustration started to mount as she wondered where could they be, and she ran towards the throng of people helping to douse the flames coming from one of the buildings. Reaching the nearest man, she grabbed him by the shoulder.

'Have you seen Jeremy Thomas?'

The man shook his head. 'Sorry, not since before the air raid.'

'Where was he when you saw him last?'

He pointed towards the gate. 'I think he was going to meet his wife.'

'What about Aled Davies? He's—'

The man interrupted her. 'I saw him carrying a Waaf into the medical unit.'

Breathing a massive sigh of relief, Cadi pounded towards the base hospital, only stopping when she heard someone shout her name. Turning quickly, she ran towards Aled. 'I can't find Jez. I've asked around, but it seems no one's seen him or Annie since before the attack.' Her bottom lip trembled. 'Where *is* he, Aled?'

Aled's jaw flinched. 'He wasn't at his post when the air raid sounded – I know because I asked a Waaf, and she said he wasn't there.'

Cadi sagged with relief. 'Thank God for that.'

'I was on my way to see if Annie was in her kennel—' Aled began, but Cadi cut across him.

'I've already looked, and she's not there.' She glanced up at Aled's face. 'You're worried, aren't you? You'd not be looking for him otherwise.'

Aled laid a reassuring hand on her shoulder. 'No news is good news.' But deep down he was indeed worried, because he knew that if Jez were unhurt he would have tied the dog up as soon as the all-clear sounded and run to help where he could. A sudden thought caused him to brighten up. 'I bet you Annie's run off, and Jez has gone looking for her.'

Cadi couldn't help feeling doubtful; she knew her husband kept the dog tethered at all times, for her own good. 'Do you really think so?'

He nodded. 'She hates loud bangs, but that's nothing compared to a proper assault. She'll have been scared out of her wits; might even have broken her collar. I reckon she'll be hiding either behind or under one of the buildings, and Jez is probably trying to coax her out – especially if the building's on fire!'

He began racing over to the burning hut, Cadi close on his heels, but after a quick scan they could see neither Jez nor Annie. 'We need to do a proper search,' he told her. 'I'll work my way around the outskirts on the east side, and you take the west. If we haven't found them by the time we meet, we'll continue our search in ever decreasing circles until we do.'

Trying to feel as confident as Aled sounded, Cadi did as he instructed. Scouting every building which was raised off the ground, she would stop periodically to call out to Jez and Annie. In the distance, she could hear Aled doing the same. It did occur to her that if Jez was looking for Annie, they might have missed each

150

other somehow, but she had a sinking feeling that they couldn't find him because something terrible had happened. Even if Annie had been hiding, surely she'd have come out by now?

As she continued to walk, her attention was caught by a line of holes going towards one of the shelters. Curious as to what had caused the marks, she walked over. Bending down, she pushed her finger into one of them and dug out a spent bullet. Standing up, she followed the trace of bullet holes until she got to the last one. A puzzled look crossed her face. Why had they ended so abruptly, when the German pilot appeared to be heading straight for the shelter? The answer came to her when she saw a pool of dark liquid a little further on.

Tears already forming, she looked along the trail of blood towards the bushes, and saw an open hand protruding from under the lower branches.

Screaming Jez's name, Cadi flew towards it, and nearly tripped over Annie, still lying faithfully by her master's side.

Tears flooded Cadi's face as she collapsed on to her knees beside her husband. Blinded by her emotions, she didn't see Aled as he dashed towards them, or the expression on his face when he looked down at Jez. Instead, shaking Jez by the shoulder, she pleaded with him to wake up, whilst Aled yelled for someone to bring a stretcher. As they waited for help to arrive, he knelt down beside Cadi, who stared up at him, through soulless eyes. 'He's not waking up and I don't know what to do.'

Aled's words caught in his throat. 'Help's on its way. We'll soon have him in safe hands.'

Seeing two men running over with a stretcher, he gently pulled Cadi to one side so that they could get to Jez. Watching earnestly over their shoulders, she wrung her hands anxiously. 'Is he going to be all right?'

Taking great care, they slowly rolled Jez on to the stretcher, and the extent of his injuries became clear. She stared in horror at his wounds, as the men carefully removed him from the bushes.

Running alongside the stretcher as they hurried him into the medical unit, Cadi stared at the blood-streaked wedding ring on Jez's limp hand. Seeing a host of doctors as well as nurses running to his aid, she clasped the hand in hers. 'Jez, it's me, Cadi ...'

A doctor ushered her firmly but politely out of the way, and one of the nurses steered her to one side. 'Do you know him?'

Tears trickling down her cheeks, she nodded slowly. 'I'm his wife.' Her guts wrenched as she heard the nurse give a sharp intake of breath.

'I understand that you want to be with your husband, but it's important that the doctors are free to work on him. Is there anyone who can look after you?'

Aled, who had been standing to one side with Annie, stepped forward. 'I'll stay with her.'

'Can't I at least come in the hospital?' Cadi pleaded.

The nurse nodded. 'We've a room where you can wait' – she looked at Annie – 'but I'm afraid you can't bring the dog in.'

Cadi spoke in leaden tones. 'Her name's Annie, and she never leaves his side ... you can't take her away from him now.'

Seeing that the nurse was about to object, Aled took her to one side and spoke in lowered tones. 'I'm no doctor, but I can see he's in a bad way, so do you not think you could bend the rules just this once? It's not as if we're taking her into the operating theatre. You can see how much it means to his wife.'

The nurse agreed, albeit reluctantly. 'All right. But if anyone asks, I know nothing.'

Aled gave her a grim smile. 'Thank you.' Looking over his shoulder, he gestured for Cadi to bring Annie over to join them.

As they entered the hospital, the nurse pointed them in the direction of the waiting room, before fielding another nurse who had come over to object at Annie's presence. Cadi entered the room, but Aled hung back. 'I'll be with you in a minute.'

He approached the nurse, who was eyeing him expectantly. 'Can you make a phone call for me, please?'

'Certainly. Who to?'

'RAF Fiskerton. Can you let them know that Sergeant Cadi Thomas has been delayed and that she needs to stay with her husband?'

Nodding, the nurse was about to rush off when Aled put an arm out to detain her. 'Sergeant Thomas has close friends at Fiskerton, one of whom is Mr Thomas's sister.'

The nurse gave him a sympathetic look. 'Don't worry. I'll make sure they handle the information sensitively.'

'Thank you.' He took a moment to gather himself before joining Cadi in the waiting room. He'd seen many men shot up, but Jez had to be the worst he'd seen outside of a dogfight.

He entered the room to see Cadi comforting Annie, who was whining quietly.

'I've spoken to the nurse, and she's going to inform RAF Fiskerton of your whereabouts.'

'Thank you.' Keeping her face close to the dog, she kissed the top of her soft, silky head, then looked up through tear-brimmed eyes. 'I knew Annie hadn't got away from him, because he promised me he'd never let her off leash again.' She brushed away a tear before it had time to fall. 'The pilot of the plane was trying to shoot them before they got to the shelter.' Her eyes narrowed. 'Why would anyone do that? Why target an individual, when your orders are to disable a base?'

'Jez and Annie were in the wrong place at the wrong time,' said Aled simply. 'As for why the pilot did what he did, only he knows the answer to that.' He stroked the setter's head. 'We've always taken the mickey out of her for being a scaredy cat, but not today. Today Annie showed us she has the heart of a lion.'

'She loves him more than she loves herself,' said Cadi. 'She put her life on the line to stay with him because she knew...' Unable to finish the sentence, she fell into silent tears.

Aled stared at his feet. He didn't need Cadi to complete the sentence; he knew exactly what she was trying to say.

The door to the waiting room opened, and one of the doctors who'd run out to Jez came in. 'Mrs Thomas?'

Nodding, Cadi gripped hold of Aled's hand. 'Yes?'

'I think you should come and see your husband.' He glanced at Annie. 'Is this the dog I've been hearing so much about?'

154

'Her name's Annie,' said Cadi automatically. 'And yes, she belongs to my husband.'

'You can bring her too.'

'But the nurse said we weren't to take her out of the room ...' Cadi began, but Aled hung his head. He knew there was only one reason why the doctor would make such an exception.

'That was then, but now I'm saying she can go with you.' He glanced at Aled. 'Are you related to Mr Thomas?'

Aled shook his head. 'No, but he saved my life once.' He looked at Cadi. 'If you need me, I'll be right here.'

Before they entered Jez's room, the doctor spoke plainly to Cadi. 'I'm afraid I have to tell you, Mrs Thomas, that whilst we've done all we can, I'm afraid it's not enough.'

Cadi heard Aled curse softly behind her, and she spoke in hollow tones. 'How long?'

The doctor's voice was grave. 'We've sent for his mother, but it's highly unlikely she'll make it in time to say goodbye.' He looked at her with deep sympathy. 'I'm so sorry.'

Cadi walked into the room as though she were in some awful dream, none of which was really happening. Heading straight for Jez's bed, she glanced at the nurse who had allowed Annie to stay. 'Can he hear me?'

The nurse nodded. 'We think so.'

Taking Jez's hand in hers, she brushed his fingers against her cheek, kissing his knuckles as they passed her lips. 'Hello, cariad. It's me, Cadi.' She smiled down at him, her eyes glistening with tears as she spoke. 'I've brought Annie to see you. She's been ever such a brave girl.' Still holding his hand in hers, she gently brushed the hair from his face before kissing his forehead. 'Oh, Jez, I love you *so* much. Please …' Seeing his eyes flutter, she held his hand close to her chest. 'Jez?'

He opened his eyes the merest fraction of a slit, the sides of his mouth tweaking as if he were trying to smile. Kissing the knuckles of his fingers, Cadi gazed lovingly at him. 'I *knew* you'd wake up. Oh, my darling man, I love you more than words can say.'

When Jez spoke his voice was only just on the cusp of her hearing. 'I love you too.'

Leaning forward, Cadi kissed him on the lips, her heart aching as she felt him try to respond. She blinked, sending tears cascading down her cheeks. 'You've got to fight this, Jez. I don't want to be on my own.'

He opened his eyes a fraction more, and fixed her with a pleading gaze. 'You must promise me something,' he whispered.

'Anything,' Cadi responded, squeezing his hand.

'Find happiness with someone else. I couldn't bear to think of you ending your days alone.'

'But I don't want anybody else,' sobbed Cadi. 'I only want you, so you see you *can't* —'

Jez interrupted her. 'Please, Cadi. Just p-promise me …'

Seeing his eyes begin to close, Cadi spoke fervently. 'I promise, my darling …'

A faint smile wavered on his lips as he took a small, peaceful breath. 'I love you, Cadi Thomas.'

She smiled through her tears. 'And I love you too.' She felt his hand go slack in hers as the light faded from his eyes, and let out a cry of anguish as she flung herself across her husband's chest. And Annie, still sitting beside her master, gently licked his limp hand before raising her muzzle and letting out a howl so mournful there was no mistaking its meaning.

Hearing Cadi's cries, Aled burst into the room and rushed towards the bed, only to be fielded by the nurse, who was shaking her head. Leading him back into the waiting room, she said, 'She needs to let the pain out. I know it's hard, but you must leave her to grieve.'

Aled glared at the woman, his eyes shining with unspent tears. 'I can't just leave her on her own.'

'You'll be here for her when she needs you, but right now she needs to be with her husband.'

Aled stared at the nurse through glassy eyes. 'He saved my life. Where the hell was I when he needed me most?'

The nurse smiled compassionately. 'You couldn't have saved him no matter how quickly you'd got to him. His injuries were too severe.'

'I could've done something.'

The nurse raised a sharp eyebrow. 'Not unless you'd taken his place.'

Aled stared at her. 'In a heartbeat, if it saved Cadi from going through such pain.'

The nurse looked confused. 'Are you related to Mrs Thomas?'

Aled shook his head. 'No, but we grew up in the same village.' He could still hear Cadi's sobs. 'Are you sure I can't do anything to help her?'

'She'll come to you when she's ready.'

Aled eyed her doubtfully. 'Maybe if it was someone else, but Cadi's a strong, independent woman who doesn't like to rely on others. I worry she might try to carry this burden on her own.'

'Mr Thomas's family has been informed, and they're on their way. Your friend won't be on her own for much longer.'

Aled stared at her incredulously. Was she purposely denying Cadi a source of comfort? 'She needn't be on her own now, because I'm here.'

'I hope you don't think I'm speaking out of turn, but you're just a friend ...' began the nurse, but Aled intervened.

'I'm not *just a friend*, I'm more than that. We've been through a lot, me and Cadi, and we've always been there for each other. I've never let her down before, and I don't intend to start now.'

The nurse spoke kindly. 'If you really want what's best for Mrs Thomas, you'll give her space to grieve.'

The door behind them opened, and Izzy came in. Tears streaming down her face, she looked straight at Aled, a frown creasing her brow. 'Why aren't you in there with her?'

'Good question,' said Aled, glaring at the nurse.

'I'm sorry, but unless he's family ...'

Izzy took him by the hand. 'He is as far as I'm concerned.'

She led Aled back to Cadi, and the three held each other as they mourned Jez's passing.

June 1944

Cadi stared blindly into the grave, tears trickling down her cheeks, as the vicar read the committal. His words washed over her, but she waited for him to finish before stepping forward. Clasping a single rose between her fingers, she kissed the petals before allowing the flower to fall on to the lid of the coffin. Beside her, a black ribbon replacing her collar, Annie snuffled at Cadi's fingers. Stroking the smooth hair of the dog's head comforted Cadi somewhat, but Annie would be going back to Rhos with her parents after the wake, and it would be a long time before she saw Jez's dog again. Turning to her mother she spoke unsteadily, her voice hoarse with emotion. 'Jez loved roses because they reminded him of me.'

Jill slipped her arm around her daughter's shoulders. 'You were his Rose Queen.'

Cadi fingered the brooch of delicate roses that Jez had given her as a Christmas gift. 'He loved hearing me tell how I'd been crowned Rose Queen, because he said it was the start of my journey to Liverpool, and had it not been for the carnival I might never have come his way.'

At Cadi's side, Maria dabbed the tears from her eyes. 'You made Jez happier than I ever thought he could be,' she told Cadi. 'I'll never forget the way he brought you to me, after saving you from Eric. I knew there and then that he'd found the love of his life.'

159

Cadi's lips trembled. 'I wish I could've saved him the way he saved me.'

Jill squeezed Cadi's hand. 'That's all poor Aled's been saying, but the truth is neither of you could've saved him.'

Cadi turned to her mother. 'What's Aled been saying?'

'He's beating himself up because Jez saved his life, but when push came to shove he couldn't save Jez. I've told him over and over that there's nothing he could've done, but it doesn't make the slightest bit of difference. As far as Aled's concerned he's let you both down.'

'But that's ridiculous,' Cadi sniffed.

Jill wagged a chiding finger. 'You were saying the same thing yourself just a few moments ago, so what's the difference?'

Cadi opened her mouth to argue before shrugging helplessly. 'I wish I could've done something.'

'Which is only natural,' said Jill, 'but you're going round in circles, and that won't do you any good. You need to move forward, not live in the past.'

'Only I don't want to move forward,' said Cadi softly.

Jill glanced over the top of Cadi's head to Maria, who stepped forward. 'Jez wouldn't want you to live in the past, Cadi you know he wouldn't.'

Cadi shook her head. 'I hear what you say, but I'll never be happy again, not without Jez beside me.'

Jill kissed the top of her daughter's head. 'I know it feels like that now, but you'll not feel this way for ever.'

'I will,' said Cadi fervently 'because no one can bring him back.' She watched as Aled took some soil from the box and sprinkled it into the grave. Grey-faced and hollow-eyed, he looked as though he'd not slept since the day of the attack, and it worried her that he was still on board the *Ulysses* as rear-gunner. She said as much to Jill and Maria.

'He's a different man from the one I met back in the Greyhound,' said Maria, arching her brow as she looked at Cadi. 'I know it was a while back, but ...'

Cadi shook her head. 'I've never seen him look so ill. He's carrying a terrible burden.'

'Why don't you have a word with him, luv?' said Jill. 'Tell him the same as we've told you, that working as a rear-gunner is too dangerous a position to be dwelling on things that were out of his control.'

Nodding, Cadi walked over to where Aled was talking to two of Jez's colleagues. Making his excuses, he turned to greet her.

'Have you got a minute?'

He nodded. 'Of course. What can I do for you?'

She spoke quietly. 'You can stop blaming yourself for not being able to save Jez.'

Rubbing his hand across the back of his neck, he glanced at the sky before looking back to Cadi. 'He put his life at risk to save me ...'

Cadi interrupted without apology. 'Because he could, and had you been able to do the same I know you would have done, but they were totally different circumstances.'

'I just feel as though I've let him down,' said Aled. 'You too, come to that.'

161

'Why me?'

'Because you've always been there for me,' said Aled. 'Warning me about Daphne, even though you knew it could cause ructions.' He hesitated. 'I wish I could've done something to help you the way you've helped me.'

'You helped me to look for Jez, and you never left my side when we were waiting to hear ... news. You might not think you did much, but you really did. Just being there made the world of difference.'

He pushed his hands into his pockets. 'You do know that if you ever need me, all you have to do is call?'

She threaded her arm through his. 'Of course I do.' She hesitated. 'I hope you don't mind my saying, but you look as though you've not slept in a month of Sundays.'

'I'll be fine,' said Aled. 'It's you I'm worried about.'

She squeezed his arm in hers. 'Stop worrying about others and start looking after yourself. You're no good sitting at the back of the plane if your mind's elsewhere.'

'Easier said than done,' Aled confessed. 'I can't get that day out of my mind, no matter how hard I try.'

'I'm the same,' said Cadi. 'I keep reliving the moment we found him, over and over – I believe the Canadians refer to it as Groundhog Day.'

Aled puffed his cheeks out. 'Why do we do it to ourselves, when it doesn't make the blindest bit of difference to the outcome?'

'All part of the grieving process, I suppose,' Cadi said. 'When something happens so quickly, it can be hard to make sense of, especially when there was no reason for him to die.'

Aled gritted his teeth. 'That bloody pilot ...' Cursing himself inwardly for voicing his inner thoughts, he shook his head. 'Sorry. I didn't mean to ...'

Cadi patted his forearm. 'Don't worry. I do it all the time.'

Trying to steer away from the day of the attack, Aled changed the subject. 'Are you going to continue in the WAAF?'

Cadi looked at him in surprise. 'Of course I am. Why wouldn't I?'

He shrugged. 'Too much, maybe?'

'Better than sitting at home feeling sorry for myself,' said Cadi, adding as an afterthought, 'wherever home is.'

He eyed her speculatively. 'What do you mean, "wherever home is"?'

'I suppose I feel lost without him,' said Cadi, sliding her arm out from Aled's. 'I know Maria would have me back in the Belmont, and my mother would want me back in Rhos, but I don't feel as though I belong anywhere other than the WAAF. Does that make sense?'

He nodded. 'Perfectly.' He paused as Marnie came over to join them.

She smiled at Cadi. 'I was so sorry to hear about Jez, Cadi. He was a lovely man. If there's anything I can do ...?'

Cadi returned her smile. 'I wish there was, but it's going to take time.' She glanced meaningfully at Aled. 'Make sure he takes care of himself, won't you?'

163

Marnie arched a doubtful brow. 'I'll try my best but I don't know whether he'll listen to me.'

Cadi indicated her parents, who were standing by a taxi, waiting for her to join them. 'Sorry, but I think I'm needed. I hope I'll see you both at the wake?'

Marnie slid her arm through Aled's. 'Of course.'

For Cadi, the rest of the day passed in a dreamlike fashion. She nodded in all the right places, shook people by the hand, accepted their condolences, and did her best to hide the fact that she wanted to run away and pretend that none of it had ever happened. It was only her close friends who knew how she was really feeling. Coming over with a glass of water, Poppy said quietly, 'We're right here with you.'

'Thanks, Poppy. I don't think I could've done this without you and the girls.'

'All for one,' said Izzy, who had walked over.

Cadi's lips hinted at a smile. 'That's what Jez used to say, do you remember?'

'The four musketeers,' said Izzy.

Cadi blinked. 'How am I meant to carry on?'

'One step at a time,' Poppy told her. 'You've got to learn to live life without Jez, and that's not going to be easy, but we're going to be with you every step of the way.'

Cadi twizzled the wedding band on her finger. 'I haven't the strength to take it off. I know I should, because I'm not married any more.'

'You're still Mrs Thomas,' said Poppy.

Bill and Maria walked over to join them, and Bill placed his arm around Cadi's shoulders. 'I should imagine you're exhausted; I think we should call it a night, and say goodbye to our guests.'

Cadi stared around her. 'Can they not stay just a little longer? It may sound silly, but I'm not ready to say goodbye to anyone yet. It feels as though once the wake's over, that's it. Life as normal' – she laughed without mirth – 'whatever that is.'

Bill squeezed her shoulders. 'You make it sound so final, but Jez'll never be gone when there're still people who remember and love him.' He took Cadi's hand and placed it against her chest. 'Jez's memory, his thoughts, his love, are buried deep inside you. If you ever want to see him, you only have to look in your heart to find him. That's why you feel close to him when we're around, because there's a little bit of Jez in all of us.'

Maria nodded. 'Bill's right. We've all got memories of Jez, and half of us wouldn't be here today if it wasn't for him.' She smiled fondly at Cadi. 'Whenever I see you, I remember the way he used to gaze at you, all soppy.'

'Like a lovesick puppy,' Poppy agreed.

Maria gave Cadi a sidelong glance. 'You know you'd be more than welcome to come and work for me in the Belmont?'

'Thanks for the offer, Maria, but I feel closer to Jez when I'm part of the air force,' said Cadi. 'It's good to be busy, and my job keeps me on the go from dawn to dusk.'

'I think Cadi's doing the right thing,' said Bill. 'When me and the lads were making our way back to Blighty, we didn't have any time to stop and think about things. It was only when I got back that it truly hit home. Having time to think isn't always a good thing.'

Cadi made her point. 'I used to have dreadful nightmares after the Greyhound got bombed. So much so, I feared they might haunt me when I had to sleep in a room full of strangers, but I was always so tired it was quite the opposite.'

Maria looked up. 'And how do you sleep now?'

Cadi breathed out. 'Truthfully? I don't get much sleep, and when I do it's never for long.'

'And you still go out in the car,' said Maria. 'If you're not careful you'll wind up causing an accident.'

'Normally I'd agree with you, but I'm never tired now, not even the teensiest bit. I go to bed wide awake, and I'm like that the whole day through.'

'It'll catch up with you at some point,' said Maria, 'and when it does, you need to ask for time off, so that you can rest properly.'

'I will,' Cadi promised.

They spent the rest of the evening swapping stories about Jez, and Cadi found herself smiling, just a little, when they discussed incidents such as the time Jez had asked the taxi driver to take him to Hillcrest House before realising how it must have sounded. With everyone having more than one story to tell, it was getting late when they said their final goodbyes. The last people to leave were Aled and Marnie.

Taking Aled in a warm embrace, Cadi held him tight. 'Thanks for everything, Aled. Make sure you take your time on the journey home.'

Leaning back from their embrace, he smiled. 'If you ever want to talk, just call.'

'Only if you promise to do the same.' She turned to Marnie. 'Thanks for coming. Aled won't admit it, but I know today's not been easy for him.'

'Stiff upper lip and all that,' agreed Marnie.

Cadi closed the door behind them and slid the bolts across, before turning and seeing that everyone but Poppy had gone upstairs.

'Aled looked as worn out as yourself. Do you think he's coping after what happened?'

'Not in the slightest,' said Cadi, 'but I've had a good chat with him, and he's promised to stop blaming himself.'

'And are you going to listen to your own advice?' asked Poppy tartly.

'I'm going to have to,' said Cadi, a tad reluctantly, 'because blaming myself doesn't bring him back.' Her cheeks reddened as she prepared to make a confession to her oldest friend. 'But how do I stop feeling guilty? And I *know* Aled feels guilty too. He's not said as much, but he doesn't have to: I can see it in his face, the same as I see it in my own every time I look in the mirror.'

Poppy stared at her, her eyes rounding. 'Guilty about what?'

Cadi lowered her gaze. 'About being alive.'

Poppy threw arms around her friend. 'Oh, Cadi, you mustn't feel guilty about being alive, because it's a blessing, something to be thankful for.' She hesitated. 'Can I speak frankly?'

Cadi nodded. 'Of course you can.'

'Not appreciating every day that you wake up is an insult to Jez, because he doesn't have that privilege.

Being alive is something to celebrate, not regret.' She paused as she found the words. 'Jez would be mortified if he thought you intended to spend the rest of your days in mourning. He wanted you to be happy, you said so yourself.'

Cadi knew that Poppy was talking about Jez's last request: that she should not end her days a widow. 'I know I promised him, Poppy, but I really don't know if I can ever keep that promise.'

Poppy eyed her sternly. 'Then you're not the woman I take you for. The Cadi I know would never break her word, especially not to someone she loved so dearly.'

Cadi blinked against the tears which started to form. 'You're making it sound as though I'm ungrateful.'

Poppy shrugged. 'I did ask you if I could talk frankly, and you agreed I could. To be honest, Cadi, feeling guilty that you're not lying in the ground next to Jez *is* being ungrateful.'

'I can't help the way I feel,' cried Cadi.

'No, but you can stop living in what should have been, and start living your life as it is now.' She gave her friend a sympathetic smile. 'I'm not trying to hurt you, or to be mean – I'm trying to do the exact opposite.'

Cadi nodded miserably. 'I know you'd never try to upset me, and you're telling me all this for my own good, and you're right, of course you are. I promise I'll do my best to stop living my life mourning what should have been.'

Poppy smiled. 'That's all any of us want to hear. Don't forget Bill's words: if you ever want to know what Jez would think, say or do in any given situation, all you have to do is look inside your heart to find the answer.'

Cadi enveloped Poppy in a warm embrace. 'Thanks, Poppy. You really are the best friend a girl could have.'

Aled placed his arm around Marnie's shoulders as they walked towards the car. 'I'm glad that's over with.'

She glanced up at the underside of his chin. 'I didn't realise that Cadi was a blonde.'

Aled looked confused. 'What on earth has the colour of her hair got to do with the price of fish?'

'Nothing,' she said slowly. 'I was just surprised, that's all.'

'Do you not remember the day we were carol singing outside the church, and Jez came storming over because he thought you were Cadi?'

She nodded.

'Well, you must've realised the two of you look a little alike, for him to make that mistake,' said Aled reasonably.

'I didn't really think about it at the time,' Marnie admitted, 'mainly because I didn't know who he was.' She fell into silent thought as she contemplated Jez's reasons for thinking that Aled might be with Cadi. 'What made him think I was her, though? We might look a tad similar, but there's lots of blue-eyed blondes in the WAAF. What made Jez assume that I was Cadi?'

'Because you were standing next to me.'

Marnie felt her cheeks begin to warm. She didn't like asking these sorts of questions when Aled had just buried his friend, but something wasn't sitting right with her. 'You were about to kiss me at the time. Does that mean that Jez thought you were about to kiss his fiancée? And if so, what on earth would make him think the two of you would behave in such a manner?'

'Because he'd behaved like a jealous idiot, and he was paranoid in case he'd pushed Cadi into the arms of another man. Only we sorted that out when I gave him a lift to Chester train station.'

Marnie was itching to say that there must have been more behind Jez's assumption than Aled was admitting, but pushing for an answer now might make her out to be as jealous as Jez had been. On the other hand, she was only asking these questions because she had seen the way Aled looked at Cadi during the funeral. Granted he and Cadi had been through a lot, and they were good friends, but there was something in the way that Aled was looking at her which seemed to be deeper than friendship. She briefly considered speaking her thoughts, then cursed herself inwardly. She'd never been the type to be jealous, until she'd found her former beau in the arms of another. Was it her own insecurities that were making her see things that weren't there? True, her cheating rat of an ex had taught her to be on her guard, but up until now she had thought Aled to be true blue. She tutted to herself. The affection which Aled was showing for Cadi was only to be expected after everything that had happened. She felt a shiver run down her spine as she imagined how awful it must've been for the two of them to find Cadi's husband. She knew the experience had prematurely aged Aled; if anything he was probably feeling kinship with Cadi because of the trauma they had shared.

As they walked, Aled found himself wondering why Marnie had brought up the subject. She'd never asked him about Cadi before, so why now? Surely it couldn't be down to hair colour? Had he said or done something to make Marnie feel insecure? He glanced down at her. 'Is everything all right? Only you've never really been interested in Cadi before.'

'Just curious, I suppose,' said Marnie, crossing her fingers deep within her pocket.

Aled found this doubtful, but with nothing further coming he would have to take her at her word. He knew her ex had cheated on her with another woman, but surely Marnie wouldn't think Aled capable of doing the same thing? Especially not with his friend's widow? Admittedly there was a time when Aled would've jumped at the chance to be Cadi's beau, but that was a long time ago, and a lot of water had passed under the bridge since then. Now, he saw Cadi as no more than a very good friend, and he loved her as such.

Chapter Six

July 1944

Just as she had every night since Jez's death, Cadi had woken to find herself covered in sweat, with her heart pounding in her chest, and her stomach churning itself into knots.

The girls had told her to go and see the doctor, and Cadi had done just that, only to be told what she already knew: the nightmares would fade in time, and she should start looking after herself before she became too ill to drive. But how could she eat when her heart still ached for the man she had loved with all her heart? The doctor had also told her to take some time off, but Cadi had said this would just make her worse, and that keeping busy in the WAAF was the only thing that kept her going. Bill had been correct when he said that time to think wasn't necessarily a good thing, which was why she was currently in Scotland.

Swinging her legs out of bed, she put her greatcoat over her shoulders and headed for the ablutions. Being on a remote airfield, far away from everyone she knew, held one big advantage. Nobody knew her from Adam, so she didn't have to suffer sympathetic looks, or get special treatment, or have people ask her how Jez was doing, only to apologise in embarrassment when she explained what had happened.

Filling the sink with water, she washed briefly before drying herself with a towel. Seeing her face in the mirror above the sink, she hastily averted her gaze rather than acknowledge her gaunt cheeks and pasty complexion. Remembering her conversation with Aled the previous evening, she gazed cautiously up at her reflection. Aled's voice had been full of concern, wanting to know if she was all right, and asking if she needed anything, just as it was every time he rang. Cadi had done her best to convince him that she was coping well under the circumstances, but when he offered to come and see her she had used her constant travelling as an excuse, saying that meeting would be too difficult. She could hear by the hesitation in his voice that he wasn't altogether convinced, but, ever the gentleman, he had respected her wishes, saying that he would come and see her when she was more settled.

Aled wasn't the only one on her case. Poppy and Izzy were constantly trying to persuade her to eat, saying that Jez would be worried if he could see her now, but all they had achieved was to make Cadi hide away from her friends as well as everyone else. She tutted irritably to herself. It wasn't as if she didn't eat anything; it was only breakfast that she skipped, and she'd rather skip breakfast than try to force it down just to please her friends. She grimaced as she recalled the few times she'd eaten breakfast in order to please them, only to end up spending the morning with her head down the toilet.

Having washed and dressed she headed to the cookhouse, where she grabbed a quick cup of tea before heading out to the car. Today she would be making the long journey to RAF Ilfracombe. A beautiful part of the country where she wouldn't be asked questions by anyone who knew her.

She was a good way into her journey when she pulled over to let a lorry through. As it passed by, she found herself checking to see whether the driver was Kieran O'Connell. It was the first time she had thought of him since she'd lost Jez. She tapped her finger against the steering wheel as she drove on. If she remembered rightly, the plan had been to tell Daphne what Kieran was capable of, so that she could warn his belle – if he had one, of course. Since losing Jez, the whole debacle had paled in significance, which was only to be expected, but it didn't take away from the fact that they were allowing Kieran to get away with murder if they did nothing to stop him.

She imagined the map in her mind's eye. Ilfracombe wasn't far away from Chivenor; if time allowed she'd be able to call in on her way to her next destination.

She reached Ilfracombe just as the sun was setting. Shattered after the long drive, she quickly checked in at the office before heading over to the ablutions, where she had a quick wash before retiring for the night. As she snuggled between her sheets, she went through the conversation she would have with Daphne the following day. Doubtless the other woman would be curious as to why Cadi wanted to speak to her, but would she see Cadi's request as being helpful or interfering? Would she even listen to what Cadi had to say, or would she walk away before she'd had a chance to finish? Might she accuse Cadi of interfering in Kieran's life the way Cadi had accused Daphne of interfering in Aled's? Or would she heed Cadi's advice and speak to the other woman? If she did, Cadi would have to warn her to be careful of Kieran's temper. She pursed her lips, thinking. She supposed she was asking Daphne to do something pretty risky, when you considered what type of man he was. Could Cadi really ask her to get involved? Only what choice did she have? She hesitated. There was one alternative, of course. If she approached Daphne, she could find out who Kieran's belle was and talk to her herself. Quite frankly, she'd welcome an outburst from Kieran, as it would give her the perfect opportunity to get rid of some of her anger by telling him what she thought of men who bullied women.

As she drifted off to sleep, images of Kieran shouting the odds formed in her mind. A fleeting smile of satisfaction crossed her lips as she imagined herself with a megaphone announcing to the entire base that Kieran O'Connell was a toerag, as he left the RAF with his tail between his legs. Within moments of her drifting off to sleep, however, the vision had morphed into that of Jez, but this time he wasn't the only one who'd been struck by bullets. Cadi twisted in her sheets as her sleeping eye fell on Annie's bloodstained body lying next to her master's.

Haunted by her nightmares, Cadi woke early the next morning and was up betimes, ready for the day ahead. After the usual cup of tea to start off her day, she headed to the office, where she was given a package to take to RAF Okehampton. Pleased that Chivenor was en route, Cadi headed off.

Arriving in Chivenor some twenty minutes later, she showed her pass to the guard and was let through. Once parked, she quickly called in at the office to say that she had come to visit Daphne, and asked if somebody could point her in the right direction.

'Go to the motor pool. Someone's bound to know where she is,' said the Waaf on duty.

Thanking the girl for her help Cadi wandered over to where she could see numerous vehicles all parked in the same spot. As she made her way between them, she kept an eye out for Kieran as well as Daphne. She definitely didn't want to bump into him unawares. As she tried to decide what she would say to him if she did, she spied him in the distance, and tutted beneath her breath. He was talking to Daphne. Should she approach Daphne with him there, or would it be better to wait until she could get her on her own? She nodded to herself. It would be better to wait; that way, Kieran couldn't bully Daphne into silence as soon as Cadi had left. Tucking herself out of sight, she jumped as a voice spoke to her from behind.

'Can I help you?'

Turning, she smiled briefly at a man who was watching her with mild interest. Embarrassed that he might think her to be spying, she explained her presence. 'I'm waiting to speak to someone.'

He looked over to Daphne and Kieran. 'Let me guess: it's summat to do with Kieran O'Connell?'

She eyed him sharply. 'What makes you say that?'

He looked thoughtful. 'There's summat shifty about him, and rumours are rife concerning his dealings.' He jerked his head towards Daphne. 'But the women fall at his feet. They're like putty in his hands.'

Cadi's jaw flinched. 'Only because they don't know him as well as I do. If they did, they'd steer well clear.'

'You know him, then?' he said, his voice rising with intrigue. 'What did he do before signing up, do you know? Only no one here seems to, and he's very guarded when it comes to life before the war.'

Cadi smiled grimly. 'I'm not surprised. Let's just say he hasn't the rosiest of pasts, and if you know what's good for you you won't delve too deeply.'

He raised his brow. 'So we were right to be suspicious?'

She nodded. 'Only that hasn't come from me.'

He glanced back in the direction of Kieran and Daphne. 'Are you here to warn his fiancée?'

Cadi's eyes grew round. 'He's engaged to someone? Looks like I got here in the nick of time.' She faced the man squarely. 'You say you thought him shifty, and mentioned something about his dealings, but what makes you think he's up to something illegal?'

'His attitude,' replied the man simply. 'And he's work-shy. He's always making excuses why he can't do summat or other, and he doesn't seem bothered when people point it out to him. You get the feeling he's here because he has to be, as though he's got no other choice. Yet when you try and quiz him for answers, he's vague with his replies.' He adjusted the cap on his head. 'He always seems to have plenty of money, but where does it come from? One of the corporals told him to sod off back to Ireland if he didn't want to do his bit, and Kieran flipped his lid. Started shouting the odds, saying that the feller didn't know who he was talking to, cos if he did he'd know to keep it zipped.'

'Kieran was speaking the truth for once,' said Cadi darkly. 'Your friend doesn't know exactly what kind of man he's talking to.'

'You seem to know an awful lot about him,' said the man. 'What's he done?'

Seeing that Kieran was walking away from Daphne, Cadi brought their conversation to an end. 'My advice would be to treat him as though you're playing with fire, because if you get involved with Kieran O'Connell that's exactly what you're doing.'

Without giving him a chance to quiz her any further, she hurried after Daphne, who was heading towards one of the huts. Cadi waved to get her attention, and Daphne visibly deflated. 'Oh, for God's sake. I don't know what you want, but I'm not interested.'

'Don't worry,' said Cadi, 'it's nothing to do with you.'

'Makes a change,' said Daphne tartly.

'It's about that feller you were just talking to. Kieran O'Connell.'

Daphne was shaking her head. 'Whatever it is you have to say, I suggest you don't bother, because I'm not interested.'

'Well you should be,' snapped Cadi. 'He's bad news, and from what I hear he's engaged to one of the girls on your base.'

'You know full well who he's engaged to,' said Daphne fiercely. 'That's why you're here, so that you can plunge the knife in, and give it a good twist. Well, I won't let you do it! You're just jealous, you always have been and you always will be.'

'If I knew who he was engaged to I wouldn't be standing here wasting my breath on you,' said Cadi. 'The only reason why I'm involving you in any of this is so that you can point me in the right direction. Kieran O'Connell is dangerous, and he's only after one thing, which is money. And Kieran isn't the only name he goes under.'

Daphne shook her head, her eyes narrowing. 'Don't even pretend that you know him. You think his name's Micky, which is complete poppycock!'

Cadi gaped at Daphne. 'How do you know?'

'I know that you've been asking questions, because the cook told me.' She glared at Cadi. 'Why can't you leave sleeping dogs lie? Is this your sick idea of revenge for me spilling the beans to Jez? If so, then you can forget it. I've had a gutful of your interfering, and I'm not prepared to listen to a damned word that leaves your lips.'

'I'm trying to help,' said Cadi. Keeping her tone lowered, she tried to make Daphne see sense. 'This has got nothing to do with you, so I fail to see why you're being so obnoxious.'

Daphne stamped her foot. 'If you don't leave this minute, I'm going to telephone Jez and let him know that his wife's being an interfering witch – yet again!' Seeing the stunned look on Cadi's face, she continued, 'Although I dare say I'm not telling him anything he doesn't already know. I honestly don't know what he sees in you—'

Before Daphne could go any further, the words bolted from Cadi's lips. 'Jez passed away in May.'

Daphne's defiant attitude dissipated, leaving her momentarily speechless. Her cheeks flushed with colour as she stammered an apology. 'I'm – I'm sorry. I didn't know.'

Cadi spoke in leaden tones. 'Just tell me who Kieran's engaged to, and I'll do us both a favour.'

Daphne continued to stare at Cadi. 'What I don't understand is why you came back, after the cook told you you'd got it wrong?'

'Because he turned up at RAF Little Snoring and started bandying threats around, saying that if I didn't keep my mouth shut he'd make Raquel's life a living hell.' Not wanting Daphne to know the ins and outs concerning Raquel's past, she had deliberately fudged this bit. She eyed Daphne beseechingly. 'Daphne, you've met Kitty: she wouldn't say boo to a goose. He scared the living daylights out of her. God only knows how he knew where to find her.'

Daphne's cheeks grew warm. She'd told Kieran where Kitty worked, and it was possible that Cadi was speaking the truth, at least in some part. Kieran had said something about stopping Cadi and her pals from upsetting Daphne; was this his idea of protecting her from them? She wondered what it was exactly that Kieran had said to Kitty.

Not wishing to admit that she had been the one to give away Kitty's whereabouts, she tried to deflect Cadi with a different question. 'But why would he go to all that trouble?'

'Because he wants to marry his way into money, and he's worried I'll scupper his plans before he's got his foot through the door.'

Daphne rolled her eyes. 'Well, you've obviously got that wrong, because I'm flat broke.'

Cadi's jaw practically hit the floor. '*You*?'

Daphne tutted impatiently. 'As if you didn't know.'

'I really didn't,' Cadi gasped.

Daphne heaved an impatient sigh. 'Well, now you know the truth you can do one, because Kieran loves me for me, not my money!'

Cadi was utterly flummoxed. They'd obviously got hold of the wrong end of the stick, but even so, she couldn't stand by and watch Daphne make yet another mistake. 'You can do better than him,' she said softly. 'I know we've not always seen eye to eye, far from it, but I'd not wish the likes of Kieran on my worst enemy.'

Believing that Cadi was talking out of grief, Daphne took several deep breaths before speaking. 'I'm sorry that you've lost Jez, really I am, but you can't go round interfering in other people's lives just because yours has gone wrong.'

Cadi lifted her head to say that that wasn't the case, but what was the point? She had told Daphne what Kieran was really like, and she still didn't want to listen. Besides, Cadi could hardly argue her point when Daphne hadn't a penny to her name.

With nothing more to say, she rounded the conversation off. 'I dare say you're going to tell Kieran that I paid you a visit, so whilst you're about it, can you pass on a message? Tell him that *everyone* knows about his trip to Kitty, and that Raquel has a threat of her own. If he should try to cause trouble, she won't hesitate to tell all.' Cadi half-turned before addressing Daphne over her shoulder. 'And Daphne, if he ever gives you cause to pause, don't hesitate. Get out whilst you can.'

Hearing Daphne's retreating footsteps, Cadi made her way towards her car, wondering all the way why Kieran had set his sights on Daphne. Could it really be that he'd decided to turn over a new leaf? Maybe the fire had caused him to see the error of his ways, and he was making amends for all he'd done wrong? After all, with Ireland remaining neutral, he could easily have gone back to his homeland, just as the corporal had suggested. She supposed that Paddy might have done just that, whilst Kieran had stayed to fight. Raquel was keen to hide her old life; maybe Kieran was the same. They reckoned that stranger things happen at sea, and maybe in this instance they were right. Remembering the corporal's words, she shook her head. Kieran wasn't the sort to turn over a new leaf, because he didn't think he'd done anything wrong in the first place. The men had all seen through him, but not the women, and there could only be one reason for that. Kieran was playing his cards close to his chest, whilst securing himself a lucrative future. Just what part Daphne had in that, she couldn't be sure, but at least she'd warned her.

When Daphne entered her billet she turned to close the door, and saw that Cadi had gone. Sitting down on her bed, she took a moment to gather her thoughts. Jez's passing had clearly affected Cadi, which was why she was acting so irrationally. *Misery loves company*, Daphne told herself. *That's why she's come all this way, because she wants you to be as miserable as she is.*

There were just one or two sticking points. Why did Cadi think Kieran was called Micky, and why had he supposedly threatened this Raquel – whoever she may be? And just how did he know Cadi? He certainly wasn't from Rhos, or Liverpool. Kieran was from … she paused. Kieran had never actually said where he was from, just that he had been moving around quite a bit before signing on. With him being Irish, Daphne had immediately asked whether he was a traveller, but he had laughed, saying that he had dealings up and down the country, all of which he'd put on hold for the duration of the war. He'd never actually said what he'd been dealing in, but neither had Daphne asked. As far as she was concerned, Kieran relished the idea of running a farm, and that was all she needed to hear. With hindsight, though, maybe she should have asked more questions. She pursed her lips to one side. If she were to tell Kieran that Cadi had called by, she would have to tell him what Cadi had said, including the part about him going to see Kitty in RAF Little Snoring. Her tummy turned a somersault, because she felt certain that this bit, at least, was true. It seemed obvious that Kieran had taken her words to heart when she'd said that Kitty was part of the reason why she and Aled had split up. The more she thought about it, the more sense it made. Kieran had gone to warn Kitty off, and Kitty had vastly exaggerated the tale to Cadi. Just where this Raquel came into it was a mystery to Daphne, but she supposed that was what happened with Chinese whispers.

If she were to get to the bottom of this, she would have to speak to Kieran. Rising to her feet, she set off in search of him, and it wasn't long before she found him helping to unload a wagon full of kitchen supplies. When he saw her approaching, he stopped what he was doing and leaned against the tailgate of the wagon.

'Can't keep away, eh?'

She smiled. 'I've had a visitor.'

'Anyone I know?'

Daphne paused. 'Cadi Thomas, the one I told you about.' Not wishing to appear totally naïve, she added, 'Kitty's friend.'

His face impassive, Kieran barely hesitated before replying. 'Let me guess: she's here to defend her little pal?'

Daphne gave an inward sigh of relief. At least he wasn't going to try to deny that he'd been to see her. 'So, what happened?'

Kieran continued to lean casually against the back of the lorry. 'Harris asked me to take some stuff to Little Snoring. As soon as I heard the name I remembered what you'd said about that Kitty woman and how she'd ruined things between you and your ex. I probably shouldn't have, but I thought I'd call in on her, just to give her a friendly warning to keep her nose out of our business.' He held his hands up in a placating fashion. 'I know I shouldn't have interfered, but you've got to be careful with people like that, and I was damned if I was going to stand by and let her ruin what we have.'

Daphne was positively beaming. Cadi had blown things out of proportion, probably jealous that Kieran would go to such lengths to protect their relationship. 'I knew it was a pile of old tosh the moment she started speaking.' She tutted angrily. 'She even pretended she didn't know we were an item.'

Kieran thought on his feet. 'I don't know what Cadi said to you, but I told Kitty that we were together,' he lied. 'I can't believe she wouldn't tell Cadi.'

Daphne's eyes narrowed. 'I *knew* she knew, but she kept denying it. What is wrong with that woman? I know she's lost her husband, but even so.'

Kieran's brow shot towards his hairline. If Cadi's husband was the same feller who'd come to Hillcrest the day Kitty had set the place on fire, then Kieran could only assume he must have been killed whilst on duty. 'I did hear a few of the airfields had been targeted. I've always said we're like sitting ducks.'

Daphne shrugged. 'She didn't go into detail, and I didn't ask ...' She gazed thoughtfully at Kieran. Daphne hadn't mentioned that Jez was in the RAF, and whilst it was pretty much a given that most young men were in one of the services, Jez could've been in the Army or the Navy for all Kieran knew. She shrugged it off. Cadi's poison was causing her to overthink things.

'I think the whole matter is best swept under the carpet,' Kieran went on. 'This Cadi's obviously still mourning the death of her husband, and hitting out in any way she can.'

'You're right,' conceded Daphne. 'I only told you because I've learned the hard way not to keep secrets.'

He waved a dismissive hand. 'Idle gossip between folks who have nowt better to do with their time. I blame myself for going there in the first place. I should've kept well clear, then she wouldn't have had any reason to call in.'

'Shall I see you later?'

He nodded. 'Of course.'

She was about to turn away when she changed her mind. Throughout the whole business, Cadi had spoken about Kieran as though she'd known him from somewhere else, yet Kieran had never done the same. Why? She eyed him sheepishly. She didn't want him to think she didn't trust him, but on the other hand, she didn't seem to know Kieran as well as Cadi did.

'Cadi thought your name was Micky, and she seems to think she knows you from somewhere. In fact, she talks as though she knows quite a lot about you. Are you certain you've never met her before?'

She had expected him to be upset with her for questioning him in such a fashion, but she hadn't expected him to look so angry. Taking her by the elbow, he jostled her away from the lorry so that the others might not hear what he had to say.

'As I've already told you, my name's Kieran and I don't even know anybody by the name of Micky. And whilst I'm about it, I think I know who I have or have not met, and I'm telling you straight, I've never met Cadi or any of her cronies before. But if you'd rather believe them over me, you only have to say, and we'll call the whole thing off.'

Daphne had gone quite pale. The last thing she wanted was to have Kieran break off their engagement. 'I'm sorry. I didn't mean to upset you.' She shook her head. 'This is what people like Cadi and her pals do. They whisper in corners, and cause people to question themselves. I'm sorry if it sounded as though I doubted you, because I really don't. I just thought she might've bumped into you somewhere, perhaps seen you from a distance, and concocted some farcical tale as a result.'

Removing his cap, Kieran smoothed his hair down before placing it back on his head. 'Well you should've said

186

so then, instead of making me out to be a liar,' he said in sulky tones. 'Either that or kept your mouth shut.'

'I promise I'll never mention them again,' said Daphne earnestly, 'not one single word. I don't want this to come between us.'

'Neither do I,' said Kieran, 'but I won't be questioned over my integrity, and if you can't trust me we should call it a day now, *before* we get wed.'

Daphne wrung her hands anxiously. 'I *do* trust you, and I'll swear it on a stack of bibles if you want me to. I can't apologise enough, Kieran. I don't know what came over me.'

Relenting a little, he put his hands into his pockets, whilst a faint smile settled on his lips. 'Fair enough. Sorry if I got a little heated, but it seemed like a real smack in the chops after I went out of my way to defend you.'

Cursing herself inwardly for ever broaching the subject, she smiled gratefully at him. 'How about we go for a meal tonight, by way of an apology?' she suggested. 'My shout.'

He rubbed his hand back and forth over his chin, pretending to consider her proposal. 'I suppose that would be all right.'

Grateful that the matter seemed to be behind them, Daphne bade him goodbye and headed back to her hut. Kieran watched her go before returning to the lorry. When Daphne had mentioned Cadi, he'd known that Kitty must've spilled the beans despite his threats. If he'd denied the encounter Daphne would have been sure to smell a rat, so he had decided to play along and see where it took him. After all, if he and Daphne were to split, it would be inconvenient, but there were plenty more women in desperate need of the attentions of a sympathetic Irishman. He hadn't pressed Daphne for details of her conversation with Cadi, but it sounded to him as though Daphne had sent the other woman off with a flea in her ear. *Whatever went on*, Kieran told himself, *Daphne must have made it plain that she didn't believe her, and Cadi obviously didn't spell out how she knows me, probably because she doesn't want Daphne knowing what Raquel used to do for a living.* He grinned. They were so busy trying to contain their own skeletons they couldn't tell Daphne the whole truth, which is why she was confused. *You've got away with it,* Kieran congratulated himself, *they'll not come bothering you again. Seeing Kitty was the best thing you could've done, because they've made themselves look untrustworthy.* He whistled softly beneath his breath as he continued with his work. Nothing could stand in his way now. As far as he was concerned, the future was looking very rosy indeed.

As Daphne headed back to her hut, she chastised herself for questioning him. She knew that Cadi and her pals were nothing but troublemakers, so why on earth had she taken any notice of what they said? She winced as she recalled Kieran's suggestion that they break off their engagement. *If I'd allowed that to happen, it would've been two men which Cadi had seen off,* thought Daphne bitterly, *and this time, I'd only have myself to blame. I knew she spoke falsely, so why on earth did I listen to her at all?* She sighed heavily as her treacherous inner voice spoke over her thoughts. *Because there's more to this than meets the eye. Cadi speaks without hesitation when it comes to Kieran, yet when I ask him a plausible question he blows his lid. Which would suggest that he does know her. Question is, why is everyone being so secretive about their past encounters?* .

An older Waaf entered the hut. Saying a brief hello to Daphne she had started to walk to her own bed when Daphne stopped her.

'If you knew a friend of yours was courting a wrong 'un, would you tell them?'

The woman, whose name was Abigail, nodded. 'Course I would. Why d'you ask?'

'Because that's what I'd do too,' said Daphne, 'but I'd also let them know why I believed him to be a wrong 'un.'

'It would be odd not to,' conceded Abigail. 'You can't go making accusations unless you're prepared to explain yourself.'

'So, under what circumstances would you not give them the full story?'

Abigail gave a knowing smile. 'That's easy. If you're only getting half the story, it means they've got summat to hide.'

'That's what I thought,' said Daphne, before lapsing back into silence. She'd established that Cadi was telling half-truths, but what could have happened that would cause her to clam up? She hesitated. Cadi had asked Daphne to pass on a message from a woman by the name of Raquel, but if she'd relayed the message she would've been confirming that she thought Kieran was a liar. *Maybe that's it*, she thought. *Maybe the secret surrounds this Raquel.* That's when it hit her like a ton of bricks. Raquel must be Kieran's ex. Ex-what she wasn't exactly sure, but it made sense that whilst Kieran didn't know Cadi, Cadi could know of him through this Raquel woman, and it must be Raquel who was filling Cadi's ear with poison, saying all kinds of rubbish about her ex because she wanted to pay him back, probably for dumping her. *And Cadi was stupid enough to take the woman at face value*, thought Daphne. *I bet this Raquel is so besotted with Kieran she keeps a photograph of him, and that's how Cadi recognised him, only she got the name wrong ... unless of course he'd changed it in order to escape from a possessive woman, and he couldn't admit it even to me, because he doesn't want to risk word getting out.* She nodded slowly. Should she warn Kieran that Raquel knew of his whereabouts, or should she leave sleeping dogs lie? She envisaged Kieran's wrath and her mind was made up. She would keep quiet, and hope Cadi and Raquel stayed away.

August 1944
Several weeks had passed since Cadi's confrontation with Daphne, and now her travels had taken her to RAF Fiskerton, where she had already arranged to meet up with her friends. The nightmares had almost stopped, and she was pleased to hear the approval of the guard on the gate when she pulled up outside the base.

'Good to have you back, Sergeant Thomas. Life on the road seems to suit you down to the ground, or at least you look a lot better than you did the last time I saw you. Are you here for a while?'

Cadi shook her head. 'Fleeting visit, as per usual.'

He waved her through and Cadi lost no time in seeking out Poppy and Izzy. 'Let's go to the NAAFI for summat to eat,' she suggested. 'I've got heaps to tell you.'

Eager to hear her news, they followed her to the NAAFI, where Cadi ordered a plateful of liver and onions with mashed potato, along with a slice of Victoria sponge for pudding.

Poppy grimaced as she sat down opposite Cadi. 'I'm pleased to see that you've got your appetite back, but I don't know how you can eat that stuff. It makes me go green around the gills.'

'Nowt wrong with mashed potato,' Cadi smiled.

'Oh, ha ha. You know full well that I was referring to the liver.'

Izzy frowned. 'I thought you hated liver and onions?'

Cadi gathered her cutlery. 'I did, but nowadays it seems to be the only thing that whets my appetite.'

Poppy nodded knowingly. 'Liver is full of iron. I reckon it's your body's way of letting you know you need more energy.' She hesitated, before adding tentatively, 'Does this mean the nightmares have stopped?'

'Kind of, or at least I don't have them as often as I used to.' Cadi hesitated momentarily before snapping back into the conversation. 'But back to the business at hand. When I was in Devon a few weeks back, I thought I'd pop in to see Daphne.'

Izzy eyed her with intrigue. 'I'd forgotten all about her.'

'So had I, but when I pulled over for a lorry it reminded me of the day I saw Micky – or Kieran, I should say.'

'So, what did she say?' asked Poppy. 'Did she know his fiancée?'

Cadi laughed. 'She should do, seeing as it's her.'

Poppy's jaw dropped. 'You're kidding?'

'Nope. I heard it straight from the horse's mouth.'

'But why is he with Daphne?' queried Izzy, 'I didn't envisage her as being wealthy.'

'Your guess is as good as mine,' said Cadi, 'not that it matters, considering she didn't believe a word I said.'

'She probably thought you were only saying it to get your own back for what she did to you and Jez,' said Poppy.

Cadi finished her mouthful whilst nodding. 'You've hit the nail on the head, because that's what she said, more or less word for word.'

'There's no helping some people,' said Izzy.

'Was that it?' asked Poppy. 'Or was there more?'

'Not really, because our theory of his marrying for money kind of fell flat on its face after I knew he was engaged to her.' She shrugged. 'Even Daphne thought it was laughable. I did wonder whether he'd seen the error of his ways—'

Izzy choked on a mirthless laugh, cutting Cadi short. 'Men like Kieran *never* see the error of their ways. They're just like my dad, always out to diddle someone or other. I wouldn't trust him if he swore it on a stack of bibles.'

'That's what I figured,' said Cadi, 'not that it makes any difference to the outcome. So I left her to it.'

Izzy puffed her cheeks out. 'I would say she's reaping what she sows, but no one deserves to be with someone like that.'

'I agree, which is why I warned her to be careful, no matter whether she believed me or not.'

Poppy grimaced as she watched Cadi take a slice off the liver. 'Did she ask how you knew him?'

'No, because I didn't want her spiteful tongue judging Raquel.'

Poppy pulled an uncertain face. 'So you told her that he was bad news, but you didn't tell her why? No wonder she was sceptical.'

'I'm not having her know my family's business. She should've taken me at my word. I've never lied to her, or given her cause to distrust me,' said Cadi flatly.

'Daphne's judging you by her own standards,' said Izzy. 'Without proper explanation, she assumes you're lying.'

'I know,' said Cadi softly, 'but if she knew that your mam used to be a you-know-what, I just know that she'd relish poking fun and drawing comparisons between myself and Raquel. It shouldn't matter, but it does.' She hesitated before adding, 'More so now than ever.'

'I'd like to think that Daphne wouldn't be so petty,' said Poppy, 'but I'm afraid you're probably right. She would use the knowledge as payback, and tell anyone who stood still for long enough that your mother-in-law used to be a prostitute.'

'I'm still glad I went, though,' Cadi concluded, 'because at least I can look myself in the eye and say "I tried".'

Izzy folded her arms on the table. 'You never know, your words might've planted a seed of doubt in her head. If she's lucky, the penny'll drop before she says "I do".'

Poppy spoke her mind. 'Even if you told her the truth, she'd say you'd got it all wrong and that Kieran was an innocent landlord, and Raquel and Dolly were using his premises for prostitution without his knowledge.'

Cadi gaped at her. 'You're right! That's just the sort of thing she'd do.'

'Not only would you be left looking like a trouble-maker, but Kieran would come out of it smelling of roses, whilst you, Jez and the rest of us would be painted as the bad ones,' said Izzy.

Cadi spoke in disbelieving tones. 'How can anyone be that blind?'

'There are none so blind as those who will not see,' volunteered Poppy.

'Then that's that,' said Cadi.

'We've no other choice,' Izzy agreed.

Poppy watched as Cadi cleared the last of the liver from her plate. 'It makes me happy to see you polishing your dinner off, even if I can't stomach the stuff.'

Cadi reached across the table to hold Poppy's hand. 'I'm going to be all right. You just have to be patient with me.'

They got up from their table and made their way to the tub of hot water where Cadi dipped her irons. Poppy watched as she shook the water from her cut-lery. 'It's been so lovely to see you. It seems as though you never have time to stop and chat these days.'

'I like to keep busy,' said Cadi. 'That way I don't have time to dwell on things – it probably helps me to sleep better, too.'

'Only you're going to have to slow down sooner or later,' said Poppy.

Cadi held the door open as they passed through. 'At this point in time, I opt for later.'

Outside, Izzy put her arm round Cadi. 'You can't run away from what's happened.'

Cadi nodded. 'I know, but the thought of standing still scares me.'

'Burning the candle at both ends is a recipe for disaster,' said Poppy. 'You need to hope and pray you never fall asleep at the wheel.'

Cadi knew they were right, especially in the mornings when she often felt light-headed and dizzy. She'd never fallen asleep at the wheel, but she knew her concentration wasn't what it used to be. 'I'll see if I can get some local runs.'

Izzy wagged a reproving finger. 'Don't give me that malarkey. You know full well that as a sergeant you get to call the shots. If you really want to keep busy, why not dive into the admin side of things here?' She rolled her eyes. 'Goodness only knows there's plenty of it.'

Cadi ran her tongue across her bottom lip. Izzy had made a valid point: there was plenty of paperwork, enough to keep her going day and night. 'Do you know, I think I might just do that.'

Poppy beamed. A different tack might be the thing that got their friend back on track. She hated seeing Cadi look so dreadfully thin, but if she was permanently based in the offices at Fiskerton they'd be able to keep a closer eye on their friend.

September 1944

It had been several weeks since Aled had last spoken to Cadi, and even though he'd gone to the NAAFI intending to pick up the phone on a few occasions, he'd been reluctant to do so, fearing that he might appear overbearing. Today, however, he had done it.

Holding the receiver to his ear, he replied 'RAF Fiskerton' as the operator repeated her question, and stood in silent torment as he waited for someone to pick up at the other end. He was about to replace the receiver when Cadi's voice came down the line.

'RAF Fiskerton, can I help you?'

Aled blinked before replying. 'Cadi?'

'Is that you, Aled?'

He nodded before remembering she couldn't see him. 'Yes. I wanted to give you a quick call, to see how you are.'

Cadi felt sorry for Aled, as he obviously cared for her, but at the same time she found it hard to speak to him from the heart. Heaving a sigh, she made the decision to tell him the truth. 'Better than I have been.'

Aled's heart plummeted into his boots. 'Then why on earth did you tell me you were all right when I spoke to you last?'

'Because I didn't want you to worry,' said Cadi openly.

'And is that why you've been avoiding seeing me?'

'Sort of. I've not exactly been looking my best ...'

Aled tutted irritably. 'I don't care what you look like as long as you're all right.'

'That's what I meant,' said Cadi quietly. 'You see, I haven't been too well.'

Aled clapped a hand to his forehead. 'I'm coming over.'

Cadi shook her head hastily. 'No! Not because I don't want you to see me, but because I'm doing better now, and I don't want you rushing off half-cocked, like Jez the night of the car crash.'

Remembering the accident, Aled relented slightly. 'All right, but how about I come and see you in a couple of weeks?'

Cadi grimaced. She would very much like to see him, but what would other people say if they saw her with another man so soon after Jez's death? *She'd* know that there was nothing in it, but the thought of the gossips drawing their own conclusions was more than she could bear. 'Give me a call in a couple of weeks, and we'll go from there.'

Relieved that she hadn't said no outright, Aled agreed before bidding her goodbye.

Taking a seat, he ran his mind over their conversation, and with images of Cadi looking more like a ghost than a person haunting his mind, Aled vowed that he would see her before the year was out, no matter what.

Ever since her last encounter with Cadi, try as she might Daphne couldn't stop herself from reflecting on the other woman's words. The stubborn part of Daphne wanted to put it all down to jealousy and payback for the trouble she had caused between Cadi and Jez, but there was something in Cadi's demeanour which forced her to think otherwise. For a start, her old nemesis had been a shadow of her former self; with her gaunt cheeks and pale complexion she appeared far older than her years. Daphne sighed ruefully. Quite frankly, Cadi didn't look as though she had the energy to seek revenge. *If Kieran's as bad as she makes out, surely the best form of revenge would be to sit back and watch you marry him*, Daphne thought to herself, *so why intervene? And if this Raquel really is his ex, why not just tell me?* Cadi had spoken of Raquel without bothering to explain what her beef with Kieran was. If Cadi *really* wanted to cause trouble and was making stuff up with that end in view, then surely Raquel was also a figment of her imagination? And if that was true, then why didn't she make up some elaborate story about what Kieran had supposedly done to this imaginary woman? *And if Kieran's so innocent, why didn't he demand to speak to Cadi so that he could put her on the spot and show her up for the liar she is? Because that's what I'd have done*, Daphne told herself. *Yet he visited Kitty, and had it out with her instead.* She rubbed some polish on to the toe of her shoe. If Cadi was lying, then she was doing a pretty rubbish job, but if Daphne were to believe that Kieran was innocent, then threatening a woman he'd supposedly never met before would be alarming to say the least. Her mind turned back to the cook. When she had mentioned a man called Micky, Kieran had tried to laugh it off, but Daphne knew there was something wrong somewhere along the line. His face had spoken before his lips had a chance to deny the claim; if he wasn't Micky, then he definitely knew someone by that name. She wished now that she hadn't been so quick to dismiss Cadi's accusations, and that she'd asked more questions, such as *Who is Raquel?* Cadi's last words, advising Daphne that if Kieran ever gave her cause to pause she should get out whilst she could, entered her mind. She was making it sound as though Kieran was someone to fear, yet he'd never been anything but kind and gentle … she stopped. Apart from when she'd questioned him, of course. Instead of trying to understand why Cadi was saying such terrible things about him, he'd turned on a sixpence, accusing Daphne of believing Cadi's lies, which was ridiculous. Daphne was the one trying to work out why Cadi would make up such a farcical tale, and if Kieran was innocent surely he'd have done the same? Picking up the other shoe, she began to brush the polish off. *I'll find out where Cadi's based and go and see her for myself,* she thought. *I'll tell Kieran what I'm planning to do, so that he can join me if he wants. After all, if he's telling the truth and the two of us turn up, Cadi won't have a leg to stand on, but if he's lying I'll be able to tell from the look on his face.*

She removed the remainder of the polish from her shoes before slipping them on to her feet and heading off to find Kieran. *If he threatens to break off our relationship, just because I want to go and see Cadi, then I shall know he's got summat to hide. On the other hand, if he decides to come with me, I shall have it out with Cadi once and for all, and I'll be able to marry Kieran knowing that he's true blue.*

Standing outside his hut, she found herself hesitating before rapping her knuckles against the door. Why was she feeling so nervous? If Kieran was telling the truth, she had every right to confront Cadi, so why worry as to what his reaction might be?

'Hello, gorgeous.'

Startled, Daphne turned to see Kieran smiling down at her. Holding a hand to her chest, she composed herself. 'I wanted to have a quick chat.'

He slid his arms around her waist. 'Should I be worried?'

'I've decided to go and have it out with Cadi.' Seeing his smile dissipate, she continued with haste, 'I thought we could both go, to shut her up once and for all.' She pouted irritably. 'She shouldn't be allowed to bad-mouth you when you've done nothing wrong.' She hesitated. 'Aren't you worried she might be spouting her rubbish to all and sundry?'

Rather than being angry, Kieran wrapped his arms even further around her waist, whilst gazing into her eyes. 'I don't care what she has to say, and neither should you.' He paused. 'I've been having a think, and I reckon you're right about not waiting for me to speak to your father before we wed.'

Her frown deepened. 'Are you suggesting what I think you're suggesting?'

He nodded. 'I reckon we tie the knot as soon as we can book ourselves into the register office.'

Daphne gave a hesitant smile. 'But you were ad-amant that you wanted to speak to my father first. Why the change of heart – not that I'm complaining, mark you.'

'I remembered what you said about Cadi's hus-band; none of us know how long we've got, so why wait?'

Daphne should've been dancing inside, but she couldn't help feeling that he'd only suggested getting married straight away because she'd told him that she intended to go and see Cadi. 'I don't expect we'll get in for weeks, if not months,' she mused.

'Then I shall make it my top priority,' said Kieran. 'How about we call in at the register office to make an appointment, or, if they've a cancellation, get married there and then.' Kieran wasn't surprised to see that his fiancée was looking doubtful, but rather than giving her time to get suspicious he played his ace. 'Think of what it would be like for us to go and see Cadi as a married couple. That way we would really show her that we mean business.'

He had only said it to put the ball back into his own court, but it was all Daphne had to hear. If Kieran was willing to confront Cadi whilst standing at Daphne's side, then he *had* to be innocent.

October 1944

Aled smiled as Marnie's voice came down the line.

'How's tricks?'

'Busy! Way more so than my last posting.'

'I think it's the same for everyone,' said Aled. 'We hardly seem to touch down before we're off again. What's Devon like?'

'Beautiful! The sea is bluer than the sky, and the little towns and villages are adorable. You should come for a visit – if they ever give you leave again.'

'I'm saving my leave for Christmas. I thought you might like to come to Lincoln so that we could spend it together, maybe stay in a hotel in the city?' said Aled. He had thought the idea quite romantic, but judging by Marnie's response he'd got it wrong.

'Why Lincoln? Why not Devon or Rhos?'

'Lincoln's a beautiful city, and you might get to see some of your old chums, plus I've only got four days, so I don't want to spend most of it travelling.'

Marnie fought the urge to point out that she, too, didn't want to spend most of her break travelling, but as it was his suggestion to spend Christmas together she let it slide. 'Chums? You mean Izzy and Poppy?'

'Amongst others.' He hesitated. Up until now, he'd assumed that Marnie liked the girls, but perhaps he'd got the wrong end of the stick. 'I thought you liked them, or have I got that wrong?'

Marnie sighed. 'I do, it's just …' There was an audible pause before she continued, 'Just ignore me. I'm being silly.'

'So does that mean you'll come?'

Feeling that it would be petulant to say otherwise, she agreed. 'I'd love to, but only if you come and see me in Devon come the new year.'

'Splendid!'

'Now that we've got that sorted, how's everyone at Finningley bearing up?'

'Jez and Annie were a big part of life at Finningley, so it seems empty here without them, despite the fact the place is teeming with new faces.'

Marnie didn't want to mention Cadi, but she knew it would be churlish not to. 'How's Cadi? Have you seen much of her?' She crossed her fingers around the phone wire, hoping his answer would be no.

'Not since the funeral,' said Aled, 'but we have spoken over the phone, and to be honest, I'm worried about her.'

'Why, what did she say?'

'That she's not been too well, but she's doing much better now.'

Marnie frowned. 'Then why are you worried?'

'Because she'd been insisting that everything was fine until I spoke to her a few weeks ago – that's when the truth came out. She's not been doing at all well, but she hadn't said anything because she didn't want to worry me. I wanted to go and see her at once, but she insisted I wait a few weeks rather than rush off half-cocked.'

Marnie spoke slowly. 'You make it sound as though you were intending to drop everything there and then.'

'I was,' Aled admitted.

The crease on Marnie's brow deepened. Hearing that Aled had wanted to rush to Cadi's side wasn't the news she'd been hoping for. 'If she doesn't want to see you, I suggest you respect her wishes. She has plenty of friends to talk to, not to mention family.' Fearing that Aled might suggest Cadi join them in Lincoln she hastily added, 'So she won't be on her own for Christmas.'

Aled could easily imagine Cadi insisting she wanted to be on her own for Christmas. 'Cadi's fiercely independent, always has been, always will be – especially if she thinks her presence might spoil it for others.' He fell momentarily silent before adding, 'I've just had a cracking idea.'

Marnie grimaced, fairly certain that she knew what was coming next. 'Oh?'

'Why don't we invite Cadi, and ask Poppy and Izzy to join the three of us for a meal when you come over at Christmas? She won't be able to say no if we all insist.'

Marnie tutted beneath her breath. She hadn't seen Aled for months, yet he wanted to invite three other women to their reunion.

'Couldn't we have Christmas on our own? I've not seen you since June.'

'I understand that sweetheart, but this will be the perfect excuse to see how she's doing first hand.'

'I'm sure she'll be just fine,' Marnie pouted.

The operator cut across their call. Their time was up.

'Be fair. You've got the rest of your life with me; Cadi's just lost her husband.'

Marnie sighed. 'Just let me know when and where.'

Aled beamed. 'I promise I'll make it up to you. Ta-ra, Marnie.'

Hearing the receiver click down at his end, Marnie frowned at the earpiece. 'I love you too.'

Replacing the receiver, she cursed herself inwardly for bringing Cadi's name into the equation. Had she kept quiet, she could have been spending Christmas alone with her beau, but as things stood, in all likelihood she'd be spending it with Aled *and* Cadi, and what's more, if she objected, it would look as though she was being petty. *Next time, I shall learn to keep my big mouth shut!* Marnie told herself. *Either that or spend every holiday with Cadi in tow.*

Meanwhile, making his way towards the hut for debriefing, Aled congratulated himself on his plan to invite Cadi over for Christmas. He could hardly envisage her saying no, if he said that Marnie was coming up from Devon to see her. It would give him the perfect excuse to check on her and make sure she was taking care of herself as she insisted she was. Cadi was a strong, independent woman, and Aled feared she would choose to remain quiet rather than ask for help. He felt his cheeks grow warm. He might well be worried that Cadi wasn't coping, but in truth he'd been plagued by nightmares himself, all of which ended with Aled reaching out to Jez, who slipped away from him. He had thought it wasn't affecting him until Tom had unwittingly suggested that Aled might reignite the torch he had once held for Cadi now that she was a widow. Furious that Tom would suggest such a thing, Aled had rounded on him.

'Keep your thoughts to yourself,' he had snapped. 'I would *never* take advantage of Cadi. And if I had my way, Jez would still be here. He was a decent bloke and he didn't deserve to go out the way he did.'

He had meant every word, and Tom had apologised. It had taken Aled a moment or two to calm down before making an apology of his own. It had been unfair of him to react the way he did, and he'd only done it because he was afraid that many people would be thinking the same thing. After all, there was a time when he'd have leapt at the chance – had it been under different circumstances. But he'd buried his feelings for Cadi a long time since, something that hadn't been easy for him to do, but it was either that or spend the rest of his life on his own. He had met Marnie, and they were very happy together, and even if they hadn't been he still wouldn't make a play for Cadi, because he respected her too much.

Sometimes, Aled told himself now, *there can be too much history for a relationship to work, and I think that could well be the case when it comes to myself and Cadi. Another time, another place, and who knows what could've happened, but not now. Not any more.*

Paddy Finnegan reached the gate to his latest posting. He'd lost count of the number of times he'd been reposted, not that he cared: new postings gave him the chance to slip under the net before it closed in. Not that they could ever prove anything, Paddy had made sure of that, but every time he moved the petty thefts would stop. Moving from station to station also brought plenty of opportunities to hunt for his brother, and whilst he'd not heard so much as a whisper of Micky's whereabouts, it was only a matter of time before he caught up with him. It still infuriated him to know that Micky had gambled their money away as though he hadn't a care in the world while leaving Paddy high and dry. It was Micky's fault Paddy was stuck in the RAF, and not living the high life with the earnings they'd accrued in Portsmouth. He often pictured what he was going to do to Micky once he found him, and he imagined it would take an army of men to prise his fingers from his brother's throat.

As he passed through the gate, he immediately noticed that some of the buildings were peppered with bullet holes. *Sitting bloody ducks*, Paddy thought ruefully. *If I do find Micky it'll probably be in the obituaries.* He climbed down from the cab of his lorry and entered the office. As the Waaf looked up from her work, he jerked his head in the direction of the building marked by flak. 'I see you've been having fun and games.'

The Waaf pulled a grim face. 'We have that; we also lost a few of our boys.'

He nodded thoughtfully. 'No one under the name of Micky Finnegan or Kieran O'Connell, I hope?'

She shook her head. 'Are they friends of yours?'

He signed his name in the book. 'You could say that. We've lost contact along the way.'

206

'Part of the beauty of being in the RAF is bumping into people you'd lost contact with.' She smiled at the handsome Irishman. 'Since being in the services I've met school pals that I hadn't seen in years! I can keep an eye out for them if you like.' Hesitating, she took a pencil and began to write. 'Micky Finnegan and …'

'Kieran O'Connell.'

'That's right.' She folded the paper and tucked it into her book. 'Shall I tell them you're looking for them?'

He grinned delightfully. 'Nah, I'd rather surprise them.'

Failing to notice the wicked glint in his eye, she said 'That's nice' before telling him how to find his hut. 'Someone'll come along and tell you what's what in a bit, and if you need anything else just let me know. I'm Melanie by the way.'

He winked at her. 'Thank you, Melanie. It's a rarity to meet such a helpful soul, and a beautiful one at that, might I add.'

A warm blush spreading along her neckline, she smiled coyly. In Melanie's opinion, women would be lining up to help the handsome Irishman. 'My pleasure.'

Stepping outside, Paddy hefted his kitbag over his shoulder before making his way towards the hut. As he walked, the aircrew from one of the planes strode past, deep in conversation. *Stuck up, pompous gits,* thought Paddy, *always thinking they're better than the rest of us. I used to earn ten times what they're on, yet there they are all high and mighty, whilst riskin' their necks for pennies.* He gave a short snort of contempt. *And they reckon they're better than me!*

He entered the hut and asked the nearest man which beds were free before selecting one. Paddy knew that the beds were only vacant because someone had lost his life. He fervently hoped he wouldn't be next in line.

Aled waited with bated breath for Cadi to pick up the phone. He had no idea why he was so nervous – it wasn't as though he was doing anything wrong, especially as it was her suggestion that he telephone her back in a couple of weeks, which was precisely what he was doing.

Hearing her voice come down the line, the frown disappeared from his forehead. 'Cadi? It's me, Aled. I thought I'd give you a quick ring to see how you're doing now.'

Cadi stood in stunned silence. She'd totally forgotten she'd told him to call back. 'I'm still doing well. You?'

'All the better for hearing your voice, but I'd feel better still if I could see you for myself, which is why Marnie and I thought it might be nice for us all to get together in Lincoln this Christmas. What do you say?'

Cadi had been intending to work over Christmas, but maybe this would be the ideal opportunity to have a break and stop being so hard on herself. 'I'm game if you two are, but are you sure you don't mind? I wouldn't want to intrude.'

'Not at all!' said Aled. He had been expecting her to turn him down, so hearing her accept his offer so freely had taken him by surprise. Swept up in the moment, he found himself asking her out for lunch. 'Why don't

I take you out for a meal this weekend? If you're free, that is.' Hearing the silence that came down the line, he cursed himself for being so pushy. He was about to politely retract his offer when Cadi accepted. He blew a euphoric sigh of relief. 'Marvellous! Have you any idea where you'd like to go?'

Cadi was nibbling the inside of her bottom lip. Was she doing the right thing? Part of the reason why she wanted to see Aled again was because she missed male company. True, she was surrounded by men in the RAF, but they were men who were after relationships, whereas Aled was already spoken for, and she could enjoy his companionship without fear of repercussions. 'Izzy likes the Wheatsheaf Inn in Waddington.'

'Then the Wheatsheaf it is! And now that we've got that settled, how are things in general?'

'It's getting easier,' admitted Cadi. 'I've got a new desk job, so I'm not rushing round like a headless chicken any more. I found it incredibly hard to sit still at first, but I'm getting used to it, and I'm using the time to process what happened, which is something I'd been trying to avoid. Only I know now that you need to do that in order to come to terms with the past.'

'Sounds like you've got a hold on things,' said Aled, pleased to hear that she really did seem to be doing as well as she claimed.

'I'm certainly getting there, thanks to Poppy and Izzy,' Cadi told him. 'They've been marvellous.'

'Good friends are worth their weight in gold,' Aled agreed. He glanced at his wristwatch. 'Looks like our time's nearly up, so shall we say I'll see you at eleven o'clock sharp, outside the gate to your base?'

'I shall see you there.' She hesitated. 'Thanks for suggesting this Aled. It'll be good to have time out from work.'

'My pleasure.'

They said their goodbyes and Cadi headed back to Poppy and Izzy, who were halfway through their dinner. Settling back into her seat, she told them about her phone call whilst she tucked into a plate of pie and mash.

'I'm glad you said yes,' mused Poppy, 'because he's always cared about you, and you him.

'I know, and I felt mean turning him down last time, but I didn't want him to see me looking ...' she paused, 'unwell.'

'Like a stick insect,' said Poppy. 'But you don't look like one any more – thank God.'

Cadi smiled. Hearing her friend say that was music to her ears. 'Do you really think I look better?'

'Much,' agreed Izzy.

'Talking about Jez is going to be difficult,' said Cadi slowly, 'but it's inevitable that we will; it's only natural. I wonder if he feels the same.'

'Probably. Men find it a lot harder to talk about these things than women,' said Poppy.

'Very true,' agreed Izzy. 'How do you feel about meeting him after all this time?'

'I'm looking forward to seeing someone who was close to Jez, but I'd hate people to get the wrong idea, thinking that I'd start courting so soon after his passing.'

Poppy pulled a stern face. 'If you hear of anyone spreading gossip, just you point them my way, and I'll soon put them straight. There's nothing wrong with spending time with a close friend, be they male or female, and I honestly think it will do you both the world of good to get together and talk.'

'Thanks, Poppy.'

'Jez wanted you to be happy,' said Izzy, 'and if spending time with an old pal makes you happy, then he'd be delighted.'

Cadi smiled gratefully at her friends. 'Thanks, girls. Just having your support these past few months has helped me immensely. I don't know what I'd have done without you.'

'We're only glad to see you smile again,' said Poppy.

'I still have more bad days than good, but it's better than having all bad days,' admitted Cadi. She scraped up the last of the mashed potato on to her fork. She was looking forward to seeing Aled, and if anyone should say anything, she'd tell them to mind their own business before sending them Poppy's way.

Aled was on his way to meet Cadi when he had to stop for a lorry which was blocking the road. Stepping out of his car, he approached the driver, who was leaning against the cab whilst enjoying a cigarette.

'You can't just leave that there whilst you have a fag break,' said Aled, indicating the lorry with a wave of his hand. 'I've got places I need to be.'

The driver shrugged in a nonchalant manner. 'It's knackered, so it ain't going nowhere, and neither are you.'

Aled stared at him in disbelief. 'You can't just leave it there.'

'I know that,' snapped the driver, 'but until the mechanic comes up with the right part there's not a lot I can do about it – and before you start, we can't just tow it out of the way because the towin' ring's busted off.'

Aled glanced around at the small crowd of frustrated – or just nosy – passers-by which had gathered. If he were to wait for the mechanic, he could be there for hours. After a brief headcount, he instructed the surly driver to get back into his cab.

The driver stared at him before laughing scornfully. 'What you goin' to do? Push me out of the way?'

Aled signalled to those standing closest by. 'Who's with me?' Placing his hands on the bonnet, he waited whilst several others joined him, all chattering excitedly about the challenge which lay ahead.

When everybody was ready, Aled braced himself. 'On the count of three. One, two, *three* …'

At first it seemed that the lorry was going nowhere, but after a moment or two the wheels slowly turned, and as they gathered momentum the vehicle became easier to push. Once it was out of the way, Aled signalled for everyone to stop. 'That'll do!' He thanked them for their combined efforts and jumped back into his car, leaving the driver of the lorry to mumble something about patience being a virtue.

As he drove down the narrow country lanes, Aled debated what he would say to Cadi when he arrived at Fiskerton. He was keen not to upset her, or appear insensitive, but at the same time he knew that it was important to talk about these things, after experiencing the loss of the *Ulysses'* mid-gunner. The crew had gone from boasting that they were the luckiest in their squadron to having to face up to a bitter dose of reality. Not knowing how to deal with their tragedy, they had avoided talking about their loss, and when Tom had come along as their new mid-gunner they had found it difficult to speak to him too. But you can't be part of a crew if you don't communicate, so they had no option but to address the subject of that fateful night, and it was only when they did so that things began to get easier.

You should've insisted on seeing her sooner, Aled told himself; *at least that way you'd have known that you'd done everything you could.* He conjured up an image of his parents, as well as Cadi's, all eyeing him doubtfully. They all knew he'd been keen on Cadi; would they approve of this rendezvous? His jaw tightened. Whether they approved or not shouldn't concern him. Cadi was all that mattered, and if she was happy to meet him, then it was nothing to do with anyone else.

Chapter Seven

Cadi twisted her wedding ring round her finger as she waited for Aled to arrive. In some respects she couldn't wait to see him, but in others she feared the very sight of him would take her straight back to the day of the attack – and she *never* wanted to go back there.

Feeling her tummy flutter, she held a hand to her stomach to calm her nerves. Ever since gaining her appetite back, she'd suffered from one stomach complaint or another. Poppy was sure it was the amount of liver Cadi was getting through, but Izzy insisted that Cadi still needed to build up her strength after hardly eating for such a long period of time.

Seeing the car come into view, she stepped forward to greet Aled as he drew up alongside her. Glancing around to see if anyone was watching, she opened the passenger door and got in.

Aled smiled. 'Someone's eager for the off.'

'I've been telling myself repeatedly that there's nothing wrong with meeting an old friend, but in truth I still worry what people might think or say. Not because they'd be right,' she added hastily, 'but because I don't want anyone questioning my love *or* my loyalty to Jez.'

He checked over his shoulder before pulling away from the kerb. 'I did wonder what your parents and mine might think,' he said truthfully, 'but I wouldn't worry about what folk on base will say. I think most of them know better than to gossip when someone's lost a loved one – they leave talk like that to the fishwives.'

She arched her brow. 'You worried about our parents?'

He shrugged. 'I suppose it comes from living in a small community. You know what it's like being in a village.'

She eyed him thoughtfully. 'I worried that seeing you might bring the memories flooding back. Not that they ever went away, but you know what I mean.'

He glanced across at her before turning his attention back to the road ahead. 'I do indeed, but however painful it is, it will do us both good to talk. We went through this huge, life-changing moment, but never talked about it.' He hesitated before adding, 'I should've insisted on seeing you sooner. I'm not saying I'd have been the answer to all your problems, but I might've been able to do something to help, even if it was just being a shoulder to cry on.'

She smiled softly. 'I knew you'd be there like a shot if I asked, but I didn't want you worrying about me when you're surrounded by the Luftwaffe.'

'But I did worry about you, and I suppose I always will.' He glanced across at her. 'You said you'd been unwell, and I can see you've lost weight.'

'I was, but that's all in the past. I'm eating properly now, and I'm pleased to say it's beginning to show.'

He gave a surprised cough. 'You mean you were thinner?'

She grimaced. 'Quite a bit. I completely lost my appetite after Jez, and the nightmares didn't exactly help matters. I used to wake up every morning with my stomach in knots.'

'But you're better now?' Aled was eager for her reassurance.

She nodded. 'Lots.' Wishing to move on to a more cheerful topic of conversation, she smiled brightly at him. 'How's Marnie? Is she still enjoying the Devonshire sea air? I heard she was quite excited about going there.'

Aled pulled into the car park of the Wheatsheaf Inn. 'She certainly likes being by the sea. Not that she gets much time to enjoy it, being rushed off her feet as she always is.'

Cadi waited for Aled to open her door before stepping out. 'I like being by the sea. It's one of the things I miss about Liverpool – you're only a tram ride away from Seaforth Sands.'

'Jez said summat about you wanting to run a pub when all this was over. Have you given any thought as to what you want to do now he's no longer here?'

She walked through the door which Aled was holding open for her. 'Sort of. Maria wanted me to leave the WAAF and work for her in the pub, but I don't think I could. Too many memories. As for running a pub? Not on my own, that's for certain.'

Aled approached the barman. 'A pint of mild for me, and …' He turned expectantly to Cadi.

'A lemonade for me, please.'

Nodding, the barman began pouring the drinks.

'I might open a tea room,' said Cadi, 'because that had been my original plan.'

'In Liverpool?'

'I suppose so. There's not really much call for a tea room in Rhos.'

He smiled. 'I guess not.' Paying the barman for their drinks, he followed Cadi over to a table. 'Have you talked to anyone about what happened?'

She took a small sip of her drink before answering. 'Only about my feelings, but not anything else; you?'

He shook his head. 'Marnie knows I was with you when you found him, but that's all.' He watched Cadi as she turned her wedding ring round on her finger. 'I think that talking about things helps ease the pain, but if you'd rather not ...'

She looked up. 'What we went through was terrible, and no one should have to find their husband – or their friend – the way we did. I can't talk about it with the girls, because I don't want to upset them any more than they already are. I guess I felt the same about you. Bad enough living it without reliving it.'

'But at the same time, it has to be acknowledged,' said Aled, wiping the froth from his top lip.

'And you can't do that unless you talk about it,' agreed Cadi. She folded her arms on the table top. 'I keep seeing the bullet holes which led me to him.'

Aled grimaced. 'I keep seeing you on the ground beside him ...' He hung his head. 'I'd do anything to bring him back.'

Reaching across the table, she closed her hand over his. 'I know you would, and if love could've kept him alive he'd have lived for ever, but we can't keep treading the same path of if onlys and what ifs because ...' she indicated her gaunt features, 'this is the result.'

He smiled dubiously. 'Easier said than done, though.'

'Most definitely, but do you really think Jez would like to see either of us this way?'

'No.'

She looked towards the bar. 'Shall we take a look at the menu?'

Getting up from his seat, Aled fetched a couple of menus, which they perused in silence before Aled snapped his shut. 'I fancy the pie and chips; you?'

Cadi wrinkled her nose. 'The pastry'll give me terrible heartburn, so I'll have sausage and mash, please.'

He got to his feet again and went to the bar to place their order.

Watching him, Cadi decided she couldn't be more pleased with her decision to join him for lunch. Talking to someone who was with her on the day she'd found Jez was helping enormously. Just knowing she wasn't on her own with her feelings made her feel less lonely.

When Aled returned it was with two more drinks.

'So, have you got any news? I know you've switched roles, but is there anything else I should know about?'

Cadi nodded. 'I know Jez told you about my run-in with Daphne, but there've been further developments.'

He cocked an eyebrow. 'Now why doesn't that surprise me?'

Cadi went on to explain how the man Daphne was engaged to was one of the Finnegan brothers, and everything that had transpired as a result.

'Flippin 'eck,' breathed Aled, 'that girl seems to attract trouble.'

'More to the point, she won't listen to reason,' said Cadi. 'I know a lot of people would say that she deserves it after everything she did to us, but ...'

'You've not got a vindictive or spiteful bone in your body,' said Aled, before adding bitterly, 'which is more than I can say for Daphne.'

'Good intentions are no use if someone doesn't want to listen to reason, so it doesn't matter what I say or do, Daphne thinks I'm doing it to cause trouble, and that's it.'

Aled shook his head. 'Daphne was desperate for a farmer as a husband. There's no way she'll let this Kieran feller slip through her fingers, and certainly not on your say so.'

'But the Finnegans are evil,' said Cadi. 'I know she hasn't got two pennies to rub together, but I still think he's after her for the wrong reasons.'

Aled rubbed his chin thoughtfully. 'Maybe he sees the farm as a ready-made home with plenty of money to be made out of the stock.' He gave a short, grim chuckle. 'And if he does, he's in for a big surprise.'

'I'm rather afraid you've hit the nail on the head,' said Cadi. 'But what will he do when he realises he's made a mistake?'

Aled shrugged. 'You know him better than me; what do you think he'll do?'

'I reckon he'll walk away, taking what he can with him, and leave Daphne heartbroken but whole,' Cadi told him frankly.

'Problem solved, then,' said Aled. 'Maybe it'll teach her not to jump in with both feet.'

'You say *problem solved*, but does she really deserve to walk into a loveless marriage?'

He smiled affectionately at her. 'I would tell you not to waste your time worrying over the likes of Daphne, but I know I'd be wasting my breath.'

Cadi grimaced fleetingly. 'Life's too short to waste it on idiots like Kieran, full stop. So if I can think of a way to help her, I will.'

November 1944

Paddy Finnegan was hating his new station, which was proving to be far busier than his last posting. If it wasn't for the fact he'd be homeless without a penny to his name, he'd have walked out without so much as a backward glance. Quite honestly it baffled him how anyone could live a decent life on the so-called wages that the services handed out, and he utterly loathed emptying the latrines and delivering the coal, because he thought such tasks beneath him, something that should be done by the Waafs.

He had complained bitterly, claiming that he'd been earmarked for the worst jobs solely because of his nationality, but they'd rebutted his statement, saying that he only got the worst jobs because stock didn't tend to go missing when he wasn't the one making the run. He'd huffed and puffed, claiming that they were a bunch of liars, and that someone in his unit was setting him up to look like a thief, but of course he knew they were speaking the truth. And when he was no longer carrying stock, he wasn't able to continue with his sideline.

As he reversed the coal lorry, his eyes flickered up to the man who had made him look a fool only days after his arrival.

Pompous git, he thought to himself, *showing off in front of the rest of them, then swanning off like he was the cock of the walk.* He watched as the man in question walked past the car he and his crewmates shared. An evil smirk tweaked Paddy's lips. He'd always believed that revenge was a dish best served cold, and since it had been a couple of months now he thought that today was as good a time as any. But what to do? He screwed his lips to one side as he pictured the coal falling into the feller's car, but try as he might he couldn't come up with a plan which would make it look like an accident. Tutting beneath his breath, he stared at the car as though willing an idea to present itself. As his eyes travelled from the back seat to the bonnet, he came up with the brainwave of removing one of the spark plugs. Not only would the men never be able to find the culprit, it would also prove to be a huge inconvenience: it would take time to pinpoint the cause of the engine failure, and then they would have to source a new spark plug, which could take some time. He checked to make sure there was no one else around before driving over and parking the lorry at such an angle that the front of the car was hidden from view. He quickly jumped out of his cab and popped the bonnet to set about removing the spark plug. As he worked, he imagined their faces as they tried to start the car. As far as Paddy was concerned, men who flew planes hadn't an ounce of common sense, so they would probably assume they were out of petrol before checking the engine. The spark plug removed, he got back into his lorry and drove away before anyone could discover what he had done. Or at least that's what he thought. What he didn't realise was that he had been watched.

Keen that nothing should spoil his plans to spend Christmas in Lincoln, Aled had been about to check the car for oil and water when he saw one of the drivers eyeing it intently. Curious as to why the car was the object of such fascination, he hovered in the background, just out of sight. It was the man who'd given him short shrift the day Aled had asked him to move his lorry. Aled had gathered from his surly attitude that he was a wrong 'un, and this opinion was confirmed by his crewmates when he told them of the encounter. Due to the number of petty thefts which had been happening on the base, they never left anything of value in the car, but the driver didn't know that, and if Aled could catch him red-handed as he searched their car for goodies he would be able to call him out as being the thief.

Seeing the man move the lorry forward, Aled was beginning to think that he'd got hold of the wrong end of the stick until the driver pulled up in front of the car. After that there wasn't a doubt in Aled's mind that he really was up to no good. Melting into the shadow of the wall behind him, Aled watched the man in the reflection of the window in the building opposite. If his suspicions were correct, he was about to catch the Irishman in the act. Craning his neck to get a better view, Aled was so engrossed in the task in hand that he didn't hear Tom approaching.

It was clear that his friend was spying on someone, so Tom kept his voice lowered. 'What's going on?'

Nearly leaping out of his skin, Aled glared at Tom. 'You're going to give someone a sodding heart attack if you creep up on people like that.'

Tom raised a fleeting brow. 'Considering you're obviously spying on that chap, I could hardly announce my presence.'

'I caught him staking out the car,' hissed Aled. 'I'd lay money on it that he's the one responsible for the recent spate of thefts.'

'Is he one of the new fellers?'

Aled nodded. 'He's the surly bugger I had words with the day I went to see Cadi. I knew he was a wrong 'un from the moment he opened his mouth.'

Tom was also now spying on Paddy via the reflection in the window opposite. 'Why do you suppose he's lifted the bonnet?'

Aled continued to watch the man. 'Beats me.'

Tom turned to face him. 'Aren't you going to confront him?'

Aled shook his head. 'Not yet. I want to make sure he's done summat before I start throwing accusations. He's a weaselly blighter who's got an answer for everything, and I don't want to give him the heads-up.'

They both watched as Paddy closed the car bonnet and got back into his cab, and Aled waited until the lorry had pulled away before gesturing to Tom to follow him. 'Let's go and see what the bugger's been up to.'

The two men approached the car and Aled lifted the bonnet. Casting an eye over the engine, he pointed to the gap where the spark plug had been. 'The sneaky git!'

Tom appeared confused. 'What would he want with a spark plug? It's not as if it would fit his lorry, and he hasn't got a car of his own, has he?'

'Not that I know of. He's done it to cause me a headache, that's what,' Aled snapped. 'He's obviously still narked at me for showing him up that time.'

Tom pointed to where Paddy was parking. 'C'mon. Let's go and see what he has to say for himself.'

When they reached the lorry Aled knocked on the cab door to gain Paddy's attention. Irritably, Paddy wound the driver's window down. 'What do you want?'

Aled held out his hand. 'We want our spark plug back. We saw you taking it from the car so there's no point in trying to deny it.'

Paddy slapped the spark plug into Aled's outstretched hand with a condescending snort. 'Talk about not being able to take a joke! I didn't even know it was your car.'

'Oh, I can take a joke, but not one that could've ruined my Christmas,' Aled snapped.

Paddy pulled a face. 'It was a prank. Hardly the crime of the century.'

Aled folded his arms across his chest. 'Maybe not, but there have been an awful lot of thefts around here lately – although I must admit this has been the pettiest so far.'

Paddy glared at him. 'I didn't nick it. I did it for a laugh; I had every intention of putting it back.'

'Really? Then why nick it in the first place?'

'As I've already said, I didn't nick it. Blimey, if I'd known you hadn't got a sense of humour, I'd not have bothered.'

Aled fixed Paddy with an accusing stare. 'So you did know it was my car?'

Paddy rolled his eyes. 'Figure of speech.'

Aled glared at him. 'And a liar to boot.' He held the spark plug up. 'If I find you near my car again, or anything else of mine for that matter, I won't hesitate to report you.'

Cursing himself inwardly for being caught practically red-handed, Paddy wound his window back up. He knew he'd lose his temper if he continued to talk to the air gunner, and he wasn't prepared to do time for someone who was probably going to get shot down before the month was out. Placing the lorry in gear, he drove off.

Tom shook his head. 'Doesn't he realise how serious summat like this is?' He glanced at Aled. 'He's lucky it was you that caught him and not any of the others.'

Aled shrugged. 'I don't want the hassle, and I reckon I've said enough to keep him off my back.'

Seeing the upset, one of the Waafs who worked in the office walked towards them. 'Oh, dear. Has Prince Charming been giving you grief?'

Throwing the spark plug up into the air, Aled caught it one-handed before replying. 'Hello Melanie. It's nothing we can't handle.'

'Prince Charming?' scoffed Tom. 'You need to kiss a few more frogs if that's your idea of charming!'

Melanie smiled. 'He might give you lot the run around, but he's very different when it comes to the ladies.'

'Is he now?' said Aled. 'Well, you'll need to keep your hand on more than your ha'penny with him around.'

She looked startled. 'Oh?'

'We've just caught him nickin' the spark plug out of our car,' said Tom defiantly. 'He said he only did it for a laugh, but we reckon there was more to it than that.'

Melanie shot them both a meaningful glance. 'Are you sure you didn't do anything to upset him?'

'Only pushed his wagon out of the way when it was blocking the road,' said Aled. 'You'd think he'd have been grateful.'

'Finnegan's certainly a rum character.'

Aled stared at her. 'Finnegan as in Paddy Finnegan?'

She nodded. 'Yes, why?'

Aled's face clouded over. 'If it's the feller I'm thinking of then he's a lot more trouble than we gave him credit for.' He hesitated as he tried to recall the name of the man Daphne was engaged to. 'I don't suppose he's ever mentioned anyone by the name of Micky, or Kieran?'

Melanie nodded slowly. 'First day he arrived, he asked if I'd come across two men by the name of Micky and Kieran. He said they were friends of his he'd lost touch with.'

Aled blew his cheeks out. 'They're not his friends, because they're one and the same person. Micky, aka Kieran, is Paddy's brother, and if Cadi's suspicions are right they've had the mother of all fall-outs.'

Tom and Melanie exchanged glances. 'He's using an alias?'

'To hide from Paddy,' said Aled, 'or at least that's what we think.'

Tom raised his brow. 'What's he done, or shouldn't I ask?'

'I'm not sure what he's done to Paddy, but he's engaged to my ex.'

Tom burst out laughing. 'Punishment enough!' But his face fell when he saw that Aled wasn't laughing.

'If it were anyone else I'd agree with you, but even Daphne doesn't deserve someone like that.' Aled rubbed his chin in a thoughtful manner. 'This calls for some careful consideration.' He glanced at Tom and Melanie in turn. 'Please don't mention any of this to anyone else, will you? Only I need to keep it under my hat until I know what I'm going to do.'

Melanie agreed without hesitation. 'What should I say to Paddy next time he comes asking about Micky or Kieran, which he does at least once a week?'

'That you don't know anything,' said Aled. 'Paddy shouldn't be a danger to anyone but Kieran. All I can tell you is he has a dark background, which I'm pretty sure he doesn't want anyone knowing about, and should we let on that we're on to him he might turn nasty.'

The Waaf stared at him thoughtfully. 'I know the fellers who work with Finnegan would love to see the back of him. They reckon he's a surly so-'n'-so who wouldn't get out of bed if he didn't have to.'

'He's not joined up out of the goodness of his heart, that's for sure,' said Aled. 'He's done it because he had no choice, which is surprising considering the brothers probably left Portsmouth with a stash of cash.'

She gasped. 'What did they do, rob a bank?'

Aled shook his head. 'It was their money. It's how they earned it that bothers me.'

Tom folded his arms across his chest. 'Who's told you all this?'

'Cadi. Don't ask me how she knows, because it's not for me to tell you, but needless to say they weren't friends of hers – far from it.'

'But why not go straight to the authorities?' queried Tom.

'Because the Finnegans are a nasty piece of work, and I don't want to do anything that might have repercussions for Cadi or her friends. They know far more about the brothers' shenanigans than I do, and their evidence could make the difference between a slap on the wrists and doing time at His Majesty's pleasure.'

'You think they've done enough to land them in jail?' said Melanie.

'I do, but I'd have the devil's own job proving what they used to do. I need Cadi for that.' He fell silent as a sudden thought entered his mind. 'Please tell me Paddy's not courting any of the girls on base?'

Melanie shook her head. 'Not that I know of.'

'Good. He may have the gift of the gab, but it's just a front.' Falling into silent contemplation, Aled wondered whether he should telephone Cadi directly or wait until he saw her. An image of Paddy or one of his friends – if he had any – overhearing their conversation entered his mind, and he immediately knew the answer. He would send her a letter, telling her that Paddy was at Finningley. That way she'd have the information without running the risk of Paddy's finding out she knew. 'I'll write to Cadi and we can go from there.'

Tom pulled a doubtful face. 'I'm not sure the RAF will do much about Finnegan's past misdemeanours unless he's wanted for murder.'

Aled grimaced. 'And that's why I need to speak to Cadi. I want to make sure that I'm playing with the right cards before I lay my hand down.'

Cadi sifted through her mail, noting the correspondent of each of her letters until she got to the last one. A confused look etched her face as she wondered why Aled would be writing when he would be seeing her in just over a couple of weeks' time. Keeping her fingers crossed that he wasn't writing to cancel his visit, she slit the envelope open and read the letter within, her eyes growing wider as she finished each sentence. She pushed the letter into her pocket and rushed off to find Poppy and Izzy.

After a couple of minutes' searching, she eventually found her friends chatting as they stood beside one of the cars. Seeing Cadi approach in such an earnest manner, Izzy was the first to speak. 'Blimey. What's got you all hot under the collar?'

Cadi produced the letter from her pocket. 'I've received this from Aled. I think you should take a look.'

Apart from emitting occasional gasps, both girls read the letter in silence.

'Flippin' Nora,' breathed Poppy. 'What are the odds?'

'That's what I thought,' said Cadi. 'I wonder what he wants with Kieran?'

'More to the point,' considered Izzy, 'why doesn't he know of his brother's whereabouts? Because I don't believe that claptrap about him losing touch for one minute!'

'Me neither,' said Cadi. 'It sounds very much as though Kieran's doing his best to avoid Paddy.'

'Well, I'd bet a pound to a penny that Kieran did a runner with the money, and that's why Paddy's after him,' said Poppy plainly.

Cadi's brow shot towards her hairline. 'I don't know whether even Kieran's stupid enough to steal from Paddy. He must know that his brother wouldn't let summat like that lie.' She blew her cheeks out. 'Paddy would wring his neck!'

'Hence why he threatened poor Kitty,' said Izzy.

Cadi leaned against the car. 'So how do we play this to our advantage?'

'I reckon you definitely tell Kieran that we've bumped into his brother,' said Poppy. 'Then, if Kieran looks worried, you can blackmail him into breaking things off with Daphne, as well as steering clear of the other women on the base.'

'I like your thinking,' said Cadi, 'but what do we do about Paddy?'

Poppy shrugged. 'Leave sleeping dogs lie. The less he knows the better.'

'What a massive stroke of luck, though,' mused Izzy, 'because I don't think you'd ever have persuaded Daphne to leave Kieran. But this should do the trick, with no harm done.'

'She'll be disappointed when he calls things off,' conceded Cadi, 'but better that than marrying a heartless pig.'

'How do you intend to break it to him?' asked Poppy curiously. 'Cos I dare say he's not going to take the news well, especially when you try to blackmail him.'

'I haven't been on car duty for ever such a long time,' said Cadi, 'but I can easily arrange to put myself down for the next run going that way.'

Poppy considered. 'This is only a thought, mind you, but what if we're barking up the wrong tree? What if it's Paddy who's trying to steer clear of Kieran?'

Cadi shook her head decidedly. 'Paddy was looking for Kieran ...' She tailed off as Izzy picked up Poppy's train of thought.

'That's certainly the way it looked, but who's to say he wasn't checking that Kieran *wasn't* on the same base?'

Cadi cursed softly. That idea hadn't crossed her mind, but if the girls were right she'd be shooting herself in the foot. What was more, he might threaten to marry Daphne there and then if she didn't tell him where Paddy was. After a moment's thought, she nodded. 'I could swap information? Tell him of Paddy's whereabouts once he'd broken things off with Daphne?'

'But once he knows where Paddy is, he'll be able to do what he likes. There won't be a thing we can do to stop him from getting back on track with Daphne – that's even if he does break it off, cos we'll only have his word for it.'

Cadi tutted beneath her breath. 'Why do these things always have to be so complicated?'

'Everyone who knows the Finnegans suspects them of pilfering goods and selling them on through spivs,' said Poppy. 'If we could actually catch them in the act, we could get them out that way, with no harm done, as Izzy said.'

'But that could take for ever,' said Cadi. Falling into silent contemplation, she could almost hear Jez's voice as his face came into her mind. *'The Finnegans are a slippery pair of customers. Paddy's the stronger of the two, and undoubtedly the brains behind the business, whereas Kieran's more impulsive. If either of them has stolen money off the other, then Poppy's right and it's Kieran that's nicked it from Paddy, which explains why Paddy's looking for him. But once you've let the cat out of the bag there's no putting it back, so you have to be sure you're using the information where it'll have most impact. Ideally you want the Finnegans out of your lives, and whilst Daphne might be head over heels about Kieran at the moment, she's not altogether stupid. Give her time and she'll work it out for herself, especially as you've already sown the seeds of doubt.'*

Izzy nudged Cadi gently. 'Penny for them?'

'I was wondering what Jez would say if he was here.'

Poppy slid her arm through Cadi's. 'We could always rely on Jez to shoot from the hip.'

Izzy blinked as the sun came from behind a cloud. 'So, what do you reckon he'd say?'

'Give Daphne time to work things out for herself, and as for who's hiding from who, it's more than likely that Kieran's hiding from Paddy, because he's the weaker of the two. But keep shtum until you know for sure.'

Poppy nodded thoughtfully. 'I think Daphne might see through Kieran's lies – after all, she can be pretty devious herself.'

Cadi nodded slowly. 'Takes one to know one.'

'Exactly.'

Izzy grinned at her friends. 'So, are we agreed?'

'Sit on the information for now,' said Cadi, 'until we know what's what.'

Poppy gave her the thumbs up. 'Sounds good to me.'

With that decided, Izzy eyed Cadi curiously. 'Do you often turn to Jez?'

'Only when I need him most,' said Cadi. 'Bill was right when he said that we each carried a piece of Jez in our hearts.' She smiled faintly. 'I only wish that I could hold him just one more time.'

Standing outside the door to the register office, Daphne looked down at the small, and rather pathetic, bouquet of flowers that Kieran had managed to get for her. The day had not started off well, when she had telephoned her parents to tell them of her intended wedding. She had deliberately waited until it would be too late for them to join her, and her father had demanded to know why.

'You can't really blame them for being upset,' said Kieran, 'and in all honesty, I don't know why you didn't tell them sooner, especially when we set the date a month ago.'

Not wanting to upset or insult her fiancé, Daphne chose her words carefully. 'He's set in his ways, and can be very old-fashioned – not to mention bullheaded – when it comes down to it.'

'All the more reason to invite them along, then,' said Kieran. 'Your father wants to meet the man his

daughter is about to marry, and that's only natural ...'
He hesitated. 'You're not ashamed of me, are you?'

Daphne looked up sharply. 'No. If anything it's the other way round.'

Kieran stared at her. 'Why would you be ashamed of your parents? From what you've told me, they're both hard-working pillars of the community.'

She sighed wretchedly. 'They are, but Dad's fussy when it comes to the farm.'

Kieran tucked his thumbs into his trouser pockets. 'I could've reassured him that the farm would be in safe hands; shown him that I'm willing to learn, and told him that I intend to build a better future for his daughter.'

She felt her tummy flutter. 'Trust me, it's better this way.'

Kieran had had doubts in the past that Daphne's farm might not be all she'd made it out to be, and her hesitance to invite her parents to the wedding was reaffirming his concern.

'When you say your father has a farm, how many acres do you mean?' He'd asked her the question before, and she'd been vague in her answer. Was there a farm at all, or had she made it up to impress him?

'It's complicated.'

Kieran cupped his chin between his forefinger and thumb. 'How can it be complicated? Surely land doesn't change in size?'

'When war was declared, Dad was given more land to farm, but that might change when the war's over.' She shrugged. 'I don't know how much he farms now, because I haven't asked.'

Kieran stared at her. 'Nobody just gives their land away, war or not.'

'Extended it then,' said Daphne, 'for the war effort.'

Kieran furrowed his brow. 'You're not making any sense. How do you extend your land?'

'The landlord,' said Daphne simply.

The crease between Kieran's brows deepened. 'I thought you said the farm was your father's?'

She nodded. 'It is – well, practically, anyway.'

'How can it be his, when he doesn't even own it?' snapped Kieran. 'Does he own the livestock?'

'He's an arable farmer.'

Kieran tutted irritably. 'No wonder you didn't want me to meet him.'

She eyed him accusingly. 'What do you mean by that?'

'You made it sound as though your father was all but gentry.'

'I most certainly did not!'

Kieran – who had no intention of marrying a woman who had nothing to offer – walked towards the door that led out of the register office. 'And you had the nerve to call me a liar.'

Catching hold of his arm, Daphne gaped at him. 'I didn't call you a liar, someone else did, and I merely told you what they'd said. And I never lied about my dad owning the land; you were the one who made that assumption.'

Kieran ripped his elbow out of her hand. 'Thank God I learned the truth before I said "I do", because I most definitely do *not*.'

'Why? Because you thought I had money, or because you think I'm a liar?'

Kieran laughed sarcastically. 'Take your pick. It still works out the same.'

Furious, she caught hold of his elbow again and yanked him round to face her. 'Cadi was telling the truth, wasn't she? You were only marrying me because you thought I had money – or rather my family did.'

'Cadi is a nasty little liar, you said so yourself, and all I can say is it takes one to know one. If you want my opinion you're all half-baked; quite frankly you deserve each other.'

But Daphne wasn't listening. She'd been led to the altar by a man who'd lied his way into her life, then had the audacity to make her out to be the untruthful one. 'That's why you pushed for us to get married: cos you worried that I'd learn the truth from Cadi.'

'You don't know what you're talking about.'

She stared icily at him. 'You're right, I don't, but I'm going to find out, because there's more to you than meets the eye.'

Grabbing her by the arm, he dug his thumb into the crook of her elbow, causing her to cry out. 'You've heard the expression don't go askin' questions, because you might not like the answers?'

She nodded as tears pricked her eyes.

'Maybe you should heed that advice.'

Pushing her away, he had turned to leave when Daphne said something that stopped him in his tracks. 'You may think you can bully me into silence, but you can't bully Raquel.'

Kieran spun round to face her; his eyes glowing with anger. 'What did you say?'

Swallowing, Daphne slowly walked backwards to the safety of the register office, which was full of another wedding party. 'Cadi asked me to pass a message on from Raquel. That should you come causing trouble, she won't hesitate to tell all.'

Kieran folded his arms across his chest. He couldn't throttle Daphne with so many people nearby, but he could threaten her. 'You're playing dangerous games for someone so ignorant.'

'Oh, I'm not playing. A lot of people knew we were getting married today, and they'll want to know why we didn't go through with it. I'm not having them believe your version of events when I know the truth, cos quite frankly, *Micky*, I'm glad I found out that you're a dirty little liar, and God knows what else, before I tied the knot.'

Hell hath no fury like a woman scorned. Kieran knew the saying, and he had no doubt that Daphne would make as much trouble for him as she had for Cadi and her pals. But what to do? If he treated her the way he had Kitty, he knew Daphne wouldn't hesitate to shop him to his superiors. He glanced at a car which had pulled up beside the kerb, and a look of pure malice crossed his face as he turned his attention back to Daphne.

'Considering you believe me to be some kind of gangster, you aren't half throwing some stupid accusations around. I hope you take better care when you're behind the wheel.' His mouth smiled, fleetingly, whilst his eyes bored into hers. 'Goodbye, Daphne. I think we're best leaving each other alone, don't you? Only I'd hate for us to fall out, in case you had a nasty accident afterwards.'

She gasped. 'You wouldn't!'

Kieran shrugged. He wore a puzzled frown, but his lips were smiling again. 'I don't know what you mean.'

Daphne turned on her heel without saying another word. Cadi had said he could be dangerous, and she was right. Kieran had scared the living daylights out of Kitty, and whilst she didn't know the ins and outs of his visit to the other girl, Daphne shuddered to think of the lengths he might have gone to in order to ensure her silence.

I'm glad I found out the truth before I married him, Daphne told herself. *I only wish I'd listened to Cadi instead of accusing her of trying to cause trouble.* She turned her thoughts to Cadi's friend Raquel. Kieran had only turned really nasty when Daphne had mentioned that name. She wondered what the other woman's connection was to Kieran, and what Raquel knew that he so desperately wanted to keep quiet?

With everyone knowing that she and Kieran were supposed to be getting married, Daphne decided not to return to base until much later that same day, and when she did eventually walk into the NAAFI she found a table far from the others, hoping to be left alone. It was no use: Abigail wandered over to see whether the rumours were true.

'Kieran said you'd both had a change of heart. Are you all right?'

Daphne shot the other girl a dark glance. 'I am now.'

Sitting down opposite her, Abigail placed her hand over Daphne's. 'Did you really both have a change of heart, or was it just Kieran?'

Daphne laughed without mirth. 'Well, it was Kieran who called the whole thing off.'

Abigail sat upright. 'You don't seem upset?'

'If someone stopped you from jumping into a fire, would you be upset?'

A look of doubt crossed Abigail's face. 'I'm confused.'

If Daphne were to tell Abigail what Kieran was really like, she knew she would be opening a can of worms, and she didn't fancy facing the consequences. She smiled dismissively. 'It's nothing; we just weren't right for each other. Good job we realised before we made a big mistake.'

Abigail stared at Daphne. Ever since Daphne had arrived at the station, she had been outspoken and forthright with her opinions. If she was opting to remain quiet, then Abigail would bet a pound to a penny that it wasn't her choice. 'Has he got you over a barrel?'

Careful to avoid eye contact, Daphne removed the engagement ring from her finger and thrust it into her pocket. 'Not me, no.' She glanced up at Abigail. 'I've had quite a day of it. Do you mind if I sit on my own for a bit?'

Abigail got up from her seat. 'If you ever need to talk, you know where I am.'

'Thanks.'

As Abigail walked away, Daphne mulled over Cadi's words of warning, and whether she, too, would warn another woman if Kieran made a play for someone else. *Not without finding out the facts first*, Daphne told herself. *No one's going to listen to you when you're only giving half the story. That was the problem with Cadi; had she been straight with me, I would never have let things get*

239

this far. Only how could she speak to Cadi without letting the other woman know that she'd been right all along? She breathed out wearily. Cadi didn't need Daphne to tell her something she already knew.

She glanced up as two Waafs entered the NAAFI. One of them looked in Daphne's direction before giggling and nudging her friend, who responded the same way. Daphne got up from her seat. She had no idea what, if anything, Kieran had said, but she wasn't about to sit waiting to be judged by others. As she had no idea where Cadi was based, she would telephone Kitty at RAF Little Snoring, and find out *exactly* who Kieran O'Connell was.

Kitty was in the kitchen rolling out the pastry for the officers' mince pies when she was hailed by a Waaf who had come in through the back door.

'You've a phone call in the NAAFI – someone by the name of Daphne.'

Wiping her hands on her apron, Kitty looked to the cook, who heaved a sigh. 'But don't be long,' she warned as Kitty followed the Waaf outside.

Kitty shot the Waaf a sidelong glance as they made their way to the NAAFI. 'Are you sure she said Daphne?'

The other girl nodded. 'Why, don't you know her?'

Kitty pulled a face. 'I only know one Daphne, and I can't think why she'd want to speak to me; unless …'
She hesitated as she opened the door to the NAAFI. Thanking the Waaf, she headed for the phone.

Picking up the receiver, she spoke tentatively. 'Hello?'

'Is that Kitty?'

'Speaking.'

'It's me, Daphne. Look, I'm really sorry – about Kieran coming to see you, I mean. I had no idea he was going to do that ...' Daphne went on to explain how Kieran had said and done all the right things to pull the wool over her eyes, and how things had come to a head when she told him that her father didn't own the land he farmed. 'It was like someone lifting a veil. Everything became crystal clear, and I realised that Cadi had been telling the truth all along.' She blew her cheeks out. 'You should've seen his face when I called him Micky. Talk about angry – he was livid. It was bad enough when I passed on Raquel's message, but the straw that broke the camel's back was when I told him I was going to find out the truth: that's when he really flipped his lid. He told me in no uncertain terms that I was not to go asking questions because I might not like the answers.' She paused before continuing. 'He also said he'd hate for us to fall out in case I had a nasty accident; but he was smiling when he said it.'

Kitty hissed inwardly. 'He never!'

'I'm afraid so, which is why I need to know exactly what it is he's done, so that I can have the same leverage as Raquel.'

'I agree with you, but it's really not my place to say,' said Kitty.

'Surely you can tell me what he used to do for a living?' pleaded Daphne. 'I'm not going to go blabbing, but I'd like a bit of ammunition in case he threatens me again.'

Having been on the receiving end of Kieran's wrath, Kitty felt she was in no position to deny Daphne the right to defend herself. She drew a deep breath. 'He used to run a brothel, amongst other things.' Her heart hammering in her chest, she continued, 'To cut a long story short, he had to flee Portsmouth, which must be why he joined the RAF, because I'm sure he wouldn't have dreamed of signing on otherwise.'

Daphne was left temporarily speechless as she took it all in, but the more she thought about it, the more it made sense. 'It certainly explains why he's so obnoxious, surly and bad-tempered. I know the fellers on the base can't stand him. They're always saying that he's lazy, and that he shouldn't be here, but I put it down to jealousy, because he's so popular with the girls.' She gave a brief, sarcastic laugh, 'A ladies' man! If only they knew.'

'What are you going to do?' Kitty asked.

'Now that I know the truth? Nothing, because I don't want to rock the boat. But should he start getting nasty, at least I've got some information that will put him in his place.'

'What if he starts courting someone else?'

Daphne fell silent as she thought this through. 'I couldn't stand by and watch her make the biggest mistake of her life.' She nodded thoughtfully to herself. 'I've changed my mind. I'm going to tell him that should he even *think* about approaching another woman in the WAAF I shall make it known exactly who he is and what he used to do.'

'Be careful. He can turn on a sixpence,' Kitty warned her.

'Not if I tell him that I've spoken to you, and if anything happens to me you'll sing like a canary!' suggested Daphne.

'Feel free,' said Kitty, adding as an afterthought, 'and if all else fails, tell him that his brother's looking for him, and if he doesn't back off we'll let him know where he's based.'

Daphne was dumbfounded. 'There are two of them?'

'There are indeed, and whilst we're not too sure what's gone on between them, we do know they used to be as thick as thieves, yet Paddy hasn't a clue where his brother is now, which would suggest they've had a bust-up. Hardly surprising, considering what happened the last time we saw them.'

'Thank you so much for this. I really appreciate your help.'

'He threatened you verbally, but he grabbed me by the throat and threatened to snap my neck,' said Kitty. 'What sort of person would I be if I didn't try to help someone in the same boat as myself?'

Daphne stood in stunned silence. 'I – I didn't realise he'd gone that far.'

'He's capable of far worse,' said Kitty darkly. 'Be grateful you got out when you did.'

'I'm just sorry I didn't listen to Cadi sooner,' said Daphne.

The operator cut in, to let them know their time was up.

'Thanks again,' said Daphne. 'I'll be in touch.'

'Make sure you are,' said Kitty. 'If I haven't heard from you by Friday, I'll be giving the station a call to make sure you're all right.'

Thanking Kitty once again, Daphne said her goodbyes before heading out to find Kieran. A slow smile crept up the corners of her lips as she envisaged his face when she told him all she knew. Heading straight for the motor pool, she soon located him, and gestured for him to join her. She stood out of earshot from his friends, but close enough to have witnesses should she need them.

Kieran folded his arms across his chest. 'What?'

'I don't like living life looking over my shoulder, so I telephoned Kitty to find out who you are.'

If looks could kill, Daphne would've been six feet under. 'Typical fishwife,' he snarled. 'Do you seriously think I give a monkey's what any of that lot say, or you for that matter?'

She let out a short, mirthless laugh. 'No, because you haven't got a conscience. I'm here to let you know that should you even *think* about courting any of the women in RAF Chivenor, or indeed any other base, I shall tell them exactly what Cadi should've told me. That you used to prostitute women for a living, amongst other things.' She shrugged nonchalantly. 'What they choose to do with the information is up to them.' She held up a finger as she got ready to play her ace. 'And should anything happen to me, Kitty will tell Paddy where he can find you.'

The look of pure hatred on Kieran's face was replaced with one of utter shock. 'You're bluffing!' he huffed. 'My brother knows where I am.'

She arched an eyebrow. 'Really? Then why's he asking people if they've come across a Kieran O'Connell, or a Micky Finnegan?'

He stared at her, utterly perplexed as to what to say or do next. Kieran had spent his whole life threatening others; having someone threaten him was a new experience. 'Where is he?'

A half-smile formed on her cheeks. 'I thought you said he knew where you were?'

Kieran spoke in leaden tones. He couldn't afford to play games if his brother was involved; the price was simply too high. 'Why do you think I did a runner and changed my name in the first place?' He barely paused before continuing. 'If you tell him where I'm at, you'll have my blood on your hands.'

Daphne shrugged. 'You'd best hope I don't say owt then, hadn't you?' She stared woodenly at him. 'Cos according to you I'm no better than a fishwife.'

Kieran mumbled, 'You've as good as signed my death warrant,' before turning on his heel and walking towards his hut. It took him no more than a moment or two to collect what few belongings he had before leaving the station.

With Christmas fast approaching, Aled was busy making plans when he received an unexpected phone call from Marnie.

He smiled down the phone. 'Hello, sweetheart. Are you all ready for Christmas?'

Marnie placed a hand to her forehead. She didn't like disappointing people, especially around this time of year, but she had to be true to herself.

'Sorry, Aled, but I'm afraid I won't be coming.'

'But I thought you'd sorted your leave?' said Aled, adding bitterly, 'Don't tell me they're changing their minds this late in the day.'

'I'm the one who's had a change of heart, not anyone else,' Marnie confessed.

Aled was perplexed. 'Why would you do that? I thought you were looking forward to spending Christmas together?'

Marnie spoke quietly. 'I only agreed to spend Christmas in Lincoln because I didn't want to come across as jealous or petty, but I can't help the way I feel, Aled.'

He shook his head. *Not this again.* 'Is this about Cadi?'

'I know you say that you're only looking out for a friend, but I can't help thinking it's more than that.'

Aled glared at the phone. 'So you're calling me a liar?'

'Not at all,' said Marnie hastily, 'but I saw the way you were looking at Cadi at the funeral, and even though I've tried to reason things out in my mind, I know what I saw, Aled, and the love you feel for her was obvious to me even if it's not to you.'

Aled could feel the frustration rising within him. 'Of course I love her, I've never denied that, but there's loving someone and being in love with someone, and—'

She stopped him short. 'And you're in love with her.' She sighed. 'You might not want to be, it might not be the right thing, but just as I can't help the way I feel, neither can you.'

'But there's no question of being with Cadi,' said Aled. 'It's you I want.'

'I'm the choice you made,' said Marnie, 'but I'm not a fool, Aled. Jez knew you were in love with his wife, and so do I.'

'All that was a long time ago, and what does it matter, if I never acted on my feelings?' said Aled. He

246

wished he could retract the words as soon as they left his lips, but it was too late.

'Because I'm no one's second best,' said Marnie, 'and whilst I realise you didn't mean me to be, that's what I am.'

'You're not! And I'm never going to be with Cadi.'

'Maybe not,' said Marnie, 'but as I say, I'm nobody's second choice.'

'So what are you saying? That you want me to stop seeing her? Not that I am,' he added hastily.

'There's no point, when your heart belongs to her.'

Aled was nearly at a loss for words. 'Can't we try and work something out?'

'My last relationship failed because my so-called fiancé was lying about seeing someone else, but in this instance the only person you're lying to is yourself. I'm sorry, Aled, but I don't see the point in us continuing when you love someone else.'

'But I love you too,' cried Aled.

'I know you do, but you don't look at me the way you do her,' said Marnie softly. 'I'm sorry for you, because you may never have the one you truly love, but it doesn't have to be that way for me. Which is why I'm cutting myself free to find a true love of my own.'

'I do love you, you know,' he said.

'And I you,' said Marnie, 'but sometimes love just isn't enough. Goodbye, Aled. No hard feelings.'

Aled wanted to retaliate, to tell her she was wrong, but what was the use when she'd made it clear she thought they weren't meant for each other? He sighed. 'Goodbye, Marnie. I hope you find what you're looking for.'

'You too.'

Hearing the click as her receiver went down, Aled replaced his own handset, before returning to his billet. Sinking down on to the end of his bed, he gathered his thoughts. Some of the things Marnie had said were correct, but not his being in love with Cadi. Yet how could he convince her she was wrong, when she'd already made up her mind?

He turned his thoughts to the intended trip to Lincoln. It would be only natural for the girls to ask about Marnie, but what was he meant to say in response? He could hardly tell them the truth. Should he telephone ahead and cancel his visit? He heaved an inward sigh. As if Cadi hadn't gone through enough without him letting her down at Christmas. He took his jacket off and hung it up. He would have to tell her the truth, warts and all. He would assure her that whilst some of what Marnie said was correct, he had no intention of upsetting her after everything they'd been through. If she was still willing to meet, then all the better, but if not, he would have to respect her feelings.

Cadi listened as Kitty relayed the second telephone conversation she had had with Daphne.

'Blimey! I didn't think he'd go AWOL,' said Cadi. 'What else did she say?'

'That rumours are running rife, but she's told people the truth: Paddy Finnegan is Kieran's brother, and Kieran left because he feared that Paddy would kill him if he found him. Word is he's probably gone back to Ireland with his tail between his legs.'

'More than likely. I don't know why he didn't go there in the first place.'

'Me neither,' said Kitty. 'Are you going to telephone Aled?'

'Too right I am. Aled would never forgive me if I didn't fill him in on all the goss.'

Kitty laughed. 'I reckon men are worse than women when it comes to gossip.'

Hearing the operator cut across, Cadi said her good-byes. 'I'll give you a call if Aled has anything to add.'

'Make sure you do,' said Kitty. 'Not that I'm scared of Kieran turning up; he'd have to be bonkers to walk into a camp knowing people are looking for him, but I still like to be kept in the loop.'

'Right you are,' said Cadi. 'Ta-ra, Kitty.' She replaced the handset and hurried off to find her friends, eager to fill them in on Kitty's news.

Aled and the rest of his crew were making their way from the debriefing room to their billet when they stopped to watch a rumpus outside one of the maintenance huts.

Tom pointed to a man who appeared to be at the centre of the kerfuffle. 'Here, isn't that the feller who tried to nick a spark plug from our car?'

Aled frowned as he focused on the man in question. Seeing Paddy's face come into view as he wrestled with the Royal Air Force Police, Aled knitted his forehead. 'That's the one. I wonder what he's done this time? He's putting up a good fight.'

Tom folded his arms across his chest. 'It must be pretty bad to involve the RAFP.'

An airman who was closer to the fracas than Aled and his crew came over to fill them in. 'They're charging him with being a member of the IRA.'

Aled stared at him in utter disbelief. 'Are you sure?'

The airman nodded. 'Heard it with me own ears.'

'But the IRA support the Germans, not us,' said Tom. 'That can't be right.'

'I don't know the ins and outs,' confessed the man, 'but I do know they're after his brother, who's done a runner.'

Aled and Tom exchanged glances. 'I've got to make a phone call,' said Aled.

Tom joined him. 'I'll come with you.'

Not waiting to see what happened to Paddy, the pair hastened to the office, where they might have a bit of privacy. Opening the door, Aled picked up the telephone and asked the operator to put him through to RAF Fiskerton. He spoke to Tom as he waited for Cadi. 'It has to be a false rumour. There's no chance that two men running a brothel in the south of England are working for the IRA. It just doesn't make sense.'

'That's what I figured,' agreed Tommy. 'It sounds more like someone spreading false rumours to get the brothers in shtuck.'

'On the other hand, why's Kieran done a—' He broke off as Cadi's voice came down the line.

'Cadi!'

She smiled. 'Aled? Have I got news for you!'

Aled shook his head. 'If it's about Kieran absconding, we already know.'

With the wind taken out of her sails, Cadi deflated. 'Who told you?'

'Some feller, whilst we were watching Paddy getting arrested by the RAFP,' said Aled. Hearing Cadi's sharp intake of breath, he quickly continued before she could cut him off. 'Apparently they reckon Paddy and Kieran are members of the IRA.'

Cadi gasped again, and began to cough. After taking a moment to regain her composure, she spoke in a disbelieving voice. 'Are you sure you got that right?'

'Positive. I take it you don't know anything about it?'

'Not a dickie bird. Raquel never said anything, but I dare say she wasn't privy to their disreputable past.' She hesitated. 'It would explain why they changed their names before coming to Britain, and why they never returned to Ireland.'

Aled intervened. 'You think they were running away from someone back in Ireland?'

'Having had first-hand experience of the brothers, I'd say there's not much that frightens them, but the IRA are a different kettle of fish. I reckon they've done something to hack them off.'

'The police must have good reason to suspect a connection to the IRA,' Aled pointed out. 'Given everything we know, I would guess that they're former members who had to get out of Ireland fast.'

'If we're right in thinking that Kieran double-crossed Paddy, then maybe he did the same to the IRA?'

Aled spluttered in disbelief. 'Nobody's that stupid. I know I've not met Kieran for myself, but I've met Paddy, and ...' The memory of the Irishman removing the spark plug from his car without ensuring he wasn't being watched came to mind. 'Scrap that. If Paddy's the sharper of the two, then I'd say it's more than likely they've done just that. And Kieran might even be stupid enough to think they wouldn't bother to track him down in England, so it was safe to use his middle name.'

'Paddy's definitely the thinker out of him and his brother,' said Cadi, who was recalling the night Paddy had thought on his feet whilst his brother lay on the floor nursing his nether regions.

Aled spoke slowly. 'There might be one person who knows ...'

'Daphne,' Cadi agreed.

'When was the last time Kitty spoke to her?'

'Not sure, but there's no chance she's said anything to Kitty, because Kitty would've been straight on the phone to let me know.'

'I suppose it's neither here nor there, really,' said Aled, 'because whatever the outcome, I don't think you'll be seeing the Finnegans again any time soon.'

Cadi had a horrible thought. 'Unless the rumours are unfounded, in which case Paddy could be out for blood, and who knows who he'll gun for?'

'But who'd spread a false rumour like that?'

'My first thought would be Daphne, but I don't think she's that naive,' conceded Cadi. 'My next thought – if I were the Finnegans – would be that one of us had decided to get revenge for what they did to Raquel and Kitty.'

'Only you haven't,' said Aled.

'We know that, but they don't,' said Cadi. 'But I dare say they've made a few enemies since entering the RAF, and we *know* they left a score more behind in Portsmouth. Quite frankly, it could be anyone.'

'Someone needs to speak to Daphne so that we can be prepared should they come making accusations,' said Aled. 'I could telephone her if you like?'

Cadi shook her head. 'Sorry, Aled, but I'd rather she didn't know that you and I were still in touch. She knows about Jez's passing, and I'd hate her to think that we were in cahoots romantically.'

'I hadn't thought of it like that,' said Aled after a moment, 'but it's imperative that you all know what's going on with the Finnegans.'

'I'll ask Kitty to give her a call,' said Cadi. 'She's got good reason to fear comebacks, and Daphne knows that.'

'Good thinking. Do let me know what happens, won't you?'

'Of course!'

Aled gave her a mischievous wink. 'I must say, life's a lot more exciting with you in it,' he noted. 'It was pretty boring before you came along.'

She smiled. 'I seem to recall you saying something along those lines the last time I saw you in Speke. I suppose, in hindsight, you were right.' She hesitated. 'Is Marnie looking forward to spending Christmas in Lincoln?'

Aled grimaced. He'd been meaning to call Cadi to let her know that he and Marnie were no longer an item, but had been putting it off. He drew a deep breath. 'I'm afraid Marnie won't be joining us.'

'Oh, heck. Why not?'

Aled wanted to say that he'd rather not talk about it, but Cadi would find out sooner or later, so he ploughed on. 'Unfortunately, she doesn't think I'm committed to the relationship, so she broke things off.'

Cadi remained quiet, not knowing quite what to say. It took her a moment or two to find the right words. 'Oh, I'm sorry. Have you any idea what would make her think that? Only I thought you made a perfect couple, and I know you'd taken her to meet your parents.'

He felt his cheeks grow warm. 'I've tried talking to her, but she won't listen to reason.'

'Do you think it's being posted at opposite ends of the country?'

Glad that Cadi couldn't see the colour of his cheeks, he continued without answering her question. 'We've not had a cross word since the day we met, so I had no idea she felt the way she did until the last time we spoke.'

'Perhaps she's going through a hard time at work?' Cadi suggested. 'Do you think it would help if I had a word?'

'No!' Realising he had been a little sharp, Aled added, 'I'd rather just leave things lie.'

'Sorry, I shouldn't have suggested it,' said Cadi. 'I just hate to see her make such a big mistake.' She paused. 'Are you still coming to Lincoln?'

'I had intended to,' said Aled, 'if that's all right with you, of course?'

'You can come and drown your sorrows with me and the girls,' said Cadi. 'We can cry on each other's shoulders.'

'I couldn't think of a nicer shoulder to cry on.'

'Maybe you'll meet the next Mrs Davies whilst you're down here.'

Aled shook his head. 'I think I'd rather stay single, thanks all the same.'

Cadi thought it a real shame that someone as nice as Aled seemed to have such bad luck with women. Especially with Marnie, who had struck Cadi as a perfect match for her old friend. She sighed inwardly. Sometimes people didn't realise what they had until it was too late.

Having gone through the details surrounding Kieran's disappearance with the RAFP for what felt like the millionth time, Daphne returned to her billet, exhausted from repeating the same answers: No, she didn't know he'd been in the IRA, no, he hadn't told her where he was going, no, she didn't know he had a brother until recently, and no, she hadn't warned him that the net was closing in on him. She had told them everything she knew about Kieran, including his threatening behaviour towards Kitty, and Cadi's having warned her that he was bad news.

Laying on her bed, she wondered if the RAFP had quizzed Kitty and Cadi in the same manner as herself. *Probably not, because they weren't daft enough to get engaged to a gangster*, Daphne thought bitterly. Leaning up on one elbow, she looked to the door of her billet. There was no way Kitty could know that Kieran was involved with the IRA, because she would've said something when she'd been ratting him out to Daphne, but Raquel on the other hand …

She hurried to the NAAFI and headed straight for the telephone. Hearing Kitty's voice come down the

255

line at last, Daphne got straight to the point. 'Who's Raquel?'

Kitty had been expecting questions, but not about Raquel. 'I've just had Cadi on the phone, so I'm assuming this has summat to do with Paddy Finnegan's arrest for his involvement with the IRA?'

Paddy's arrest was certainly news to Daphne, although she supposed with hindsight it was only natural that the police would tar Paddy with the same brush as his brother. Taking a deep breath, she explained that the RAF had put out a warrant for Kieran's arrest as soon as he went AWOL. In doing so, his name had come up as a man wanted in connection with the IRA. 'All hell broke loose,' sniffed Daphne. 'They didn't believe me when I told them that he'd jilted me at the altar, saying instead that I'd warned him to leave before they arrested him. Which is ridiculous, because he was only brought to their attention by going AWOL in the first place. They tried accusing me of being involved with the IRA myself, which is ludicrous.' Her bottom lip trembled. 'I can't prove I knew nothing about it, so there's nothing to stop them from giving me the third degree. I was hoping that Raquel might know summat which would get them off my back, because you did say she'd threatened to tell all.'

Kitty blew her cheeks out. 'Sorry, Daphne, but Raquel's as clueless as the rest of us. She only meant that she'd tell everyone about the brothel and the other activities carried out within its walls; she knew nothing about them being involved with the IRA.'

Daphne rested her forehead on her hand. 'I don't know what else I can do or say to get them to leave me alone. I thought being left at the altar was bad enough, but this is a hundred times worse.'

'If you think this is bad, imagine what it would have been like had you married him.'

Daphne gave a small exclamation. 'It doesn't bear thinking of.'

Kitty thought for a moment before saying slowly, 'If the RAFP want information on the Finnegans, they'd be better off approaching those they used to do business with in Portsmouth.'

'Only we've not got any names to give them—' Daphne began, before being interrupted by Kitty. Even down a telephone line, Daphne could tell that she was grinning.

'We don't, but I know a woman who does. Leave it with me!'

Chapter Eight

Christmas Eve 1944

Standing in the reception at the White Hart, Aled was waiting for the receptionist to finish seeing to another customer before booking him in. Having questioned himself at least a hundred times as to whether he was doing the right thing, he found his attention being drawn to the door of the hotel. He knew his intentions were honourable, and that he had no other agenda than to see Cadi through a difficult time, but Marnie's words lingered in his thoughts. Was he looking at her with anything other than affection for an old friend who'd gone through a hellish time? And would other people think the same as Marnie? He couldn't bear the thought of Cadi's friends telling her to be careful whilst he was around, because nothing could be further from his mind. Coming to a decision, he picked up his bag and headed towards the door, just as Cadi and the girls came through.

Stopping dead in his tracks, he smiled awkwardly as Cadi wrinkled her brow. 'Going somewhere?'

Glancing at his kitbag, Aled looked round at the faces eyeing him so expectantly.

'Don't let the thought of spending Christmas with a gaggle of women drive you out,' said Poppy. 'Mike and Geoffrey will be here soon.'

Aled rubbed his hand over the nape of his neck. 'It's not that ...' he began, but Cadi cut him short. Stepping forward, she lowered her voice so that only Aled could hear.

'Is this to do with your break-up with Marnie?'

Aled gave her a rueful look. 'I'm worried that people might think I have ulterior motives.'

Cadi eyed him sternly. 'Well, if they do, they can jolly well come and see me, because I know you'd never ...'

He held up a hand to silence her. 'I wasn't entirely truthful with you over the phone. Marnie broke things off because she thinks I'm in love with you.'

Cadi gaped at him. 'Since when?'

Aled glanced at the girls, who were deep in conversation, before looking back at Cadi. 'Can we talk somewhere a bit more private? I don't like airing my dirty laundry in public.'

Nodding, Cadi turned to her friends. 'Why don't you go ahead and get us a table, and I'll wait with Aled.'

When the others were out of earshot, Aled ran his tongue across his bottom lip. 'I wasn't going to say anything, but her words have been playing on my mind, and I couldn't help but worry that she might not be the only one who had the wrong impression.'

'But I've only ever met her once,' said Cadi. 'How on earth did she get hold of the wrong end of the stick?'

'Because she'd never seen you before, she hadn't realised that you both have blonde hair,' said Aled. 'We'd only just left the wake when she started raking

259

up the past; talking about the day Jez turned up to the Christmas carol concert in Rhos.'

Cadi nodded slowly. 'He mistook Marnie for me, so when you leaned in for a kiss ...'

'Precisely!' said Aled. 'She wanted to know why Jez would think I'd try to kiss you.' He waved a dismissive hand. 'She asked a few more questions, but I thought I'd laid the matter to rest when I assured her it was Jez's insecurities getting the better of him.'

'So why on earth did she agree to come to Lincoln?'

'Because she knows that unlike her ex I'd never cheat on her, but in the end that made no difference, because she's convinced that I'm in love with you.' He hung his head in embarrassment. 'I told her I used to carry a torch for you, but those days are long gone, and that she was the only woman for me, but she wouldn't listen. In her mind, she's second best.' He rolled his eyes. 'She even said she felt sorry for me, because I was in love with a woman I could never have. I tried to tell her that she'd got it all wrong, but there was no talking to her.'

Cadi held a hand to her forehead. 'Aled, I'm so sorry.'

He looked perplexed. 'What've you got to be sorry about?'

'That Marnie saw our love in a romantic sense, and not for what it is.'

He breathed a sigh of relief. 'Thank you. That's precisely what I was trying to tell her. You're one of my oldest, closest friends, and we've been through a lot together. I'd have the compassion of a lump of coal if I didn't love you, the same as you love me.'

'Are you sure I can't say anything to convince her she's got it wrong?'

He shook his head. 'She'll probably say that you're as blind as me. You see, when I tried to tell her how I felt, she said she knew I truly believed what I was saying, but she could see beyond that.'

Cadi slipped her arm through his. 'We're going to have to develop some pretty thick skins if we're to ignore the gossips.'

He shot her a sidelong glance. 'Has anyone said anything to you?'

Her brow shot upwards. 'No. Because they know I'd give them a thick ear if they even tried to question your motives.' She tutted softly. 'Not that I'd do that to Marnie, because I know what it's like for someone to feel insecure. Poor old Jez felt that way for ever such a long time, as did Daphne. People act in the most peculiar ways when they feel their affections are being threatened. Marnie's just doing what Jez would've done.'

'Only unlike Marnie, Jez fought for you,' said Aled sullenly. 'I guess that's why I'm not bothered about trying to heal things over, because when all's said and done, if she doesn't believe I'm worth standing by, then did we ever really have a relationship?'

Cadi grimaced. 'I'm afraid I can't answer that one.' She fell silent as the receptionist caught their attention.

Following Aled over to get his key, Cadi came to a conclusion. 'If there's one thing Jez taught me, it's not to have secrets. The girls will know summat's up, so if you don't mind I'll fill them in whilst you put your things in your room.'

He nodded. 'Thanks, Cadi.'

Seeing the girls seated at a table in the restaurant, Cadi went over to join them. 'I'm going to put this as briefly as I can,' she said, taking a seat between Izzy and Poppy. 'Marnie broke up with Aled because she thinks he's in love with yours truly, and her words have been playing on his mind. That's why he was about to leave when we walked in.'

Poppy tutted. 'Maybe he was once, but that was ages ago.'

'She's mistaken his love for me with him being *in* love with me,' said Cadi. 'Poor old Aled's done every-thing he can to convince her that she's wrong, but she dumped him anyway.'

'Well I think she's being silly,' said Kitty. 'You have to grab love with both hands, because you never know ...' She fell silent as her words caught up with her, and turned rounding eyes to Cadi. '... I'm so sorry, Cadi, I never thought ...'

Cadi smiled sadly. 'Sorry for what, telling the truth?' Seeing Aled walk into the restaurant, she beckoned him over whilst saying quickly, 'He knows I've told you, because I don't like keeping secrets.'

Ronnie and Kitty moved up so that Aled might fit a chair in between them. 'Should my ears be burning?'

Poppy cast him a sympathetic smile. 'Sorry to hear about Marnie. I know her ex put her off men for a long time, so she's probably suspicious of every woman she sees.'

Aled pulled a downward smile. 'You'd think so, but she's been fine up until Cadi. She's so convinced, she even said that she felt sorry for me because I was blind to my own feelings.' He gave a short laugh. 'Pretty insult-ing when you think about it.'

Poppy nodded slowly. Had Marnie got hold of the wrong end of the stick, or was she bang on the money? It seemed strange that Marnie hadn't been jealous of any other woman than Cadi, and Poppy doubted that she would have thrown her relationship away without good cause.

Her thoughts were interrupted as Kitty picked up a menu from the table. 'So, who wants to hear the latest on Daphne?' she asked, a broad grin crossing her cheeks.

Izzy smiled knowingly. 'I already know, because I've spoken to me mam, but I didn't want to take the wind out of your sails so I promised to keep shtum.'

Kitty went on to tell the girls how she'd spoken to Dolly before talking to the officer in charge of her unit. 'Once Dolly gave me the go-ahead, I spoke to Officer Pilkington, who set the ball in motion. The police have been to see Dolly and she's given them the details of every man who ever had dealings with the Finnegans. She was delighted to put the fox amongst the chickens, because she could finally get even with the two men who corrupted innocent girls for their own profit.'

'Does anyone know what's happened to Kieran?' asked Ronnie, from the edge of her seat.

'Not so much as a whisper,' said Kitty. 'From what I managed to glean, they think he's gone back to Ireland.'

Aled spoke thoughtfully. 'And what about Paddy?'

'He's protesting his innocence, saying that the IRA are after them for no reason, and that's why they fled Ireland and started calling themselves Finnegan.'

Aled and Cadi exchanged knowing looks. 'That's exactly what we thought,' said Cadi, adding, 'apart from the bit about having nothing to do with them. The IRA don't chase you for no reason. We reckon the Finnegans were up to their necks with the IRA.'

'If it's true, and Kieran has gone back to Ireland, I don't fancy his chances much,' Aled put in.

'Dead as a dodo as soon as his foot touches Irish soil,' Ronnie agreed. 'I know he's thick, but that's plain suicidal.'

'If he thought he was dead anyway, then maybe he took his chances,' said Izzy. 'Ireland's a big country, and he probably guessed Paddy wouldn't return, so at least he'd be safe from him.'

'One man opposed to a huge organisation?' said Cadi. 'Where's the sense in that?'

Kitty pulled a face. 'We are talking about Kieran, don't forget.'

'Serves him right for getting mixed up with them in the first place,' said Ronnie. 'Especially after the way he treated those girls at Hillcrest, *and* poor Kitty.'

Cadi nodded. 'You reap what you sow, and in Kieran's case the harvest is long overdue.'

When Kieran left RAF Chivenor, he had no idea of the trouble he had caused. Knowing he was unpopular, he didn't think anyone would be bothered that he'd gone; in fact he rather thought they'd welcome the news. Oblivious of the fact that the authorities had been alerted to his connections with the IRA, he thought of himself as being of no interest, not only to the RAF but to the civilian police as well.

It was only when he reached Holyhead that he learned the extent of the trouble he was in. Hearing one of the officers stationed in the port remarking that they had been alerted by the RAFP to a man who had gone AWOL and was believed to have connections with the IRA, Kieran had hastily left the harbour to search for a different crossing.

Taking refuge in one of the dockside pubs, he made enquiries and was pointed in the direction of a man who was known for transporting illicit goods. After a brief chat, they agreed a price and the man made a quick phone call before taking Kieran to his vessel.

Relieved that he had found a way of crossing the Irish Sea without drawing the attention of the authorities, Kieran boarded the ancient-looking fishing boat, and they were soon under way. Following the man's instructions, Kieran hid down in the bow, where he slept until they reached a sandy beach just south of Drogheda the following day. The smuggler woke Kieran and informed him that they would have to reach the shore by rowing boat, which he had already launched. Kieran stepped unsteadily into the boat, taking care not to drop the false papers he had acquired when he first left Ireland. They were nearly on the beach when the man told Kieran to disembark.

Stepping into a foot of water, he made his way up the beach, clutching the papers proclaiming him to be Micky Finnegan to his chest. As he neared the sand dunes, he turned to see that the boatman was waving to someone out of his range of vision. As his gaze met Kieran's he quickly began to row away from the shore.

Realising that something was amiss, Kieran hastened into the dunes. Treading his way through the thick sand, he had barely got amongst the beachgrass when a heavy hand landed on his shoulder.

'Well, if it isn't Kieran O'Connell. Or should that be Micky Finnegan?'

Kieran turned round frightened eyes towards the stranger, who was smiling at him in a most unpleasant manner. 'Y-you've got the wrong man,' he stammered. 'I'm ...'

The man laughed scornfully. 'Are you not? So what's the name on them papers?'

Kieran's Adam's apple bobbed nervously in his throat. 'It wasn't me! It was me brother, Paddy, it was him that made me do it.'

The man gave him a wry smile. 'You've the loyalties of a hooded snake, Kieran.' He took his hand off Kieran's shoulder. 'It's time we were making a move. Mr White's a man of little patience.'

Nodding, Kieran took a couple of steps alongside the man before bolting in the opposite direction. He had no idea where he was running to, but he didn't care as long as he got away. Harry White was not the sort of man to be crossed, and there was no doubt in Kieran's mind that White would hold him accountable for his actions, no matter how long ago.

To Kieran's surprise, the man didn't follow, but stood in the dunes laughing. It was only when he heard the shot ring out that Kieran realised why the man hadn't bothered to give chase. Kieran may have been fast on his feet, but even he couldn't outrun a bullet. He fell heavily, and as the sand entered his mouth he felt the darkness descend.

*

It was Christmas Day and Cadi was talking to Poppy and Izzy outside the NAAFI.

'I appreciate the offer, but I don't see why you should miss out on Christmas just because of me,' Cadi insisted. 'I know they say that misery loves company, but it would only make me feel worse than I already do.'

'But we won't have a good time, knowing that you're unhappy,' said Poppy.

Cadi laid a reassuring hand on her friend's shoulder. 'I'll be happier if it's just myself and Aled,' she gave a soft laugh before continuing, 'because he's as miserable as me at the moment.'

'I don't like the thought of not being here for you, but it's not about me,' said Izzy. She pulled a rueful face. 'Christmas will never be the same again, will it?'

Cadi gave her a friend a sympathetic smile. 'No, but it will get easier – not that it feels like that at the minute.'

Hearing several people break into song, she took her friends in a warm embrace. 'I rather think that's my cue to leave.'

'You know where we are should you need us,' said Poppy.

Nodding, Cadi turned towards the gate, where Aled was just pulling up in his car. As she took her place in the passenger seat, she gave him a grim little smile. 'I don't care where we go, as long as I don't have to listen to people singing carols and being happy.'

He pushed the car into gear. 'I thought we might go for a walk along the canal; we shouldn't bump into too many people down there, not today.'

Cadi brightened. 'Good idea. I love canals, and it's one place I never went with Jez.'

'So, no memories,' conceded Aled. 'I must admit, I suggested the canal because it's somewhere I never took Marnie, either.' He glanced over his shoulder before pulling out on to the road. 'How're the girls?'

'Down in the dumps, which is understandable, but I think they'll feel better not having me around, and I know I'll feel better not pretending to be happy. Kitty is spending the day in Waddington with Ronnie, but I made sure I telephoned to wish them a merry Christmas before coming out.'

'That was very good of you, but I'm sure people would understand if you kept a low profile.'

'Jez loved Christmas – it was his favourite time of year – and so did his nan. It upsets me that I'm not celebrating something he loved so much, but it's not the same without him.'

'I wish there was something I could do to make you feel better,' said Aled.

She glanced across at him. 'I take it you've not been in touch with Marnie?'

He shook his head. 'No point. Much like yourself, I'm feeling bad enough as it is, without having her tell me that I'm living a lie.'

'Doesn't she realise that you've had a terrible year? Surely she could've waited until after Christmas—'

But Aled cut her short. 'Sorry, Cadi, but contrary to Marnie's conviction, I'd rather not live a lie, no matter how painful the truth. If she doesn't want to be with me, then I'd prefer to know about it sooner rather than later. There's no sense in prolonging the agony.'

'Have you told your parents?'

He pulled a face. 'Mam was furious, saying that Marnie was being selfish, but in truth she's just worried that I might change my mind about returning to the farm.'

Cadi watched him closely. 'And is she right?'

He tapped his finger against the steering wheel. 'I'm not staying in the RAF when all this is over, and as I don't know how to do anything other than farming I don't see that I've much choice. Besides, whether I like it or not, farming's in my bones.' He glanced sidelong at her. 'If you're stuck for work you can always come and work for me.'

Cadi laughed. 'And get covered in you know what every day? It was bad enough that day you drove past me in the tractor and I got soaked in it.'

Aled pretended to take offence. 'Surely you're not still harping on about that?'

'Eau de cow poop,' giggled Cadi, 'what's not to like?'

'I prefer to think of it as the smell of the countryside,' chuckled Aled. 'Or clean living.'

'I wouldn't call the stuff you covered me in as being clean.'

Aled raised his brow. 'Aye, I seem to remember that you didn't seem too chuffed at the time.'

'All I remember is you laughing your head off,' said Cadi. She began to giggle. 'My dad tried to convince me that you'd only done it because you liked me.'

Aled burst out laughing. 'Your father must have some pretty strange ideas when it comes to courting.'

Cadi laughed until the tears came. 'My poor mother.'

Pulling into the car park close to the canal, he turned to look at Cadi. 'I have to say you look a lot better than you did back in October.'

Wiping the tears from her eyes, she nodded. 'My appetite's come back with a vengeance, and I'm eating lots of the good stuff.'

'It shows,' remarked Aled as he got out of the car. 'Jez would be pleased.'

She smiled as he took her hand to help her from the car. 'That makes me happy, because I know he would've been dreadfully upset to see me the way I was.'

He closed the passenger door. 'What changed do you think?'

'I don't really know. One day I was feeling green around the gills, and the next, as hungry as a horse. I know that losing Jez knocked me sick to my stomach, but even though the pain's still there it's bearable now.'

'How do you feel otherwise? I hope you're not still blaming yourself?'

She shook her head. 'I've come to terms with the fact that I couldn't have done anything differently. What's more, had I not found him when I did, I'd never have had the chance to say goodbye.' She cast him a sidelong glance as they passed a couple of boats that had moored up for the festive period. 'How about you?'

Aled struck a stone with the toe of his boot, sending it bouncing down the path in front of them. 'I beat myself up for the longest time, but much like yourself, I came to the conclusion that I couldn't have done anything differently, so rather than torture myself for something I had no control over I decided to turn my focus on you.'

She stared at him in amazement. 'Me?'

He pushed his hands into his pockets. 'I couldn't save Jez, but I can look after you, whether it be moral support, a shoulder to cry on ...' he shrugged, 'or anything really.'

Cadi nodded slowly. 'Is that why you suggested coming up for Christmas?'

'I couldn't bear the thought of you pretending to be happy when you were anything but, but I know you wouldn't have wanted to disappoint your friends.'

'Jez would be pleased to know that you were keeping an eye out for me.'

'I'm glad I can do something for him.' He fell silent for a moment before adding, 'I wish I had a relationship like yours and Jez's, but no matter how hard I try mine seem doomed to fail.'

She tucked her hand into the crook of his elbow. 'I know you said you've sworn off women, but you will find someone, given time.'

He pushed out his bottom lip. 'Maybe, but I'm not even going to *think* about women until I'm settled back on the farm.'

'Probably a good idea,' said Cadi. 'You've got enough to concentrate on without worrying about a new belle.'

'I need a woman to see me in my overalls and think, yep, that's the man for me.'

Cadi mulled this over for a moment or two before voicing her opinion. 'I bet there's loads of women in the village who'd jump at the chance to be a farmer's wife.'

He smiled vaguely. 'There was only one village woman that ever piqued my interest, and she's off limits.'

Cadi squeezed his arm. 'Poor old Aled. Life's not been fair to either of us, has it?'

He pulled a grimace. 'I dunno so much. At least I'm alive. There's plenty of aircrew who never made it past their first operation.'

She nodded grimly. 'I always said I preferred Jez to be a mechanic because he had both feet safely on the ground. Had he been aircrew I could've lost him a lot sooner than I did, so at least we had some time together.'

'Every cloud,' said Aled.

Clasping the locket which hung around her neck, she blinked back the tears before they could form. 'I wish I had something other than jewellery to remember him by.'

'You've got your memories,' said Aled. 'No one can take them away.'

'You can't hold a memory.'

Aled squeezed her arm in his. 'True, but you can treasure them.'

Having spent the day away from the festivities, Cadi and Aled joined Izzy and Poppy for an evening meal in the NAAFI, at Fiskerton. Cadi and Poppy saved a table while Aled and Izzy collected their meals, and waited until they returned with their laden trays before going up to queue themselves.

Standing behind Cadi, Poppy placed her hand on her friend's waist. 'So, how's the day been for you?'

Cadi turned to face her. 'Not too bad. Certainly better than it would've been if I'd gone home, or back

272

to the Belmont, because I know they'd have showered me with sympathy, and that would only have made me feel worse.'

'How was Aled? He's changed an awful lot since we moved to Liverpool. Mind you, I suppose we've all changed a fair bit since then.'

'He's definitely changed since the day we found Jez. Aled always used to be quick with the compliments, a real charmer, but that seems to have vanished. I think the whole experience has aged him, much as it did me.'

'All that business with Marnie couldn't have helped,' Poppy supposed.

'Not really. He just said that it wasn't worth trying to change her mind, and it'll be a long while before he even contemplates courting again.'

'Not surprising, after his last two attempts. When is he going back?'

'The day after Boxing Day.' She hesitated. 'He suggested we could go for a drive to Skegness tomorrow.'

Closing her eyes, Poppy inhaled deeply as though smelling something wonderful. 'Oh to be by the sea!'

Cadi looked wistful. 'I know we won't be able to go down to the beach, but we'll still be able to see the sea, and I've not done that since we left Liverpool.'

Poppy waited while Cadi ordered her plate of sausage and mash before continuing. 'I've got to hand it to him, he's doing a marvellous job of taking your mind off things.'

Cadi placed her plate on the tray. 'I suppose he's a crutch for me as much as I am for him. Poor Aled; he really thought his future lay with Marnie.'

Also opting for sausage and mashed potato, Poppy watched the cook ladle gravy over her food of choice. 'He's a handsome man who stands to inherit his father's farm, and I bet he's not short of a bob or two either. He'll be fighting them off with sticks when he decides to start courting again.'

'He deserves to be happy,' said Cadi, as they took their trays over to join the others.

'Do you still worry that people might think ill of your meeting up with him?'

Cadi shook her head. 'Not in the slightest. Anybody who thinks he has an ulterior motive should take a good look at him. The poor man's completely exhausted and I'm not surprised. His role is demanding.' She slowed down so that she might finish their conversation whilst still out of earshot of their table. 'I can't imagine what it must be like to go out every day not knowing whether you'll be coming home. Especially when the odds aren't stacked in your favour.'

Poppy knew that losing Jez had all but broken Cadi. Aled might be her rock now, but what if he were to find another belle? It would only be natural for him to want to spend every waking moment with his new love, and Cadi had already lost two of the most important people in her life. If she were to lose Aled, Poppy feared it might prove to be the straw that broke the camel's back.

It was the evening of Boxing Day, and Cadi and Aled had stopped off at a country pub to have a late dinner.

'Thank you so much for taking me out. It's really helped to take my mind off things,' said Cadi as she

274

scanned the menu. 'I was dreading Christmas, but it's not been half bad.'

'I'm glad I've managed to cheer you up, even if it's only a little bit. I had reservations about whether I was doing the right thing by coming on my own, but I'm glad I did,' said Aled. 'There would have been no sense in the two of us being miserable. Had I stayed in Finningley, I would have been surrounded by happy couples exchanging presents and snatching kisses under the mistletoe: not what I want to see after losing Marnie. And if I'd gone home I'd have had Mam telling me how there's plenty more fish in the sea, but no one wants to hear that when they've just come out of a relationship.'

Cadi grimaced. 'Mam and Maria were hinting about me moving on not long after I lost Jez, but I'm sure they only did it because they don't like the thought of me being on my own.' She furrowed her brow. 'Why is it that everyone seems to think that you can only be happy if you're in a relationship?'

'I guess it's the natural order of life,' Aled supposed. 'First marriage then kids.'

'Well, I won't be doing either of those for a long time yet, if ever,' said Cadi. She smiled shyly at him. 'And thanks for taking my mind off Christmas. I really do appreciate it, and because of you next year might not be too bad.'

'I hope you don't think that I'm comparing my break-up to your losing Jez, because I know they don't come close, and in all honesty I feel a bit of a fraud licking my wounds when they're nowhere deep as your own.'

Cadi gave a grim smile. 'We're both nursing broken hearts.'

He glanced at the bottom of his menu. 'Talking of broken hearts, I see they've run out of custard!'

Cadi shook her head. 'Thinking of pudding and you've not had your mains yet!'

'Life's not worth living without pudding,' Aled chuckled. He glanced at her over the top of the menu. 'I bet you'll have fish and chips.'

Cadi looked mildly impressed. 'I will indeed, but how did you guess?'

He closed the menu before laying it on the table. 'I remember you saying fish and chips was your favourite, especially when you're close to the sea.'

Cadi wrinkled her forehead. 'Only we're not by the sea.'

He grinned. 'I know, but we're not far from the canal.'

The barmaid approached, pencil and pad in hand. 'Are you ready to order?'

'We are indeed,' said Aled. 'Fish and chips for two, as well as an extra couple of rounds of bread and butter, please.' Noting their order, the barmaid gathered their menus and headed back to the bar, and Aled indicated Cadi's empty glass with his own. 'Would you like another lemonade?'

Cadi nodded, and rested her chin on her knuckles as she watched Aled walk to the bar. To an outsider, it looked as though he hadn't a care in the world, but she very much doubted that was the case when he was sitting in the gunner's turret. Recalling John's words, she spoke her thoughts as Aled returned with their drinks. 'When Jez and I got married, I remember your father telling us how you were still flying by the seat of your pants, and treating the whole thing as though it were some big game. Have you always been like that?'

'I was until we lost our mid-gunner,' admitted Aled. 'It took a while for the crew to get back into the swing of things, but given time you go back to feeling as though you're invincible. If I'm honest, I don't think we'd be able to get back into the plane unless we thought that way. But losing Jez showed me that none of us are safe.'

'Because he was a mechanic?'

'Yes. Much like you, I'd always thought those on the ground were safer than the rest of us. I know that airfields come under attack, but I've never known anyone on the ground to die, apart from Jez.' He shrugged. 'I've lost many friends in aircrew, it almost goes with the territory – in fact I'd say it was to be expected, really – but not ground crew, and not the way Jez went.'

Leaning back in her seat, Cadi gazed into the glass of lemonade. 'You mean being hounded by a pilot who gunned him down on purpose?'

Aled nodded slowly. 'There's a big difference between someone taking a lucky shot and someone literally gunning for you.'

'It took me a long time to come to terms with that,' said Cadi. 'I kept asking myself why he'd chosen Jez in particular, but of course he hadn't. Jez was in the wrong place at the wrong time; it could've happened to any one of us had we been within his sights. The pilot of the Messerschmitt didn't know him from Adam. He was purely doing what he had been instructed to do. To create hell on earth, while destroying the base along with our morale. I dare say our boys do exactly the same to them when they go over there, the only difference being we didn't start this war, they did.'

Aled gazed steadily at Cadi. 'You're right. When we go over there we bomb them, the same way they do us. I don't feel bad about it, because they've left us with no choice. If we didn't retaliate they'd see it as a sign of weakness, and, believe me, they wouldn't stop until they'd wiped out every man, woman and child. It's the same when we're under attack: I don't stop to think of them as someone's father, son or husband, I just make sure that I'm the one who comes out on top, else it would be my family mourning and not theirs.'

They both fell silent as the barmaid arrived with their food. Placing the plates down on the table, she smiled expectantly at them both. 'Would you like any salt or vinegar?'

Covering her mouth to hide the half-eaten chip, Cadi nodded. 'Both, please.'

The woman quickly returned with the condiments, and Cadi sprinkled salt over her chips before passing the cellar to Aled. 'Everyone's saying that the war's going to be over soon,' she said. 'Do you think they're right, or is it wishful thinking?'

Aled appeared to be deep in thought as he placed some of his chips on one of the rounds of bread and butter. 'I'd say a huge part of it is wishful thinking, but at the same time I can't see it going on for much longer, not at its current pace.'

'I hope you're right, and that 1945 will be the year we finally see peace return to our world,' said Cadi. 'I dread to think what state the country will be in if we have to stick this out for another year.'

'I've been saying that too,' said Aled.

Cadi sliced her knife through the crunchy batter. 'Fish and chips used to be Jez's favourite, and the crunchier the batter the better. He'd have loved this.'

Aled was about to speak when they heard the all too familiar sound of the air raid siren. Lifting the bar flap, the barman called for everyone to head for the cellar, and Aled picked their plates up whilst Cadi gathered the cutlery. 'No sense in letting good food get cold,' he said as he followed the barmaid down the steps.

Taking a seat on one of the benches, Cadi smiled weakly at Aled. 'The last time I sheltered in a pub cellar was when we lost Carrie in the Greyhound.'

Aled gave her a reassuring smile. 'It's bound to be a false alarm, so try not to worry; lightning doesn't strike in the same place twice.' He handed her plate over. 'You'll feel better once you've got that down you.'

Cadi had taken a bite of the fish when the barman began to descend the steep steps. Losing his footing, he dropped the till, which crashed noisily down the remaining steps.

Her heart pounding in her chest, Cadi shot the barman a furious look as she swallowed the fish, and turned to Aled. 'Jez had been bringing the till down when the Greyhound got hit. The blast knocked him clean off his feet. I thought history was repeating itself for a moment there—' Suddenly, a wave of pain engulfed her entire body, and she grabbed hold of Aled's hand and squeezed it tightly. Struggling to regain her breath, she turned round eyes to Aled. 'What the hell was that?'

Aled stared at her, his face full of concern. 'What happened?'

She swallowed. 'That pain. I've never felt anything like it.'

Aled looked at the fish. 'It can't be the food, you've only had one bite.'

Cadi shook her head fervently. 'Definitely not the food, although I can't say what—' She stopped as another wave of pain took her over. Panting heavily, she stared fearfully at Aled, her gaze pleading for help. 'It's just happened again.' Her bottom lip trembled as tears formed in her eyes.

Kneeling down in front of her, Aled held her hands as he tried to reassure her. 'Where does it hurt?'

'My stomach,' she managed in between gasps. Another spasm racked her body, and she let out a low groan. 'Not just my stomach, it's everywhere...' Screwing her eyes shut, she cried out as the pain took the words from her lips, and as soon as it had passed she looked at Aled through frightened eyes. 'What's wrong with me?'

Still holding her hand in his, Aled used his free hand to push her hair back from her face which was beaded with sweat. He had little medical knowledge, but he knew that his mother had lost her brother from a burst appendix when they were children. Cupping the side of her face in the palm of his hand, he spoke in low, reassuring tones. 'I think you might have appendicitis.' Seeing the fear in

Cadi's eyes, he quickly glanced at the other people sheltering in the cellar. 'My friend is in need of urgent medical attention. Is there anyone here who can help?'

There was a general shaking of heads, and a ripple of 'No's' swept the cellar walls.

With tears beginning to fall, Cadi looked pleadingly at Aled. 'Am I going to die?'

Swallowing, Aled attempted to lift Cadi into his arms. 'Not on my watch. I'm taking you to hospital, air raid or no air raid.'

Much to his surprise, Cadi was shaking her head. Her cheeks flushed with embarrassment, she looked down at her skirt, which was wet through.

'I can't go in this state.'

'Bugger that,' said Aled. He slid his arms underneath her, but the barmaid who had just entered the cellar, was shaking her head.

'You can't move her, not in an air raid.' She smiled at Cadi. 'How far gone are you, luvvy?'

Cadi gasped, as yet another wave of unbelievable pain swept through her. When she could speak again, she said, 'What on earth do you mean by that?'

The barmaid turned to her husband, the landlord of the pub. 'I'll need lots of clean towels, and hot water. I'm no midwife, but I've given birth to my fair share.'

Nodding, the landlord disappeared to do his wife's bidding.

Cadi stared at the woman, her eyes rounding. 'Too right you're no midwife, cos if you were, you'd know I'm not pregnant!'

The barmaid smiled kindly at Cadi. 'I wouldn't have had you down for it when you walked in, but there's plenty who carry a baby well.'

Aled stared at the woman as though she were talking in a different language. 'What the hell are you on about? Cadi's not pregnant, she's got appendicitis, and hot water and towels will do sod all for that. We need to get her to a hospital before ...' He fell silent, unable to complete the sentence.

Cadi gaped at him. 'Before *what*?'

The barmaid laid a gentle but firm hand against Cadi's stomach. 'I know this must be scary. Gawd only knows, I'd be the same in your position, but this baby is coming whether you like it or not.' She broke off as her husband returned with a selection of assorted towels, sheets and blankets, and she instructed him to divide the cellar into two by using a couple of sheets. 'Keep everyone on the other side of that curtain, and I'll help this young lady bring this baby of hers into the world.'

Aled stared at the woman in disbelief. 'She can't be having a baby. You must've got it wrong.'

The woman indicated Cadi's stomach with a jerk of her head. 'That ain't Scotch mist in there.'

Grasping hold of Aled's arm, Cadi turned a tear-streaked face towards him. 'Please don't leave me, Aled. I don't want to die on my own.'

He smoothed her hair back from her face as he knelt beside her. 'You're not going to die, and I'm not going to leave you.'

He looked at the barmaid, who was kneeling at Cadi's other side. 'This is really happening, isn't it?'

She glanced up at him. 'I can see the baby's head.'

Aled swallowed hard before turning his attention back to Cadi. 'Are you sure you want me here?'

As another spasm engulfed her, Cadi held his hand in a vice-like grip. 'Don't you dare leave me, Aled Davies.' Panting hard, she fought to control her emotions, which were threatening to get the better of her. 'I can't do this. It's going to have to wait for another day or two, until I can get to a hospital ...'

'I'm afraid you don't get to call the shots. Your baby is ready to be born, and you're going to have to push, but only when I tell you to.' The barmaid slapped a wet cloth into Aled's outstretched hand. 'Mop her brow, and for God's sake don't let her go to pieces, cos I can't do this on my own.'

Nodding, he turned his back to what he later described as the 'business end' and focused on Cadi. 'You know I'd never leave you, so you needn't worry about being on your own. I'll see you right, no matter what happens.'

She broke into a fresh bout of tears. 'How could I not have known.' She stopped speaking as the barmaid told her to push, not that she needed telling; the urge to push was so overwhelming she was finding it difficult to only do so when instructed. Panting heavily, she gulped back her tears. 'Jez is a father and he didn't even know.'

Aled glanced up to the ceiling of the cellar. 'He knows. He'll be up there cheering you on, telling you that you're doing a marvellous job and that he's proud of you.'

She gripped Aled's hand so tightly his knuckles whitened. With the barmaid instructing her to give one final push, Cadi roared like a lioness as she brought her baby into the world.

It was many hours after the air raid siren had given the all-clear, and the landlord and his wife had very kindly allowed Cadi the use of one of the rooms in their B&B.

Holding her baby boy, who was swaddled snugly in a clean towel, Cadi beamed through her tears as she gazed down at the precious bundle. Hearing someone knock on the door, she called for them to enter.

A woman wearing a midwife's uniform came in, and spoke cheerfully to Cadi and Aled. 'I hear you've had quite a surprise.'

Cadi, who had hardly taken her eyes off her son, glanced up momentarily. 'You can say that again. My husband was killed in an air raid in May and I hadn't the foggiest idea that I was pregnant until today. How is that possible?'

Feeling awkward, Aled thought he should make his position clear to the midwife. 'I'm a friend of the family. I was here to help Cadi through her first Christmas without Jez.'

The midwife waved a carefree hand. 'She's lucky you were.' She walked over to the baby, and smiled approvingly. 'Considering he's premature, he's a bonny lad. I'm surprised you had no symptoms, but that's a cryptic pregnancy for you.'

Cadi stared at her blankly. 'What's a cryptic pregnancy?'

The midwife took the baby from Cadi and examined him whilst she spoke. 'It's when a mother doesn't have the normal symptoms that you'd expect with pregnancy, such as lower back pain, or morning sickness—'

Cadi cut her short. 'But I was sick a few months ago. I did go to the doctor, but he said it was down to the stress caused by the sudden loss of my husband.'

The midwife rolled her eyes. 'Doctors don't know everything.' She glanced at Cadi's stomach. 'I'm assuming you didn't have a baby bump?'

Cadi shook her head. 'Not even slightly.'

'She was eating liver like it was going on ration,' Aled put in.

Standing, the midwife wrapped the baby up before turning to Aled. 'It's often the way with pregnant ladies. I need to check Mrs Thomas over, so if you wouldn't mind stepping out for a few minutes?'

Aled got to his feet. 'She's all yours.' He smiled at Cadi. 'I'll just be on the other side of that door should you need me.'

'Thanks, Aled.'

Outside the room, he sank down on to the floor. It had been a long night, and he'd hardly left Cadi's side. Hearing someone ascending the stairs, he gave a nod of acknowledgement as the landlord came into view. 'The midwife's in with her now,' he said as the landlord sat down next to him.

'Poor mare. What a thing to happen to you, especially after losing your husband,' said the man. 'I gather she's a sergeant in the WAAF, and she obviously had no idea that this was coming, so what'll happen when her leave's up? Because I can't see them letting her back on base with a babby in her arms.'

Aled rested his head in his hands. 'God knows. I'll make a few phone calls, let everyone know who needs to know, and go from there.' He shrugged. 'She's a Liverpool lass at heart, but her family hale from the hills, so she could always go back there if need be. Personally I reckon she'll opt to stay with her husband's adoptive family in Liverpool because that's where she was calling home before joining the WAAF, and I know they'll be eager to have her.'

He spoke slowly. 'How do you know her, if you don't mind my asking?'

Aled shook his head. 'Not at all. We grew up in the same village, and met again not long after I joined the RAF.' He gave the man a sidelong glance. 'Her husband would have made a brilliant father. Why is it that all the good ones die young?'

The barman blew his cheeks out. 'I've been asking myself that since the war began. We've three sons, all of them serving in France. We've been lucky so far, but we live in constant fear of receiving a telegram.'

'Poor Cadi's lost two family members, the first being her husband's grandmother when they were sheltering in a pub cellar. Her husband – or fiancé as he was then – had been carrying the till down when the blast knocked him off his feet.'

The landlord clapped a hand to his forehead. 'So when I dropped the till ...'

Aled nodded. 'I think it sent her into early labour.' He rolled his eyes. 'And there I was insisting she had appendicitis.'

They looked up as the midwife came out of the room and closed the door behind her. 'Considering she had no idea she was pregnant, both mother and baby are doing well, but she's extremely anxious about what's going to happen.' She glanced at the landlord. 'Is there any chance she could stay here overnight?'

He nodded fervently. 'Course she can.'

Aled plunged his hand into his pocket as he got to his feet. 'I'll pay for her room and board.'

The landlord waved him away. 'Put your money away, son. This one's on the house.'

Thanking him for his generosity, Aled went back into the room, where he found Cadi lying on her side, with the baby beside her.

'I've just been talking to the midwife and the landlord,' he explained. 'She says you're doing really well, under the circumstances, and the landlord says you can stay here overnight.'

Cadi heaved a sigh of relief. 'Can you do me a favour?'

'Telephone Fiskerton?'

She nodded. 'Someone's got to, and I haven't got the strength.' She indicated her son. 'How do I explain this one? They'll think I've gone stark raving mad.'

He laid a reassuring hand over hers. 'Don't worry, I'll sort everything out. You just stay here and look after yourself and ...' He hesitated. 'Have you thought of a name yet?'

She gently stroked the baby's face with the tip of her forefinger. 'Oscar Dewi.' She smiled at Aled. 'Oscar was Jez's middle name, and of course Dewi after my father – we decided on names a long time ago, which was a good job when you think about it.'

'It certainly was.' Leaning forward, he twitched the swaddling to one side. 'Welcome to the world, little Oscar. You're going to be seeing a lot of me, cos I'm your Uncle Aled, and I'm going to take good care of you and your mother whether she likes it or not!'

Cadi called after him as he turned to leave the room. 'Thank you for everything, Aled. I don't know what I'd have done had you not been with me. In fact, I do know what I'd have done – I'd have gone to pieces, that's what. You're a real star, you do know that, don't you?'

Thankful that she couldn't see his face, he blushed. 'Anyone would've done the same in my shoes.'

Her brow rose to her hairline. 'I beg to differ. Not many husbands would choose to be in the same room when their wives are giving birth, let alone friends. You went above and beyond for me, and I'll never forget that.'

It was several weeks after the birth of the baby, and Cadi's life had changed beyond recognition. After Aled had telephoned Fiskerton, word had spread like wildfire and it wasn't long before everyone knew of Oscar's unexpected arrival. Fiskerton had let her go without any disciplinary action for leaving her duties, and Cadi had opted to live in the Belmont, where she said she felt closer to Jez.

'I do wish you'd consider bringing him home to Rhos,' Jill had said when Cadi rang to give her mother the news. 'It's too dangerous in the city.'

'It's safer here now than it was during the early years,' said Cadi reasonably, 'and I feel it's where I need to be. But don't worry, Mam. I promise to take plenty of photographs and you can come and see him whenever you want.'

'But he has a family here,' objected Jill. 'Grandparents as well as three uncles.'

'And would you see him working down the pits, just like his grandfather and uncles?' said Cadi. 'Because there's very little choice for him in Rhos, you know there is.'

It had been enough to sway her parents into respecting their daughter's wishes, and with no more to be said on the subject they had set about making arrangements to come and see their grandson in Liverpool.

Raquel had been overjoyed to hear that she was a grandmother and with her being based in Burtonwood she saw Oscar on a fairly regular basis. The girls had rushed over to the pub the very next day so that they could meet Oscar for themselves.

'He's better than a puppy,' Poppy had cooed, causing everyone to laugh.

'He's the most beautiful baby I've ever laid eyes on,' Izzy had agreed. 'Jez would be proud as punch.'

They had both made a real fuss over Aled for being there for their friend, but he had dismissed the praise, saying that he was just in the right place at the right time.

Now, as she stood in the kitchen to the Belmont, Cadi rocked the baby's crib with the toe of her shoe as she rolled out a sheet of pastry.

'Aled's been marvellous,' she told Maria. 'But even though I know he means well, I don't want him to think Oscar's his responsibility.'

Maria pulled a face. 'Have you ever thought that this might be his way of making things up to Jez?'

Cadi nodded fervently. 'I'm positive it is, but I have to make him see that he's done more than enough already, by being there for me. It's impractical for him to spend the rest of his days looking after me and Oscar, not when he's got his own life to lead. On top of which, Oscar and I will need to make our own way in the world without relying on anyone else.'

Maria leaned over the cot and smiled. 'He's the image of his father.'

Cadi placed the pastry in the tray, then used a knife to slice off the excess. 'I see Jez every time I look into Oscar's eyes. It makes me feel as though I've got him back, if only a little bit.' She hesitated. 'Is it silly of me to think that Oscar was Jez's parting gift to me?'

Maria held a hand to her heart. 'Not in the least. In fact, I think that's a lovely way of looking at it. Because a baby is a gift.'

Cadi flattened the pastry down with pie weights before placing it in the oven to blind bake. 'I had no intention of leaving the WAAF until I was demobbed at the end of the war,' she reminded Maria. 'I scoffed at the suggestion that I should come back to the Belmont to recuperate after losing Jez because I wanted to keep my focus on seeing the war out. But having this little one has changed my whole perspective.'

'It's called putting your family first,' said Maria. 'You knew where he had to be, and you brought him here.' She grimaced fleetingly. 'I feel ever so sorry for your parents being so far away, but you could hardly take him back to Rhos.'

Cadi gazed lovingly at her son. 'Jez and I both love Liverpool, and I want Oscar to be a Scouser just like his father. When he's old enough I'm going to show him all the places his father used to go: where we first met, where Jez used to work, and where his Auntie Izzy and Nana Taylor used to live.'

'You're doing right by him,' said Maria, 'and that's what a good mother should do. Besides, you can always take him to Rhos on holiday. He'll love it there as much as he'll love Liverpool.'

Cadi began to peel the potatoes ready for the evening meal. 'I fully intend to show him where his Auntie Poppy and I went to school, as well as where we worked before leaving for Liverpool. I want him to know that you can have anything you want in life if you put your mind to it.'

Maria smiled approvingly. 'I can't think of a better example than his mother.'

The telephone rang, and Cadi wiped her hands on a dishcloth before going through and picking up the receiver.

'Belmont Hotel, Cadi speaking. How may I help you?'

'You can start by telling Oscar's Uncle Aled how he's getting on,' said Aled.

Cadi smiled fondly. 'He's doing brilliantly. He's putting weight on hand over fist, not that he needed to, and he smiles from dawn to dusk.'

'That's what I like to hear!' said Aled cheerfully. 'And how's Oscar's mam?'

She leaned against the hall table. 'Being a mother is like flying by the seat of your pants,' she said, 'and even though we're ever so grateful for Uncle Aled's contributions—'

Guessing that Cadi was about to suggest that Aled should stop depositing cheques into her account, Aled cut across her. 'I can't see what's wrong with my wanting to spoil my adoptive nephew. It's not as if I've got any others.'

'I know you don't, and we really do appreciate what you've done for us, but if you knew me at all, Aled Davies, and by God I know you do, you'd know that I'm fiercely independent, and I don't like taking handouts, no matter who they're from.'

'I do indeed,' conceded Aled, 'but this has nothing to do with independence, or not as far as I'm concerned. The money is a gift to use as you see fit. If you don't need it for clothes, or food, or nappies, then you could always pop it into a fund for him for when he's older, I really don't mind what you do with it, as long as you use it to make your life a little easier.'

'That really is very kind of you—' Cadi began, but Aled interrupted her.

'Good, I'm glad you think so. Now that we've sorted that out, you can tell me what's going on in Liverpool, and how wonderful it is to not to wake up to reveille every morning.'

He'd changed the subject decisively, and Cadi knew it was pointless to argue. 'Liverpool's much the same. The Belmont's thriving, and we're busier than we ever were in the Greyhound. As for not waking up to reveille, Oscar would give even the most enthusiastic trumpeter a run for their money.'

Aled laughed. 'Fine set of lungs eh? He probably gets that from his mother, cos as I recall, you couldn't half give someone a good ear bashing if they'd rubbed you up the wrong way.'

Cadi snorted on a chuckle. 'I was only like that with you.' She hesitated. 'And Daphne, of course.'

He rolled his eyes. 'Not the dreaded Daphne.' Hearing Cadi giggle, he continued, 'In all seriousness, I'm glad to hear that it's working out for you, because I realise it can't have been easy leaving the WAAF and starting a new life as a mother. Especially when you weren't prepared for it – although I suppose mother-hood comes naturally.'

Cadi gave a short laugh. 'Then you suppose wrong. Motherhood definitely doesn't come naturally; it's bloomin' hard work with very little thanks.'

A smile twitched his lips. 'So sleepless nights, stinky nappies and puking babies aren't for everyone, then?'

She eyed him with amusement. 'Sounds like you've done this before.'

He shook his head, even though she couldn't see him. 'Nope, but I've birthed plenty of animals, which is stressful in itself.'

'Do you hold their hooves the way you held my hand?' chuckled Cadi.

He grimaced. 'Unfortunately not. I tend to play the part of the midwife when on the farm. I've put my hands into places no man should venture.'

She smiled, curiously. 'Aled, I had no idea you were so …' she hesitated as she found the correct word, 'nurturing.'

He pulled a face. 'I'd not be a farmer if I wasn't. Unless you're an arable farmer, the whole point is to rear animals, whether it be for meat, milk, or wool.'

'I remember you saying that Marnie might see you in a different light if she saw you up to your knees in pig poop. I agreed with you at the time, but with hindsight I think you're wrong. I think any woman who sees a man bringing life into the world sees a man that's to be admired.'

Aled's cheeks grew warm. 'Maybe I should mention that when I next ask a woman on a date.'

She ran her finger down the telephone wire. 'I thought you'd sworn off women?'

He rubbed his hand across the back of his head. 'I have – at least for the time being. I was talking metaphorically.'

'You'll find someone,' said Cadi. 'You're too great a catch to stay single, which brings me to another point. I know you're not going to like what I'm about to say, but I want you to hear me out.'

'Go on, I'm listening.'

Cadi drew a deep breath before continuing. 'Part of the reason why I wanted you to stop being so generous was because no woman wants a man who has ties to another woman, be it friendly or otherwise. You deserve to be happy, and I've already driven a wedge between you and Marnie. I know I didn't mean to, but surely you must see what I'm getting at?'

'I do,' said Aled, 'but it's my life, and when I do start courting she's going to have to accept that you're a part of it. In short, she can like it or lump it.'

'Is there nothing I can say to prove to you that you needn't feel obliged to keep giving us money?'

He scratched the newly formed stubble on his chin. 'Nope.'

Realising that it was futile to keep arguing, she changed the subject. 'So, when are you coming to see your godson?'

Aled stood in stunned silence before finding his tongue. 'Really? Are you sure?'

Cadi nodded. 'I'm as sure as eggs is eggs. It's not only what I want: I *know* Jez would've wanted it too.'

'But what about Bill? He's ...' Aled began before Cadi interrupted.

'Bill's his Grandpa Smyth – he can't be both.' She paused. 'You don't have to if you'd rather not.'

'Only I do,' said Aled quickly, 'in fact I'd be honoured. No one's ever asked me to be a godfather before. And besides, I've now got every right to spoil my godson!'

Cadi rolled her eyes. 'You've got me there.'

She could hear the excitement in Aled's voice. 'When's the christening?'

She puffed her cheeks out. 'Whenever we can get everyone together, which is going to be nigh on impossible when you think of the guest list.'

'It would be easier if you had the christening in Lincoln,' he commented, 'but I'm guessing you'll want it wherever Jez was christened.'

'Spot on! Oscar's going to be christened in the church where Jez was both christened and laid to rest.' A faint smile crossed her lips. 'Not only will it be in keeping with family tradition, but I'll feel a lot closer to Jez doing it that way.'

'I think that's a splendid idea. I don't suppose you've a date in mind? Just so that I know what leave to aim for.'

Having already discussed the matter at length with her friends, Cadi shrugged. 'When I spoke to the girls, they said they'd heard a rumour that the services were planning to cancel all leave when things really started heating up. As none of us know when that will be, I'd like to have the christening sooner rather than later. I don't suppose you've got any leave booked already?'

Aled had been pushing for leave ever since Cadi had left the WAAF, but the most he had managed to get so far was three days in March. He said as much to Cadi. 'I could've come sooner if I hadn't had Christmas off.'

'I know that Kitty's in the same boat as yourself, because she also booked Christmas off, but the others have leave owing, so it's going to take some juggling. I shall tell them all when you're off and see if they can match your dates.'

'Splendid! Who's the godmother, by the way, or should I guess?'

She laughed. 'Guess, although it's fairly obvious.'

He pretended to mull it over before putting his suggestion forward. 'Poppy?'

'Like I said, fairly obvious,' said Cadi.

'It's funny how life turns out; I remember the time you swore blind that you'd never marry, let alone have kids, yet look at you now.'

'I suppose it's called growing up,' said Cadi. 'Believe you me, I've had to do a fair bit of that lately.'

He smiled. 'We've all grown up since then. When you look back, even though we were in our late teens we were still kids who thought we knew better than anyone else – or at least I did.'

'I can't believe Poppy and I left home as young as we did,' confessed Cadi. 'Dad was right when he said that we were still wet behind the ears.' She laughed. 'I stormed out of the room, because I couldn't believe he'd said such a thing, but looking back he was absolutely right. We hadn't a clue what we were doing, and we wandered into the worst part of Liverpool like lambs to the slaughter.'

'You weren't the only one who ignored their parents' wishes,' said Aled, 'I applied for the RAF behind my parents' backs. Dad was livid when he found out what I'd done. I thought he was being unfair, not to mention denying me a better future, but of course he was only looking out for me.'

Cadi smiled. 'You didn't need looking after.'

His brow shot upwards. 'Do you really think that? Because I don't. If I'd had a bit of nous, I'd have kicked up a real fuss over my pilot's exam results, because even though I questioned it I never took it any further. How could I have been so naive?'

'Because you've not got a bad bone in your body, and it didn't occur to you that someone would do something like that to you.' Cadi tutted irritably. 'I've often wondered what you saw in that woman.'

'She was eager to be with me, and you were spoken for,' said Aled truthfully.

Cadi laughed. 'Don't try and lay the blame at my door, Aled Davies. There were plenty more fish in the sea.'

'True, but I wasn't interested in any of them,' said Aled, 'and once I knew I couldn't make pilot she seemed the obvious choice.' He shook his head. 'It's a funny old world.'

Inevitably, the operator cut across their call.

'Looks like that's us told,' he said ruefully. 'Don't forget to keep me in the loop regarding the christening.'

'Will do. T.t.f.n.'

'Ta-ra, Cadi. Take care.'

Replacing the receiver, Aled walked back to his hut. He knew that he had no obligation towards Oscar, but he wanted to do all he could to help the two of them out, and if that meant sending money every week then that's what he'd do. No ulterior motives, no hopes of getting his feet under the table; he just wanted Cadi to be as happy as she could be under the circumstances, and to know that she was not as alone as she believed herself to be. When he had first heard that she was intent on going back to Liverpool he had wanted to talk her out of it, fearing that the city – a major port – was too dangerous, but he knew that Cadi had to settle where she was happiest, and if that was Liverpool, then he would make sure he shot down every German plane within his sights, so that they might never darken its skies again.

Cadi entered the kitchen to see Maria fussing over Oscar. She smiled. 'Now why aren't I surprised to see Nana Smyth giving out cuddles?'

Maria gave her a guilty grin. 'You know I can't resist. He's only got to look at me with those big brown eyes, and I'm putty in his hands!'

Cadi placed her arm around Maria's shoulders. 'Jez always did say that you'd make a terrific mother, but

298

as far as I'm concerned you're a fantastic grandmother, and I know Jez would agree with me.'

Maria smiled lovingly at the small bundle in her arms. 'You've made me the happiest Scouser this side of Liverpool,' she told Cadi. 'Lookin' after this one is an honour, and I shall be proud to tell everyone that he's my grandson.' She stopped short, remembering the telephone call. 'Who was that on the phone?'

'Aled, and he said yes to being a godfather, but no to stopping the payments.'

Maria made gurgling noises at the baby before turning her attention back to Cadi. 'I knew he wouldn't stop the money; he cares about you too much.'

'I know, which is why I've decided to start a trust fund for Oscar. As Aled says, I can't ask his godfather not to spoil him.' She sighed. 'I hope he finds himself a woman who sees what a big heart he has, because he doesn't deserve to be on his own.'

'Neither do you,' said Maria. 'I know it's still too early for you to move on, but I'm hoping that in time you'll find someone who makes you happy, and start your life anew.'

Cadi appeared doubtful. 'Not many men will want to take on a single mother.'

'Jez would've married you if you had a gaggle of kiddies in tow, so don't go throwing yourself on to the scrap heap just yet.'

Cadi smiled, but said nothing. She knew that Maria, Raquel and her mother were keen for her to find a new beau when the time was right, but Cadi was happy on her own, and she very much doubted that would ever change.

February 1945

Aled left the debriefing room with the rest of his crew.

'What did you make of that, then?' said Tom as he jogged up alongside his friend.

Aled clapped a hand on to Tom's shoulder. 'It looks to me as though things are finally coming to a head, and if everything goes the way they're planning it shouldn't be too much longer before this whole thing is over.'

'What if it doesn't go their way?' said Tom dubiously. 'Cos if the Krauts have second-guessed our plans, or laid a trap, then we'll be sitting ducks – or lambs to the slaughter.' He blew a low whistle. 'With over eight hundred of Britain's finest darkening the skies, it's not like we'll be hard to see.'

Aled pushed his hands into his pockets. 'Bomber squadron are going to be the heroes of this war, Tom, and that's summat to be proud of. Although it does put a bit of a spanner in the works as far as Oscar's christening goes.'

Tom nodded thoughtfullly. 'I hope all this "don't book any leave for the foreseeable" doesn't go on for too long.'

'That makes you, me and everyone else in the services,' said Aled, as he turned to veer off towards the NAAFI. 'As I've had my leave cancelled I'm going to have to make a couple of phone calls, so I'll catch up with you in a bit.'

Aled's jaw practically hit the floor once he got inside the NAAFI. The queue for the phone went from one side of the room to the other. It seemed that everyone was keen to phone home and explain the new circumstances. Standing in line, he tried to think of a way in which he could see Cadi and Oscar before things got really intense. Briefly, he considered the idea of her coming to Lincoln, but it was one heck of a train journey to undertake with a small baby. He could always go to Liverpool if he wasn't flying, but he would have to be back the same day. He supposed it would be possible if he left in the early hours, and there weren't too many hold-ups. He toyed with the idea of going by car, as he had the day of Jez's funeral, but if petrol rationing had made it difficult back then, it would be even worse now.

He tapped his forefinger against his mouth as he pondered the timescale. If he did go to Liverpool he would be spending most of the day on the train. He'd only get a couple of hours with Cadi, but that would be better than nothing; certainly enough time to make sure that she was all right, and that finding herself a widowed mother hadn't had an adverse effect on her general health, as it had when she had lost Jez. Even though they now put her earlier sickness down to being pregnant, Aled still believed the trauma of losing Jez must have had some part to play in her weight loss.

For the first time in a long while, Aled was thankful that the operator was keeping a strict limit on calls, but it still seemed an age before he reached the head of the queue. Picking up the receiver, he asked for the Belmont in Liverpool, and was happy to hear Cadi's voice come down the phone.

'Hello, Aled. I'm guessing you're telephoning to say what the girls have already told me: your leave's been cancelled and you can't book any more until further notice.'

He grimaced. 'I'm afraid so, but at least it's for a good reason.'

'I really hope so, because it's unfair to ask everyone to wait indefinitely.' She hesitated. 'I love being a mum, but hearing everyone talking excitedly about leave being cancelled makes me yearn for the days when I too was in the thick of things. I know none of you can say too much over the phone, but I think it all sounds promising, don't you?'

'Very much so,' Aled agreed. 'I was thinking about coming down to see you, even if it's only for a few hours. Time permitting, of course. What do you think?'

'I think it would be lovely, but there's no way I'm asking you to spend a whole day travelling when you've got to be on your toes in the back of that plane. Good God, Aled, I'd never forgive myself if summat happened to you. And that's why I've decided to come to Lincoln for a couple of nights.'

Aled gasped. 'Are you sure that's a good idea? It's a hell of a long way, and I don't think Oscar will enjoy it much.'

'Maria has very kindly offered to come with me,' said Cadi, 'so you needn't worry about my travelling all that way with a small baby.' She grinned. 'Mind you, if Oscar decides the journey's not to his liking, we might have the carriage to ourselves should he choose to voice his thoughts.'

Aled chuckled softly. 'Every cloud, eh?'

'Exactly.'

'Any ideas as to when you're thinking of coming over?'

'We've booked a room for the last weekend in March. We may not be able to see you all at the same time, but as long as we get to see everyone at some point, I can't ask for more than that.'

'Which hotel are you staying at?'

'We're booked in at the Adam and Eve; it was the last place I stayed with Jez. It's a lovely tavern and I know the landlord well.'

'Will going back there not upset you?' Aled asked tentatively.

'No, if anything I'm looking forward to it *because* I stayed there with Jez. I find I'm happier reliving memories, than I was when I was trying to avoid the past.'

Aled brightened considerably. His friend was sounding a lot better than she had a few weeks back. 'Perhaps we can all have dinner together,' he said. 'My treat.'

'Sounds good to me,' said Cadi.

As expected, the operator cut across them, and Aled glanced at the queue behind him, which was as long as it was when he first entered the NAAFI.

'I've got to go, kiddo. There's plenty more wanting to use the phone this end.'

'I look forward to seeing you in a couple of weeks,' said Cadi. 'Give me a call whenever you've the time, but I won't expect too much, because I know how busy you all are.'

'Will do. Hwyl fawr, cariad.'

Cadi smiled. Only her family and Aled spoke Welsh to her, but she was determined to bring Oscar up to speak both languages.

'Goodbye, Aled. Hwyl fawr.'

Replacing the handset, Cadi turned to Maria, who was playing peekaboo with Oscar but took a moment to say, 'Let me guess. Another one who's been told to stay put?'

Cadi nodded. 'It really looks as though things are heating up. I don't know whether I dare to believe that we really could be coming to the end.'

Still peeping between her fingers for the amusement of Oscar, who was chortling with delight, Maria said, 'We shall all sleep a lot easier in our beds when those rotten Krauts surrender.'

Cadi pulled a doubtful face. 'I don't wish to appear pessimistic, but I've learned not to count my chickens before they've hatched.'

Maria wiped the dribble away from Oscar's chin. 'I don't blame you. I want things to go our way, of course I do, but I'm tired of getting my hopes up just to have them dashed. I take it Aled said yes to meeting in Lincoln?'

'He did indeed.' Watching Oscar gurgling happily, Cadi turned an anxious face to Maria. 'Mam always used to say you should never back an animal into a corner, because if you do, it'll come out fighting. Do you think that will be the same for the Krauts? Only if they think they're losing, surely they'll throw everything they've got at us in a last-ditch attempt to secure victory.'

Maria placed a reassuring hand over Cadi's. 'I know you're worried about your friends, because I am too, but I really think we're on the home stretch and Hitler's on his way out, which is why we're throwing everything we've got at him.'

'But what about Aled?' said Cadi. 'I just know they'll be sending him over to Germany. They'd not have cancelled his leave otherwise.'

Maria soothed Oscar, who was beginning to get tetchy. 'Aled's been lucky so far, who's to say his luck won't continue?'

'I hope so, Maria, because he's been an absolute rock since Jez passed.'

It was the last weekend in March and Maria and Cadi were anxiously awaiting the arrival of their friends in the bar area of the Adam and Eve.

Rumours were rife that the end of the war was in sight, and as Cadi had predicted Hitler had been bombarding Britain with his V1s and V2s in a last attempt to destroy the morale of the British people.

When the pub door swung open, Cadi beamed as Poppy and Izzy entered, smiling fit to burst as they hurried over to where Cadi was sitting with Oscar in her arms.

'You've no idea how much we've missed you,' Izzy told Cadi as she held out her hands for her nephew. She gave a small squeal of delight as Cadi gently placed the baby in her arms. 'I can't wait for this rotten war to be over, so that we can all be together again.' She smiled down at Oscar, who gazed happily back. 'Doesn't he look like Jez?' Izzy's eyes were shining with happy tears. 'You must be so proud of him.'

'Immensely. And we all think he looks like Jez; in fact I'd say he looks more and more like him with every day that passes.'

'He doesn't just look like Jez,' added Maria, 'I'd say that being born in the cellar of a pub is very Jez, if you know what I mean?'

'No airs and graces,' agreed Poppy, 'that was our Jez to a tee. Rough round the edges, but a prince amongst men.' She watched as Izzy continued to gaze lovingly into her nephew's eyes. 'I wish he could see us now.'

Cadi glanced around the pub. 'Who's to say he can't?' She lowered her voice so that only the three of them could hear her. 'I've worked the dates out, and we must have conceived Oscar whilst we were staying here on our sort-of honeymoon.'

'I hope he can see him,' said Poppy as she took the baby from Izzy's arms. 'What did Raquel say when she visited?'

'She cried a lot,' said Cadi; 'we both did. Having Oscar feels as though we've got a tiny part of Jez back.'

'I can't think of a better goodbye present,' said Izzy, much to the delight of Maria and Cadi who told the girls of their conversation about a parting gift.

'Great minds think alike,' said Poppy.

'Have you any news on the war?' asked Cadi eagerly. 'It's obvious that things are coming to a head, but how close are we, do you think?'

Poppy and Izzy exchanged glances. 'We really can't say, and not because we know summat we've been told not to tell, cos we don't. But it's as though we're part of a really big secret that nobody's told us about,' said Izzy. 'Everyone's running round like headless chickens, and even though we *know* summat big's about to happen, whenever we ask they say that the information's on a need-to-know basis.'

Faint lines furrowed Cadi's brow. 'Surely they can't be saying that to aircrew?'

Izzy pulled a face. 'I think Mike knows more than he's letting on, but he's probably been sworn to secrecy, and I don't like to push him, so I tend to leave sleeping dogs lie.'

'Geoffrey doesn't say much either,' said Poppy. 'I reckon they're pretty much in the dark same as the rest of us.'

'It's infuriating knowing that something's going on, but not what,' said Cadi. 'The newsreels don't tell you much, but then again I suppose they can't really, can they?'

Poppy sank down on the seat next to Cadi's. 'I think it's going to be over before we know it. Call it what you will, whether that be women's intuition, or a feeling in my waters. But enough of the war. How's this little one getting on? He's certainly gained a few pounds!'

'Hasn't he just,' agreed Cadi. 'He's just started to sleep through the night, and he's loving life.'

'Do you know what time Aled's arriving?' asked Izzy.

'He's coming over for dinner this evening,' said Cadi.

'I think it's lovely the way he's looking out for you and Oscar,' said Poppy. 'That Marnie threw away a good man for no reason.'

'If she could see how wonderful he's been with me and Oscar she'd—'

Izzy interrupted without apology. '… Say that she was right to dump him because it's obvious he's in love with you.'

Cadi opened her mouth to object and then thought better of it, because Izzy was quite possibly right. 'I have told him to stop sending money, in case his next belle gets the wrong idea, but he's determined to keep on.'

Izzy took another turn in holding Oscar. 'Have you thought any more about what you're going to do next?'

307

'I have to leave the Belmont at some point,' Cadi began, only to have Maria interrupt with an opinion of her own.

'You don't *have* to do anything. You know Bill and I would love it if you stayed.'

'You know I think the world of you and Bill, and that I'll always be grateful to you for taking me in, but I want to see Jez's and my dream come to fruition.'

Poppy stared at her. 'Surely you're not still thinking about getting your own pub?'

Cadi nodded. 'I know that after Jez died I thought I couldn't bear to do it without him, but I've changed my mind. It'll be a secure future for myself and Oscar, and I know the hospitality business inside out.' She shrugged. 'And I'm good at it.'

'I don't want to put a spanner in the works,' Izzy grimaced, 'but how will you be able to afford it?'

'Hard work and determination,' said Cadi. 'I know it won't be easy ...'

Maria shot her a chiding glance. 'Won't be easy? The brewery handing over the keys to a woman on her own with a child in tow? Try nigh on impossible. Don't forget, Cadi, I only got my name above the door of the Greyhound because Bill went off to war. Once I'd proved myself to the brewery, they were content to hand me the keys to the Belmont, but they keep a closer eye on me than they do on any of their male landlords. You must remember the time your father shopped us to the brewery for you being underage. They were willing to accept his word despite the fact he'd never set foot in the pub, but if he'd tried that with Bill in charge they'd not have taken any notice.'

But Cadi sat firm. 'They'll have to give me summat, because I'm not backing down until they do!'

They spent the next couple of hours planning what sort of pub Cadi would like, and how they would come and stay with her whenever they got the chance.

With evening fast approaching, Izzy and Poppy returned to Fiskerton, and Cadi felt that this goodbye had been like no other. 'I've never seen the girls so nervous,' she told Maria when the girls left the pub.

Maria nodded. 'Me neither. It's as though everybody knows that this is the last hurrah, and if it doesn't work ...' She shook her head sadly. 'We'd best hope and pray that it does.' She sighed. 'I thought I might take Oscar for a stroll when Aled arrives. What do you think?'

Cadi pulled a downward smile. 'What about dinner?'

'I'll get fish and chips down the road.' Maria hesitated briefly before continuing, 'You and Aled haven't seen each other since the night you gave birth. I should imagine you've got quite a bit to talk about. Besides, I'm no good at goodbyes, and just knowing that the man's going into battle' – she shuddered as a shiver ran down her spine – 'chills me to the bone.'

Cadi pulled a grim face. 'I know what you mean. Wishing him good luck doesn't quite cover it, when we know the magnitude of the task ahead of them, and what's more you can bet your life that the Germans won't give up quietly. This is going to be one hell of a fight.'

Aled walked into the pub as the last words left Cadi's lips. Smiling at the women, he waved a cheery hello before ordering himself a drink and making his way over. 'Anyone in need of a top-up?'

Maria held up a hand to decline. 'I'm going to take Oscar for a walk before it gets dark. I've told Cadi that I'll grab myself a fish and chip supper whilst I'm out.'

Aled's face fell. 'I hope you're not leaving on my account, because I fully intended for the three of us to have dinner together.'

Maria spoke quietly as she settled Oscar into the pram. 'It's lovely of you to offer, but we've been sitting in this pub for most of the day, and truth be told I could really do with stretching my legs.'

Aled glanced expectantly at Cadi, who agreed. 'I'll have a glass of lemonade, please.'

Aled went to fetch the drinks and Maria rearranged the blankets over Oscar who was starting to stir. 'Looks like I'm leaving in the nick of time,' she said, just as the baby opened his lungs to let the world know that he was awake.

Aled stepped away from the bar as Maria passed by. Leaning down, he smiled affectionately at Oscar, who had been quick to settle under the motion of the pram. 'He's looking well,' he noted, 'and so's Cadi, come to that.' He glanced at Maria quizzically. 'Is she doing as well as she appears to be?'

Maria nodded. 'She's doing better than any of us expected given the circumstances. She's made of stern stuff is that one, and she always comes up fighting. She's already set her sights firmly on the future; I just hope she gets everything she wants.'

He wrinkled his forehead. 'How do you mean?'

'She wants to fulfil her and Jez's dream of getting up a pub, but I know the trade inside out, and they won't want to give a licence to a single mother. I've told Cadi my thoughts, but she's determined that she can make it on will alone.'

Aled nodded. 'Sounds like the Cadi we all know and love, which is excellent news; and quite frankly, if anyone can persuade the brewery I reckon it's her.'

'I hope you're right and that she's successful, even though I'll miss them terribly,' said Maria. 'I've never had a baby of my own, so I've loved every minute of having this one around. The Belmont will be like an empty shell when they move out.'

Aled winked at her. 'Cadi won't see you short of cuddles.'

'I know she won't. Our Cadi's got a heart of gold, and she's forever putting others' needs before her own. I reckon it's about time things went her way for once.'

'I'll keep an eye out for her,' said Aled, 'and I'll always be around to lend a helping hand should she need it.' He beamed down at Oscar. 'I wouldn't consider myself much of a godfather if I wasn't!'

'You're a good lad, Aled,' said Maria, turning away quickly to shush Oscar, who was beginning to fidget. Aled went over to the door and opened it wide so that Maria could push the coach-style pram through unhindered.

'I hope I'll get to see you before I go,' he said as she passed by.

She smiled. 'I'll make sure I'm back in time.'

As she made her way down the pavement, Maria reflected on how sad it was that Aled and Cadi would never be a couple, purely because of their past history. *He'd make a wonderful stepfather, and he loves our Cadi with all his heart*, Maria thought to herself. *He'd do anything for the two of them. I hope they see past their history one day, because they'd make a lovely couple.*

Aled took the drinks over to Cadi, who was stifling a yawn with the back of her hand.

'Are you sure you don't want to go and put your feet up for an hour or so?' he said, laying the drinks down on the table. 'I'd quite understand it if you did, because I should imagine the journey over wasn't relaxing.'

Cadi laughed. 'That's an understatement. Oscar was wide awake the whole time, and if he wasn't squealing with excitement, he was squawking his head off.'

Aled grimaced. 'I bet you were popular.'

She wrinkled the side of her nose. 'People are very good. They could see that Maria and I were doing our utmost to calm him; a couple of the Waafs even offered to take him for a walk along the corridor.'

'That was good of them.' He jerked his head towards the door. 'Talking of Maria, she told me that you're thinking of applying for your liquor licence?'

Cadi cradled the glass in her hands. 'I am indeed. And before you say anything, I know it won't be easy, but if I've learned anything, it's where there's a will there's a way.'

Aled gazed steadily at her from the other side of the table. 'And whilst I don't doubt your capabilities regarding getting the licence, I am concerned that you'll be spreading yourself too thin by trying to work full time when you've got a baby to look after.'

'Staff,' said Cadi simply. 'I won't even think about attempting to get my licence until after the war, and as that'll release a flood of former Waafs in need of employment, I'm rather hoping I'll be inundated with barmaids who're more than happy to get stuck in.' Leaning forward, she began listing the benefits she planned to give to her female employees. 'I shall pay them the same wages I'd pay a man, and they'll work shifts, so that they don't have to work every weekend, and they'll have annual leave.'

Aled grinned. 'Where do I sign?'

She raised her brow fleetingly. 'Your mother would have my guts for garters.'

He leaned back in his chair and crossed his ankles. 'She would that; she'd probably have mine too.'

'Besides, I want female workers,' Cadi reminded him, 'so that at least some women can catch a break from a male-dominated workforce.'

He smoothed his fingers over his chin. 'Ah! Well there you have me.' He eyed her fondly. 'I don't think I've ever met a woman quite like you. Where do you suppose you get your tireless spirit from? Your mam?'

Cadi laughed. 'Maintaining a two up, two down whilst looking after four burly men *and* running your own business? I should say so. My Auntie Flo – she's Mam's sister – is also a strong, independent woman. Poppy reckons me and Auntie Flo are like peas in a pod.'

'Does she run a pub too?'

'No. She works for the War Office, and has done for donkey's years. When I first introduced her to Poppy she thought my auntie was working for the secret service as an undercover spy.' She laughed again. 'Because she was forever on the move, and she was always a bit evasive when talking about her work. But she had to be working for the War Office.'

'It sounds to me as though the women in your family are a force to be reckoned with,' said Aled, as he glanced towards the chalked menu behind the bar. 'Have you any idea what you fancy for your dinner?' Seeing that liver and onions was one of the choices, he gave her a lopsided grin. 'Or is that a stupid question?'

'Liver and onions, please,' said Cadi promptly. 'I need all the energy I can get.'

Aled smiled sympathetically. 'Them's the joys of motherhood.'

'He's a big boy with a fine set of lungs, and he's not shy of letting you know what he wants, whether it be food, a fresh nappy or a nap.'

Aled leaned forward. 'Sounds like you do more work now than you did in the WAAF.'

She blew her cheeks out. 'Way more. At least the WAAF allow you proper breaks with a good night's kip. Oscar's a hard taskmaster, but he's worth it.'

Aled went to place their order at the bar and returned a few moments later.

'I quite fancied liver and onions myself.' He ran his tongue over his lips. 'You can't beat a bit of onion gravy, and the stuff they make here is way better than the dishwater they serve up in the RAF.'

'Kitty says it's because they're providing for fewer people, which makes sense when you think about it.' She smiled softly at him. 'I know better than to ask, but I can't help it. Do you know what's going on? With the war, I mean. Only with them cancelling everyone's leave, it looks like summat big is about to happen.'

He drew a deep breath, contemplating his answer. He knew a lot more than he was prepared to say, because rumours were quick to spread, no matter how much people swore they would keep the information to themselves. 'I suppose the answer would be to watch this space. I'd love to be able to give you a timeline, but it's a bit like the age-old question, "How long is a piece of string?" I can only say that things are definitely coming to a head, but I suppose I'm not telling you anything you can't work out for yourself.'

She smiled gratefully. 'You're not, but it's nice to have my thoughts confirmed. I can't believe it's been nearly a year since Jez's passing.'

Aled shook his head, stern-faced. 'Me neither. I remember it as though it were only yesterday ...' He broke off, giving her an apologetic grimace. 'I'm guessing it's the same for you too.'

'Very much so. I'm hopeful that it'll get easier with time, but having said that, Oscar's proving to be a marvellous distraction, even though every time I look into Oscar's eyes I see Jez looking back at me, so I have a constant reminder of the love I lost – not that I need one.'

They had been so deep in conversation that neither of them had noticed the barmaid approaching with their meals. Now she placed their plates down, along with the cutlery, and addressed them. 'Can I get you anything else?'

They both declined her offer, and Aled waited for her to walk away before continuing with their conversation. 'That must be tough. Or does it make it easier?'

She shrugged. 'I'd say it's six of one and half a dozen of the other.' She sprinkled salt over her meal. 'How about you? Do you think it's got any easier with time?'

'In my opinion a year's too soon,' said Aled, 'and besides, you don't really have time to grieve when you're up to your neck in the thick of things. Which I suppose is why you were hungry for distractions.'

'Bill always said you have to have time to think in order to process things and move on,' said Cadi, 'and now that I've done just that, I can see that he's right: it does make things a little easier. I used to feel guilty about being here when Jez isn't, but Oscar changed all that, because if I wasn't here he wouldn't be either.'

'I too used to feel guilty, but when Tom reminded me that Jez would give anything to be in my position I realised that I should appreciate how lucky I am to be alive.'

'Exactly! Even knowing there was nothing you could have done, you still have to go through the process.'

Aled swallowed his mouthful of food before agreeing wholeheartedly. 'You have to come to terms with your emotion, and some find that harder to do than others.'

Cadi nodded. 'Absolutely. I found it easier to cope with Carrie's loss than I did Jez's, because whilst I loved Carrie I was *in* love with Jez, so was more emotionally invested, and that's why I found his passing harder.'

'Grief is a funny old thing,' said Aled. 'Some people bury it deep inside, whilst others mourn for the rest of their lives, like Queen Victoria.'

'I think that's why Jez made me promise not to die a widow. He couldn't stand the thought of me spending the rest of my life grieving.'

'He's right. And that's why I think running your own pub is a marvellous idea, provided you have plenty of staff to help you.'

'Good. But just because I'm thinking about moving on, it doesn't mean to say I've any desire to find myself a new husband. I honestly can't ever see that happening.'

Aled furrowed his brow. 'I don't think anyone would expect you to be thinking about that sort of thing for a long while yet.'

'For a lot of women, being married epitomises happiness, but I don't see life like that,' said Cadi. 'For me, happiness is being surrounded by the people I love.'

Aled raised his glass to make a toast. 'Amen to that.'

By the time they finished their meal, Maria had returned with a sleeping Oscar. She placed a finger to her lips as she walked over to join them.

'I'll take him through to the room, if that's all right with you,' she said quietly. 'It seems a pity to wake him up when he's sound asleep.'

Cadi smiled appreciatively. 'Thanks, Maria.'

Aled rose slightly in his chair, so that he might take one last peek at the sleeping infant. 'He's the spit of Jez!'

Cadi's eyes shone as she gazed lovingly at her son. 'He has the same colour hair, and I'm sure it's beginning to curl.'

Waving to indicate that she was about to take the baby through, Maria said her goodbyes to Aled. 'Take care, luv, and be sure to call in if you're ever in Liverpool,' she finished.

'Wild horses wouldn't keep me away.'

As Maria left, Aled glanced at his watch before turning rueful eyes towards Cadi. 'I'm afraid I'm going to have to shoot off myself.'

Cadi nodded sorrowfully. She had very much enjoyed Aled's company, and had completely forgotten he had to go back to Finningley. 'I wish you weren't going off in a plane,' she said quietly. 'I hate to think of you on your own in the back of that thing with God knows what going on around you.'

He smiled briefly as he stood up. 'You thought Jez was safe because he was a mechanic, but in truth it's the luck of the draw. Jez was bloody unlucky, but that doesn't mean to say that I will be too.'

She followed Aled out of the pub to his car. 'I know. I just wish I knew how many more sorties you'd be going on, so that I could count you down to safety.'

He placed his hands on her shoulders. 'Too many to mention, but hopefully not for too much longer.'

Cadi tried her best to appear cheerful. 'I'll set a date for the christening, just as soon as they declare peace, because even though actual demobbing will take an age, I can't see them refusing people leave in the meantime, not after everything they've done for their country.'

He winked at her. 'I'll play the farmer's son card; tell them I've got to get back home to help the old man out.'

'Do you ever wish you'd stayed in Rhos?'

He shook his head decidedly. 'Not in a million years. Although it would've saved you an awful lot of bother if I had, cos I'd never have met Daphne, and you and Jez wouldn't have had to go through everything you did as a consequence.'

She gave a half-shoulder shrug. 'What's life without a bit of drama?'

Gazing affectionately down at her, he hesitated momentarily before pulling her into a warm embrace. 'Goodbye, Cadi Thomas. Be sure to take care of yourself as well as little Oscar.'

Leaning back, her smile wavered ever so slightly. 'I promise. Mind how you go, Aled.'

She lifted her hand in farewell as she watched Aled drive away. Had she seen her friends for the last time, or would the heavens smile favourably on them all?

Chapter Nine

April 1945

It had been weeks since Aled saw Cadi last, and the crew were gearing up for what would turn out to be the last bombing campaign of the war.

Aled knew that the success of their raids meant the difference between defeat and victory, and accordingly he had aged considerably in a short space of time. The Americans had referred to the bombing of Dresden as a 'home run', and even though Aled was pleased that the mission had proved successful, he couldn't shake the images out of his mind. They had turned the city into a blazing inferno with not a building left standing; the sheer volume of devastation had been worse than anything he had witnessed to date.

Taking his position in the back of the *Ulysses*, he closed the blast doors behind him and gazed unseeingly through the glassless turret. Hearing the skipper confirm that they were clear for take-off, he shuffled around in his seat as the heavy bomber accelerated along the runway.

As they lifted off, he gazed to the spot where Jez had met his maker. He had got into the habit of dedicating each op and sortie to Jez's memory, but today he did so with greater intensity than ever before. Because today they were heading for Berchtesgaden, the reported retreat where Hitler himself was believed to be hiding. He set his jaw in a determined fashion. The thought of the man who had created such carnage hiding hundreds of miles away from the action made him sick to his stomach. The dictator was nothing but a cowardly bully, who never dirtied his own hands. If they were to take him out today, it would mean the end of the war.

The crew knew that flying over Germany would be dangerous, and weren't surprised when they met several fighters who tried to take them down, but Aled and Tom defended the *Ulysses* well, and it wasn't until the return journey that they really ran into trouble.

Whether Aled had relaxed a little in the knowledge that the operation had been successful, or whether it was fatigue from the countless sorties they had carried out over the previous days, he couldn't be sure, but by the time he realised the Messerschmitt was on his tail it had already fired off a round of bullets. Aled fought back furiously, and was euphoric when he sent the enemy hurtling seawards. It wasn't until his vision blurred that he realised something was wrong. Glancing down, he saw blood running from several wounds. Hearing the growing concern in Tom's voice as he repeatedly asked him whether he was all right, he managed to tell him he'd been hit before the world began to swim in and out of focus. Trying to stem the flow of blood, he was only grateful that he couldn't feel the pain caused by the bullets. He heard Tom instructing him to stay focused just as a world of darkness enveloped him.

May 1945

It was the 8th of May and Cadi and Maria were preparing for the party of a lifetime, along with the rest of the nation. Having got up betimes, Cadi was helping Maria to swathe the bar of the Belmont in bunting, occasionally singing snatches of *God Save the King* at the top of their lungs.

Maria held the bunting whilst Cadi climbed the ladder and began pinning the little triangles into place. 'Look at Oscar,' Maria told her. 'He can't keep his eyes off the flags.'

'I'm going to make sure Oscar knows that his father was a hero who sailed halfway around the world to fight the Nazis,' said Cadi. 'Even though at the time I hated the thought of him going away, I realise now that we might never have won the war without men like Jez.'

Maria smiled down at Oscar, who was continuing to stare at the different colours in wide-eyed wonderment. Breaking her gaze, she turned her attention back to Cadi. 'Never a truer word said, which is why I'm going to put a photograph of him behind the bar, along with his medals.' She glanced at the clock on the wall. 'What time are we expecting Raquel, do you think?'

'Around two this afternoon,' replied Cadi, her voice muffled by the drawing pins she was holding between her lips.

'She must be looking forward to seeing you and Oscar,' said Maria, passing up more bunting.

'When I spoke to her last night she couldn't wait to get here. She said she loves spending time with Oscar because it makes up for the time she lost with Jez. She adores that baby.'

'As do we all,' said Maria. 'Have you heard anything from the girls?'

Cadi smiled. 'I have indeed. Poppy said they're having a right old knees-up in Lincoln city.'

'What about Ronnie and Kitty?'

'Ronnie was granted a forty-eight within minutes of peace being declared, so she's heading back to Blackpool. As for Kitty, she's still in Little Snoring, but she plans on coming home just as soon as she's demobbed.'

'Everything's going to change now that the war's over,' Maria mused. 'Have any of the girls got a clue as to what they'll do when they're demobbed?' Standing to one side, she waited for Cadi to descend the ladder, and together they moved it further along the bar before Cadi responded.

'I know that Ronnie's going to help run the family business: a tea room on the promenade in Blackpool. I should imagine Izzy and Kitty will come back to Liverpool, but I have no idea what either of them will do for a living, and as for Poppy …' she hesitated as she ascended the ladder again, 'I reckon our Poppy'll be married before the month is out.'

Maria steadied the base of the ladder with her foot as Cadi stretched more bunting along the top of the bar. 'I'm glad they've all come through this,' she said, and hesitated. 'We've covered the girls, but what about Aled? Do you think he'll go back to the farm as he said, or stay on in the RAF?'

Cadi gave a small grunt as she pushed a pin into place. 'No idea, cos I've not heard a dickie bird. I've tried calling his station, but the woman I spoke to reckoned she'd never heard of him, so I'm guessing she's not been at Finningley long.'

Maria pulled a face. 'Churchill did say that Japan hadn't surrendered, so we have to continue the fight. Do you suppose he's gone overseas to fight the Japanese?'

Cadi tutted under her breath as the drawing pin she was using refused to go in. 'Damn and blast, I do hope not. But I suppose someone has to go, and there's no reason why that someone shouldn't be Aled.' Her shoulders dropped. 'And just when I thought everyone was home safe and sound.'

Maria pulled a grim smile. 'If it's any consolation, I'm sure the worst is over. Japan's not as big as Germany. We've beaten the Krauts, so the Japs should be a walk in the park.'

'It beats me why they're still holding out. Surely they must realise they haven't got a cat in hell's chance of winning?'

Maria shook her head. 'It's all down to national pride.'

Cadi rolled her eyes. 'So more people have to die, just so their stupid pride doesn't take a bashing? Which it will do anyway, probably more so for them having held out longer than they should.'

'We just have to hope they see sense sooner rather than later,' said Maria. 'Harking back to Aled, have you thought about approaching his parents? I'm sure they'd know if he were staying on.'

Cadi beamed as she pinned the last flag into place. 'Good thinking. I'll write them a letter, or better still I'll send them a telegram.'

Maria glanced towards the door. 'Go on. I can keep an eye on things here.'

Cadi jumped down the ladder and kissed her friend on the cheek before taking her coat down from its hook and bundling Oscar into his pram. 'Thanks, Maria, you're a star. I shan't be long.'

Pushing Oscar along the pavement she smiled at the passers-by, all of whom looked as joyous as she felt. The mood of the city had changed considerably in the past twenty-four hours, and it occurred to Cadi that she was seeing the real Liverpool for the first time since visiting as a child. Thanking an elderly man for holding the door open, she wheeled the pram into the post office and joined the back of the queue. As she waited, she overheard some of the women in the queue ahead of her saying their loved ones had already been demobbed, and hearing this brought another thought to her mind. What if Aled was already home? He had joked that he would play the farmer's son card in order to get demobbed faster, but what if he really had, and he'd kept quiet in order to surprise her? If that was the case, then she might be worrying over nothing, and she would finally be able to make arrangements for Oscar's christening in a few months' time, when she felt certain that everyone would be able to make it.

When she reached the head of the queue, she asked the postmistress to send a telegram to the Davies family, simply stating *Aled. Please telephone Cadi at earliest opportunity*. The message sent, she returned to the pub and helped Maria to bake pies and cakes for the celebration.

'It's going to be a party like no other,' said Maria. 'It's such a pity that Oscar won't remember any of it.'

'We must be sure to take lots of photographs,' said Cadi, 'and every year we'll get them out so that we can remember not just the war, but everyone we lost as well as those who came home safe.'

Much later the same day, Raquel was helping to get yet another batch of pies out of the oven. 'I've not seen this much food since I don't know when,' she said, wiping the sweat from her brow with the back of her hand.

Bill teased a small piece of crust off one of the pies and popped it into his mouth. 'We'll not need to eat for a week after we've got through this lot.' He looked at Cadi. 'Maria said you'd sent Aled's folks a telegram. Have you not heard back yet?'

Cadi waved the steam away from the oven before putting a sponge cake in to bake. 'Not a sausage, but I dare say they'll be busy with celebrations of their own. If I've not heard owt by tomorrow, I might give the village post office a call to make sure that the telegram's gone through.'

'It will've,' said Bill confidently. 'I know there's lots of people sending messages, but I have great faith in His Majesty's telegraphic service.'

Cadi frowned. She had already spoken to Poppy on the matter, and they both thought that Aled would've been straight on the phone if he'd seen her message, if only to rejoice in the good news.

'The telephones have been red hot here, but even so, everyone's managed to phone home,' said Poppy, 'so I should imagine Aled wouldn't have had any bother. What did they say at Finningley?'

'The Waaf who answered said that she'd never heard of him, but that she'd leave a message with someone who might know more,' said Cadi.

'Perhaps try in the morning when things have calmed down a bit,' Poppy had suggested. 'If they don't put you through to Aled, you could ask for Tom, because he's sure to know where he is.'

Cadi gave a small cry of triumph. 'Good thinking that woman! I know that Aled was keen to set a date for Oscar's christening, so it's strange he hasn't been in touch to learn the date.'

'Sometimes life takes over,' said Poppy. 'We're not busy in Fiskerton, but we know for a fact that other stations are still in full swing. Maybe Aled doesn't want to call until he knows when he can get leave.'

Cadi had groaned inwardly. 'Surely they'd allow him some, if only for a short while? The poor man's not had time off since Christmas, and that's far too long considering we've won the war.'

'We've not been granted any leave either,' Poppy reminded her friend.

Cadi sighed. 'I know someone's got to continue the fight, and I suppose Aled is brilliant at his job. I just wish they'd give him a little bit of time to celebrate with the rest of us.' Her previous thought came back to her. 'Do you think he might be home already and he's saving it as a surprise?'

Poppy had dismissed her suggestion without hesitation. 'Not a chance. Aled would've rung the moment he saw your telegram, and in any case he would definitely have come to see you and Oscar before going back to Rhos.'

Cadi had agreed with her, but it hadn't made her feel any better. Now, she looked at Bill, who was watching her expectantly. 'I'll not bother with the post office, because you're right, the Davieses will have got the telegram. I'll call Finningley when we've finished baking and ask for Tom. He'll know where Aled is, and if they say that Tom's not there either I'll know that our suspicions are correct and the *Ulysses* has gone to fight the Japanese.'

With all the baking done, Cadi, Raquel, Bill and Maria were busy celebrating with the rest of the locals who frequented the Belmont.

'It's lovely to see so many happy faces,' said Raquel as she placed another glass of beer on the bar.

'Oscar thinks it's all for him,' Maria cooed, jiggling the baby's chubby cheek between her finger and thumb.

'He certainly enjoys a party,' agreed Cadi. 'He's just like his father on that score.'

'And his mam,' quipped Bill, who had appeared from the cellar holding a bottle of rum.

Maria took the bottle from his hands and wiped the dust from its shoulders. 'This'll put a smile on the face of the Navy veterans.'

Bill grinned. 'It's put one on mine too.'

'Are we going to have everyone in the bar when Churchill gives his speech?' asked Raquel. 'I doubt there'll be a dry eye in the house when he makes the announcement official.'

'Of course,' said Maria. 'We'll invite them in from the streets and the parks. Everyone's welcome at the Belmont.'

Raquel glanced to Cadi, who was looking glum-faced. 'What's up, luv?'

'We're all celebrating, yet I still haven't heard from Aled. He could be fighting the Japanese, and here I am eating cake and sarnies.' She sighed irritably. 'I must say, I'd have thought I'd have heard from his folks by now. Even if he's not at home, they know I'm looking for him.'

Maria jerked her head in the direction of the hall, where they kept the telephone. 'Why don't you give that Tom a call? You did say you would.'

Cadi glanced around the crowded bar. 'I'll wait until things have quietened down a bit.'

Bill placed his hand over the pump which she was using to fill a glass with stout. 'You'll turn the beer sour with that face of yours. Get you gone and find out what's what.'

Cadi smiled gratefully as she handed Bill the glass. 'Thanks, Bill.' Taking her leave, she slipped into the back and closed the hall door to. Drawing a deep breath, she picked up the receiver and asked the operator to put her through to Finningley. As she waited for someone to come on the other end, she was wondering what she would do if they said that Tom had been demobbed when a Waaf answered the phone.

'RAF Finningley.'

Cadi was about to ask for Tom when she suddenly realised she had no idea what his surname was.

The Waaf's voice came down the line. 'Hello?'

Cadi rolled her eyes. 'Can I speak to Aled Davies, please?'

Cadi could hear muffled voices whilst the Waaf conferred with those around her before speaking into the telephone again. 'Are you sure you've got the right base? Only there's no one by that name at Finningley.'

Cadi stood in stunned silence before mumbling an apology and placing the handset down. She walked back through to the bar, deep in thought, and seeing her expression Maria sighed. 'Don't tell me Tom wasn't there either?'

Cadi put a smile on her cheeks for the customer who was handing her his empty glass, and asking her to fill it with Boddingtons. 'I don't know Tom's surname, so I had to ask for Aled, and the Waaf who answered the phone said that there isn't an Aled Davies at Finningley.'

Maria's brow shot towards her hairline. 'So you think he's been posted elsewhere?'

Cadi nodded slowly. 'It certainly looks that way, but why didn't he tell me?'

Bill strolled over to join in the conversation, tapping the side of his nose with his forefinger. 'Sounds to me like it's hush-hush.'

Raquel looked at Cadi uncertainly. 'No matter how hush-hush it is, Aled could call to let you know he's all right; he doesn't have to say where he is or what he's doing. I don't mean to be pessimistic, but I've started to wonder whether Aled has regretted some of the promises he's made?'

'Like what?' said Maria, but Cadi knew exactly what her mother-in-law was getting at.

'About looking after me and Oscar,' she said dully. A sudden thought entered her mind. 'Maybe he's back with Marnie? If she got wind that I'd left the WAAF after having Jez's baby, she might have got back in touch with him, asking if they could start over.' She shrugged. 'Aled could be keeping his distance, rather than upset her.'

Maria dismissed this idea without hesitation. 'I can't see that happening. Marnie was hell bent on going their separate ways.'

'He might've met another woman,' said Raquel. 'If so, he might've thought it best to break ties with Cadi, in case his new flame got jealous like Marnie?'

Maria acknowledged a customer with the wave of her hand whilst saying, 'He thinks the world of our Cadi *and* Oscar. I can't see him turning his back on them for anyone, but especially not for some woman he hardly knows.'

Cadi flapped her arms in a hopeless fashion. 'What, then? Because I feel as though I've been sent to Coventry without having any idea why, or else Aled's fighting the Japs. Either way, it's a no-win situation.'

'It certainly is a conundrum,' said Raquel, 'because I can't imagine what would make him behave in such a manner. His parents either, come to that.'

'Exactly!' cried Cadi. 'Why on earth are his parents ignoring me? I can't think of anything I've done, except for having Oscar.' She stopped speaking as another thought presented itself. 'Do you suppose it's something to do with my being a single parent? Maybe John's objected to Aled's helping me?'

Maria cut her off before she had a chance to continue. 'And since when did Aled listen to a word his father said? He even signed up for the RAF knowing that his father was dead against it. Besides, I met John and Gwen at your wedding and they seemed lovely to me, not the sort to turn their backs on someone who's been through hard times. Whatever this is, it's nothing to do with your being a single parent.'

'So what am I supposed to do?' said Cadi, in exasperated tones. 'Aled's meant to be Oscar's godfather, and I need to know whether he still intends to fulfil that role, cos quite frankly it doesn't look likely at the minute, does it?'

Maria took her aside whilst Raquel served another customer. 'Telephone your folks; see if they've got any ideas. Your brother Alun might be your best bet, cos he's still working on the Davieses' farm. If anyone should know what's going on, it's him.'

Cadi beamed with relief. 'Maria, you're a godsend! I've been that moidered it never crossed my mind to try my folks.' She glanced back to the phone. 'May I?'

Maria nodded. 'Course you can.'

Whilst Cadi's parents didn't have a telephone, her mother's sewing shop in Wrexham did, so Cadi dialled the operator and waited to be put through.

'Cadi!' cried Jill. 'How wonderful to hear from you. How's my beautiful grandson?'

Cadi grinned. 'Bonny – which basically means that he's as fat as butter, and as happy as a sandboy. How's Annie?'

'Missing you, of course, but she comes to the shop with me during work hours, and after work I take her for a walk up Rhos mountain, so she's never on her own.' She sighed happily. 'I can't wait to see my little Oscar. I bet he's changed loads since I saw him last.'

'I swear he changes on a daily basis,' said Cadi. 'He's already trying to crawl; I dread to think what my life will be like when he finally gains his freedom!'

Jill laughed. 'You're going to have to have eyes in the back of your head with that one, cos he's going to get up to all sorts of mischief.'

'I must say I'm glad you're at the shop,' said Cadi. 'I did worry you might be in the village.'

'I was until your brother got the tractor caught on the bunting whilst driving through the village,' explained Jill. 'As no one else had any spare string, I said I'd come and get some from the shop so that it can be hung back up.'

Cadi chuckled at the image. 'I remember Aled doing something similar to me, only it was manure, not string.' She hesitated before continuing. 'Speaking of Alun, he's the reason for my call.'

'Oh?'

'I'm trying to trace Aled. I've already sent a telegram to the Davieses' but I've had nothing back. I tried calling him at Finningley, but they said he's not there any more, so I was wondering whether Alun had heard anything from John or Gwen? Only Aled's meant to be Oscar's godfather, and I need to know when he's free so that I can arrange the christening.'

Her mother paused before replying, and when she spoke her tone was grave. 'Not a word, but we think something bad's happened because they've not come into town since before peace was declared, and Alun says you can't mention Aled's name without Gwen bursting into tears.'

Cadi felt her tummy flip. 'Oh my God, that doesn't sound good.'

'I agree. Alun says that the atmosphere on the farm has turned very sombre. Not only that, but they've given notice that they're not continuing with their tenancy.'

When she heard that, Cadi could have been knocked over with a feather. 'Bloody hell.'

'Cadi!'

'Sorry, Mam, but this is bad, very bad. I know that John said he couldn't manage the farm on his own, so it looks to me as if Aled's decided to stay on in the RAF.'

'I've heard that a lot of pilots will be going back to their old lives, but maybe Aled's considering other opportunities now the war has come to an end.'

'But why avoid me? Because there's no doubt in my mind that that's what he's doing.'

'Maybe he's ashamed that his folks have given notice because he doesn't want to go home?'

Cadi could feel herself getting annoyed. 'He should know that I'd never blame him for wanting to live his life the way he wanted.'

'I wish I could help you, cariad, I really do, but if Aled's decided to keep things to himself there's not a lot we can do about it.'

'He's being damned selfish,' said Cadi, 'and I intend to tell him so.'

'How?'

'I'm going to pay the girls a visit in Lincoln, and call in at RAF Finningley on the way.'

When Jill responded, Cadi could hear the uncertainty in her mother's voice. 'What's the point, when you know he's not there?'

'He may not be, but Tom might, and I shan't let him fob me off!'

It had been several days since the VE celebrations, and Oscar was being looked after by his doting grandparents whilst Cadi was on board the train heading to Lincoln. Having phoned the girls the previous evening so that she could tell them of her plans, she had asked them to keep her arrival to themselves so that Tom wouldn't get wind of her intended visit.

'I think you're doing the only thing you can do under the circumstances,' said Poppy. 'It's a pity you had to come all this way just to see what Aled's playing at.'

Now, as the train reached its destination, she gathered her belongings, ready to get off.

As the station came into view, Cadi wasn't surprised to see a throng of people waiting to board. *All going home*, she thought, *to pick up the pieces of their lives and adjust to life outside the services.*

Seeing her friends waving madly to her from the platform, Cadi made her way to the nearest carriage door and waited eagerly for the guard to open it. Jumping down on to the platform, she hurried over to greet them.

'I can't tell you how good it is to see you both,' she enthused as she took them in a strong embrace. 'I've missed you terribly, and I can't wait to show you how much Oscar's grown since you saw him last.' She quickly fished out the latest photographs from the recesses of her handbag, and handed them to the girls, who cooed over their nephew.

'We've missed you as well,' said Poppy now, as she gazed lovingly down at the photograph of Cadi, Oscar and Maria. 'Oh, I can't wait to give our Oscar a great big cuddle.'

'I'm so looking forward to coming home,' said Izzy. 'Wherever home is.'

'It's wherever we are,' said Cadi firmly. 'You can come and work for me in my pub, when I get it.' She looked to Poppy. 'You too, although I should imagine you have other plans?'

Poppy smiled shyly. 'Geoffrey wants us to be married as soon as we're demobbed, but he lives in Blackpool, which is miles away from everyone I know and love.'

Cadi eyed her friend reassuringly. 'You'll soon make friends, and we can always visit. Besides, Ronnie lives in Blackpool.'

Poppy's smile broadened. 'I'd forgotten that.'

Izzy nudged Poppy as the girls swapped photographs. 'I *told* you you'd be all right.'

Cadi picked up her bag, and the girls made their way out of the station. 'I'm staying in the Horse and Groom, so I thought I could drop my stuff off, and we could grab a bite to eat in the bar?'

'Good idea,' said Poppy. 'I'm famished.'

As they walked Cadi turned to Izzy. 'You never said whether you were going to join me in my new venture?'

Izzy grinned sheepishly. 'You know I'd love to, but I rather think Mike's gearing up to ask me to be his wife.'

Cadi gaped at her. 'So that's what you meant by "wherever home is"!'

'Exactly. He's been asking how I'd feel about him staying on in the RAF, and whether I'd like to travel the world.' She laughed softly. 'I think he's testing the water before popping the question.'

Cadi breathed a sigh. 'I should imagine life would be very different being the wife of a flying officer rather than a sergeant in your own right. And how would you feel about living abroad?'

'I think it would be rather fun, as long as I don't have to get up with reveille every morning!'

'Well, I think it sounds like a marvellous opportunity,' said Cadi, slowing to a halt before turning to face her friends. 'I'm happy for you both, truly I am, but with you going to goodness knows where and Poppy off to Blackpool, I'm going to be on my own, aren't I?'

Poppy shook her head hastily as she saw tears begin to well in Cadi's eyes. 'No! We'll come and see you often, and you can always come and stay with us.' She looked to Izzy for confirmation.

'You can come abroad for holidays wherever Mike and I are based,' Izzy assured her, 'and we'll come back to Liverpool whenever Mike gets leave.'

Taking a handkerchief from her pocket, Cadi dabbed the tears from her eyes. 'It just feels as though I'm losing everyone I love.'

Poppy smiled kindly. 'You've got a beautiful son, and family and friends who care about you deeply. You'll never be on your own, Cadi.'

As they began to walk the girls spoke of the good times that lay ahead, and even though they included Cadi in their plans she couldn't help but feel as though she were being left behind. *I've got Oscar,* she told herself, *but it's not the same as having a husband by your side.*

It was the following day and Cadi was sitting in a taxi, en route for Finningley. As the car neared the gate, she asked the driver to wait outside for her whilst she talked to the guard. Getting out of the car, she realised that the airman on duty was the one who'd been guarding the gate the day Finningley had come under attack.

'Sergeant Thomas,' he said, ripping off a textbook salute. His smile wavered as he remembered the last time he'd seen her. 'How are you?'

She smiled back. 'I'm doing just fine, thank you. I'm here to see Tom, the mid-gunner on the *Ulysses*, but I'm afraid I don't know his surname.'

The man nodded wisely. 'I know who you mean. If you'd like to wait, I can ring through and get someone to fetch him for you.'

Cadi was about to ask the man not to mention who was waiting for him when it occurred to her that he'd probably call her Sergeant Thomas. It wouldn't cross Tom's mind that he was referring to herself.

Keeping just out of sight, she waited until the guard stepped out of his office to let her know that Tom was on his way, and as soon as he came into view she marched towards him in a determined fashion.

'Tom!'

It took the airman a moment or two to realise that Sergeant Thomas was in fact Aled's friend Cadi. He eyed her accusingly. 'I see you're still using your rank.'

She shook her head. 'The guard was the same one who was on duty the day Jez died. He recognised me as soon as I got out of the taxi.'

Tom shoved his hands in his pockets, and it was clear from his stance that he was anything but pleased to see her. 'I would ask what I could do for you, but I guess I already know the answer to that.'

She nodded. 'I realise that my coming all the way out here might seem a little extreme, but Aled's not left me any choice. I've tried contacting his parents, but the only thing I've learned is that they're leaving Rhos.'

Tom looked at her with genuine shock. 'They're leaving the farm?'

She stared at him. 'They're giving up the tenancy. You didn't know?'

He shook his head. 'It's news to me.'

'So it seems I'm not the only one who Aled's keeping in the dark,' said Cadi. She stared Tom straight in the eye. 'Where is he, Tom?'

He stared at the floor, grim-faced. 'Have you heard the saying "Ask me no questions and I'll tell you no lies"?'

Cadi tutted impatiently. 'Of course I have. I'm not a child!'

He fixed her with a wooden stare. 'I know you're not.'

Cadi placed one hand on her hip and rubbed her forehead with the other. 'I don't understand. Why doesn't he want to talk to me? If nothing else, he should have the decency to pick up the phone and tell me that he doesn't want to see me any more, not just ignore me in the hope that I'll go away.' With Tom remaining deathly silent, she continued desperately, 'Has something happened to him? Is that why everyone's being so evasive?'

Tom stared at his boots. 'Cadi, if I were able to tell you, do you not think I'd have done so by now?'

A single tear trickled down her cheek. 'Aled was right beside me when I lost Jez, the same as he was when I gave birth to Oscar. He even held my hand. How can someone like that turn their back on you for no reason? He's acting like the spoilt, selfish little prig he was before he joined the RAF.'

Tom lowered his gaze. 'I wish I could help, I really do.' He glanced back up. 'I'm sorry, Cadi, but it might be best all round if you forget about Aled.'

Cadi stared at him through her tears. 'How can I?'

He shrugged. 'You're going to have to find a way. Ta-ra, Cadi.' He gave her a grim smile before turning on his heel and walking back the way he had come.

Cadi returned to the taxi, more confused than she had been before speaking to Tom. As she slid on to the back seat she wondered whether she should've asked Tom if Aled had a new girlfriend, then dismissed the idea. The men in aircrew were more brothers than friends; if Aled had asked Tom to keep quiet about anything, no matter how petty it might seem to Tom, she had no doubt he would obey Aled's wishes.

Back at the tavern, Cadi told Poppy and Izzy what had happened.

'There's definitely more to this than meets the eye,' conceded Poppy, 'but we're still none the wiser.'

Izzy glanced at Poppy before speaking her thoughts. 'What if Poppy and I put out a few feelers, see if anything comes back?'

But Cadi was shaking her head. 'Tom said I should forget about Aled, and maybe he's right.'

Poppy pursed her lips to one side. 'Has it ever occurred to you that Aled might be avoiding you because he wants more than friendship?'

Cadi stared at her friend open-mouthed. 'No! Aled's like a brother to me, and I'm like a sister to him.'

Poppy pulled a face. 'But what if Marnie was right, and Aled really doesn't know how he feels about you? Or rather, what if he didn't, but he does now?'

Cadi still wasn't convinced. 'Surely I'd know?'

'Not if he doesn't know himself,' said Poppy. 'Look at everything he's done for you.' She began ticking the list off on her fingers. 'He kept his distance because he knew that you loved Jez, he didn't leave your side the night Jez passed, he held your hand whilst you gave birth. If you ask me, Aled's in love with you, so much so that he can't bear to be near you in case you guess how he feels.'

Cadi stared at her friend open-mouthed. 'If that's the case, what do I do?'

Izzy spoke without hesitation. 'Leave well alone.'

Cadi sighed breathily. 'I wish we'd thought of this *before* I went to see Tom.'

'Why? It wouldn't have changed anything,' said Poppy, 'not if I'm right, that is.'

'So, I've lost Carrie, Jez and now Aled,' said Cadi sorrowfully. 'You two will be the next to go.'

Poppy linked her arm through Cadi's. 'We'll never leave you.'

Cadi smiled, grateful that the girls, at least, wouldn't desert her. But deep down her heart was aching. Losing Jez had been the single worst thing that could have happened to her, but the thought of losing Aled felt like someone rubbing salt into her wounds. He was one of the best friends she'd ever had, and she wasn't prepared to give up on him just yet.

'I know you think it best that I leave sleeping dogs lie, but we're making a lot of assumptions. I'm going to send him an invitation to the christening. If he cares about me as much as you seem to think he does, then he'll turn up to do his duty.'

Poppy eyed her quizzically. 'That's all very well, but where will you send the invitation?'

'To his parents,' said Cadi. 'If anyone knows where he is, it's them.'

Back at the NAAFI, Tom waited for the operator to connect him, and asked to speak to Aled. When Aled's voice finally came somewhat sullenly down the line, Tom filled him in on Cadi's visit.

'I'm a man of my word, Aled, you know that. But I felt a real heel lying to Cadi whilst she stood there in tears. I know you think what you're doing is the best for her, but I think you've got it wrong. She deserves to know the truth, because this is torture for her.'

'It's not my fault she came to Finningley,' said Aled, in a hoarse voice.

'That's where our opinions differ,' said Tom plainly. 'She only came because she's desperate to see you. I know you think she'll forget about you in time, but I don't think she will. Besides, she's bound to learn the truth sooner or later. If she'd asked the guard on the gate where you were, I've no doubt he would have told her, because he knows she used to be a sergeant in the WAAF.'

'But she's still none the wiser,' said Aled, his voice barely above a whisper, 'and that's the way it must stay.'

'Her family come from the same village as your parents,' hissed Tom. 'Did you know your parents were giving up their tenancy?'

'Hardly my fault,' said Aled.

'Cadi called you a spoiled selfish prig, and quite frankly, I'm beginning to agree with her. If you thought anything of Cadi you'd put her out of her misery, and tell her the truth.'

For the first time, Aled's voice came clearly down the line. 'Don't you dare try and tell me how I feel about Cadi. I think the world of that woman ...' He stopped talking as he broke off into a series of coughs.

Tom waited for them to stop before speaking his mind. 'You love her.'

'Enough to let her go,' said Aled, his tone quiet once more.

'Do you not think she deserves the chance to say goodbye?'

The silence that followed was so prolonged that Tom began to wonder if they'd been cut off, and was just about to speak Aled's name when his friend spoke again.

'Don't ask me to see the pain in her eyes, because I couldn't bear it.'

The operator cut in just then, and Tom rather thought she had been listening to the conversation by the thickness in her voice. 'I'm afraid your time is up.'

Tom could hear the grim smile in Aled's voice as he replied, 'Ain't that the truth,' and was about to say goodbye when the operator ended the call.

Aled handed the handset back to the nurse, who tried to pass him a glass of water, which he waved away. 'Is there anything I can do?' she asked, some-what timidly.

Aled raised an eyebrow. 'Not unless you want to give me one of your lungs, as well as a kidney, not to mention new legs.'

The nurse's cheeks turned pink. 'I – I'm …'

'Thought not,' said Aled gruffly.

The nurse turned away as an older, more experienced colleague approached. 'I hope you're not scaring my nurses again, Gunner Davies.'

Aled shrugged petulantly. 'If they will insist on asking stupid questions …'

'Asking someone if they can help is not stupid, but refusing their help is.'

'I don't see why,' muttered Aled. 'It's not as if she can do anything useful, such as put me back to the way I was.'

The nurse shook her head. 'She never said she could.'

'Bloody doctors are nothing but a bunch of quacks,' said Aled. 'If I were a dog they'd put me to sleep, but instead they turn me into a vegetable when they should've left me to die, cos that would've been the humane thing to do.'

The nurse strode over to the door of his room and closed it sharply before turning to face him, her arms folded across her chest. 'When you first came in your friends told me that you were a fighter, someone who never gave up, and if anyone stood a chance of surviving it was you. They pleaded with the surgeons to save your life because they knew you wouldn't waste it. To be honest, the way they were talking I was expecting someone like Douglas Bader, but instead I get the cowardly lion!'

Aled heaved himself up on to his elbows. 'How dare you speak to a dying man in that manner?'

An air of defiance swept her features. 'You can make the most of the time that's left – which, by the way, might be a lot longer than you think if you fight for it. Or you can lie in that bed for the rest of your days, which could be months or even years from now. The choice is yours.'

Aled looked horrified. 'Years?'

She nodded. 'I was a nurse in the first lot, and I saw the difference between the men that fight and the men that give in. The ones that fight faced huge difficulties, no one's denying that, but at least they're living their lives, whereas the ones who choose to shut themselves away merely exist, and it's not a pleasant existence.'

'But why did the doctors make out I hadn't a chance?'

She smiled sympathetically. 'Because of the seriousness of your wounds. But in fact no one knows how well you'll mend; what they do know is that if you give up, so will your body. As a nurse I've seen the difference a little determination can make, and I know that where there's a will, there's a way.'

He eyed her doubtfully. 'Do you really think I could make it?'

She laid a reassuring hand on his arm. 'Not if you don't try, but either way, it's got to be better than staring at these four walls.' She paused for a moment. 'When you first came to, you said something about looking after a friend of yours?'

'Cadi,' Aled muttered.

'Wouldn't you like to see her again?'

On this question, Aled was adamant. 'She must never know. If she ever learns the truth, she'll insist on looking after me, and I couldn't stand that, when I'd promised to look after her.'

'She must be awfully worried, not knowing where you are.'

'She'll get over it,' said Aled stiffly.

The nurse tried a different tack. 'You said that you were going to look after her, but what does that mean exactly?'

'I'd been putting money into her bank account on a regular basis ...' He gave a short, mirthless laugh. 'I can't even do that any more.'

'Some people would prefer friendship over money,' warned the nurse as she got to her feet. 'Do you not think she'll be hurt when the man she thought was her friend refuses to answer her calls, or reply to her letters?'

Aled clenched his jaw. He couldn't bear the thought of hurting Cadi, but if he were to do what was best for her, then that was the way it would have to be. He stared unseeingly into the distance. 'She has plenty of friends. I'm sure they'll see her right.'

The nurse indicated the glass of water which Aled had refused. 'If you're going to push away everyone who loves you, you're going to be a very lonely man; take it from someone who's seen it happen too many times before. Even if you don't want to see Cadi, the least you can do is allow your parents to visit.'

Aled's eyelids fluttered as he envisaged his mother's reaction if she were to see him bed-bound and swathed in bandages. 'Mam would just make things worse,' he told the nurse. 'She never wanted me to join the RAF, and neither did my father; I applied behind their backs. I know they'd never actually say "I told you so", but that's exactly what they'd be thinking, and they'd be right.'

'Speaking as a mother, I know that your parents will just want you to be happy.'

He gave another derisive snort. 'Which is why I don't want them visiting.'

She appeared deep in thought. 'Granted, so why don't you get your act together and stop lying in bed feeling sorry for yourself?'

For the first time in what seemed like months, Aled's lips tweaked into a smile. 'You're a hard pill to swallow, Nurse Shelby, but I reckon you're the best medicine this place has to offer!'

March 1946

It was the day of the christening, and Cadi stared down the aisle of the church with a heavy heart. Despite sending Aled an invitation, Cadi had heard nothing in reply. The man she had believed to be the best friend a woman could have, had turned his back on not just her but her son as well, and for that she could never forgive him.

Suspecting that Aled might not turn up, she had asked Geoffrey to be ready to take his place, but even though he stepped up to the mark Aled's absence cast a shadow over the occasion.

'I really don't understand it,' Maria hissed to Bill. 'He seemed so keen when he came to see them in Lincoln – more than.'

'War does funny things to people,' said Bill, 'and whilst I can understand Cadi's anger, I think she should give him the benefit of the doubt until we know what's gone on.'

'The girls think that Aled's in love with Cadi, and that he can't bear to be near her if he's not *with* her,' whispered Maria.

Bill rubbed the back of his neck with the palm of his hand. 'I s'pose it's possible.'

They fell silent as the vicar finished his piece, and Oscar bellowed his disapproval at having his forehead splashed with cold water.

Bill grinned. 'He's got a proper set of lungs on him, ain't he?'

'I've heard you holler when the water in the ewer's been colder than you expected,' Maria retorted.

'True.' He placed his arm around his wife's shoulders. 'It would've been the icing on the cake if Aled had come, but as it stands, I hope she draws a line under it and moves on.'

When the christening came to an end everyone began to make their way out of the church. Cadi left Raquel to fuss over Oscar whilst she caught up to Poppy and Geoffrey.

'Thanks for stepping in, Geoff. I really appreciate it,' she said, as she fell into step beside them.

Geoffrey placed his arm around Cadi's shoulder. 'My pleasure—' he began, before stopping short. 'Cadi?'

Cadi was staring fixedly at someone who was making his way out of the church gates. 'Who was that? I don't remember seeing him at the christening.'

Geoffrey and Poppy both followed Cadi's gaze. 'No idea. Why?'

Cadi shrugged. 'Maybe it's my imagination, but it seemed like he only left when he saw me looking.'

'Probably visiting the grave of a loved one,' suggested Poppy.

Cadi nodded, but the niggling doubt remained that the man had only left because she'd looked in his direction.

Chapter Ten

August 1950

Cadi began to wipe down the remaining table surfaces as she waited for the last of her customers to finish their meals and leave.

The war had been over for five years, and a lot had changed in that time. Poppy and Geoffrey were married, and living in Blackpool with their two girls, Maisie who was three and Annabelle who wasn't yet a year old. Izzy and Mike were also married, and just as Izzy had predicted they had moved abroad. Mike's first posting had been to Germany, where Izzy had found work as an English tutor in a public school. After a couple of years in Germany Mike had been posted to France, and it was there that Izzy found out that she was pregnant. She had continued to work as a tutor right up to the birth of their daughter Fleur, after which she had invited private pupils into her home so that she could look after Fleur whilst earning a decent wage. Ronnie had married a man called Norman, whom she had met during the VE Day celebrations, and they had expanded her family's business, opening a candyfloss stall on the promenade.

When Dave went home to Scotland he and Kitty had retained a long-distance relationship for a while, but the separation had proved too great and their relationship had fizzled out within a matter of months. Kitty had been disheartened at losing her first love until she met Arthur, a local man who worked in the tobacco factory down the Stanley docks. Their friendship had quickly blossomed into romance, and they had married within a year of their meeting.

Raquel had married Hank, one of the Americans she had met whilst in the WAAF. She refused to leave her grandson, so Hank had secured a posting to RAF Speke, and Raquel continued to work as a barmaid for Maria.

Accepting the fact that Maria's warning about the difficulties facing a single mother applying for a liquor licence had been well founded, Cadi had reverted to her original plan to open a tea room, and when the opportunity to rent a bakery on Great Homer Street came up had made sure that she was the first to view. When she entered the premises she headed straight for the kitchen, where she was horrified to see cockroaches scuttling for cover. Casting a brief eye around the rest of the room, she had moved into the shop area, where she found that the floor was smothered in rat droppings. Fearing that her dream was over before it had begun, she had turned to Kitty for advice. Kitty agreed to meet her at the bakery the very next day, and had been quick to put Cadi's mind at ease by saying that the vermin could be easily eradicated, and that she firmly believed the former bakery could become a goldmine under the right management. So convinced was she that the tea room would thrive, she had suggested that the two of them could become partners.

Cadi had been delighted at Kitty's proposal, and they had signed on the dotted line that very day. Consigning Oscar to Maria's loving care, the girls had worked like Trojans to rid the premises of pests, and they had scrubbed and painted every surface within a few weeks of obtaining the keys. Having agreed to call their new venture Thomas's Tea Rooms, it had been a proud moment indeed when they watched the men hang the sign above the door. The business had taken off at a pace which neither of them would have dared to predict, and they were soon on the look-out for more staff. Employing two girls to wait on, Cadi and Kitty had seen to the rest of the business. It had been harder than Cadi could ever have imagined, and with early mornings and late evenings she rarely had time for herself, and often wondered how she would have managed without Maria's devotion to Oscar and Kitty's expertise when it came to catering for the masses.

Today marked exactly a year since they'd begun trading, Cadi had gathered the meticulous accounts which she and Kitty kept and headed for the accountant's office. Shaking the rain from her umbrella, she had looked up to see Daphne sitting behind the receptionist's desk. The two women stared at each other in frozen horror, until Cadi broke the silence.

'I'm here to see Mr Clark,' she said, a touch primly.

Daphne nodded. 'I'll let him know you've arrived.' Cadi had turned to take a seat when Daphne spoke softly from behind her. 'I'm sorry.'

Cadi clasped the handle of her leather briefcase in both hands as she turned to face the other woman. 'What for?'

Daphne's cheeks were beginning to colour as she spoke. 'For everything. I know I've already apologised for the letter I sent to Jez, but I never apologised for confronting him after he came home from Africa, or for not believing you when you warned me against Kieran.' She gave a terse, humourless laugh. 'I suppose that was my comeuppance for everything I did.' She held a hand out to Cadi. 'I really am sorry.'

Shaking her by the hand, Cadi's lips formed a small smile. 'Apology accepted. I take it you've not seen or heard from M— Kieran?'

Daphne's face clouded over at the mention of his name. 'Vanished without a trace – thank goodness. I've not seen his brother, but I do know that he got off without any charges.'

Cadi gaped at her. 'How come?'

'They couldn't actually prove that he'd done anything other than talk to members of the IRA, which isn't illegal. From what the police told me, it was Kieran they were interested in, and they hoped that arresting Paddy might smoke him out, as it were.' She chuckled softly. 'But as we all know, Kieran's a cowardy custard who looks out for himself and no one else. Once they realised that, they had to let Paddy go.'

Interested despite herself, Cadi sank into the chair opposite Daphne's desk. 'Does anyone know where he is?'

'Sailing the seven seas on board a merchant vessel, or so I've been told,' Daphne told her.

'With the rest of the rats,' said Cadi, much to Daphne's amusement. 'Talking of rats, I don't suppose you've heard from Aled?'

Daphne looked genuinely shocked, as well as shamefaced. 'No, but I should imagine I'm the last person he'd seek out.' She eyed Cadi curiously. 'I never thought I'd hear you describe him in such a manner. Do you mind my asking what's happened?'

Cadi shook her head. 'Not at all. I've not heard a peep from Aled since a few weeks before the end of the war. His poor parents have had to leave the farm, whilst Aled's vanished off the face of the earth, leaving everyone else in the lurch.'

Daphne blew her cheeks out. 'That does surprise me. If Aled were going to confide in anyone I would've thought it would be you.' Realising how this might sound, she hastily added, 'I'm not trying to suggest there's anything between you, I just ...'

Seeing Daphne squirm as she tried to get herself out of the hole she was currently digging, Cadi cut her off mid-sentence. 'It's all right. I know you didn't mean anything by it.'

The colour in Daphne's cheeks began to fade to a lighter shade of pink. 'I'm always putting my foot in things.' She looked at Cadi quizzically before adding, 'I'm probably about to do it again, but why is Aled's absence so upsetting to you?'

Cadi went on to explain how she'd given birth, and the promises that Aled had made.

Daphne looked to be deep in thought before sharing her opinions. 'Aled's a man of his word. I really can't see him turning his back on you for anything trivial.

As for his parents, I'm guessing they gave up the farm because John couldn't run it on his own.'

'He had my brother,' said Cadi.

'That certainly does seem a bit odd,' admitted Daphne.

Cadi waved a dismissive hand. 'I've pondered over this for years, and still not come up with an answer.'

'If I hear anything, I'll be sure to let you know,' said Daphne. She was about to ask Cadi where she could be reached when the penny dropped. 'If you're here to see Mr Clark, I take it your business is Thomas's Tea Rooms?'

Cadi smiled proudly. 'It is indeed. You'll have to pop by for a cuppa.'

Daphne's lips formed a genuine smile. 'I'd like that.'

Cadi glanced at Daphne's left hand, which was bare of any rings. 'I see you didn't marry.'

Daphne gave a short snort of laughter. 'I rather lost my faith in men after Kieran, although I have started courting again recently.'

Cadi eyed her inquisitively. 'Is he a farmer?'

Daphne shook her head fervently. 'No! My desire to stay on at the farm always got me into trouble.'

Mr Clark exited his office, bringing the girl's conversation to an abrupt end.

When Cadi left the accountant, she had a spring in her step. He had been so pleased with the turnover of the tea rooms, he had approved her suggestion of buying the flat above the business, which had recently come up for sale. The move would mean that she and Oscar would have more time together, instead of her having to dash between the tea rooms and the Belmont at all hours of the day and night.

Maria and Bill were upset to see Cadi and Oscar leave, but as Maria said at the time, she had known that this day would come, and she was proud of Cadi for following through with her dream of independence.

Cadi had given up asking her parents whether they had heard what happened to Aled, mainly because it seemed pointless now that the Davieses no longer lived in Rhos. Aled's disappearance hadn't stopped the locals' tongues from wagging, though. 'Some of the girls from the bakery said they'd heard tell that Aled had run off with an African lady,' tutted Jill, in a telephone call with Cadi. 'It's utter nonsense, of course—'

Cadi had been quick to interrupt her mother. 'How do you know it's nonsense?'

Jill had paused. 'All right, so I suppose I don't know, but if I were to believe every rumour I heard, Aled would be living in a tepee with a German woman of African origin along with her ten kids.'

Cadi snorted on a giggle. 'Oh, Mam! What are they like!'

'Fishwives with nowt better to do than make up stories,' tutted Jill. She sighed. 'I don't know what's happened to him, luv, but I feel ever so sorry for the Davieses.'

Everyone had told Cadi to move on with her life, and to forget about Aled, but it was easier said than done when you had cared about someone as much as she had for him. What was more, she'd also believed him when he'd said that he would always be there for her. She had known at the time that it had been a sweeping statement, because nobody really knew what lay ahead of them, but even so, Aled had managed to convince her that she wasn't on her own. She had wanted to tell Oscar how his daddy had saved Aled's life, and how

Aled had saved Annie's – a companion whom Oscar loved dearly. And how it had been Aled who'd been with her when she found Jez, and when she'd given birth to Oscar himself, but she knew that the little boy would want to meet this marvellous friend of his parents, and she would have to admit that he was gone without trace. *It's as though he's made me erase part of my life*, Cadi had told herself, *a very important part that would help Oscar to see his father as a hero, and Aled as the friend who had come to her rescue in her darkest hours.*

Now, as she put the dishes into the sink, she heard the bell go above the door, indicating that the last customers had left. Rinsing a cloth, she trotted down the couple of steps that separated the kitchen from the tea room and cleared their empty dishes on to a tray before wiping the table down. Standing up, she wiped the back of her hand across her forehead. It had been one of the busiest days yet, and Kitty had been struck down with a horrid cold, along with their two waitresses, leaving Cadi to hold the fort on her own. Being the only one in, it had been down to her to take all the orders, make the meals, and wash the dishes. She hadn't had a minute's break all day, but with only an hour left before closing time she would soon be able to put her feet up and relax ... she corrected herself. She would be able to pick Oscar up from the Belmont, where he was being looked after by Raquel while Maria prepared the evening menu in the pub kitchen. Raquel would've given Oscar his tea, which was one less chore for Cadi, and after a quick chat to discuss their day Cadi would bring Oscar back to the flat for a bath, followed by bed, and a story to help him go to sleep. Only then would she be able to put her feet up.

Making her way back into the kitchen, she was just finishing washing the dishes when she heard the bell above the door ring once more. Hoping that it was just a customer who had forgotten something, she headed back down the steps into the tea room with her fingers crossed.

As she entered, she saw that two people had taken their seats at the table closest to the door. Trying to hide her dismay, Cadi fetched a couple of menus from under the counter and headed over. As she drew near, she smiled a welcome to the woman before turning her attention to her companion.

Her smile disappeared as the man stared back at her through hollow eyes. Clutching the menus to her chest, she struggled to find words.

'Aled.'

The woman with Aled looked from Cadi to Aled, and back again. It was clear to her that the two of them recognised each other, but it was also obvious that they were uncomfortable in each other's presence. She gave a small cough, hoping that one of them would speak, but when neither of them said anything she decided to break the ice by stating the obvious. 'I see you know each other?'

Cadi gave a short, bitter laugh. 'I thought we did, but it turns out that I couldn't have been more wrong if I tried.'

The woman looked at the dainty watch on her wrist and gave an obviously false cry of alarm. 'Would you look at that! I don't think we have got time for that cup of tea after all; maybe it's best if I take you straight to the station.' She got up to leave, but Cadi was shaking her head. She had waited over five years to speak her mind, and she wasn't going to let him run off before she'd voiced her thoughts.

Her eyes locked with Aled's as she spoke in a frosty tone. 'Five years and not a word. I nearly went out of my mind with worry. Tell me, Aled, what had I done that was so bad you never wanted to speak to me again?'

Aled shook his head. 'It wasn't you, it was me ...'

'Damned right it was you!' snapped Cadi. 'And even though I knew I'd done nowt wrong, it didn't stop me from wondering. Because that's what happens when someone breaks contact for no reason.' Tears began to form in her eyes. 'You swore that you'd be there for us, even though I told you you didn't have to be. It was you who insisted you'd look after me and Oscar; I never asked you to do that. How could you turn your back on us without so much as a phone call?' She gave the woman a reproving look before turning her attention back to Aled. 'I'm not stupid, Aled; I knew you'd get a girlfriend at some stage, but that's still no reason to turn your back on me and Oscar!'

Aled gaped at her open-mouthed before looking up at the other woman. 'I'm frightfully sorry ...'

Cadi gave him a scathing look. 'What a surprise! I didn't realise you were capable of apologising!' She shot him a withering glance. 'You knew I'd lost Jez, and yet you let the same thing happen again, because you didn't have the guts to tell me to my face. I never had you down as a coward, Aled Davies, which just goes to show how wrong a person can be.'

The woman looked at Cadi in alarm. 'I say, that's a bit strong! I don't know the ins and outs of your relationship, and I don't want to, but I can't stand by whilst you call him a coward. I think you owe Mr Davies an apology.'

Cadi stared at her in utter disbelief. '*Me?* Apologise to *him*? Have you not listened to a word I've said?'

Aled addressed the woman directly. 'I really am ever so sorry about this. If you don't mind, I think it might be better if I make my own way to the station.'

The woman was eyeing him doubtfully. 'Are you sure? I don't mind coming back for you.'

Cadi rolled his eyes. 'He's not a child, even if he has been behaving like one.'

The woman's cheeks coloured as she did her best to pretend that she hadn't heard, and Aled gave her a reassuring smile. 'I'll be fine, honestly. Thank you for all your help. I'm sure you'll keep this under your hat.'

The woman nodded before scowling at Cadi. 'Of course I will. Some of us know how to behave, even if others don't.' She left the tea room without another word, leaving Cadi to stare after her, fuming.

Turning her attention back to Aled, she folded her arms across her chest. 'Hiding behind a woman? Is that your style nowadays?'

Aled indicated the chair opposite his with an open-palmed hand, but Cadi shook her head. 'Anything you have to say to me should've been said five years ago. If I were you, I'd have left with your *friend*.'

Aled lowered his gaze. 'I understand that you're angry—'

Cadi's eyes rounded. 'Angry? Try furious. You're a selfish, self-centred pig who cares about no one but himself. You knew how much I struggled when I lost Jez, and you pretended you cared, which is worse than not caring at all. You also pretended to be delighted when I asked you to be Oscar's godfather.' She laughed derisively. 'You must have thought me an idiot! And you'd be right, because I hoped against hope that you'd put in an appearance, right up to the last minute, but you couldn't even be bothered to show your face.'

'I did,' said Aled softly. He looked up at her. 'You saw me, or at least I think you did.'

Cadi shook her head angrily. 'I've got eyes in my head. If you were there I'd have seen you!'

Aled continued to gaze at her, his eyes taking in every inch of her face. 'I was by the church gates.'

Cadi was about to refute his claim when she remembered she'd seen a stranger by the gates. 'I did see someone, but it wasn't you. It was a feller in a wheel—'

She fell silent as Aled rolled himself backwards from the table and cocked an eyebrow. 'I knew you'd seen me.'

Cadi stared at him open-mouthed as she tried to gather her thoughts. She was astounded by his condition, but that didn't mean she wasn't still angry. 'Then why didn't you say something? If you came at all, and knew I'd seen you – which you obviously did – why did you leave?'

'Because I was a coward,' said Aled. He shrugged. 'And because you deserve better than this.' He slapped the wheel of his chair with the palm of his hand.

'I deserved the truth,' said Cadi. Softening slightly, she went on, 'So, what happened?'

Aled told her how he'd been shot, and how the doctors had said that it was only a matter of time before he succumbed to the severity of his condition. 'One of my lungs had been torn through, and whilst they managed to stitch me up it's now half the size it was. My liver and kidneys were damaged, and they had to resuscitate me twice. My legs only have enough strength to support me for a few seconds. I knew you had enough on your plate without me adding to your woes and I couldn't bear to see you go through yet more grief.'

'But you're all right now?'

He held his left hand up and waggled it back and forth. 'I have my good days, and I'm not going to die any time soon, or at least I hope not.'

The last comment made Cadi smile for the first time since Aled's arrival. 'Why didn't you get in touch once you knew you were going to pull through?'

He stared at her in amazement. 'Look at me.'

Cadi stared back in disbelief. 'Did you really think I'd turn my back on you because of something like this? Did you really think so little of me?'

He laughed incredulously. 'Of course I knew you wouldn't turn your back on me, which is precisely why I stayed away.' He heaved a sigh. 'I didn't need your sympathy, and I knew you'd insist on looking after me because that's the type of person you are. I wanted more than that for you.' He glanced around the tea room. '*This* is what I wanted for you. The freedom to get on with your life, without being tethered to someone like me.'

Cadi sank down into the chair opposite his. 'Do you not think that was my decision to make? You say you had my best interests at heart, but how do you think it felt to have the man I relied on the most drop out of my life?' Her bottom lip trembled. 'I needed you to support me emotionally, not *physically*. When the war ended all my friends got on with their lives, but I was stuck in limbo because the man I had always relied on was no longer there, and I'm not just referring to Jez. But you left as suddenly as Jez, and that time I had no closure, because I didn't know where you were.'

Aled nodded slowly. 'I know, and I'm sorry, but I thought it was for the best.'

'Best for who: you? Because it wasn't the best for me. You might think your chair would've held me back, but you couldn't be further from the truth. When you turned your back on me, you changed everything. I can't talk to anyone the way I used to talk to you.'

He gazed at her, shame-faced. 'I'm sorry. I never meant to hurt you, or anyone else for that matter, and if it's any consolation I nearly came over at Oscar's christening, because watching you from a distance wasn't enough. But the thought of you seeing me in this thing terrified me.' He sighed breathily. 'My wheelchair means we live in completely different worlds. Besides, as far as I was concerned, I'd burned my bridges, and I had no right to come back into your life after treating you so badly.'

Cadi spoke coolly. 'You were never going to tell me, were you?'

Aled shook his head. 'How could I? Tom told me that you'd come to the station.' There was a momentary silence as he fought to keep hold of his emotions. 'He also told me that you'd cried, and that I was being a selfish idiot. He was right, and I knew it, but it didn't change my mind.'

'You said something about the doctors thinking the worst. What changed?'

'I surpassed their expectations when it came to my body's ability to heal. And one of the nurses kept reminding me of who I was before the accident. In fact I'll always be grateful to the nurses. They stuck by me no matter how obnoxious I became, and without their support I wouldn't be where I am today.'

At last, Cadi smiled. 'Well, you're here now, and that's what counts.'

He eyed her incredulously. 'Does that mean that you forgive me?'

'Of course I forgive you.' She took his hands in hers. 'Aled, you're one of my oldest, dearest friends, and I love you very much. I just wish you'd said something sooner, rather than suffer in silence for all these years.' She glanced from the smart pinstriped suit to the briefcase which Aled had placed on the floor beside his wheelchair. 'Am I to take it you're now working in an office?'

Aled followed her gaze. 'I am indeed. I started off working for the War Office, but the airman in me still wanted to move around, so I packed that in and started my own business working as a freelance accountant. That's why I'm in Liverpool.' He grimaced as he glanced at the empty chair beside his. 'Miss Grainger – the woman I was with – is a client of mine.'

Cadi buried her face in her hands as the colour rose in her cheeks. 'Oh, Aled! I'm so sorry. Whatever must she have thought?'

He chuckled softly. 'Don't worry. I'll clear things up with her when I get back.'

Eager to steer the subject away from her outburst, Cadi asked the next question on her mind. 'So, where are you based?'

'Pretty much anywhere and everywhere. I don't have an office per se, but I do have a nice little flat in London's Soho.' He hesitated. 'How's Oscar?'

Cadi smiled. 'He's a cheeky cherub, full of the joys of spring and not a care in the world. I'd love for you to meet him.'

Aled waved a dismissive hand. 'Kids aren't interested in old men in wheelchairs.'

Cadi was quick to put him right. 'Oscar would love to meet the man whose life his father saved, the man who saved Annie – the apple of Oscar's eye.' She met Aled's gaze squarely. 'I've not told him any of this, because I knew he'd want to meet you, and I'd have had to tell him that his hero had vanished without a trace.'

Aled covered his forehead with his hand. 'I'm so sorry, Cadi. I never realised my absence would have such a big impact.'

'That's all in the past,' said Cadi, 'where it will remain.'

He glanced at Cadi's ring fingers and saw that she had moved her wedding band to her right hand. 'I see you never remarried.'

'I've been on a few dates, but they never amounted to anything. To be honest, I never felt comfortable about introducing any of them to Oscar. It will have to be someone pretty special if I'm to feel at ease with them around my son.' She hesitated. 'You never made it up with Marnie, then?'

He gazed at her sheepishly. 'No. Mainly because I knew she'd got it right.'

Cadi tilted her head. 'Oh?'

'I thought I'd buried my feelings for you a long time ago, but when you lost Jez I guess something resurfaced.' He waved his hand helplessly. 'Not that I realised it, of course, which is why I pooh-poohed Marnie's claims. It was only after I lost the use of my legs that everything became clear. I'd never stopped loving you, not deep down, and the thought of you giving up your dreams in order to care for me was more than I could bear. But worse still was the thought of you being with someone else.' He shrugged. 'I realised that I couldn't stand by and watch another man enter your life, so I used the wheelchair as an excuse to hide.' He eyed her quizzically. 'You don't seem surprised?'

'The girls always thought that Marnie might have been right,' said Cadi, 'so I suppose it's been at the back of my mind.'

'So I was only managing to pull the wool over my own eyes,' said Aled. 'I did the same when I said there had been too much water under the bridge for us to be anything other than friends. I didn't know then that I was only using it as an excuse because I thought you'd never see me in that way.'

'But sometimes having a history can *make* a relationship,' Cadi said thoughtfully. 'It's part of the reason why my dates never came to anything. I couldn't talk to them about the day I left Rhos for Liverpool, or what it was like to hear that my father was trapped down the mine, because they'd not been through any of it with me. Not like you. You know everything about me, warts and all. That's why I find it so easy to talk to you.'

He nodded slowly. 'And we've always been able to continue with our friendship, no matter how long the breaks between meetings.'

'We just pick up where we left off.'

'Because we know each other inside out.'

'Never a cross word – until today,' said Cadi. 'And even now, we've managed to talk things through and sort it out.'

'Oldest friends are always the best,' said Aled.

She smiled at him affectionately. 'So let's not leave it another five years, eh?'

His eyes twinkled as he gazed at her across the table. 'Definitely not.'

Cadi glanced at the clock above the counter. 'What time does your train leave?'

He smiled. 'I'm my own boss, so I don't have to go back to London this evening if I don't want to, and we've still got a lot to catch up on. How about I take you out for dinner this evening?' Seeing the uncertainty in her face, he quickly added, 'Unless you'd rather not, of course.'

'That depends.' Her expression was serious, but her eyes were dancing mischievously. 'Are you asking me out on a date?'

Aled felt his cheeks grow warm. 'And would you say yes if I were?'

She gazed at him solemnly. 'Do you know, I rather think I would.'

Two dimples punctured Aled's cheeks as a smile swept his face. 'In that case, dear Cadi, would you do me the honour of accompanying me on a date this evening?'

Cadi beamed. 'That would be lovely.'

Epilogue

It had been a little over a year since Aled moved to Liverpool and Cadi couldn't stop smiling as she drove towards the train station to collect him. It seemed as though she had been walking on air since his return. They had gone on their date, and Aled had proved to be the perfect gentleman, assuring her that he wouldn't try to rush things and they would take their relationship at a pace which would suit them both.

As Maria had known Jez the longest, it was to her Cadi had turned for advice as to whether she was doing the right thing by courting Aled. Her friend had given her her open and honest opinion.

'You've been on your own for far too long,' she said. 'Aled is a lovely man, who will treat you like a princess. If you've any reservations concerning what Jez would think then you should clear them from your mind, because Jez liked Aled very much. They became firm friends, and he would want to see you with Aled over any other man, because Aled will respect your free spirit and treat you with the love and compassion that you deserve.'

Cadi was thrilled to have Maria's approval, but she needed further affirmation from the one who was unable to give it to her in person. 'Thanks, Maria. Your blessing really does mean a lot, but do you really, truly think Jez would approve?'

Maria held Cadi's hands in hers. 'I do. Think about it. Jez wouldn't have wanted to see you end up like Queen Victoria, a sad and lonely widow who mourned her husband's passing for the rest of her days. That's why he made you promise to move on with your life.' She heaved a weary sigh. 'Life is too precious not to live it. Not many people get a second chance at happiness, which is why you should grab it with both hands. Have some fun, and let your hair down. You've done nothing but work since you had Oscar, and whilst you've achieved an awful lot for a single mother I can see you're still not happy – no one could be in your position. I'm not saying you have to marry Aled or owt like that, but don't rule it out because you'd feel you were being disloyal to Jez, because you're really not. What *would* be disloyal is breaking your promise to him.'

So Cadi and Aled had begun a long-distance relationship, with Cadi travelling down to London whenever she got the chance and Aled catching the train to Liverpool as often as he could. Everything went wonderfully, and in little over a year Aled announced his decision to move to Liverpool.

'It seems silly for us both to be rushing around like headless chickens when I can easily be based up here,' Aled had reasoned as they waited for his train. 'Of course I would still travel for work, but we'd get to see each other more, instead of wasting precious hours sitting on a stuffy train.'

'I agree,' said Cadi, 'but have you thought about where you'd live?'

He wriggled his eyebrows. 'I've seen a nice little place on Ullet Road.'

'Ullet Road! Do you have any idea how expensive it is to live around there?'

He laughed. 'Of course I do. I'm an accountant, so it's the first thing I checked.' He smiled. 'I pay myself a decent wage, so it's not exactly out of my reach.'

Cadi's cheeks turned pink. 'You say you've seen a *little place* but I've been down there myself and *none* of the houses on Ullet Road are little – I don't think I've seen a single one that isn't set over two floors. Are you sure you'd be able to manage?'

Aled had taken her hand in his. 'The place I've seen is a ground-floor flat, so there are no stairs, and the doors are wide enough for my wheelchair to get through. It even has a ramp up to the front door.'

A look of intrigue crossed her face. 'It sounds as though you've already had a good look round.'

He pulled a guilty face. 'I didn't want to say anything before I'd had a quick shufti to make sure it was suitable.' He tapped the side of his wheelchair with the palm of his hand. 'There's no point in going off half-cocked when you're stuck in one of these things.'

'And as it's passed muster, what happens next?'

He squeezed her hand. 'I'd only be coming up here so that I could be closer to you and Oscar, so if you're happy with that I'll put my London flat up for sale. If all runs smoothly I could be moving up to Liverpool within the next two months.'

Cadi sighed contentedly. 'In that case, it looks as if we're going to be seeing an awful lot more of each other from now on.'

Aled's London flat had sold to the first person who viewed it, and he had moved to Liverpool the following month.

With Aled living in Liverpool, their relationship had begun to develop more quickly. It seemed that they saw each other on an almost daily basis, only parting when Aled went away on business, and Cadi missed him terribly whenever he did.

Now, as Cadi turned on to Skelhorne Street, just outside Lime Street station. Pulling up alongside the kerb, she switched the engine off and glanced at Annie in the rear-view mirror. The red setter was beginning to get excited, as though she knew why they were there. *And she probably does,* Cadi thought to herself, *because I always bring her with me when I pick Aled up*. Reaching back, she smoothed the hair on Annie's ears. Having Annie back with the family had been the icing on the cake as far as Cadi was concerned. Oscar simply adored her, and Cadi liked to think that Annie sensed Jez in Oscar, because she was loyal to a fault, shadowing him wherever he went, as though ensuring he wouldn't come to harm.

Taking her handbag, she fished around inside until she found the compact mirror which had been a wedding present from Jez. Opening the case, she gently smoothed her thumb over the engraving which marked the date of their wedding whilst she examined her reflection. She would always cherish Jez's memory, but that didn't mean that she couldn't move on with her life. Maria had been right when she said that Cadi deserved a second chance at happiness, and Aled had given her just that. Placing the mirror back in her bag, she glanced at the band of Welsh gold which adorned her wedding finger. The lonely widow had become a happily married woman for the second time, and whilst she would never forget the past, she now had a bright future to look forward to, and she intended to make the most of every minute.

Dear Reader,

A Rose and a Promise may have put me through the wringer emotionally, but I thought it important to acknowledge that not everyone survives war. Jez was an outstanding character who represented all the heroes who paid the ultimate sacrifice in order to protect the women they loved, and it would feel like a disservice if I didn't recognise that. I also had to tie up many loose ends, such as Daphne and the Finnegans. The thought of letting the dastardly brothers loose on the unsuspecting public was unfathomable, and I knew that they had to be accounted for if I were to sleep at night!

The idea for my next novel, *Winter's Orphan*, came on my last trip to London. I've always been fascinated with the city's rich history and iconic settings, one of which is Petticoat Lane. As I began my research, I quickly became intrigued by the infamous street market and its truly villainous beginnings. Probing into the lives of the folk who lived and worked down Petticoat Lane, I was immediately drawn to the captivating characters and their amazing resilience to the hell that was World War II.

To me, Libby is a true representative of that gung-ho attitude, something she displays when she loses her parents along with all her worldly possessions. If that wasn't bad enough, poor Libby, who can't swim a stroke, accidentally ends up in the icy water of the River Thames. Fearing that this is the end, she is plucked from the water by the handsome Jack, who comes to her rescue in more ways than one.

Winter's Orphan is the second in a trilogy that began with *White Christmas*, a book I wrote as a one-off, then vowed to turn into a trilogy. So how does that happen with Libby in London? She moves to Liverpool in a bid to find her long lost family; but ends up finding a lot more than she bargained for!

I simply adored writing this book, and I hope you love it just as much!

Warmest wishes,

Holly Flynn xx

Read on for an
exclusive extract of

WINTER'S ORPHAN

AVAILABLE TO PRE-ORDER NOW

PROLOGUE

Christmas Eve 1940

Libby Gilbert gasped as the icy water of the River Thames gushed into her open mouth. Spluttering as the murky liquid slid down her throat, her outstretched arms floundered above her head in a desperate attempt to find something to hold on to, but the current was too powerful, and the banks of the Thames slipped past her fingers before she could find a purchase. As her head sank below the water, Libby was beginning to think that her time was up, when she heard a large splash and a hand with a vice-like grip grabbed hold of her. Fearful that the hands might belong to her aggressor, she tried to fight him off, but he was too strong, and within seconds he had hauled her onto the bank.

Gasping for breath, she looked up at her saviour, but instead of locking eyes with a man hell-bent on revenge, she found herself gazing at a man in his late teens, with curly dark hair and green eyes, which twinkled kindly.

Seeing the anxiety in her face, her saviour took a step back, his hands held up in a submissive gesture. 'It's all right, Treacle. Jack, ain't gonna hurt you.' Seeing a cut above her eye, he leaned forward, his hand outstretched. 'You appear to have taken a lump out of yer noggin.'

As she scrambled to her feet, she attempted to scrape her hair, now plastered to her face, away from her eyes. Speaking through chattering teeth, she mumbled her appreciation. 'Thanks for rescuin' me Jack, but I'm quite all right.'

Jack eyed her studiously, his face full of concern. 'Pardon me for sayin', but you don't look it.'

She followed his gaze from her soaking wet frock, torn and muddy, to her bare feet, which were covered in cuts and bruises. 'I've lost my shoes,' said Libby. It was a fib, but she'd rather he believed she'd lost them in the water than explain why she had been running through the streets of London without any shoes.

To her relief, Jack jerked his head in the direction of the river. 'I expect they come off when you went in the water, but you can't walk round barefoot…' He was interrupted by the distant thrum of heavy bombers, making their way towards them. He held his hand out to her. 'C'mon, we'd best get us to safety before it's too late.'

Scared that her aggressor might still be nearby, she shook her head. 'Don't worry about me, I'll be fine…' She took a step forward and yelped as one of the many cuts on the soles of her feet hit the cobbled road.

Jack strode towards her in a no-nonsense manner, and scooped her up into his arms. 'Sorry miss, but I wouldn't consider meself to be much of a gent if I left you in this state, with the Luftwaffe droppin' bombs willy-nilly.'

Ordinarily, Libby would've objected to such a chivalrous act, but she knew that he was right. If she didn't get to a shelter soon, her assailant – wherever he might be – could prove to be the least of her problems. Tears slowly trickling down her cheeks, Libby felt Jack's arms tighten around her as he quickened his pace.

Ducking through the doorway of one of London's many public shelters, Jack ignored the ARP Warden who'd given a short exclamation on seeing the two of them, soaked to the skin. He took Libby to the back of the shelter and sat her down on one of the benches that lined the walls. 'Wait there, miss, whilst I get you a dry blanket.'

'My name's Libby,' mumbled Libby as she hugged her knees close to her chest. Glancing up at him through thick black lashes, she saw that he was smiling kindly at her.

'Right you are, Libby. I'll just have a quick word with me dad – he's the ARP Warden what's mindin' the door – but I'll be right back after that.'

With more people entering the shelter, Libby kept her head down in case any of them turned out to be her attacker. Watching through her downturned lids, she could see that Jack was talking quietly to an older man, who kept throwing her sidelong glances. It was obvious that they were discussing her, and it seemed that Jack was having to reassure his father about her presence. *He knows*, Libby told herself, *he can tell just by lookin' at me, and that's what he must be tellin' Jack, that he doesn't want someone like me in the shelter*. Seeing Jack break away from his father, Libby watched as he took a couple of blankets from under one of the benches and made his way towards her. She thanked him for the blanket and proceeded to wrap it around her, making sure she kept a small peephole so that she could see who was entering the shelter.

Hoping to learn something about the dark-haired beauty whom he had just rescued from the Thames, Jack tried to engage her in conversation. 'Gordon – that's me dad – was wonderin' what you was doin' in the river in the depths of winter?' Anxious that he should not appear too nosey, he winked at her, before continuing in a light-hearted fashion. 'Surely you must've realised it's not safe to go swimmin' durin' an air raid?'

She was about to reply when the curtain flap covering the door opened, and the man from whom Libby had been fleeing entered. Her heart in her mouth, Libby watched as the gruff man in his late sixties scanned the room. Trapped like a rat, she turned pleading eyes to Jack. 'Please don't let him see me.'

In answer, Jack settled down onto the bench next to her, and slid his arm around her shoulders, pulling her into his chest.

'Don't you worry your head none. If he says anythin', I'll say you're with me.'

Libby whispered 'thank you' whilst keeping a keen eye on the man who sat heavily onto the bench nearest the door. Scratching his throat, his eyes travelled over the occupants of the shelter, before settling on Libby, and Jack felt her stiffen under his gaze. Sensing her fear, he coughed into his fist before addressing the individual by way of explanation. 'My girlfriend's scared of the bombs, and who can blame her?'

The man gave a small grunt as his eyes flickered back to Jack. Apparently losing interest, he drew a watch from his pocket, flipped the case open, then closed it again before pushing it back into his pocket.

Jack's father, Gordon, took the seat opposite the man. He had no idea why his son was choosing to make up lies, but he knew it must have something to do with the young girl named Libby. Keen to keep the older man's attention away from Jack and Libby, he broke into conversation. 'I was hopin' we'd seen the last of the Jerries for one night.'

The man pulled a disgruntled face. 'Not with my luck.'

Gordon eyed him inquisitively. 'Oh?'

The man glanced back in Libby's direction. 'I got robbed by some tart, just as the first siren sounded.'

Huddling closer to Jack, Libby whispered. 'He's lyin'.'

Keeping his arm firmly around Libby, Jack pulled a disbelieving face. 'She must've been pretty feisty to get the better of a gentleman like yourself! Or did she pick your pocket?'

The man started to shake his head, before changing his mind. 'Dirty little bilge rat had it away on 'er toes before you could say "knife"!' His eyes narrowed. 'I chased 'er as far the docks, but lost sight of 'er after that.'

Gordon tore his gaze away from Libby, hoping the older man would do the same. 'Some things are more important than

money; you should be grateful you got in here before they started droppin' bombs.'

'I'll wring 'er flamin' neck if I get my hands on 'er,' the older man growled. He turned his attention away from Gordon, back to Libby. 'Pretendin' to be all nice, then runnin' off with my money. There's a name for women like that.'

Worried as to what might come out of the man's mouth next, Jack tried to change the course of the conversation. 'Maybe she was desperate?'

The man spluttered indignantly. 'What the 'ell do you mean by that?'

Keen to keep things from getting too heated, Gordon cut in swiftly. 'The lad didn't mean anythin' by it. He was only suggestin' that she nicked your money out of desperation.'

'I couldn't give a toss how desperate she was,' grumbled the older man. 'You don't rob someone before…'

Jack stared at him. 'Before what?'

Having said more than he'd intended, he brought the conversation to a close. 'What's important is she took what wasn't 'ers to take, and if I find the filthy little wretch, I'll take what I'm owed.'

Libby turned tear-brimmed eyes to Jack. 'It's not how it sounds…'

He gave her shoulders a reassuring squeeze, before hissing. 'Wait until they sound the clear; you can speak freely then.'

Libby lowered her head. Speaking freely wasn't going to be easy – not considering everything she'd just been through.

SUMMER PUDDING

**A cheap but delicious pudding, which requires
very little cooking! What's not to love?**

**If you can't buy fresh fruit, frozen will do just
as well, and you can use any mixture of berries.**

INGREDIENTS

- 300g strawberries

- 250g blackberries

- 100g redcurrants

- 500g raspberries

- 175g golden caster sugar

- 7 slices day-old white bread
  (square, medium-cut loaf)

METHOD

1. Line a 1.25 litre basin with cling film, leaving the edges
overhanging by around 20 cm – this will help you to
turn out the pudding when it's ready.

2. Wash the fruit and gently dry on kitchen paper,
keeping the strawberries separate.

(continues over the page)

SUMMER PUDDING

(continued)

3. Put the sugar and 3 tbsp water into a large pan and heat under a low flame, stirring occasionally until the sugar dissolves. Bring to the boil for one minute, then tip in the remaining fruit (except strawberries). Cook for 3 mins over a low heat, stirring 2–3 times. When the fruit is softened, but mostly intact, place a sieve over a bowl and tip in the fruit and juice.

4. Slice the crusts off the bread, then cut 4 pieces of bread in half, a little on an angle, to give 2 lopsided rectangles per piece. Cut 2 slices into four triangles each and leave the final piece whole.

5. Dip the whole piece of bread into the juice for a few seconds just to coat. Push this into the bottom of the lined basin. Now dip the wonky rectangular pieces one at a time and press around the basin's sides so that they fit together neatly, alternating wide and narrow ends up so that they fit together jigsaw-like. If you have any difficulty getting the last piece to fit, don't worry, simply trim to the right shape, dip in juice and slot in. Now spoon in the softened fruit, adding the strawberries randomly.

6. Dip the bread triangles in juice and place on top, trimming off any overhang with scissors.

7. Keep leftover juice for later. Bring cling film up and loosely seal. Put a side plate on top and weight down with cans. Leave to chill overnight.

8. To serve, open out the cling film then put a serving plate upside down on top and turn over. Enjoy with leftover juice, cream or ice cream!

KATIE
FLYNN

If you want to continue to hear from the
Flynn family, and to receive the latest news about
new Katie Flynn books and competitions,
sign up to the Katie Flynn newsletter.

Join today by visiting
www.penguin.co.uk/katieflynnnewsletter

Find Katie Flynn on Facebook
www.facebook.com/katieflynn458

HAVE YOU READ
KATIE
FLYNN'S
LATEST BESTSELLING NOVELS?

AVAILABLE IN PAPERBACK AND E-BOOK